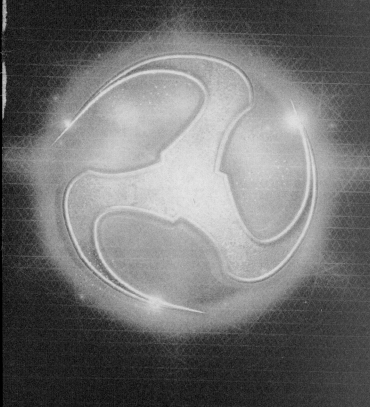

D0211755

THE KEEPER

VEGA JANE BOOK TWO
A NOVEL BY

DAVID BALDACCI

SCHOLASTIC INC.

Copyright © 2015 by Columbus Rose, Ltd.

This book was originally published in hardcover by Scholastic Press in 2015.

All rights reserved. Published by Scholastic Inc., *Publishers since 1920.* SCHOLASTIC and associated logos are trademarks and/or registered trademarks of Scholastic Inc.

The publisher does not have any control over and does not assume any responsibility for author or third-party websites or their content.

ISBN 978-1-338-05360-9

10 9 8 7 6 5 4 3 2 1   17 18 19 20 21

Printed in the U.S.A.   23
First printing 2017

Book design by Elizabeth B. Parisi

To Michelle,
who began this entire journey with a gift

"The past is but the past of a beginning."

— H. G. Wells

"Weeds are flowers too, once you get to know them."

— A. A. Milne

"To escape from the Quag means imprisonment forever."

— Madame Astrea Prine

The Quag

I T SEEMED BOTH fitting and even absurdly poetic that, hitched together like links in a chain, the three of us would die together. But having jumped off a mile-high cliff while being pursued by murderous beasts didn't leave us much choice in the matter. We had literally leapt for our lives. And now we had to land properly or our final resting place would be down there. *Far* down there.

We fell a long way, far longer than I would have liked. I glanced at my best friend, Delph, as we plunged. He was looking at me, not in stark fear but, admittedly, with a bit of anxiety. My canine, Harry Two, on the other hand, was grinning, ready for our adventure to begin.

The reason we had jumped was around my waist. My chain, Destin, allowed me to fly. But I had never jumped off a mile-high cliff and we were plunging faster than I ever had before.

I tried my best to manage the landing smoothly, though we thudded into the dirt with ample force. We all just lay there momentarily stunned. But I soon realized that while we were battered and bruised, we were alive.

I unhooked Harry Two from his harness, which had allowed him to rest suspended against my chest. I watched as

Delph slowly rose and stretched his arms and legs tentatively. Then I looked upward, all the way to the spot we had so recently vacated. If we hadn't, we would assuredly be dead.

The beasts that had been hunting us now stared down over the precipice. It was a herd of garms and a roughly equal number of amarocs. Even without being able to see them properly from this distance, I knew the scaly garms, with their own blood perpetually dripping down their armored chests, were breathing rage-filled flames at us. I'm sure the amarocs, giant wolflike creatures that apparently lived for no other reason than to kill, looked simply homicidal.

Yet none of them appeared willing to take the mile-long dive that we just had. It was worth all the coins I would ever have that these creatures could not fly as I could. I looked down and patted the chain around my waist with the letters D-E-S-T-I-N imprinted on some of its links. It had saved my life on numerous occasions already, although I had not possessed it for that long.

I could hardly believe it. I was in the Quag. Me, Vega Jane. I had lived my entire fifteen sessions in the village of Wormwood. It was all I'd ever known. I had been told that, other than the deadly Quag, it was all there was in existence. But I believed that to be a lie. There was *something* beyond the Quag, and I meant to find out what.

I was not doing this for a lark. I strongly suspected that my parents and grandfather were on the other side of the Quag. While my brother, John, still lived in Wormwood, he was not the young innocent lad he used to be. The sinister and murderous Morrigone had seen to that.

Thus, my mission in life was to get the three of us safely

through the Quag as quickly as possible. It might be an extremely ambitious goal, but it was mine nonetheless.

I breathed more normally and again looked over at Delph.

"Wotcha, Vega Jane," he said.

"Wotcha yourself, Delph," I replied, failing, despite our near deaths, to keep the smile off my face at having successfully entered the Quag.

"You reckon those ruddy beasts can get down here?" he said.

"I *reckon* I don't want to wait around to find out, do I?" I shot back.

I hoisted my tuck over my shoulder and Delph did the same with his. I kept Harry Two's harness on in case we had to take to the air quickly.

The map of the Quag that my friend Quentin Herms had left me was very detailed, but there were some troublesome lapses to it, now I could see. For one, it did not mention the cliff that we had just jumped from. And, correspondingly, I was not prepared for the valley we now found ourselves in. And yet I had seen Quentin enter the Quag one light. That's really what started this whole journey for me. He must have known what lies in here.

The map gave me general directions but did not provide a precise route to take through this place. I apparently would have to figure that out on my own. I also possessed a book, which I'd nicked from Quentin's cottage, that explained the sorts of creatures dwelling here.

Delph said, "The map has us heading generally that way." He pointed. "Toward that mountain, way in the distance over there."

I hesitated and then said haltingly, "I . . . I don't want to start that sort of trek at night. We need to find a safe place till first light."

He looked at me like I was completely mental. "Safe place? In the bloody Quag? Do ya hear yourself, Vega Jane? The Quag has many things, no doubt, but safe places ain't one of 'em, I reckon."

I looked ahead at the flat, open expanse. There were trees and bushes and long, sweeping fields of grass slowly bending in the breeze that blew off the cliff. It looked peaceful and serene and not dangerous at all. Which told me that there were probably dozens of foul things lurking in wait that could and would kill us, given the slightest of opportunities.

I looked down at my feet. Which way to step? I glanced at Harry Two, who was gazing up at me curiously, apparently waiting for me to make up my mind.

It struck me, rather uncomfortably, that I was to be the leader here. Blimey! Was I up to it? I wasn't sure that I was.

Far, far in the distance was a place the map called the Mycanmoor. It was described as a dull, dead sort of place that went on for a very long way, and which, unfortunately, there was no sure path around. The map was remarkably silent as to the *exact* perils that lay directly in front of us. But the book I'd nicked filled in some of these details.

I slipped it from the pocket of my cloak and lit a bit of candle stub to read the pages more clearly in the darkness.

Delph looked nervously over my shoulder. "'Tis nae a good idea to be lighting us up that way, Vega Jane."

"You know, Delph, you can just call me Vega. It's not like

we're flooded with folks here named Vega. As far as I can tell, in fact, I'm the *only* one."

He took a long breath and slowly let it out, his eyes big as cup saucers. "O'course, right you are, Vega Jane."

I sighed and stared down at the page. I basically had to match up the map with descriptions of the places in the Quag where the creatures described therein dwelled. It would have been much easier had Quentin Herms conveniently placed all this information in one place, but he hadn't.

I felt my spirits plummet when I fully realized how ill prepared I was. And here Delph and Harry Two were depending on me to have a plan!

Harry Two started growling. I looked down at him. His hackles were up, his fangs bared, and I quickly gazed around to see what was causing this reaction in my canine. But there was nothing in the darkness, at least that I could see.

I looked at Delph. He said, "What's got into 'im?"

And then I noticed it. My canine was breathing heavily through his snout. He wasn't seeing the danger — he was *smelling* it.

And in my experience, foul smells usually led to foul beasts.

I took a whiff of the air, wrinkled up my face and glanced sharply at Delph. "Do you smell that?"

He took in a chestful of the air and then exhaled it. "No."

I thought rapidly. I knew that scent, or at least something close to it.

And then the clouds in my mind slowly cleared.
Poison.

"What is it?" he asked nervously.

"I'm not exactly sure," I replied, and I wasn't. But I had smelled that sort of concoction before, back at Stacks, the factory where I was employed as a Finisher.

I pointed to the left. "Let's try that way."

"Shouldn't we maybe fly?" said Delph. "Get there faster, won't we? Let us . . . let us maybe see what's coming, before . . . before it *gets* us," he finished breathlessly.

We would get there faster flying. But something in the back of my head said to leave our feet firmly on the ground. At least for now.

I was one who tended to follow her instincts. They had served me more right than wrong over my sessions.

And that's when I happened to look up, and saw it. Or rather, *them*.

A flock of birds was racing in perfect formation across the Noc-lit sky. This surprised me because I did not think that birds flew at night, but perhaps things were different in the Quag. As I watched the birds soar along, something very strange happened. From out of nowhere appeared a cloud of bluish smoke.

The birds turned sharply to avoid it, but a few could not make the turn in time. And when these birds passed through the smoke and came out the other side, they were no longer flying.

They were falling.

Because they were dead.

I stood there, paralyzed. Then I felt something grip my arm.

It was Delph.

"Run, Vega Jane," he yelled. "Run!"

As we ran, I looked back once and wished I hadn't. It was a creature I had never seen for real before, but still, I knew what it was because a drawing of it was in the book.

I glanced at Delph and knew that he too had looked behind him and seen what I had. Taking to the air would do us no good. Unlike the garms and amarocs, what was back there and coming on fast was something that could fly.

It looked like our journey through the Quag was about to end before it had even truly begun.

The Kingdom of Cataphile

IT WAS A fiendish inficio behind us.

An inficio was a large creature with two massive legs, a set of powerful webbed wings and a long scaly torso out of which grew a serpentlike neck capped by a small head, which was fronted by blazing venomous eyes, and a mouth with razor-sharp fangs. If that wasn't enough to terrify sufficiently, the inficio also expelled a gas that would kill any who breathed it, like those poor birds.

I had been right in not taking to the air. We would already be dead.

Delph looked back as we sprinted along.

"It's comin' lower. Comin' to kill us!" he yelled. "Run!"

I needed to do something. Anything. Why was my brain so muddled? I had just stood there as the inficio was coming to kill us. It was Delph who had told me to run.

"Vega Jane!" screamed Delph again.

Without really thinking, I reached into my cloak pocket, pulled on my glove, and then my fingers closed around the Elemental. In its present state, it looked completely unimposing, only three inches long and made of what looked to be wood. But when I willed it to full size, the Elemental grew into a spear taller than I was, and a brilliant gold. I had been given the Elemental — along with the glove that I was required to wear while holding the Elemental — on a great battlefield from long ago, by a dying female warrior. She told me it would be my friend whenever I needed one. Well, I needed one now. I needed to do something. I refused to simply . . . die.

As I looked back, the inficio was closing fast, its clawed feet nearly on the ground. I saw its mighty chest fill with air and then it expelled a breath, which became a great cloud of blue smoke that at its center held death.

Still running, I turned and prepared to hurl the Elemental, guiding it with my thoughts. When I let it fly, the Elemental zipped past the outer edge of the smoke, and the wake caused by its speed disrupted the cloud of poison, pushing it back toward the creature that had released it. The inficio instantly soared upward. Apparently, though the beast was the source of the deadly fumes, inhaling the smoke could harm it too.

The Elemental flew back to me. Just as I grasped it, the ground under our feet gave way and we plummeted downward about fifty feet. Whatever we hit was softer than our landing off the cliff. Still, I felt myself gasp and I heard Delph do the same. Harry Two yipped once, but that was all.

I rolled onto my back and saw the dark sky disappearing behind the cover of large branches and rolls of matted grass. These elements were being hoisted into place by what looked to be a series of pulleys and ropes. But that could hardly keep the inficio at bay. I expected it to burst through this flimsy cover and destroy us.

But the inficio did not come. Instead, a heavy net fell

9

over us and we became tangled in ropes so thoroughly that I could barely move. I looked to the side and saw that Delph and Harry Two were in the same predicament. As we lay there struggling, I heard something approaching. Delph obviously did too, because he grew quiet. I willed the Elemental to shrink and placed it in my pocket and then took off the glove and placed it in my other pocket.

I reached out as far as I could and took Delph by the hand.

In a low tremulous voice, I said, "Be ready for anything, Delph."

He nodded.

Our gazes locked for a long moment. I think we realized that this might be it for us — two simple Wugs from Wormwood attempting to cross the insanely treacherous Quag. It seemed so absurd right now. We never stood a bloody chance.

"I'm so sorry, D-Delph," I said, my voice breaking as I finished.

Surprisingly, he smiled and rubbed my hand gently, which sent shivers up my spine. He said, "'Tis all right, Vega Jane. At least, well, at least we're together, eh?"

I nodded and felt a smile creep to my face. "Yes," I said.

I looked beyond his shoulder and saw lit torches set into holders on the rock walls. This gave the place a shadowy, vaporous illumination. It only added to my sense of fear and foreboding. What would be coming for us now?

I looked past Delph and stiffened.

There were dozens of pairs of eyes looking back at me from barely ten feet away. As my vision adjusted to the feeble light, I could see that they were smallish creatures with fierce, grimy faces and strong, toughened bodies. But their backs were bent and their fingers dirty and gnarled, perhaps from heavy toil.

As they grew even closer I received another shock. They had mats of grass growing on their exposed arms and necks and on their faces.

I heard Delph quietly mutter, "Ruddy Hel?"

The column of little creatures transformed into a circle and they surrounded us. I heard one of them call out in a series of grunts. When the net started to lift, I realized that he had been giving the instruction to do so.

The weight of the ropes lessened and we all three struggled to rise.

Quick as a flash, the creatures whipped out weapons and held them at the ready: small swords, lances, pickaxes and long, lethal-looking knives. And about a dozen of the creatures held small bows with sharpened arrows tucked onto strings ready to fire.

We could now see our captors quite clearly. Not only was grass growing on their bodies and faces, but their hair was grass as well.

Outnumbered as we were, I thought a friendly if direct approach best. I said, "Hello. I'm Vega. And this is Delph and Harry Two. Who are you?"

They all stared blankly back at me. Their faces were small and wrinkly, but their eyes bulged and were quite painfully red. I could see now that they were dressed in a hodgepodge of dirty clothing: trousers held up by stout rope, old shirts, frayed kerchiefs, stained vests, old coats and peaked hats. Some had on nicked metal breastplates. Others had metal coverings held on with leather straps over their thighs. One bloke sported a cap made of rusty iron.

We drew back because the little creatures were moving forward, tightening by considerable degrees the circle they had formed around us. They were jabbering and grunting, and a pair of them poked us with their little blades.

"Oi!" I cried out. "You can keep those ruddy things to yourselves."

The creatures drew even closer.

I took a sudden step forward. This obviously surprised them, and as a group they jumped back. The one who had spoken before grunted again to his fellows. He was taller than the others and seemed to possess an air of authority. I turned my attention to him and said, "Can you speak my language? Can you speak Wugish?"

And I received another shock. One so great I thought my heart had stopped.

Slowly walking toward us was, well, he looked like us, meaning like a Wugmort from Wormwood. He had all the applicable parts and he had no grass growing on those parts.

"Cor blimey," muttered Delph, who obviously had also seen him.

The male stopped right outside the circle of creatures, who had respectfully parted to allow him to pass.

I said, "Are you a Wug?"

The male stopped barely five feet from me. He was tall and had on a green cloak and I could see pointed shoes poking out from under the hem. He was elderly; his hair was white, as was his beard. His face was lined and remarkably pale; in fact, it competed with his hair for which was whiter.

Then it occurred to me that if he lived down here, the burn of the sun would never touch him.

"Not anymore," he answered in a high-pitched voice. "I left long ago." He looked at the creature that had grunted before, and started speaking to him in a fast, guttural speech that was impossible to follow.

Again, my mind was seized with dire thoughts. Was this bloke inhabited by the Outliers? Or was he an Outlier himself? Back in Wormwood we had been told of these fiendish Outlier creatures that supposedly lived in the Quag. We had been warned they wanted to invade Wormwood and kill us all. And it had terrified all Wugmorts because we had heard these creatures could look just like us and could even inhabit the minds of Wugmorts and make them do their bidding.

The male pointed to his right and said, "This way, if you please."

My heart in my throat, we headed in that direction and the creatures followed.

We passed from the large, tall cave to a small tunnel, which was nevertheless well lighted with torches on the wall.

When we entered a high, broad room of stone, the male stopped so abruptly I almost walked into him. He motioned Delph and me past him and into the cavernous room. Harry Two obediently followed.

When I looked around, the breath seized in my lungs.

There were little niches in all the walls that rose up as high as I could see. And in each of those niches was a —

Skull.

It was as if hundreds of sightless eyes were staring at us.

I looked over at Delph and found him gazing upward too. Poor Harry Two started to whine. The entire space reeked of death.

The male turned to look at me. "Do you know what they are?"

I nodded, my stomach churning. Had he brought us here because our bones would soon be joining these? "Wug skulls," I said fearfully.

"Look more closely," he said with a sweep of his hand.

I stared more fixedly at the skull closest to me and then at numerous others. I looked back at the male.

"These aren't Wugs."

He said, "They are creatures of the Quag who seek to harm us."

I crept closer to another skull on a lower niche. It was undoubtedly a frek. I recognized the jawbone and the long fangs. Next to it was an amaroc. I had seen a skull of one of those at Delph's place in Wormwood.

I looked back at the male. "Did you kill them all?"

He chortled. "Not personally, no."

"How, then?" I asked.

The male looked me up and down. "Who exactly are you?"

"My name is Vega. This is Delph. The canine is Harry Two. We're from Wormwood." He said nothing to this. "Have you been here long?" I asked.

"Longer than your tally of sessions."

"You have retained your Wug speech nicely," I observed.

"Indeed," he said, staring at me.

"What do you call this place?" I asked.

He looked around. "The Kingdom of Cataphile of course."

Delph said, "What's a c-cat-cata-whatsis? And who's the bloody king?"

"A cataphile is a collector and keeper of bones. And as you can see, we fit that criterion rather fine. As for the king, here I am. At your service."

He gave a sweeping bow to us.

"*You're* the king?" I asked incredulously.

"King Thorne," he answered with a dignified air.

I said, "How do you go from being a Wugmort to being a king here?"

He spread his hands. "Well, I largely fell in a hole, as did you." He took on a dreamy expression. "There is much to be said for falling in a hole. It opens up a world of possibilities." He paused. "'Tis a humble, darkened kingdom, but 'tis my own. And thus makes it right and just and plenty, and, most notably, my home."

Delph and I exchanged nervous glances. I was beginning to think this bloke was more than a bit barmy. "And what are *they*?" I said in a small voice, with a glance at the creatures with grass growing on them.

"They are ekos. That is the Wug translation anyway. They are the highest form of life down here. Except for me of course."

"I know there are other creatures dwelling on the surface of the Quag. But you mean there are other forms of life down here?"

"Oh, yes. The Quag has an abundance of life of all kinds. But come. We will give you refreshment and a place to sleep." He turned.

I stood there openmouthed. *Refreshments and a place to sleep? The Kingdom of Cataphile?* I had imagined the Quag to be many things, but not this. It was turning out to be, well, quite civilized. But then again, I was still very much on my guard.

"We ought to be going, Vega Jane," muttered Delph.

The king whirled around and looked at me with a face as though I had just told him I was a garm in disguise.

"Jane? That is your full name? Vega Jane?"

I nodded. "Yes."

"And are you related to Virgil Jane?"

"He was my grandfather. Did you know him?"

"Yes indeed. Is he well?"

"No. He suffered an Event." I now knew this to be untrue, but I had no reason to share that with him.

"An Event? Well, well. And Virgil too, of all Wugs."

He turned to one of the little ekos and grunted a few times. Several of them raced off. He turned back to us. "As for leaving this night, I'm afraid that is impossible. The Quag is a dangerous place even at light. At night you will not survive. Now, are you hungry?"

He didn't wait for an answer but headed off at a good clip, passing through another opening in the stone.

We hurriedly followed, with the remaining ekos right at our heels.

I drew close to Delph and began to whisper. "I don't like this bloke. He looks like a Wug, but how can he be?"

"Right," Delph hissed back. "We woulda heard if a Wug left for the Quag. Like with Herms."

"He might be an Outlier."

He shot me a glance. "Thought there was no such thing."

"Who knows for certain, Delph? I was prepared for freks, garms and amarocs, not a Wug who has his own bloody kingdom of ekos with grass growing on them. None of this was in the book of the Quag that I found at Quentin Herms's cottage."

"Aye, which means we have no idea what's coming, Vega Jane, once we get away from here."

If *we get away from here*, I thought miserably.

A Beastly Meal

THE PLACE WE were taken was a large, low-ceilinged cave roughly forty feet long and twenty wide. Light came from fired smoky candles that were lined up on a table struck from solid rock, with rough-hewn wooden chairs all around.

Thorne pointed to the seats and said, "Please, be comfortable. The meal will be along presently."

He took a seat at the head of the table. There was a large *T* carved in the back of his seat. For the king, I imagined. Delph and I shared a contemptuous look. What a ginked-up git.

I said, "The grass that grows on the ekos?"

Thorne smiled approvingly. "Oh, you noticed that, did you?"

Well, I could hardly miss it, I thought. "So what is its purpose?"

"It helps them do what they do," he replied in a casual tone.

A noise in the doorway made us turn in time to see four ekos carrying in a large platter. As they drew closer into the spread of candlelight, I could see what was on it: great clumps and claws of some beast with feather and fur still attached. My stomach gave a lurch. But around the "meat" were potatoes and asparagus and beans and peppers and purple onions. And I was fairly certain that was a rutabaga staring out at me from under what looked to be a furry thigh.

"Blimey," breathed Delph with a disgusted look.

Metal plates were thrust in front of us, with rude forks and knives metal-forged as well. One ekos, the tall one from before, served Thorne personally. Then I reckoned it was up to us to do the same for ourselves.

I avoided the clumps and claws and filled my plate with the vegetables and covered them with what I recognized as parsley and basil leaves. Delph did likewise, though I did see him tear off a chunk of meat that looked rather well smoked. A goblet of water was placed next to my plate by the hand of an ekos, so I got a much better look at the grass growing on it. In fact, some of it brushed against my hand. It felt hard and prickly.

I drank some of the water, and Delph did also. I let a bit of my rutabaga fall to the floor for Harry Two. Delph followed with a slice of his meat.

"A fine canine," said Thorne as he worked on what looked to be a wing, casually plucking off feathers as he did so.

"Thank you. So you have water resources here?" It was not an idle question. We needed water to survive our journey through the Quag.

"An underground stream. Quite tasty."

Delph spat a piece of hardened skin from his mouth and muttered something about, "And why can't the bloody food be the same?"

Thorne pointed to the half-eaten joint of meat in Delph's large hand. "What you have is a bit of attercop. Don't actually care for it myself. But the buggers are plentiful up on the surface of the Quag and quite easy to trap."

"Attercop?" said Delph quizzically. "Never heard of it."

"Well, you might know it by another term: spider?"

With an enormous cough, Delph expelled his mouthful of meat and it hit the wall opposite.

I looked at Thorne, fearing his reaction to this.

For a long moment, Thorne simply stared at Delph, and then he looked at the slop of spider meat sliding down the wall of his eating room. When he glanced back, he burst into a fit of laughter, which we soon both joined.

After we had quieted, Thorne rubbed his eyes. "Delightful," he said. "Never cared much for spider myself, as I said. Chewy, you know. And then of course, there is the question of the venom. Stick to the rutabagas. They never lead you astray, the noble rutabaga. Nothing dodgy about dear old rutabagas."

We continued to eat our meal, now chatting pleasantly.

I said, "You mentioned there were other things living down here?"

"Well, there are the ekos of course. Quite civilized." He stroked his beard with his index finger. "Then there are the gnomes."

"The *gnomes*?" I said. I had never heard the term.

"Yes, yes. Well, sometimes I call them the unders, you know, because, well, they dig *under* the rock for things that we require. Quite the sharp claws they have."

"And that's all the creatures living down here?" I said in a prompting tone.

He scowled. "Well, there are the bloody grubbs."

"Grubbs? What do they do for you?"

"Do for us?" He bent forward and his expression became so still, it was like he had been transformed to rock. "They attack us," he said quietly.

"Attack you?"

"Yes," he said, his eyes narrowed to slits. "They want to kill me."

"But why?" I asked.

He turned back to his meal without answering. Delph and I exchanged a puzzled glance. This bloke was definitely mental. I felt the hairs on my neck start to tingle.

"And what do the grubbs look like?" Delph asked nervously.

Thorne turned a very serious eye to him. "They look like the last thing you would ever want to see coming at you from out of the dark, milad. Bloody ger-rubbs," he added in a disgusted voice.

"Where are they?" I said breathlessly. "Down here somewhere?"

"I'll tell you where they are. They are where you least expect them to be." He struck the stone tablet a sharp blow with his palm, which caused Delph and me to jump nearly out of our chairs. Delph accidentally spilled some of his water. Harry Two immediately started lapping it up.

"Now you must give me news of good old Wormwood," said Thorne as he washed down a mouthful of food with the contents of his goblet. I wasn't convinced he was drinking simply water, for he filled his goblet from time to time from a silver flask resting at his elbow. "For instance, who is Chief of Council now?" he asked.

"Thansius."

"Good for him. Well done, Thansius."

"So you knew him?" I asked.

"Yes. He was a good friend of Virgil's too." He took a sip from his goblet.

"And Morrigone's," I added.

This had a remarkable effect on the Wug. The color drained from his face and he choked on his draft. Regaining his breath, he said, "Morrigone, eh?"

"If it was a long time ago that you left, she might have still been very young. Or perhaps not even born yet."

"Yes, I do believe that she was born actually."

Watching him curiously, I said, "Morrigone is on Council now."

He chortled, but there was no mirth in his eyes. "What else?" he asked.

Delph said, "Well, we been building this —"

I cut in. "I worked at Stacks, as a Finisher, as I said. Delph was at the Mill."

Delph shot me an inquiring glance, but I ignored him. The truth was I didn't want Thorne to know about the Wall. If Thorne was an Outlier or his mind had been taken over by them, the last thing I wanted was for him to learn about the enormous wall we were constructing around Wormwood to keep those very Outliers out!

I decided to get to the most important issue I wanted to ask him about. "I never heard of any other Wug heading into the Quag. It is forbidden."

"Many things were forbidden," replied Thorne in a more sober tone. "And yet *you* appear on *my* doorstep. What cause brings you into the mysterious Quag?"

22

"Curiosity," I said immediately. "We wanted to see what was in here."

"And beyond," added Delph. My kick was too slow to forestall him.

"There is *nothing* beyond the Quag," said Thorne sharply, eyeing us warily.

"So you've been to the other side of the Quag?" I asked innocently.

"No, I've never been past here."

"Then how do you know there —"

He rose abruptly. "I believe that we all are extremely tired. Now your sleeping quarters are ready." He grunted and the same large ekos appeared.

"Luc here will show you where. Off you go and pleasant sleep to you both." He hurried away.

Luc grunted once. Harry Two gave a bark in reply. Apparently satisfied that we understood, Luc turned and walked through the passageway. We hurried after the creature with grass for skin and grunts for words.

Delph whispered, "Are you sure 'bout all this?"

"I'm sure of nothing, Delph. Absolutely nothing."

I had never spoken truer words.

Bars of Bones

W E WERE LED to a chamber that was cold and filled with shadows that seemed to flicker and move about. There was one torch on the wall and a lit candle on a wooden box next to a hard pallet on which lay a blanket and a pillow.

I looked at Delph, who stood in the doorway.

"Is it just the one, then, for the both of us?" he said, eyeing me nervously.

When I shot him a glance, I had to hide a smile because his face turned scarlet and the big Wug quickly glanced away.

Males.

However, Luc was already pulling on his arm and pointing farther down the passage and grunting quite madly.

"Guess not," I said with a tiny wave. "Suppose these are just my digs."

I thought I saw Delph let out a sigh of relief, which I wasn't quite happy about for some reason.

He said, "Look, anything comes up, just give a holler. I'll be here faster than . . . well, pretty bloody fast, I can tell you that," said Delph, somewhat anticlimactically.

"Brilliant, you do the same," I said, feeling uneasy even as I said the words.

Delph disappeared with Luc, and Harry Two came over and settled down next to the wooden pallet. I dropped my tuck in the corner, sat on the rude bed and took off my cloak. Underneath was my chain, which I would not be taking off. In the pocket of my cloak was the Adder Stone, which healed pretty much anything. Along with the Stone was the glove. My shrunken Elemental was in my other pocket.

I pulled from my cloak the ring Thansius had sent me before I escaped into the Quag. It had belonged to my grandfather. It had been found at Quentin Herms's cottage. I was told my grandfather had suffered an Event, which basically meant that one vanished into, well, nothing. But that had been a lie. I had learned that my grandfather had left Wormwood of his own accord.

On the ring was the symbol of the three hooks. I had no idea what it meant. I thought I might find out in the Quag. I thought I might learn a lot in the Quag. If the place didn't kill me first.

I lay back on the bed and held the ring up to the flickering candle. The hooks glistened and glowed in the soft, bluish light. My grandfather had the very same symbol on the back of his hand. I had also seen this exact same ring on the finger of the dying female warrior who had given me the Elemental.

I put the ring on. It was too large for any of my fingers except my thumb, where it rode snugly. As I looked at it on me, I couldn't help but think that I had just made some sort of unconscious decision committing me to something.

I felt my eyes close, the rise and fall of my chest started to slow and I collapsed into a deep sleep. But right before I completely drifted off, I could hear Harry Two's contented snores as he lay beside me on the floor.

My dreams were not pleasant ones. In every crevice of my mind, I seemed to encounter danger. Time passed and I slept on. When I finally awoke, I started to rise, but something held me back. I opened my eyes. And gasped.

I was in a cage!

I sat up and looked around. Delph was lying next to me, still asleep. What had been keeping me from rising was Harry Two. His paw was still protectively on my shoulder. The bars of the cage were stark white. As I drew closer to them, I could see why. They were made of bones.

I instantly drew back when I heard a laugh, a familiar one.

I looked to the right and there sat Thorne on a huge chair carved from still more bones. And all around the cage were ekos bearing weapons.

He pointed at the cage bars. "As you can see, we do make use of our little, uh, trophies here in the Kingdom of Cataphile."

With a thrill of horror, I saw four items resting on a slab of rock next to his seat. Destin, my chain, the Adder Stone, my grandfather's ring and the glove I had to use when holding the Elemental. I touched my cloak and felt the small outline of the shrunken Elemental still in my pocket. They must not have noticed it or else thought it of no importance.

I spoke loudly. "Why are we in here? And why did you take my things?"

This roused Delph, who slowly sat up and then leapt to his feet.

26

"What the —" he began, but I shushed him and then turned back to Thorne.

"Why are you doing this to fellow Wugmorts?"

Thorne pointed in turn to the Adder Stone, the chain, the ring and the glove.

"What are these things, Vega Jane? I would dearly like to know."

"Why?"

"Well, how else can I make use of them?"

"You're *not* to make use of them. They're mine," I said heatedly. I felt woozy in the head and I suddenly knew why. "You put something in our water to make us fall asleep," I said accusingly.

He picked up the ring. "I have seen this before. On your grandfather's finger."

I grabbed the bars of bones and shook them. "Let us out of here! Now!"

"You are in no position to make demands, my silly little female."

"I'm not silly and I'm definitely not little," I shot back.

"To me, you're nearly invisible, so insignificant are you."

"Well, then I guess you don't need me to tell you what they are, if I'm so bloody insignificant."

He stood up and strolled over to the cage, stopping a foot away, and smiled maliciously.

"You must think things through a little better."

He pointed at Luc, who held a bow with an arrow perched on the string.

He grunted and Luc came forward.

Thorne said, "I just ordered Luc to kill the canine."

"No!" I screamed and immediately thrust myself between Luc and Harry Two as Luc began to take aim.

"Move out of the way, Vega, it's only a blasted canine," said Thorne.

"He's *my* canine and I'm not moving. So you can just go to Hel!"

He grunted again and four more ekos came forward with their bows and surrounded the cage. They all took aim at Harry Two. I couldn't be in four different places at once, so I ended up covering him entirely with my body.

"Vega Jane!" shouted Delph, and he put his big body over both of us.

Thorne drew closer to the bones, a dangerous smile playing over his lips. "There is a mile-long drop from a cliff when entering the Quag to get to my kingdom. How did you manage it?"

My glance betrayed me. I looked past him, to the objects he'd taken.

"I see," he said. "Now, which one?" When I didn't answer, he pointed at Luc while keeping his gaze directly upon me. "One grunt from me, Vega, and Delph is no more. I will add his bones to your cage. With his size, they'll fill all the bloody gaps. Now, which one?"

"Vega Jane, don't," shouted Delph.

Thinking quickly, and already having sized up Thorne as vain and arrogant, I said, "I'm sure *your* secrets are far more amazing than my pitiful ones."

Thorne appraised me for about a sliver. "You know, I think you've hit on something there. I actually think it appropriate to show you how my mind works. Then you will understand that it is futile to resist me."

He grunted in rapid succession and the ekos sprang into action.

The bone cage was opened, and with pokes and prods from swords and spears, we were herded out of it.

Delph grew close to me and whispered, "He's a mad 'un, Vega Jane."

"I know he is."

"We got to get out of here."

I nodded again, but I couldn't think of a single way for us to accomplish it.

Thorne led us down another passageway until we came to a far larger cave than the one we had left. I heard the sound of something pounding into rock long before we reached it. As we came into the space, I could barely believe my eyes.

It was a mountain of rock underground. And swarming over it were little creatures in work clothes and sporting red woolen caps and high leather boots that covered most of their short legs.

"The aforementioned gnomes," said Thorne, pleasantly enough.

The gnomes stopped what they were doing and turned as though hooked together, to stare down at us from their mountain.

"Come closer," said Thorne enticingly. "I'm sure our little friends would simply love to meet you."

Well, neither Delph nor I wanted to move closer and

meet anything, but the prods in the back from the ekos forced the issue.

When the gnomes came more fully into view, I flinched. It wasn't just that their faces were deathly pale and prunish and evil-looking. It was their hands. Or, rather, where their hands should have been.

Instead, they had long claws that looked as strong as metal. They were curved and deadly sharp, although they were covered in dirt from their work on the rock.

Their lips curled back like attack canines, revealing yellowish-black teeth that were rotted and misshapen. I put a hand down in front of Harry Two because I was afraid he might go after them. And as strong and brave as he was, he would have no chance against a hundred gnomes with sabers for hands.

Thorne grunted rapidly and the gnomes fell back as the armed ekos advanced on them. So, I thought, the gnomes were obviously kept in check by force.

I glanced at Delph and could tell he was thinking the same thing.

Thorne said, "Do you know what they're mining off that rock?"

I looked at him. "No."

He clapped his hands together and one of the gnomes ran off but was back in a jiffy, hefting a large bucket made of wood and encircled with metal bands.

Thorne took it from him as the gnome respectfully swept off his cap and bowed. I could see that his hair was bushy and filthy. And from the smells wafting off the thing, I could tell that bathing did not occupy a sliver of the creature's time.

Thorne held up the bucket so that I could see inside. It was filled with blackish powder.

"Still don't know what it is?" asked the king in an amused tone.

Delph answered, "Looks like morta powder."

Thorne seemed impressed. "Well, well, brains and brawn. But you're not exactly right. It's not *yet* morta powder, but it will be." He pointed to the high rock the gnomes were working. "That stone has two of the three elements necessary to make the powder. The third is charcoal, which must come from trees on the Quag's surface. I brought the requisite formula with me here, and the ekos, once I trained them up a bit, are delightfully efficient in doing the appropriate mixing, compression and other tasks necessary. Indeed, they are quite good at building many things." He thrust the bucket back into the gnome's claws and waved him off with a casual flick of his hand.

The creature instantly obeyed, but as I kept my gaze on him, I could see him look back with a sullen expression as he clacked his claws ominously against the bucket's side.

Thorne clapped his hands, and the gnomes returned to their work. I marveled at how rapidly they tore through the rock and dirt with their claws. They were like ants flitting through grains of sand.

Thorne led the way down another passage. We arrived at a large, stout wooden door with a blackened iron keyhole. Thorne produced a key and opened it. We filed inside and as I saw what was there, I gasped.

It was a large room, and from floor to ceiling, it was filled with mortas. Tall, short and even some in-between models I

31

had never seen before. They were all shiny and looked in perfect working order.

"You would need furnaces and Dactyls to make these," I noted.

"We have both," replied Thorne. "Plus a great many other skilled ekos. They have proven themselves quite adaptable to my teachings."

Thorne walked over to a corner and patted a thick-barreled contraption that was bracketed by two wooden wheels. "We call this a cannon," he said. He pointed to another section of wall, where many crates were stacked. "And powder and ammunition for the weapons."

Delph was staring upward at the shelves and stacks of shiny mortas.

He said, "What d'ya need all these for?"

But somehow I already knew the answer.

"War," I said. "You're planning on going to war."

Thorne smiled, even as Delph exclaimed, "Cor blimey!"

I added, "And you're not going to war against beasts in the Quag."

Thorne shook his head and smiled even more broadly. "What would be the point?"

I finished my horrible thought. "You're going to war against Wormwood."

Blood from a Stone

WAR? AGAINST WORMWOOD?" exclaimed Delph. He stared over at Thorne like he wanted to rip him apart. "Are you nutters?"

Thorne gave him a withering look. "I can assure you that I am in full possession of my faculties, my brawny bloke."

Thorne's statement had hit me as hard as a collision with a garm. I felt sick to my stomach. Through my mind flashed the horrors that would result from what Thorne was planning. My village of Wormwood, all the places I knew so well, Stacks, the Care, Steeples, Council building, Loons, and my old family home, all lay in ruin. And starker still, I saw piles of Wugmorts dead from morta wounds. Even mighty Thansius and magical Morrigone.

Chiefly, though, I saw my brother, John, lying dead, his eyes frozen, his features still, his magnificent mind gone for all time.

With cold dread but a steely resolve I turned to Thorne.

"There is one problem," I said firmly.

Thorne studied me, his eyes crinkling and an arrogant smile playing over his lips. "Oh, you think so?" he asked. "Do tell."

"It's a *heavy* problem," I said cryptically, though I could tell he knew exactly what I meant.

"Oh, yes, indeed it is," replied Thorne. "You've laid the mallet directly on the nail head, Vega. I can see that you've inherited the brains of your grandfather. You're thinking of the mile-long rise we will need to reach the top of that cliff, eh?"

Delph said emphatically, "You can't climb it. Not with all those mortas, cannon and ekos."

"Quite impossible," agreed Thorne.

"And ya can't go to war without your bloody army," Delph said, a triumphant look on his features.

"Well, I won't have to, will I?" said Thorne patronizingly. "Let me show you."

The room we now entered through a massive portal, which Thorne unlocked, was far larger than any we had seen so far. My gaze quickly flitted to what dominated even this enormous space.

"What in the Hel is that thing?" gasped Delph.

There was a huge structure, rectangular in shape and made of wood, that looked rigorously constructed. It reminded me of the water vessels fisher Wugs used back in Wormwood, only far larger. It could easily carry hundreds of ekos. Connected to its sides were long, stout ropes. But suspended over it, high in the air, was something that dwarfed even the mammoth wooden carrier. It was black and roughly the shape of a circle, though it was thinner at the base and wider at the top. The stout ropes from the wooden structure were connected to a frame that was in turn attached to this thing. It was flattened and suspended by other ropes from the high ceiling.

"That, my fine Wug," said Thorne, "is the culmination of many sessions of work." He waved his hand at it. "It is, in fact, an aero ship."

Delph looked at him blankly. "An aero ship?"

"It flies." He pointed up. "Aero. Up there."

"How?" demanded Delph heatedly.

I could feel waves of anger rising off him. I gripped Delph's arm tightly and looked at him, trying to calm him before he did something we might all regret.

Thorne motioned to the flattened, suspended object. "That is what I term a bladder. Once it is filled with heated air, the bladder will lift the underneath carriage quite easily. And I have fashioned certain controls that will allow me to guide its path. By my calculations, it will lift my army and all its equipment in a very few excursions. Then, we will make our way to Wormwood. Our *triumphant* march to Wormwood, rather."

"But how are you going to get this contraption out of here?"

He pointed upward again. "Much as the hole you fell in? Well, we have dug up to the top there, though it's well covered now. The hole we have fashioned is far large enough for my aero ship to be launched through."

"Why do you want to attack Wormwood?" I asked fiercely. "You're a Wug."

"Well, the truth is I didn't choose to leave Wormwood. I was forced to leave."

"Really?" I snapped. "And you, such a nice bloke and all."

"Enough," he barked, his mad eyes narrowing. "I've told and shown you all that I plan to. I require answers from *you*. And I will have them now!"

He grunted several times and Luc brought over Destin, the Adder Stone and the glove. "It's your turn to speak." Thorne grunted once more and we were surrounded by bow-and-arrow-wielding ekos. Half took aim at Delph, the other half at Harry Two. I couldn't defend them both at the same time. I had no choice.

Delph gazed at me. I could tell he knew what I was going to do. He shook his head, but I ignored him. If I lost Delph, there would be no point going on anyway.

"The chain allows one to fly. The stone can heal wounds."

He looked suitably intrigued, if a bit skeptical of my words.

"Indeed? And the glove?"

"I had the pair but I lost one when we were running from beasts in the Quag. It has no powers," I added, which was perfectly true.

"Well, let's try one out, shall we?" he said.

He grunted a few more times, each one louder and more authoritative than its predecessor. Several ekos shot forward and picked me up clean off the ground.

"Stop!" shouted Delph, but he and Harry Two were instantly surrounded by a wall of armed ekos.

I shouted, "It'll be okay, Delph." I knew what I was going to do.

The ekos carried me back into the room where the mountain of rock and the miner gnomes were located. Thorne followed us, as did Delph and Harry Two, at the sword ends of the trailing ekos.

Thorne tossed the chain to me. "Now *prove* your statement," he said.

I wrapped the chain around me even as the ekos clambered up the mountain of rock, carrying me all the way to the top. They were strong and their grasses scratched and irritated my skin. We reached a ledge at the very top of the rock. The ekos set me down. I heard grunts from below. Thorne was obviously giving his final instructions. The git needn't have bothered. I wasn't going to wait to be forced off the ledge.

When a pair of ekos reached out to me, I pushed them away so hard they fell back against the rock wall. "Bugger off!" I cried out.

I looked down at Thorne with as much defiance as I could possibly muster, which wasn't hard.

And then I jumped.

I soared straight downward. I looked at no one other than Thorne. I wanted him to see the revulsion on my face. He looked stunned, which ordinarily would have made me smile. But my anger was such that all I could do was stare daggers at him as I fell. At the last instant, I lifted my head and shoulders and pointed my arms upward. I soared over them and then lifted up, up, up, until I landed back neatly on the ledge.

The ekos all drew away from me.

I looked triumphantly at Thorne.

He smacked his hands several times by way of applause and then beckoned me to join him below. I jumped once more and landed nimbly right next to him.

He looked at me slyly. "From where did you come by such a remarkable thing as that?"

"You know Stacks?" He nodded. "It has rooms that are secret. I found it there."

He looked lost in thought for a moment. "And Stacks was not always what it is now."

"That's right. Did Julius Domitar tell you that?"

"Alas, Domitar and I did not see eye to eye on much."

"Well, my respect for him just increased a hundredfold."

"You would do well to hold your tongue, Vega," he said, sounding dangerous. He pointed to Delph. "Say you are sorry for disrespecting me."

"I'm sorry." However, my stubborn features, I know, betrayed this as a lie.

"There is a price to be paid for lying to King Thorne."

He grunted to the group of ekos and before I could react, it happened.

One of the ekos shot an arrow into Delph's thigh. He screamed and toppled to the rocky ground, holding on to the shaft that had suddenly sprouted from his limb.

"Delph," I screamed.

I rushed to him. Blood was pouring out of him far too fast. I ripped off part of my sleeve and used it to try and stanch the bleeding. But it kept pouring out. Delph's face turned chalk white and he stopped screaming. He sank flat to the floor.

Harry Two stood in front of us both, his fangs bared as though daring any of the ekos to come closer.

"Oh, Vega?"

I turned to look at Thorne. He was casually holding up the Adder Stone.

"Might you want to try this? Your purported healing rock?"

Now I knew why he had Delph shot. As a way to prove that what I had said about the Adder Stone was true. As well as to punish me for my disrespect.

I held up my hand. "Toss it here, quickly."

"Sorry, I don't think that was quite what I was looking for," he said smoothly, his manner unhurried.

Swallowing both my pride and anger, I said in a pleading voice, "Please, King Thorne, might I have the Stone to help my friend? Please, O King?"

"Now, that's better. See what a bit of respect and politeness can manage?"

He threw the Stone to me. I caught it and instantly waved it over Delph's leg, thinking good thoughts. Not only did the wound heal, the arrow slid free from his thigh and dropped to the rock without a smidge of his blood on it.

Delph's breathing returned to normal, though he was still deathly pale. He slowly rose from the floor.

"'Tis okay, Vega Jane," he said, but the fear was evident in his eyes. "Thanks for doing the Stone over me."

In a breathless voice I said, "Don't thank me, Delph. It was my fault you got shot."

When I turned, Thorne was right next to me.

"What did you have to do to cause such a cure?" he asked.

"Don't tell him, Vega Jane," shouted Delph. I looked over at him. Again, I had no choice. A dozen arrows would be flying at Delph if I didn't.

"You wave the Stone over the wound and think good thoughts."

"Does it work on all living things?" he asked eagerly.

39

I knew why he asked this. He would want it to heal the ekos in case any were injured during his attack on Wormwood.

"I've used it on my canine."

"Can it bring back the dead?"

"No," I said emphatically. "Nor can it regrow limbs that have been lost. I tried that once and it didn't work."

"Pity," he said, snatching the Stone from me. "But still, it has its uses, I'll grant you that. You will of course teach me how to fly with the chain."

I was about to scream out, *The bloody Hel I will, you king of the gits,* but I refrained. I might just take an arrow to the head. "It will take time," I said evenly. "It's not easy to train someone up to fly."

"Well, it's not like you're going anywhere. Ever again."

Despite the clear menace behind his words, I breathed a bit easier, though I didn't let my features express this. At least we would be allowed to live, until we could figure out a way to escape this place.

Thorne made sure to pocket the Stone and the ring.

He did not, however, take the glove. When he wasn't looking, I slipped it into my cloak. From out of the corner of my eye, I caught a gnome staring at me as I did this. It was the same bandy-legged creature that had fetched the bucket for Thorne. At first, I thought he was going to tell on me, but he just looked at me stonily before turning away to jabber with one of his mates.

I marched along behind Thorne with Delph and Harry Two at our heels and the brigade of armed ekos bringing up the rear.

Delph whispered, "Why'd you tell him about the bleeding Stone? And show him what Destin can do?"

"Delph, he would have killed you if I hadn't."

"So?"

I was so stunned I stopped walking. A prod in the back from an ekos made me start up again, but I looked at Delph in astonishment.

"You wanted to die?"

"I want you to survive, to get through this here place."

"I'm not getting through it without you," I replied heatedly.

"I'm not that important, Vega Jane. Not really. You're the one what needs to live. Like the female what gave you the Elemental said."

"Not important?" I hissed back. "You're all I've got, Delph. I can't go through the Quag without you. I won't."

His face grew red and he looked away. I knew Delph so well that I understood he was searching for the right words to say back to me.

"Well, neither will I," he said. "Both or nothing, eh?"

"Yes."

He drew closer to me. "Then what I'd do is get him up high-like with Destin and when the bloke least expects it, drop the prat."

I nodded slowly. This plan was certainly tempting. But if we killed the king, what might his minions do to us?

Thorne led us back to the room where we had dined. Lit torches still lined the wall. He sat at the table, drew a knife, sliced open his finger and then waved the Stone over it and,

I supposed, thought good thoughts. The wound instantly healed.

He smiled. "We will begin the flight lessons next light," he said. "You will be taken back to the cage until then."

Thorne was intelligent, crafty, vain and mercurial. A difficult combination to corral, but I needed to try. "Surely you have sufficient guards to watch over us without resorting to that," I said. "You'll be invading Wormwood soon enough with your mighty legions. Compared to that, I doubt that the three of us will pose much of a challenge. We are totally in your power."

Thorne rubbed his beard while I stood there watching him. I could hear Delph breathing heavily next to me, no doubt wondering if another arrow would soon be finding its way into his body because of more insolent remarks from me.

However, my plan worked and we soon found ourselves back in the room where I had slept.

The ekos left the three of us there, but I noted that a pair of them was stationed right outside the opening to the room.

I sat on the wooden pallet with Delph next to me. Harry Two sidled up to me. As I petted him, Delph said in a low voice, "It's not enough for us to escape this place, Vega Jane. In his blasted aero ship, Thorne can fly right over the Wall."

"We'll never let that happen, Delph. Never!"

"So you got a plan?" he asked eagerly.

"Um, it's forming right now in my mind," I said lamely. I lay down on the pallet. "I just need to sleep on it is all."

"Sleep!" exclaimed Delph incredulously. "Are ya daft? How can you think of sleep with all this goin' on and all? I'll not sleep a wink. Nae a *wink*!" he added emphatically.

"Brilliant, then you can keep watch."

I closed my eyes, and Harry Two settled down next to me.

As I expected, shortly thereafter, I heard Delph's soft snores. He was stretched out on the hard floor next to the pallet, sound asleep. His features were peaceful. I doubted that would last, but I was glad he could have that feeling for now. I pulled the blanket off the pallet and covered him with it.

I took another look at Delph's features and, despite our desperate circumstances, I felt myself go a bit willy. He was very tall, about six and a half feet, with huge shoulders, long dark hair, a wide forehead that crinkled when he was embarrassed, which was often, and eyes that were deep and brooding. He was so brave. And, well, just such a good Wug. He had never let me down. Never!

And then my heart felt like it had been split in half. Delph was expecting me to have a plan, to lead him and Harry Two out of here. And also to save Wormwood from the mad king. Yet I had nothing. I was not a leader. I was a loner. I had always been a loner, more comfortable up my tree back in Wormwood with only my thoughts as companions. But now . . . ? I felt crippled by the absolute certainty that I was going to let both Delph and Harry Two down.

I lay back on the pallet knowing full well that sleep would not be coming for me.

I had no plan. And without a plan, we had no chance to survive.

The Flight of the King

WE WERE ROUSTED from our beds by rough hands that pulled us awake.

It was a group of ekos, led by Luc.

"All right, all right," muttered Delph as he stood, towering over them.

I stretched and felt kinks in my arms and shoulders pop. I had been dreaming something, but I couldn't remember what. They pushed us out of the chamber and down a poorly lit passageway. I could hear the sounds of digging and I figured that Thorne's minions labored all light and night. He struck me as *that* sort of king.

We filed into a dark chamber with a dirty, pebble-strewn floor. Here, we were forced at sword point to sit on our bums and wait.

Within a few slivers, Thorne walked in. He was dressed in trousers, boots and a long, loose shirt.

"Can we get something to eat?" I asked.

"After we've flown," said Thorne. "It is early yet; your hunger will hold."

I bristled at this, figuring that his belly was no doubt always kept full.

"Do you have the chain?" I asked, biting back my anger. I didn't want Delph struck with another arrow.

He lifted his shirt and I saw it strapped around his waist. Seeing my chain on him made my face flush. He smiled at my obvious discomfort. "To the winner go all the spoils, Vega."

"Right," I said briskly. "Well, let's crack on."

We were joined by a dozen ekos. They all carried short-barreled mortas and pouches of powder and ammo. We made our way up a set of steps in the same chamber that we had fallen into the previous night.

With the cranking of gears, and ekos straining on ropes below, the ceiling canopy rose, revealing the blue sky. As we clambered onto the surface of the Quag, the dozen ekos raced past us and formed a perimeter, their weapons ready and their gazes scanning both sky and land. They looked like they had done this before. Then they removed their peaked caps and put them in their pockets.

Next, they sank down into the long grasses. Except for their eyes, they were completely invisible. Now I understood the grass on their arms and heads. They had adapted to their environment.

I shot a glance at Delph and saw that he had noted this too.

"Blimey," he said. "Figger me dad would have liked to seen that."

I nodded and glanced at Thorne. He was scanning the skies, and then his gaze swept the area we were in. He grunted at an armed ekos, who came forward and relinquished his weapon to Thorne. Thorne expertly examined the morta, raised it to his shoulder, swiveled around, aimed into the air and fired. A moment later a bird fell from the sky, mortally wounded.

Thorne handed the morta back to the ekos and gave me a derisive look. "Unlike you, Vega, I came into the Quag armed and ready. However, when I fell in the hole, I thought I was finished. But when I fired off the first morta round at the ekos, they scattered like dormice. After that, they came back to me on their knees and it's been that way ever since. That was the easy part, actually. The hard part was teaching the blighters to do things, make things. I plan to return to Wormwood in triumph. That's the only thing that's kept me going all this time. Now let's get on with my lesson, Vega. How do you want to proceed?"

"I have to go with you," I said.

"How is that possible?"

I indicated the straps still hanging from my chest.

"Why can't you just tell me what to do?" he countered.

"Fine," I said. "You jump straight up or get a running start and leap into the air. You point your hands where you want to go. Shoulders and head up to gain height. Reverse that to go down. Right before you touch the ground, slip your feet downward so you can land on them. But if you botch any of that while you're up there by yourself, we'll need something to pick up the pieces of you with."

Thorne, if it was possible, paled even more than he already was.

"Let's try it your way first," he said with as much dignity as he could muster.

I held out my hand. "Let me have the chain, then."

"Why?" he asked.

"If I'm controlling the flying, I need to have the chain."

He lifted his shirt, removed it, handed it over and then stood with his back to me while I strapped him into the harness.

He glanced back at me. "Just remember, Vega, that your friend and your canine will be surrounded by my ekos. If anything happens to me, they die."

I turned away so he would not see the utter hatred on my face. "I understand."

Destin, I could tell, had been ice cold while around Thorne's waist. Now the links warmed to my touch. That gave me comfort.

"Because we're tied together, we're going to have to jump straight up. Just mimic my movements. Right, then, on the count of three. One . . . two . . . three!"

On the last number, I kicked off hard, and so did he, albeit a little late. We rose awkwardly into the air and then quickly gained both speed and height.

I slowly lifted my feet into the air, drawing his with mine. We leveled out and soared along. The wind pushed harshly into my eyes and they started to water. From my cloak pocket I pulled out the goggles that I had used at Stacks. Thorne had not taken these from me because there was nothing special about them. But with the goggles on, I could see clearly and not be troubled by the wind in my eyes. Thorne's long hair blew into my face, but I tucked it under the harness's leather straps and it stayed there.

Thorne said, "This is absolutely incredible."

Though I despised him, I nearly laughed at the wonder in

his voice and words. It was exactly how I had felt when I first took to the air.

I led him through the same drills that I had with Delph. We stayed up for a while, doing ascents and descents, changing direction, soaring around trees and over small hills. While Thorne gazed around spellbound, I was taking in every detail and comparing it to the map of the Quag I had in my head and to what I had seen from the cliff when we first entered the Quag.

And with what I was seeing, I thought I might be sick.

The dark, fog-shrouded river I had spotted to the west from the cliff had moved to the north. The forested mountain to the north that had looked blue had shifted to the east. And the rocky slope was no longer even there.

I said to Thorne, "What is that mountain in the distance?"

"I have no idea, having never been there."

"I suppose it's always been there, though," I said. "I mean, whenever you've come up and looked at it, the thing's been right where it's always been?"

He turned his head and I could see a faint smile. "If you're referring to how things in the Quag have a tendency to move themselves, then yes, I have noticed that."

I exclaimed, "How can a mountain or river move? It's impossible, isn't it?"

"You will find that nothing in the Quag is impossible," he sneered.

It seemed barmy to believe such a thing was true, but the facts were literally staring me in the face.

I was ripped from my musings by screams. I looked down. A very young ekos was being chased by two freks. The other ekos were firing their mortas, but the ekos and its pursuers were well out of the weapons' range.

"Idiot creature," snapped Thorne, who was looking down now. "Ah, well, let's do some more maneuvering, Ve—"

However, I had already gone into a steep dive.

"What do you think you're doing?" screamed Thorne.

The little ekos could never outrun the freks. They were gaining with every leap of their long limbs. In less than a sliver, he would be done for.

I aimed so that I would approach from the rear. I slipped Destin from around my waist as Thorne continued to struggle.

"Up, up!" he screamed in my ear.

"No!"

Down below I could see full-grown ekos racing along, their mortas aimed. And there was another ekos — a female, by her appearance — that was running faster than any of them, though she had no morta. I concluded that was the little ekos's mother. She was grunting so loud I knew it was her way of screaming for her young. Whether beast or Wug, a mother would sacrifice anything for her young.

I swooped in behind the freks and used Destin to swat them on the sides of the head. They were instantly bowled over by the blows. I put on a burst of speed, dropped the hand in which I held Destin and soared over the little ekos.

"Grab it," I called down to him. He looked up, the fear so painful to see in his small face.

"Grab it!" I screamed, indicating the chain.

I heard growls behind us. The freks had recovered. I looked back. They were gaining. I looked ahead. A huge stand of trees was just ahead. I had to pull up.

"Go! Go!" screamed Thorne, trying to snatch at the chain that I kept just out of reach. "Leave the damn creature. Leave it!"

"Take it," I yelled at the little ekos, ignoring Thorne. Then, something occurred to me. I grunted. I didn't know exactly what I was grunting, but I figured it was better than jabbering at the poor, terrified thing in Wugish.

He reached out his little hand and his fingers closed around Destin. I instantly pulled up and we did a sharp bank and headed in the other direction, missing the trees and leaving the freks far below.

When the freks turned to follow us, they were met head-on by a mass of morta-firing ekos. I heard shot after shot and then listened to the sounds of two large demonic beasts thudding to the dirt for the very last time.

Good riddance to the bloody things.

We were flying back when I heard a scream. I looked down. The little ekos had lost his grip on the chain. He was plummeting to his death. I went into a dive, but I knew I was too far away to catch him in time. The little ekos was going to die. My heart sank.

Like a blur, Delph came racing into view. He leapt, soaring several feet into the air, his long arms stretched to their limit.

"Yes!" I screamed in joy.

Delph caught the little ekos before he hit the ground. He rose and carried him over to his mother.

The mother took her young in her arms, first hugging and kissing and then scolding him in severe grunts. Then she went back to hugging and kissing him again.

"You imbecile!" roared Thorne at me as we touched down. "You could have gotten me killed. And for what? A bloody ekos? I should have you —"

He stopped because the ekos had surrounded us. Then Luc, accompanied by the mother, approached and knelt down. Each took one of my hands and kissed it.

Then they did the same to a mightily embarrassed Delph.

The mother ekos dragged her young one over and grunted at him until he did the same. When I looked down into his tiny, unwrinkled face, I noted that his eyes were as red as the far older ekos. I smiled, showing each of my teeth. And then my smile deepened when the little creature put his arms around me and squeezed tightly.

Delph was so tall that the little ekos just gripped his legs when he next went to hug him.

Thorne, who, I observed, had been studying all of this quite closely, said kindly, "All right now, it's all over. Everything is fine. The little . . . lad is safe." He made some quick grunts and then pointed at me, and then at himself.

It seemed to me that a few of the ekos looked at us somewhat doubtfully after this. When I asked Thorne what he had said, he assured me that he had given us full credit for the rescue.

Delph whispered, "And if you believe that, I'll sell you a bloody jabbit for a pet."

"Enough flying for this light, Vega," said Thorne. "I have no doubt I will get the hang of it soon enough. And then I will have no more need of your assistance, just your chain. Or, rather, *my* chain." He snatched Destin away from me and then pushed and prodded us along until we descended once more into the darkness beneath the Quag.

We were led back to my chamber, and guards were posted outside. However, a few slivers later, the mother ekos came in carrying a large wooden tray. Luc was behind her. She put the tray down on a stone slab and smiled at us.

On the tray was a pitcher of water and what looked like milk. Some goblets, breads, some meat and a few hard-boiled eggs and a fat tomato, all sliced. And two loaves of bread that oozed warmth. And there was a bowl of nuts and some hunks of different cheeses, which filled the chamber with their deliciously pungent smell.

I smiled and tried to grunt in return, which made her laugh. She reached her grassy arms around me and gave me a hug. I hugged her back. Luc came over and embraced me too. Then the couple, tears in their reddened eyes, departed.

"Blimey," said Delph as he sat down and started digging into the meal. "I think we made some friends this light."

I knelt next to him and poured us out goblets of milk. It was cold and tasted fresh. We were so hungry that we didn't speak — we just chewed, drank and swallowed. I had given Harry Two his share, which he was happily devouring on the stone floor. I finished my meal and sat there idly rubbing my canine's ears.

Delph finally pushed away from the tray after finishing a long drink of milk, and looked at me. "So what be in your head, Vega Jane?"

I took a deep breath and then just let it out. "What be in my head is that we have to get out of here before old King Thorne runs out of use for us. But first we need to find out more of his plan to attack Wormwood. And I still want to know how he got down that cliff."

"Why is that so important to you?" he asked.

"Because I don't like unanswered questions. Thorne is evil. You saw how he was going to let that little ekos die."

Delph nodded. "I guess royalty don't care about ordinary blokes."

"Well, Luc and the female cared."

"Aye," Delph said. "'Tis a bit comfortin', though, ain't it?"

I gave him a perplexed look. "What is?" I asked.

"Well, creatures what got grass growing on 'em and talk in grunts got feelings like us. Care 'bout each other. All I'm saying. Comfortin'."

There was a lot going on in Delph's head. And that, for me, *was* comforting.

I eyed the doorway, where I could now see Luc taking a peek at us. An idea struck me.

"I think this night would be a great opportunity for us to do a little exploring."

"Exploring!" exclaimed Delph. "And how do you 'spect us to do that?"

"Like you said, we made some friends here."

Luc Speaks

THE MOTHER EKOS and Luc entered our chamber later to retrieve the meal tray.

I said, "I know you can't understand me, but thank you."

"It is we who need to thank you, Vega," said Luc as the female ekos nodded.

"You can speak Wugish?" I asked Luc in astonishment.

"King Thorne taught me as a way to prevent him from losing the speech himself. And I taught my daughter here, Cere."

Cere added, "We do not speak Wug to the others. King Thorne forbids it."

"And it was your son that was nearly killed by the freks?" I asked.

She nodded, and tears clustered in her eyes. "But for you and Delph, Vega, little Kori would be no more." She placed a grassy hand gently against my cheek. "Despite what King Thorne said, we knew that to be true."

Delph said, "So what load-a rubbish did the mighty 'king' say then, eh?"

Luc answered, "That it was *his* idea to save Kori."

"He tried to stop me from saving him. He's an evil Wug."

"Yet we all fear him too much to ever oust him," said Luc.

Delph scoffed. "There're lots of you blokes. And only one-a him."

"But he is the king," said Cere in a trembling voice. "And he sleeps behind a door made of iron. And he has recruited spies among us who report to him. Any signs of rebellion are quashed."

"Surely the ekos would rally around you, Luc," I said.

He lowered his head. "No, Vega. That would not happen."

"Why not?"

He would not look at me as he said the words. "Thorne works us hard, no doubt. But he has taught us skills and he keeps us safe."

"You could do all that without him," I pointed out.

"Yet many ekos worship him," added Cere. "I don't know why, really, because he is a cruel one, but they would follow him anywhere."

I looked at Delph and then back at Luc. "That seems very odd," I said. "I mean, he's not exactly lovable, is he?"

"Well, it is mostly because he has broken our will, our spirit," Luc explained. "Such a thing is greater than any weapon."

I thought about this but could think of no ready reply. I decided to change the subject. I said, "We must escape from here. But before we go, I would like to find answers to questions I have. Will you help us?"

Luc looked at Cere, who stared up anxiously at him. Finally, he nodded. "You saved little Kori, so we will come back this night. And then you will have your answers, Vega."

LATE THAT NIGHT, we could hear footsteps approaching. And a sliver later, along the outer stone passageway, we could both see the shadows created by a light coming our way. Then Luc appeared in the opening to our chamber holding a flickering candle in one hand. Cere was behind him, looking pale and frightened.

He said softly, "Tread lightly. There are eyes in the least likely places."

The guards that had been stationed outside our chamber were no longer there. I figured that was Luc's doing. The three of us followed him back down the passageway. I had told Harry Two not to bark or otherwise make undue noise. I could have sworn he nodded his head at me as I finished speaking.

We flitted down the cold passage. I did have one comforting thought. I had on my cloak. And in my cloak were my glove and the Elemental.

We reached a spot where three corridors intersected and Luc led us down the one on the far left. We reached a wooden door, which Luc unlocked with a fat bronze key that he unclipped from a blackened iron ring on his wide leather belt. He pushed the door open and ushered us in before closing the portal behind us. The chamber was dark, but it brightened considerably when Luc used his candle to light the torches suspended on the wall.

I gaped.

And so did Delph.

And we did so for good reason.

The chamber was vast, with high ceilings. And strewn throughout were broad, scarred and stained wooden worktables overflowing with what looked to be intricate tasks in progress. There were old worm-eaten plank shelves, literally bursting with strange objects, and piles of parchment, scrolls and leather-backed tomes. And an old desk packed with drawers and cubbies that were, in turn, bulging with scrolls and parchment. And there was a wooden swivel chair tucked into the kneehole. And on a series of low tables were bottles, scales and other delicate instruments that I had seen and used at Stacks to do my job as a Finisher.

"He couldn't have brought all this with him from Worm-wood," I said.

Luc said, "He did some of the parchment, ink, scrolls and a few of the instruments and tools you see. The rest came later. And the furniture we built according to his design after he showed us how. Thorne taught us a great deal. All he asked in return was our freedom." Luc finished in a resigned tone.

As my gaze spanned the place, it came to rest on something suspended from a long metal chain affixed to the ceiling in one far corner. It was a skeleton. And next to the skeleton and attached to the wall was the outer layer of the thing — the skin. And now I believed I knew how Thorne had made it from the cliff down to here.

"That's an adar," mumbled Delph.

"*Was* an adar," I corrected. "That's how Thorne managed the cliff. He *flew* down like we did."

"It's a big 'un," noted Delph. "Bigger'n I've ever seen."

I turned to Luc. "This is his . . . what, workshop?"

"Well, he calls it a *laboratory*," said Luc. "He spends most of his time in here, working away, talking to himself, sometimes cackling like he's gone barmy."

"I think he *has* gone barmy."

I walked around the chamber and eyed some drawings that had been fastened to the walls. These were maps of Wormwood, down to the smallest details. In the precision of the words and pictures I sensed cunning and genius, but also a sickness of the mind. It gave me chills just to look upon the parchment and to envision the mad Wug bent over his terrible obsession for the destruction of his former home.

These maps had been drawn for a very clear reason. They were going to be used as the basis of attack. I noted Thorne's scribbles and margin notes all over the parchment pages. There was an area noted as the landing place. He would probably send out his aero ship at night and make his landings at that spot while Wormwood slept. Then when his army was fully on site he would attack and take them all by surprise.

There were arrows pointing at Stacks and Steeples and the Council building, with references like "first target" and "use for prisoners," and with a shiver I read the word *Destroy* written over both the Care and hospital. I wondered why, but then it occurred to me that in a war, the side that could not take care of its citizens or treat their wounds would likely not be victorious.

I looked at Delph, who had been peering over my shoulder. He looked sickened by all of it.

"A nutter, Vega Jane, a nutter who wants to kill. We got to stop 'im."

I looked at Luc. "Can we go to the aero ship now?"

We made our way quickly through a number of passageways until I was hopelessly lost. But when I looked back at Delph, he nodded.

"I know where we are," he whispered. "It's just up there on the left."

Sure enough, Luc and Cere stopped and turned to the left and passed through another opening in the wall. The aero ship towered over us like an enormous beast waiting to strike and then devour. There was no one else here.

We drew nearer to the huge wooden carriage that would hold both troops and their weapons. It was then that I noted the series of holes in the sides.

"What are those for?" I asked.

In answer, Luc pointed against one wall. "How he plans to steer it. Look."

Delph and I saw the long oars with large, flat rectangular ends neatly stacked there.

Luc showed us how they worked and then took us through the rest of the aero ship, pointing out the contraption that filled the huge bladder with heated air, and the steering mechanism. And how vents in the bladder released air and allowed the aero ship to descend.

I nodded in understanding. "And what's the cause of your reddened eyes?" I asked.

"Mixing the morta powder," he said. "Powder dust gets in 'em."

"But Kori has red eyes too. Surely he doesn't make —"

"Thorne don't care how old or young one is, Vega," said Luc. "We all have to work."

My blood boiling at this revelation, we went back out in the passage. I said expectantly, "The grubbs?"

He nodded wearily. "Aye, the grubbs."

And I observed, as he said this, that he placed one large hand on the hilt of the short-barreled morta that rode on his belt. He turned to Cere and said, "You best head on back. Kori will be missing you."

Cere gave him a worried look. "Luc, think what you're doing. If Thorne finds out!"

"You just go on, Cere. Go on now," he added sternly.

With a baleful glance back at us, she quickly disappeared down the tunnel.

"Let's be off, then," Luc said firmly, but I could see the fear in his eyes. Not because of the grubbs, I didn't think, but because of the king.

I glanced at Delph. I could tell he was thinking exactly what I was.

Luc could be killed for helping us. But I didn't know any other way to do this. And I did have a plan. Well, part of one anyway.

Delph was expecting me to lead. Hel, I was expecting me to lead. I just hoped I wasn't leading us to our doom.

The Plight of Grubbs

I COULD BOTH FEEL and hear my heart pounding as we walked down that long, dark passageway. We had gone far enough, perhaps a half mile, that I could just tell we were entering areas that were far removed from the life of the Kingdom of Cataphile denizens. Luc was walking in slow, measured strides, his gaze swiveling from side to side. When I looked at Delph, he was glancing over his shoulder.

"Luc," he said, turning back around. "Do grubbs attack anything?"

"No. Not without a reason."

I looked at Delph. "So let's not give them a reason."

Luc's steps slowed as we neared what looked to be a blank wall. I thought perhaps Luc had taken a wrong turn down here, when I heard it. I suppose that's when we *all* heard it. And then felt it.

Rumblings, and the ground under us starting to shake. Dirt and stone dust from overhead cascaded down. We started to cough and gag. I had turned to run back the way we had come when I felt a hand on my arm, holding me in place.

Luc said, "It's all right. Just their way is all. They've heard us approach."

The next moment, the wall in front of us collapsed, revealing a hole. In the hole was a face, which took up the entire opening. A pair of dull yellow eyes was staring at me. When the mouth opened, I could see enormous jagged teeth far more lethal-looking than any knife I'd ever seen.

Luc looked at the creature and said some words that I had no way of understanding. They appeared to be a cross between grunts and hisses. Then he turned to look at us. "They know Thorne's not with us. No need to worry now."

I looked down at the morta. "Then why do you have that out?" I asked.

"Well, grubbs might've struck first and *then* found out Thorne wasn't here. Pays to be cautious when dealing with anything as big and unpredictable as a grubb. That one there weighs about a ton."

I crept forward and rested my gaze on the grubb. It gazed back at me.

"Why is the grubb staring at me like that?"

"Well, you look like Thorne. A Wug, I mean."

"Can you tell it that while I am a Wug, I'm not a Wug like Thorne?"

"Already did, Vega. It's why it hasn't tried to kill you."

My stomach lurched and I found myself backing up a pace or two.

"Its name is, well, no use saying it, you won't be able to pronounce it, much less remember it. We'll just call it Grubb."

"Hello, Gr-Grubb, sir," said a panicky Delph.

"Matter of fact, 'tis a female, Delph," said Luc. "You can tell by the eyes. Yellow for the females and blue for the males. Don't know why, just the way it is."

Luc marched forward and patted the grubb on its, or, rather, *her* head. The grubb let out a sound that I had heard before. But then it had been a feline purring.

"Peaceful creatures," said Luc. "Keep themselves to themselves. They tunnel down here. Can eat through rock faster'n gnomes with their claws can."

"They eat rock?" gasped Delph.

I watched as Harry Two sidled over to the grubb and sniffed it. My canine was perilously close to those enormous teeth and I was about to call him back, when Harry Two licked the thing.

Before I could move, a long, slithery tongue appeared between the jagged teeth and the grubb licked Harry Two back. I moved forward and cautiously put out a hand, stopping and looking questioningly at Luc.

"G'on, then," he said encouragingly. "Grubb knows you're okay."

I patted the grubb's head and then Delph joined me in doing so. It was far softer and not nearly as slimy as I thought it would be. It was like touching a cattail down by the pond back in Wormwood. I could see that it was about twice the size of a creta, which was very large indeed. It must eat a lot of rock.

As we were petting the grubb, Delph's and my fingers touched. I looked up at him and he down at me. We smiled at the same time.

"Like being down at the pond in Wormwood," he said. "You remember?"

"I was just thinking of the cattails we used to rub," I said, blushing a bit.

The grubb licked Delph's hand.

"She's taken a right shine to you, Delph," said Luc.

"What?" gasped a thoroughly wonked Delph. "No, I don't think . . . why, what business is it of yours if Vega Ja—"

I felt so badly for Delph that I interrupted him and said, "I think he means the *grubb*, Delph." I could feel my cheeks afire.

Delph stared openmouthed at me for what seemed ten slivers. His face held so many different expressions, one tracking another, that it was all I could do not to laugh, though I was as embarrassed as he.

"Oh, right, o'course he does," he said in a voice he was trying so hard to make firm that it wobbled badly.

"Um, why do they hate Thorne so?" Delph asked, keeping his gaze away from me.

"Well, they have good reason." Luc pointed to the creature's skin and then rubbed it. "Its hide is strong. But it can also do something else."

"What?" I asked.

"It can expand. Big as you want it to. It's why Thorne kills 'em."

"He kills them?" I exclaimed.

"Slaughters 'em, more like it. Least he did."

"Why is the skin so important to Thorne?" Delph asked.

"For the bladder," answered Luc.

"The bladder, on the aero ship?" I said. Then I realized what he meant. "He uses the grubb's skin to make the bladder?" I added, horrified.

Luc nodded. "Has 'em stitched together. And the grubb's blood? It hardens good and stout when you mix it with a few other ingredients. Where the needle holes are in the bladder when they stitch the hides together? Thorne uses the blood concoction to seal 'em so no air leaks out."

I turned to look at the grubb. While I knew it probably could not understand us, I sensed a deep misery in its eyes. *Her* eyes.

Why did there have to be Wugs like Thorne? Whose only interest was furthering their own goals and not caring a whit about the effect on others? I whispered this thought to Delph.

He nodded and said quietly, "'Tis a good lesson for us all, Vega Jane."

Luc said, "But he hasn't caught a grubb in a long time now." "Why?"

Luc said his next words in a low voice. "'Cause I come and warn 'em and they go hide." He shook his head sadly. "They might not be much to look at, I know. But underneath that hide, they've a heart as big as any you're likely to ever see."

I looked back at the grubb and could see that her yellow eyes were filled with moisture. When I shot a glance at Luc, he had anticipated my question.

"A grubb can sense things like we never can. They can feel what we're feeling. I don't know if we give off a scent or what, but they know. They just know. She understands that we're sad. And so she's sad too. And with that sadness, it also tells her that we're, well, that we're good creatures, not bad."

I had never been referred to as a creature before. But then again, a Wug was just one thing among many other living things, I reckoned.

I turned to look at the grubb and gently rubbed her face. I said, "I think you're very beautiful." And I smiled.

The purring sound filled the passageway again.

I smiled even more broadly, and though I couldn't be sure, it seemed that she was smiling back at me.

"Now she senses happiness," explained Luc.

I said, "Thorne said they've tried to kill him, many times. How?"

"They can tunnel through anything. Never know where they might pop out. Only thing gives 'em away is the sound of their tunneling."

"So I'm sure Thorne, being as cunning as he is, takes precautions?"

"Patrols down the passageways and has things on the wall that measure the smallest of vibrations. Gives him early warning when and where they might be coming. And his sleeping chamber is lined with iron. Grubbs can work their way through iron, but it takes a while. Plenty of time for Thorne to get away, but even so, early on, they came close to getting him."

He looked at the grubb, and his face became embarrassed. "Right more courage than I got."

"But you warned them against Thorne," Delph pointed out. "That takes courage."

"Not the same, is it?" said Luc. "No, not the same."

"It's Cere and Kori, isn't it?" I said. This statement made Luc glance at me. I continued. "He'd hurt them, right? If you turned against him? She was worried that you were showing us these places. She's afraid Thorne will find out."

Luc slowly nodded. "He has ekos fiercely loyal to him. They'd kill their own flesh and blood. I think he's done something to their minds, but I have no proof of that."

A great many thoughts were swirling through my head. I turned to Luc, my determination resolute. "How long did it take Thorne to build the aero ship?"

"Ten or more sessions, close as I remember. Lot of work."

"Ten sessions," I repeated, and then smiled. That was a good thing, I thought. "And if he can't catch any more grubbs, he can't build another bladder or aero ship."

Delph whispered in my ear, "What are you planning to do, Vega Jane?"

"Escape this place *and* make sure he can't attack Wormwood," I said flatly, as though it were obvious. And it was to me.

I had expected Delph to simply nod in agreement. Only he didn't.

"'Tain't that simple, Vega."

"What?" I said, startled.

"What about the ekos and gnomes?" He rubbed the face of the grubb. "And these here creatures?"

"I don't understand you, Delph."

"You heard Luc. Thorne has spies. Those loyal to him. If we escape and ruin his plans, you think he won't take it out on them? On Luc, and Cere and little Kori?"

I couldn't look at Delph because I knew he was right. My heart was being torn in half with this dilemma. "We . . . we can't save everyone, Delph. It's impossible."

"Well, we can try," he replied matter-of-factly.

I started to snap something back at him, but then I realized that he was entirely in the right. I felt both relieved by this but also like a mountain had settled upon my shoulders. We had come in here with the goal of surviving the Quag. Now we would be committing to saving a bunch of others as well. But Delph was right. We had to at least try.

I said slowly, "We *can* try, Delph. But I'm going to need help. I can't do this alone."

"That's why ya got me, Vega Jane."

The King's Secret

FOR THE NEXT five lights, I carried Thorne in the harness and taught him the intricacies of flying. And each night, we were visited by Luc, sometimes accompanied by Cere. They had continued to provide us with information about Thorne.

Delph and I were doing our best to come up with a plan. We had parts of it in good shape, but how could we ensure that once we left, Thorne would be king no longer?

And I did have one unanswered question that was driving me mad.

Why did Thorne want to go to war with his own kind? What would make a Wug hate other Wugs so much? I talked to Delph about this one night.

"Well," he said. "Seems to me that to answer that question, we need to know why the bloke came into the Quag in the first place. Pretty desperate thing to do. And he told us that he was forced to leave."

"That's right. Although I think he *had* to flee. If he had done something bad they would have put him in Valhall, not made him go into the Quag."

"Whatever he did musta been pretty bad, then, to make

him choose the Quag. They were probably going to lop off his head if he stayed in Wormwood."

I shivered a bit. That had almost happened to me.

"So maybe one ties into the other?" I said. "He's getting back at them for making him leave?"

"Way I see it, yeah."

An idea came to me. I quickly told Delph about it.

He said thoughtfully, "It may work, but we need to know more."

"We know who to ask, then," I replied.

The next night, I queried Luc if he knew why Thorne had come into the Quag.

Luc said, "Well, when he's been far into the bottles of mead some nights, I've heard him say things. Spouting off names and such."

"What names?" I asked anxiously.

Luc rubbed his cheek, staring off. "Me— Let me think now. Mer. No, Mur–Murgatroyd. Yes, that was it. Murgatroyd."

The name meant nothing to me. I looked at Delph, who shook his head.

"Anything else?"

"He would go on about Wugs not seeing him for the great leader he was. Oh, he did mention another name, 'cept you already know it."

"What?" I asked.

"Virgil."

"They were friends, I guess."

"In his mead cups, he didn't sound none too friendly toward him."

I puzzled over this for a bit. "Luc, is there any way I can get into Thorne's sleeping chamber?"

"Don't see how. Keeps it locked when he's out of it and locked when he's in it. Why?"

Delph said, "We think the reason he came into the Quag might be in there."

"Aye, if he wanted to keep it secret, that would be the place, for no one goes in there but him."

"Can you at least show us where he sleeps, Luc?" I asked.

We passed through quite a few corridors until I was hopelessly lost, but I knew Delph probably wasn't. I looked back at him to confirm that he could find this place again if need be. He gave a quick nod.

Luc stopped at the beginning of a passage and pointed down the corridor of stone. It was well lighted and thus I could easily see the massive door at the end, set directly into the rock wall. There were no guards posted outside the door, yet it looked impenetrable.

On the return journey, I spoke to Luc in a low voice. At first he was not receptive to my ideas, but I could sense that the courage and spirit Thorne had taken from him was slowly returning to the head ekos.

As soon as we got back to our little chamber, Luc left us.

"We *have* to get into Thorne's sleeping chamber," I said. As I said it, I felt the collywobbles in my stomach, like a million moths were flying around in there.

Delph nodded. "Thorne's become quite a dab hand at

71

flying. Which means he won't need us much longer, will he? Then we'll be bones on a wall."

"Luc will help, but I need a way to get into his room while Thorne isn't there."

"Then what you need is to get him outta his room."

I frowned. "Brilliant, Delph. I wish I would have thought of that. Well done," I added sarcastically.

"No, I mean you need a distraction."

"What sort?" I asked curiously.

"He's afraid of grubbs, right?"

"Well, yeah, they want to kill him. So?"

"So we start with that and build our plan."

"You got some grubbs that'll do your bidding?" I asked skeptically.

My cloak was hanging on a peg on the wall. He reached in one of its pockets, put on my glove, pulled out the Elemental and willed it to full size.

"The Elemental?" I said, completely puzzled.

He nodded. "With this I get to pretend I'm something that I'm not."

I smiled as I finally understood what he meant. "A grubb," I said.

THIRTY SLIVERS LATER, Delph and I peered around the corner of the passageway leading to Thorne's chamber. Delph was holding the Elemental.

"Luc is all ready to go," I said.

Delph nodded, exhaled a long breath and said, "You best be getting on, then."

I hurried down the passageway and secreted myself in a

niche that would keep me hidden from view. I leaned out, looked back down the passage at Delph and nodded. Then I squeezed myself back into the niche.

I saw the Elemental blast past me, its turbulent wake snuffing out the torches on the wall as it sailed by. Then it struck the door a terrific blow, knocking it down. Moments later, in the near darkness now, I saw it zoom back toward Delph.

There were screams and shouts and I knew Luc had done his task as well. Ekos up and down passages were crying out that the grubbs were attacking.

The next sliver, I heard him.

It was Thorne shouting orders, and I shrunk back as far as I could in the niche when he raced past me in the now darkened passage, a short-barreled morta in one hand and a flickering candle in the other. He was in his sleeping clothes, his hair wild and flying around his face. He had Destin around his waist.

As soon as he was well past me, I turned and ran toward his chamber. I didn't know how long I would have, but I doubted it would be long.

The illumination from the candle I had brought and just now lighted showed that the chamber had few furnishings. A bed, a nightstand, and an old wardrobe set against one wall. There was nothing on the bed except a pile of sheets and blankets; a pillow was lying on the floor.

I looked at the narrow crevice between the floor and the bed — nothing. Then I hefted the mattress.

Yes!

Wedged in among the ropes that supported the mattress was a book.

I snatched it free and put the mattress back in place. I looked down at the book.

Log of Experiments?

I opened it to the first page. There was neat handwriting that I knew to be Thorne's, having seen samples of it in his laboratory. I read down some of it quickly, but I could make neither head nor tail of it. I looked down at the mattress. It had been a labor lifting it and I was pretty strong. The book of experiments was full; there wasn't an empty page left in it. I doubted that Thorne would take it out often just to look at it. And thus he probably wouldn't notice it missing. I knew it was a risk, yet this might be the only chance I had. I thrust it into my cloak and continued on.

I found nothing in the nightstand. That left the wardrobe. I pulled open the wardrobe doors and rifled quickly through the clothing hanging there. Next, my fingers frantically tugged at drawers, but I found nothing in them.

And then my hand closed around the box.

It was in an open cubby at the bottom of the wardrobe. It was wooden with carvings that made no sense to me. I opened the box and gasped. Inside was my grandfather's ring, along with the Adder Stone. My first thought was to take them, but Thorne would surely miss them. Unlike the book under the mattress, these objects were new to him and far more easily accessed. On the other hand, I might not get another chance to retrieve them. It was an agonizing choice. Finally, I decided to leave them there, and continued to rummage through the box. My fingers closed around a picture of three Wugs.

One was evidently a younger Thorne. He was standing next to a grown female. Perhaps this was the Murgatroyd that

Luc said he had heard Thorne mention. And next to her was a very young female who looked both familiar and foreign to me. There was the hint of something I recognized in the eyes and around the jawline, but the rest of her didn't jog anything in my mind.

I turned when I heard footsteps and then a morta was fired off. With the labyrinth of passages down here, the echoes played funny tricks on one's hearing. I couldn't really tell how close Thorne might be. Another loud explosion caused me to jump and I dropped the picture. I waited, holding my breath, to see if another explosion would come. When it didn't, I picked up the picture, and this time the other side was facing me. I looked at the handwriting scrawled on the back. I held the candle closer so I could read it clearly.

Thorne, Murgatroyd and —

My breath caught in my throat. *Morrigone.*

Thorne was Morrigone's *father.* And Murgatroyd was her mother. The likeness among them tallied. When I looked at the picture once more, I instantly recognized the younger Morrigone and wondered why I hadn't the first time.

Morrigone had told me her father suffered an Event when she was six sessions old. He had been down near the edge of the Quag, she said, hunting for a certain type of mushroom. Yet he hadn't suffered an Event. He had done something bad that had caused him to escape punishment by entering the Quag.

What had happened to Murgatroyd? Morrigone had never mentioned her.

I quickly remembered, though, that Julius Domitar *had* mentioned her, only not by name. He had said that it was

Morrigone's job to take care of Wormwood and all Wugs in it. He said that such tasks were often passed down in families and that Morrigone's *mother* had done it before her.

So Murgatroyd had been Wormwood's protector prior to Morrigone assuming the role. Then *what* had happened to Murgatroyd? I needed to know.

The shouts and running feet were growing closer and I knew my time here was limited. Only there was one more thing in the box that needed my attention.

I pulled out the sheet of parchment. It was a letter addressed to Thorne. The handwriting was precise and clear. While I could tell the paper was very old, the ink was still as clear as the sky on a brilliantly bright, cloudless light.

I read the contents of the letter quickly, slowing as I neared the end. When I saw the signature at the bottom, I thought my heart would stop. So many things started to make sense to me. Then I heard Thorne's voice and shot a glance over my shoulder. He was very nearly at the door.

Which meant I was trapped.

Nothing from Something

I LOOKED FRANTICALLY AROUND. There was no space under the bed. The nightstand was too small to conceal me. There was only one option. I put out my candle, jumped up into the wardrobe and shut the doors. I was trying to shrink myself behind the clothing when I heard Thorne enter his chamber.

At first, I dared not move. The box was still in my hand. As I bent over to set it down, the contents inside shifted, making a slight sound. I held my breath, hoping beyond hope that he had not heard it. A sliver went by and I finally let out the breath. I figured it had been the ring sliding around that made the noise. I slowly opened the box and felt for the ring in the darkness. My fingers closed around it and I slipped it on. Then I set down the box and waited.

I heard Thorne muttering to himself. He seemed to be spending some slivers around the fallen door. That made sense, I thought. How could so paranoid a Wug safely go back to sleep exposed, particularly after such an attack? Then I heard grunts and more grunts. A group of ekos apparently had joined their king. I heard a great deal of huffing and puffing and then something hard hitting something else hard.

The grunts continued for about a sliver and then there were multiple footsteps going away. Then silence.

As I stood there in the wardrobe, I thought about what to do. Finally, I reached an answer. My plan would be to wait until he fell soundly asleep and then make my way out of the chamber through where his door had once been.

His mutterings continued and I grew more and more curious as to what the bloke was doing. I found that if I leaned forward, I could see through a slight gap between the two wardrobe doors. The chamber was lighted now because Thorne had evidently lit the wall torches when he'd returned.

My hopes of escape plummeted.

Thorne had had the ekos lift the door and place it in its opening. While it was no longer a perfect fit, there was no crevice big enough for me to fit through. I would have to stay here all night and wait for Thorne to leave next light, or risk knocking the door over as soon as he was asleep.

Then, suddenly, I had a far greater problem.

Thorne was heading right for the wardrobe.

I saw with a thrill of horror that his nightshirt was filthy. He was going to put on a fresh nightshirt to replace the dirty one.

I shrunk back as far as I could, though I knew it couldn't possibly be enough. In my anxiety I nervously twisted my grandfather's ring around and around on my thumb. The doors were flung open and I caught a breath and closed my eyes, waiting for the blow to fall.

Nothing happened. I opened my eyes. Thorne was staring right at me, our faces barely a foot apart. But he made no reaction. It was as if he couldn't see me at all. He pulled out a clean nightshirt and closed the wardrobe door. A sliver later, I heard him settle into his bed. I stood there trying not to breathe, but also trying to sort out what had just happened.

If Thorne could see to take a fresh nightshirt and then climb into bed, how could he possibly not see me? I ran a hand down my leg. I was solid enough. Then I rubbed my finger against the ring. In twisting it around and around, I had reversed it. The part of it with the strange three-hooked design was facing downward, and the ring's band was exposed on the top side of my thumb.

I had worn the ring before and nothing special had happened. But I had never reversed the ring before, I thought. In twisting the ring around as I'd done, had I been, well, rendered incapable of being seen? It seemed an impossible thought, but what other explanation was there?

So could I sneak out of here? I would still have to move the door to get through it. Thorne would certainly know someone or something was there. Or I could stay here and wait for first light. I decided to chance it.

I glanced through the crack once more and saw Thorne in bed. He had kept one candle burning, but the chamber was only partially lighted by it. I waited twenty more slivers until I started to hear his breathing deepen. When a soft snore escaped his lips, I counted to ten and then quietly opened the wardrobe door. It gave a little creak, which sounded to me like the scream of a garm on the hunt.

I froze, awaiting Thorne possibly springing up and wondering how his wardrobe had managed to open its own door. But he didn't stir. I closed the door behind me after sliding the box with the mystic carving back where I'd found it.

I looked up at the massive chamber door. I tried to wedge my head through an opening between it and the wall, but I couldn't fit. The ekos had leaned it back against the wall so that there were only crevices on either side. There was a hole dead center in the door where the Elemental had hit it, only it wasn't large enough for me to climb through. And anyway, it was too far off the floor for me to reach.

I placed my fingers inside one of the crevices, set my feet and pulled. The door didn't budge. It would have been easy with Destin around my waist because of the exceptional strength it conveyed to me. But my chain was around Thorne's waist and I seriously doubted I could strip it off him without the bloke noticing. I almost cried out when I heard the whispery voice from the other side of the huge door.

"Wotcha, Vega Jane?"

It was Delph.

I crept forward and put my mouth right next to the crevice.

"He's in here asleep, but I can't get out."

"Stand back," he said.

"What are you going to do?" I breathed through the crevice.

"Same as I did before."

The Elemental struck the door dead-on less than a sliver later, and it toppled inward. I was through the opening so fast that I could see the Elemental smack back into Delph's outstretched glove. Then he disappeared down the hall, running for his life. I was also running for my life down the passage because morta rounds were exploding out of the chamber I had just escaped. I turned for a moment and saw Thorne in the open doorway. He had a short-barreled morta in either hand and was blasting away. And though I might be invisible, I was still flesh and blood. One round zinged past my ear. Another splattered off the wall, and a piece of stone shattered off, hit my arm and cut it. I kept running and didn't stop until I was back in our sleeping chamber. Delph was already there, bent over, his big chest heaving in and out.

The full-size Elemental was on the floor. Delph had forgotten to shrink it and Thorne might be here any sliver. I snatched the glove off his hand, hefted the golden lance and willed it to its tiny size.

Delph nearly jumped to the ceiling. It was then I realized that he could not see me. He had just seen the Elemental and the glove suspended in air.

I spun the ring around until it was back to its normal position.

He stared at me like he'd seen an adar flying around the room.

"How — how — how —?" Poor Delph couldn't finish. He was shaking too badly.

"It was the ring." I held it up.

"How can a bloody ring make you . . . make you not there?"

I twisted the ring and vanished. I knew I had vanished because Delph was looking around to see where I'd gone. I put it back once more and reappeared. "I don't know how it does it, Delph. I'm just glad it did so this night. Otherwise I'd be dead." This made me remember what I'd discovered.

"Delph, I have so much to tell you."

I told him about the picture first.

He scratched his chin and said, "So you think Thorne is Morrigone's father?"

"I'm sure of it. And Murgatroyd is her mother. *Was* her mother. She's dead."

"Well, how do you know that?" he asked.

"Because of the second thing I found. It was a letter. From Virgil to Thorne."

"What letter?"

"Virgil accused Thorne of *murdering* Murgatroyd with poisoned mushrooms. He said he was going to see Thorne executed for his crime. And he mentioned Morrigone in the letter. He said that Thorne had robbed her of her mother. *That's* why Thorne had to flee Wormwood."

"Bloody Hel," exclaimed Delph. "That bloke just likes to kill, don't he?"

I sat down on the pallet next to him. "Murgatroyd was like Morrigone. It was her job to take care of Wugs and Wormwood. I bet that made Thorne jealous. I bet he also knew what else she could do. The same things Morrigone can do now."

"Ya mean magic-sorcery stuff?"

"I wonder if Morrigone even knows what really happened to her mother?"

"Makes me feel kind-a sorry for her," said Delph.

I had never thought I would feel sorry for Morrigone. But if Thorne had murdered Morrigone's mother? What a weight to carry in one's heart.

I was surprised that Thorne had not turned up to check on us by now. But perhaps he was chasing down grubbs in some far-off part of his kingdom. At least it would give us some time to think.

Thorne was undeniably a monster. And he had to be stopped. Now. But how? Then I remembered. The book I had taken from under Thorne's mattress. Maybe there was something in there.

I pulled the book out and showed it to Delph.

"Blimey," he said. "Experiments?"

We started reading the book together. It was filled not only with words but with drawings. We both turned pale and then I felt sick to my stomach.

They were drawings of cut-up ekos, gnomes and grubbs. The drawings of young ekos, their bodies all disfigured, made me sick. I had to look away.

"He's . . . been experimenting on *them*," Delph said.

"Someone's coming," I said in a hushed voice. I looked down at the ring. The blasted ring. If I was found with it? And the book!

I gazed around, searching for a hiding place. But there was really nowhere. Then something nudged my hand. It was Harry Two. I looked at my canine and he looked back at me. I took the ring off and he opened his mouth. I placed the ring inside and he closed his snout. I slid the book of experiments under him and Harry Two lay right down, his big body covering it completely. I blew out the candle, and the chamber was plunged into darkness. Delph and I quickly lay down and pretended to be asleep.

A few moments later, Thorne stalked in, followed by a number of ekos. They were carrying torches and mortas. Luc was one of them. I sat up, stretched and let out a yawn.

"What is it?" I asked sleepily. "What's all the fuss now?"

Thorne came to stand over me. He looked first at me, then at Delph. His gaze swept over but did not linger on Harry Two, who lay there on the floor with his snout between his front paws.

"What's all the fuss *now?*" said Thorne. "What do you mean by that?" he added suspiciously.

"Well, there was this commotion before. Screams. Morta shots. Then it quieted down. And then it started up again. But then it quieted down again. Until you blokes showed up."

Thorne kept peering at me. "Have you been here all this time?"

I nodded and said, "Where else would we be?"

Thorne looked at Luc, who said, "'Tis true, my king. They never left here. 'Twas the grubbs come back, no doubt."

"Hmm, I wonder," said Thorne. There was a look in his eyes and a dangerous sound in his tone that made my skin turn cold.

"I want them searched," he said, pointing at me and Delph.

"What are we looking for, my king?" said Luc.

Thorne roared, "I'll know it when I see it, Luc. Just do it."

Now I knew he had discovered the ring missing. I didn't know about the book. Perhaps he hadn't looked under his mattress. I put on my blankest expression and prayed to Steeples that Delph was able to do the same. I took a chance at glancing over at him and discovered that Delph had slumped back down and looked like he was asleep.

I was so proud of him!

We were searched and nothing was found. Of course they never thought to look in my canine's mouth for the ring or under him for the book. Thorne was not pleased, I could tell. And neither was I, at least not entirely. Now I knew Thorne would believe there were traitors among his number. And the last thing I wanted was to bring peril to Luc and his family. As Thorne stalked off, Luc gave me a tremulous glance that only heightened my fear for him.

I reached out my hand and Harry Two obediently opened his mouth and allowed me to retrieve the ring. I wiped it off and put it on, careful to keep the three-hook side up so I wouldn't vanish. Then I took the book back and looked down at it.

"An awful, terrible Wug," said Delph solemnly.

"I know. But with this book, I think we have a chance to make sure he's an ex-king, Delph."

"How d'ya mean?"

"This is proof of the evil things he's been doing to the ekos and gnomes."

His features widened in understanding. "Right, we can give it to Luc and he can . . . he can use it to fire up the ekos like. There's no way they'd remain loyal to Thorne after learning he's been killing their own kind like that."

"But first we have to make sure that Thorne can never attack Wormwood."

"This has to end soon, Vega Jane," said Delph. "He knows we're up to something. We'll never get another chance."

"It will end soon, Delph. It will end next light in fact."

Delph looked at the ring.

"There's a lot more to your grandfather than we thought," he said.

"I think there's a lot more to *everything* than we thought," I said back.

And I did not mean this in a good way.

Gone

THE NEXT LIGHT found us outside for another go at flying Thorne around.

As I readied for our flight, he looked at my arm.

"Cut yourself, did you?" he said pointedly.

I shot a glance at where he was pointing. There was blood on my sleeve from where the stone fragment blasted off by the morta shot had hit me.

"I caught it on a jag of rock."

He gave me a dismissive look and stared up at the sky, which was quickly turning dark and foreboding. "Looks like a storm is coming. Shall we get on?"

When I started to strap Thorne into the harness, he shook his head.

"Positions reversed this time, my dear. I shall carry *you*."

Since I had no choice I allowed him to harness me up and then we kicked off and sailed upward.

The ride up was bumpy as the winds pummeled us. We quickly became soaked as the rain began pelting down. I was glad of my goggles. A skylight spear shot sideways above us and the accompanying thunder-thrust was nearly deafening. I felt Thorne tense above me. It seemed the bloke was scared of a bit of rain and noise.

"Everything okay, O mighty king?" I asked snidely.

He didn't answer. Instead, I felt him wriggling above me. I couldn't tell at first what he was doing. But then it became quite clear as the harness started falling away from him. He had unbuckled it from around his torso. And since he was the only thing keeping me up, that presented a bit of a problem for me. A problem I solved by reaching back and grabbing Destin with one hand.

Unbalanced, we immediately went into a dive.

"Let go," he roared, kicking at me.

"Not bloody likely," I yelled back.

We swooped, barrel-rolled, somersaulted and plunged across the stormy skies.

He kept kicking at me and I kept parrying the blows.

Then I grew tired of that and drew back my fist and walloped him across the face. Blood from his nose spurted so fiercely that it splattered over both of us.

He looked down at me in shock. "You broke my damn nose."

"Here's another just for the Hel of it."

I punched him again, giving him a black eye, and then I added a kick in his belly for good measure. I was a female, 'tis true, but I was tougher than just about any male of my acquaintance, including this git!

He gripped my hand with both of his and tried to peel my fingers from the chain. He managed to pry three away. So I turned to face him and wrapped my legs around his torso. With my legs supporting me, both my hands were free. And I used them to sound effect.

I struck Thorne over every part of his body I could reach. All the hatred, loathing, disgust and just sheer fury I had pent up for this bloke was finally unleashed. I was hurting him for every vile thing he'd done to us. For every ekos and gnome he'd cut up. For every grubb he'd killed. For murdering Murgatroyd. And simply for being the biggest, most evil prat I'd ever had the misfortune to meet.

After a dozen hits, I thought I had very nearly knocked him out. But there was more fight in the old Wug than I gave him credit for. I didn't see the blow coming in time. His fist slammed against my face so hard I thought I felt all my teeth loosen. Thorne was old but he was big. Another blow to my face caused blood to fly from my nose and my face to puff up. I felt woozy and sick. But I was not about to let this git beat me. Thinking he had an advantage, he threw another blow, but I blocked it with my arm, the pain rattling up and down the limb. Then, keeping one leg wrapped around him so I wouldn't plunge to the ground, I drew my other leg back and kneed him in a spot no male ever wanted to be hit. He groaned and went limp.

"Oh no!" I cried out.

Though I had won the fight with Thorne, our combined equilibrium had now been upset by his nearly being unconscious. We fell into a steep dive. I bent my head back and looked down. The only thing I could see was a mass of tree canopies coming at us sickeningly fast.

Thorne must have seen this and roused himself. "You're going to kill us both," he screamed between the gap in his teeth I had caused by knocking a front one out.

"Well, you were trying to kill me," I shouted right back.

I spun us around so that I was on top. I gripped Destin with both hands, like the reins on a slep, and arched my neck and shoulders. Foot by foot we started to point up. As we finally soared upward, my boots brushed the tops of the tree canopy.

Then a skylight spear and accompanying thunder-thrust struck so close that it jarred me loose from Thorne. He seized on this opportunity by grabbing me by the hair with both hands and ripping me away from him. Then he let go, which was perfectly fine with me because unbeknownst to him I had slipped Destin from around his waist while he was mauling me.

I secured Destin around my waist and looked up just in time to see Thorne falling like a boulder.

The mighty king was screaming like a frightened baby Wug.

"Help me, Vega!" he screamed.

Part of me didn't want to do a thing. Let him fall and good riddance to the jumped-up git. But another part of me couldn't let the bloke die, at least not like that.

I suppose that's what separated the likes of him from the likes of me. And the fact was, a fast death was not justice enough for him. Not by a long shot.

I pointed my head and shoulders downward and shot that way as if I was propelled from one of Thorne's cannons. I grabbed him by the hair, to see how he liked it. When we landed, we hit softly enough to barely cause a stumble.

The next moment, a short-barreled morta was leveled against my head.

I had beaten Thorne to a bloody pulp. His face was swollen, nearly unrecognizable. And I'm pretty sure I had cracked a rib or two in addition to my facial injuries.

"I just saved your life," I snapped.

"And I'm about to take yours," he said, a completely deranged look on his bloody face.

The next instant, he was lying facedown and his morta had flown away. I looked down at Harry Two, who was perched on Thorne's back. Harry Two then bit Thorne in his left buttock. The king screamed before I coshed him on the head with my booted foot, knocking him out.

"Come on, Harry Two," I said urgently. "Quick."

I snatched up the harness, which had hit the ground near us, and donned it. Harry Two jumped into my arms and I quickly buckled him in. I jumped straight up and we soared into the stormy sky like a fired arrow.

I pointed us in the direction where I knew Delph was. A skylight spear shot near us and I rolled over and then zipped downward.

"Vega Jane!"

Delph was there running for his life. I knew this to be true because a group of ekos was right behind, firing their mortas at him. I pointed us straight at him and Harry Two and I rocketed toward the ground. At the last possible moment, I leveled out, reached down and gripped Delph's outstretched hand. We soared upward and then did a long backward arc before we both bent our shoulders forward, propelling us to speeds I had never reached before. We would need every bit of it because we had only slivers to execute our plan.

We streaked down the shaft through which we had both previously fallen and landed at the bottom. The only ekos there was Luc. This wasn't by happenstance. Delph had arranged it earlier with the head ekos, who had simply ordered the other ekos away. I freed Harry Two from the harness and gripped Luc's arm.

"The aero ship," I said.

After grabbing our tucks from the sleeping chamber, we followed him down a passageway. Then I abruptly stopped.

"Wait a mo'," I said. I put on my glove, willed the Elemental to full size and took aim.

Delph pulled Luc back and said, "Cover your ears."

I let the Elemental fly and it soared straight ahead and smashed into the towering wall of skulls. There was a terrific explosion and the bony masses collapsed downward, creating a mess of crushed bones on the rock floor. When the dust settled, there wasn't a single pair of eye sockets staring back at us from that hideous collection.

"Bugger off, O mighty King," I shouted to no one in particular.

We arrived at the aero ship's chamber a few slivers later. Luc unlocked the enormous door.

"I'll get the oars," said Delph.

But a sound made us all turn.

It was Cere and little Kori at the doorway.

"Thorne is returning," Cere said breathlessly. "And I have never seen him this angry." She paused, her face quivering. "And from words I have heard, Luc, he knows we have betrayed him. We will not live past this light."

"Yes, you will," I said firmly. I pulled the book from my tuck. "This is the proof you need, Luc. If this doesn't turn your kind against your prat king, nothing will."

Luc took the book, opened it, flipped through a few pages, and his features paled. His expression then turned to one of disgust. And from that to anger. It was as if I could see Luc's courage filling back up inside him. He closed the book and looked up at me.

"I knew that Thorne was mad, but I never suspected . . . this evil."

Delph said, "But you musta known ekos and gnomes were going missing?"

"Aye, but Thorne blamed it all on the grubbs. I can see now it was his way to turn our races against each other."

"He's a cruel monster, Luc," I said. "I don't know what else we'll face in the Quag, but I doubt we'll confront anything more evil than Thorne." I paused. "So what are you going to do about it?" I asked bluntly, tapping the book.

"Do?" said Luc. "Do?" Luc seemed to be swelling right before our eyes, growing into something, or perhaps back into the bloke he had once been.

"We are going to take our lives back. And free us from a bloody king who never should have been allowed to lead a blade of grass."

We exchanged tearful hugs.

As we drew apart, Luc said, "Thank you, Vega. You have given us the chance to fight and take back what is ours. Now go. And good luck to you in your journey."

Luc locked the door behind him. We could hear shouts and running feet in the distance.

While Delph grabbed the oars, I ran over to the aero ship, jumped inside the carriage and started fumbling with the contraption that forced air into the bladder. "Can you figure out how this works?" I called out to Delph.

"I know how it works" came a voice.

I whirled around to see the gnome who had looked at me funny that one light. He came forward from where he had been hidden in a crevice of rock.

"Who are you?" I asked.

"Sieve," he answered.

"And how come you can speak Wugish?" I asked.

"Easy enough. I listen to Luc and the king," he replied smoothly. "No one much notices us gnomes. So you hear things, you do."

"Can you fill it with air?"

He hopped into the carriage and did something with the contraption such that a flame erupted in its belly. There was a whooshing sound and I noted the bladder was rapidly beginning to fill as the heated air was propelled into it.

I turned to Sieve. "How long?"

"Not long," he said. "As you can see."

The ropes holding the carriage in place were already straining against the lift generated by the strengthening buoyancy.

Delph stared up toward the ceiling and his features collapsed. "And how do we open that so we can actually get this thing out?"

I looked where he was looking. It was only then that I noticed there was no opening.

"Damn," I screamed. Our plan was apparently full of holes.

But Sieve pointed to a dark corner where a metal lever was wedged between two large gears. "That's how. It'll open the roof. Plenty of room to get out."

Now I looked at him suspiciously. I didn't care for blokes who were that agreeable. Give me stubbornness or outright deceit any light and I will readily accept it. But casual kindness will bedevil me all night long.

"Why are you helping us?" I demanded.

He smiled and said with a slight hiss, "I don't much like the company of kings." He held up one of his clawlike hands. "I like to get in the dirt. Why we gnomes get along with the grubbs, I 'spect. And I saw you give that book to Luc. I heard what he said. No more bloody king." He clacked his claws several times more in apparent delight at the thought.

Delph pulled on the lever, and a hole opened up directly above the aero ship, which was nearly ready to go.

I glanced at the locked door as footsteps hurried toward it. "Delph, quick! He'll have a key."

We rushed over to some heavy crates built from thick wood stacked next to the door and wedged them against it.

We hurried to the carriage and climbed in, throwing our tucks in too. Delph had already slid the oars through the holes in the sides of the aero ship. There was a knife in a leather sheath inside the carriage. I pulled it out and looked at Delph. "To cut the ropes holding us down."

He nodded and looked upward at the now full bladder. The ropes were mightily creaking and straining to keep the ship tethered to the ground.

There came an almighty crash against the thick door but it held fast with the added weight of the crates behind it.

"Cut the lines," cried Sieve. "Do it now or you will surely perish."

I started hacking the ropes as fast as I could, but they were stout.

Another great crash came and the door split a bit, yet still held.

I heard Thorne roar, "Fetch the cannon!"

Delph grabbed the knife from me and starting sawing at the ropes like a Wug possessed. I looked up and saw the still stormy sky through the opening. Delph had three more ropes to slash. Harry Two clambered up onto the edge of the carriage and began to gnaw at one of them.

I looked around the interior of the carriage for the steering mechanism and the oars that would allow us to navigate. I mentally went through our plan and discovered about four thousand things that could go wrong.

When I heard the cannon being rolled down the passageway, I called out to Sieve, "How are you going to get out of here?"

He held up his claws and smiled, once more showing his stained, pointy teeth. "S'long as I have these, I have a way out."

Then he turned and attacked the rock wall behind him.

Harry Two had cut through his rope. Delph was just about done with his, which left only one.

I gripped it in my hands and pulled with all the strength that Destin provided me. The metal peg that the rope was attached to had been driven deep into the rock. But with one mighty tug, it came free. I fell over backward and hit my head on the fire contraption. I rose up at the same time the carriage did. It was a surprisingly fast ascent. But not fast enough.

The roar of the cannon came an instant later, followed by the door and the crates being blown aside as though they weighed nothing.

Delph screamed.

Harry Two barked.

I ducked.

The cannonball shot between the carriage and the bottom of the bladder.

When I rose back up, I couldn't believe our good fortune.

It had missed us completely and we were very nearly through the opening that would lead us to the outside. But when I looked at Delph, I knew I'd been wrong. The cannonball had hit the rock wall, and a chunk of stone had flown off and slashed Delph's arm. He had dropped to the carriage's bottom, clutching his limb. The blood was pouring down his front.

I knelt beside him and held out the Adder Stone.

"Where'd you get that?" he cried out, his face twisted in pain.

"Nicked it from Thorne's robe when we were cartwheeling across the sky."

I waved it over Delph's wound and thought good thoughts and the blood ceased and the slash healed. Then I used it to fix my wounds from fighting Thorne. I heard shouts and looked over the edge of the aero ship.

Thorne was down there with his fist upraised and his features awash in fury. I could only smile, though, as I looked at his battered face and broken nose.

Then I saw movement to the right of Thorne. It was Sieve. He had stuck his head out of a hole, apparently to see what was going on.

Before I could utter a warning, Thorne, who seemed to have eyes in the back of his head, had turned and fired his morta. The projectile caught Sieve full in the face. He slumped down in the hole, dead.

"You bloody murderer!" I screamed at Thorne.

"I will kill you too!" he roared back.

Then we were through the hole and out into the open expanse of the Quag, where we were quickly slammed by the wind. It was pushing us back toward the cliff. That was not what I wanted.

"Delph," I called out. "The oars."

He dropped down onto the bench, gripped an oar in each hand and pulled.

"The other way!" I shouted over the blasts of the storm.

"Right," he said, and he reversed his sitting position and tugged on the oars.

I snatched the wheel and did my best to guide us where we needed to go.

Every sliver, I looked down at the ground to see what was going on. Then I finally saw what I knew I would. Thorne and his army of ekos. They were about fifty feet behind us.

"Okay, Delph, you can stop rowing."

"Are they catching up?"

"Yes."

He dropped the oars and joined me at the side of the aero ship.

I looked ahead of us. The Quag had changed yet again. The mountains, the river and the ridges all had exchanged places. I could feel a current of energy in the air. And for some reason, I didn't think it was from the storm.

I looked behind us. A column of ekos was aiming their long-barreled mortas directly at the aero ship. Thorne was right behind them, gazing up at us with great delight. I turned to Delph and nodded.

He gripped the cord dangling near the wheel and pulled it, releasing the air from the bladder. We began to lower.

I hoisted Harry Two into the harness. "Delph, take my hand. It's time."

He grabbed our tucks with one hand and gripped my hand with his other. I led him over to the far side of the carriage, away from Thorne and the ekos.

We held hands, each of us looking at the other.

"If this don't work," said Delph.

"It will work," I said firmly.

"Right, but if it don't, well." He leaned down and kissed me on the cheek.

The mortas fired and projectiles tore into the bladder, riddling it with holes.

"Now!" I screamed. I kicked the contraption holding the fire, knocking it over. The wooden carriage quickly became ablaze.

We clambered up on the edge of the carriage and leapt.

Another round of mortas fired off, blasting into the carriage.

I looked behind us and saw that the aero ship was starting to fall.

Right before we were about to hit the ground, I straightened out and we zoomed along just above it. I looked back again and saw the aero ship hit the ground with a tremendous crash, and as the remnants of the bladder fell on top of the carriage, there was a mighty explosion. The flash of light and geyser of smoke towered above us.

Well, I thought, that was the end of Thorne's chance to attack Wormwood. Even if he somehow managed to escape Luc and the other ekos, he would never be able to build another aero ship.

When the smoke cleared away, Delph called out, "Vega Jane, look!"

I turned and saw a sight I will never forget.

Hundreds of armed ekos were racing toward Thorne and his much smaller band. And leading them was Luc. And held aloft in his hand was . . . the book — the proof of Thorne's crimes against the ekos, unmistakably written out in the miserable bloke's own hand.

I turned to Delph, a smile a mile wide on my face.

He gazed back. "I think this is the end of old King Thorne."

"Bloody well overdue," I said firmly.

I turned back around and flew along as fast as I could. About three miles farther on, I was exhausted from toting Delph and Harry Two and our bags of supplies. I aimed my head and shoulders down and we landed a sliver later.

I unhooked Harry Two from the harness and we all sank to the ground and just lay there. I was astonished that we were actually alive. As I looked over at Delph, I could tell he was thinking the exact same thing.

He said, "Well, we done it, didn't we? All the things coulda gone wrong with our plan and we done it." He looked down. "'Cept for Sieve gettin' killed."

"I know, Delph. We never would have made it out except for him. But he died fighting against Thorne. He was very brave."

"Suppose you're right, Vega Jane."

Harry Two gave a sharp bark and we both jumped. But my canine was grinning. It was like he was agreeing with me.

I touched my cheek. "You kissed me right there, before we jumped."

He glanced down, his eyes half-shut. "I . . . I . . ."

I reached over and kissed him on his cheek in the exact same place he'd kissed me.

"Thank you, Delph."

He opened his eyes fully and gazed at me. "For what?"

"Just for being you. Which is pretty bloody wonderful."

And then it happened. From nowhere a dark cloud descended upon us. I could see nothing. I heard Harry Two bark. I heard someone gasp. And then the cloud was gone.

And so was Delph.

Seamus

I JUMPED TO MY feet and screamed. "Delph? DELPH!"

I looked frantically around. He was nowhere. He . . . he was gone. The cloud! I looked to the sky. There was nothing up there except the storm. I rushed around in all directions. I looked behind trees and rocks, and raced over little knolls with Harry Two right behind me. I kept calling out for Delph until my lungs were exhausted. I collapsed to the dirt, my mind racing so fast I couldn't think clearly. Then, as the slivers passed and there was still no Delph, I started to weep, and then cry and then sob. I sobbed so hard I vomited.

I lay there in the dirt, Harry Two curled protectively around me.

I just kept mumbling over and over, "Delph, Delph, Delph. Please come back. Please come back. Please."

But Delph did not come back. He was gone.

I slowly rose from the ground and picked up my tuck. That's when I realized that Delph's tuck was gone. How could that cloud? How could . . . ?

The vile Thorne had told me that nothing was impossible in the Quag. Thorne! Could he have . . . ? But if it had been Thorne, he surely would have taken me too.

As Harry Two and I walked slowly along, I looked down at my feet. I focused on placing one foot in front of the other. I was trying to block out everything else. Most of all, I was trying to not think about Delph not being next to me. I still couldn't quite fathom how it had happened. I even stopped and closed my eyes once, and then opened them, hoping that my nightmare would be over and there Delph would be.

He would look at me with his silly, endearing grin and say, "Wotcha, Vega Jane?"

But he wasn't and so he didn't.

I was just a fifteen-sessions-old female from Wormwood who felt like bawling her eyes out because her best friend was gone.

Only I couldn't. I had no tears left to shed.

I looked ahead. The Quag stretched endlessly.

I looked above and my jaw dropped. The storm was still raging and skylight spears and thunder-thrusts had grown so ubiquitous as to be quite unremarkable. But there was something else in that sky.

It was a huge flying creature nearly the size of the inficio. I didn't know if it was ally or foe. Then, as it swooped lower, I got a better look at it. It was a firebird. Its plumage was a mess of brilliant colors that shone like a beacon even in the darkness of the storm. Its beak and huge claws were hideously sharp. Quentin's book had said that a firebird could be either enemy or ally. I couldn't afford to find out which right now.

"Run!" I cried out to Harry Two.

There was only one possible escape. I saw the opening in the rock up the first ridge. I sprinted toward it, looking over my shoulder for the gigantic bird. But the skies were so dark now and the rain falling so hard that I couldn't see much of anything.

We reached the cave opening and I stopped. Rushing headlong into a dark, confined space in the Quag might be the last thing I ever did. I took a moment to light my lantern and reached in my pocket for my glove, gripped the Elemental and willed it to full size.

I lifted the tuck over one shoulder. With the lantern in my other hand, Harry Two and I cautiously slipped into the mouth of the cave. We had gone about twenty paces when I heard a sound. It was not the growl of a beast, nor could my nose detect a foul odor of any kind. It was more like someone mumbling.

"Hello!" I called out. "Who's there?"

Next moment the mumblings stopped. I did not take this as a good sign. My hand tightened on the Elemental. I crept forward with my canine next to me. The cave was deep and the farther we went into it, the higher and wider it became, until I could easily stand straight up.

"Hello?" I said again.

Something raced across the passage in front of us and plunged into darkness on the other side.

I dropped the lantern and aimed the Elemental. "Come out right now or else I'll . . . I'll hurt you," I said, my voice cracking embarrassingly.

Inch by inch the thing came back into view. I picked up my lantern, holding it high and lighting the passage more fully. The creature was small and it wore a hooded cloak.

"Who are you?" I said breathlessly.

"They calls me Seamus," it replied in Wugish. "What be you, dearie, dearie?" He curiously eyed the Elemental cocked in my hand.

"I'm Vega Jane." I added, "Could you tell me what you are?"

He lowered the hood. "Me's a hob, me is."

I knew this as soon as he dropped the hood. I'd read about hobs in Quentin's book on the Quag. And there had also been a picture. The hob was about half my height, thick in figure with a small but wide jaw, a stout nose, and brown eyes set close above the nose, peaked ears like my canine, only longer and fuller and pinker on the inside. The fingers that had lowered the hood were long, curved and spindly with sharp-looking nails. The bare feet revealed at the hem of the too-short cloak were large and hairy. His cloak was ragged and dirty, and his face, hands and feet not much cleaner.

"I'm a Wugmort," I said.

He inched closer and once more eyed the Elemental. I had forgotten I was still aiming it at him. I lowered it.

"Why's you want to hurt things, dearie, dearie?"

"I don't, unless they want to hurt *me*."

"Hobs don't hurt nobodys."

Quentin's book had said hobs would help you. All you had to do was give them little presents from time to time, though I had no inkling what an appropriate gift might be. "I've heard that of hobs," I said. "Do you live in this cave?"

"Till I moves on."

"It's stormy outside," I said.

"Storms and storms let a hob roams and roams," he said nonsensically.

105

"Do you live in the Quag?"

"What, this here place, you mean?"

"Yes."

He gave me a crooked grin, revealing misshapen teeth. "Where else would I live, dearie, dearie?"

"You can just call me Vega."

"I could if I would if I could."

My head started to throb.

"You says you's a Wugmort? What's that, dearie, dearie?"

"Wug for short. It's what we call someone from Wormwood. It's a village. The Quag surrounds it."

He nodded, though I wasn't sure he even knew what I was talking about.

"Look," I said, "I have a friend, Delph. We were sitting together a ways from here when a dark cloud came down and covered us. When it lifted, he was gone. Can you help me find him? I have to find him. I have to."

Instead of answering, the hob turned his back on me and ventured farther into the cave. I hurriedly grabbed my tuck and lantern and Harry Two and I followed him deeper into the bowels of the place.

We came to a little chamber that was outfitted with a couple of crates, a rolled-up blanket, a bucket and two lighted candles perched on rocks.

I looked around and set my tuck and lantern down and then sat on a crate. It was cold in here and winds from the storm were managing to reach us even this far, causing the candles to flicker. I shivered and drew my cloak closer around me. The next moment I felt terrible guilt. Poor Delph might be out in the storm with nothing over his head.

"You cold, dearie, dearie?" asked Seamus.

I nodded.

He sat down on a crate, drew his hand in his cloak pocket, and what he pulled out of it made me fall backward off my seat and caused Harry Two to start barking.

Seamus ignored this commotion and placed the small ball of blue fire he held in his hand on the dirt, sprinkled a bit of something he had pulled from his other pocket on the tiny tendrils of flames, and they immediately grew to over a foot in height.

I regained my seat and said, "How did you do that?"

He looked up at me with an innocent expression. "Do what?"

"Pull fire from your pocket?"

"I pulls it, I does. Does yousey?"

"No, I does notsey," I said before catching myself. "I mean I do not. I *can't*. Where did you learn to do it?"

"All hobs cans pull fires from their pockets. We just cans, dearie, dearie. We just cans." He finished this statement off with a cackle.

I drew closer to the flames and felt immediate and deep warmth even though it was not a large fire. Flashing through my mind was a remembrance from many sessions ago.

My mother and father and my brother were sitting in front of the fire back at our modest digs in Wormwood. We had eaten our usual small meal. We never had much in terms of things. But I remember sitting on the floor in front of that fire and looking around at each of them, my father with his ready smile, my mother with her kind ways, and my brother staring at a spider in the corner of the ceiling and silently counting its legs, and thinking I was the luckiest Wug there ever was.

The memory faded and I refocused. "Can you help me find my friend?" I said again. I pulled some tins of food and a jug of water from my tuck. "Would you like some of my food and water?" I asked. I had no idea if this would constitute a proper gift, but I had to try.

"What you gots, dearie, dearie?"

"Smoked meat, cheeses, breads, fried pickles, vegetables and some apples and pears, among other things."

He looked disappointed. "Is that alls?"

I looked down at my foods and wondered how there was nothing he fancied. I rummaged around in my tuck and, in doing so, brought out a tin of chocolates that I had purchased from Herman Helvet's shop back in Wormwood. Quick as a flash, Seamus seized the tin and sniffed it.

"This be what Seamus wants, dearie, dearie."

"The whole tin?" I said, stunned.

He answered by using one of his fingernails to slice right through the metal top. He plucked out the chocolate on top and bit into it. He smiled, showing off his pile of crooked, darkened teeth. He devoured that chocolate and then finished off another. "Onesy-twosey for Seamus, saves the resties for later, I will."

He put the tin down and held his hands over the flames. I stared warily at those quite sharp fingernails that had so easily cut through my tin top.

His eyes became more hooded still as he leaned back against the wall and huddled in his cloak. I listened to the storm raging outside and drew closer to the flames. Could

Delph find shelter? Would something find him first? I shivered.

"Can you help me?!" I said. "Please!"

He said nothing but continued to stare at me with half-lidded eyes. Though the look was a bit creepy, I decided to carry on.

"Seamus," I said, "I've given you sweets." When he still didn't say anything, I drew out my Quag book and opened it to the page on hobs.

I read, *"A hob is a force for good. It will befriend those in need. All one has to do is be kind to the hob and provide it a gift and it will serve the giver faithfully."*

I stopped reading and held up the book so he could see the drawing.

"Where did you gets such a thingy?" asked Seamus as he stared curiously at the picture.

"From someone who's been in the Quag and knows of blokes like you," I shot back.

His gaze darted to the tin of chocolates that sat next to the crate. As his hand reached out for it, Harry Two shot forward to perch in front of it, his fangs bared.

Seamus quickly withdrew his hand and said sullenly, "No needs to be like that. Seamus is a good hob, he is. Like the wordsies say."

"So you can help me, right?" I eyed the tin of chocolates. "I'm really worried about my friend."

Seamus clucked. "You should be, dearie, dearie." And then he added without a trace of his claptrap, singsong speech, "For 'tis a dangerous place, this is."

We stared at each other over the smoky flames of the ball

of fire. It was suddenly so silent in the cave that I thought the storm must have ceased.

"He disappeared in a cloud," I said again. "What might you know about that?"

Seamus put a finger up to his mouth as though signaling he was deep in thought. I watched him through the smoke of the conjured flames.

"There's a place," he said. "There's a place rounds here."

"What place?" I snapped, my fear of what might be happening to Delph growing with each breath I took.

"A cottage."

I gaped at him. "What is a *cottage* doing in the Quag?"

On this he fell silent and closed his eyes completely.

"Seamus, what is a cottage doing in the Quag? Does someone live there?"

"Maybe someones does and maybe someones doesn't."

"Are you a good hob or not?" I said heatedly.

"I is a good hob."

"So answer my question. Please."

He opened his eyes and looked at me grumpily.

"'Tis a female that lives there," he said, again with none of the claptrap.

"Dearie, dearie?" I said, my eyebrows hiked.

He sat up and looked at me. I mean he looked at me for what seemed like truly the first time.

"Who's the female in the cottage?" I asked.

"Why you be here?" His tone was suddenly both aggressive and accusing.

"I asked first. And you're a hob who has yet to show me kindness, despite the tin of chocolates."

He pointed at the flames. "You were cold and now you're not!"

"And you've had two of my chocolates." I picked up the can and tossed it to him. He caught it neatly. "And nearly a full tin to spare."

He considered this, his features turning sulky.

"Don't know her name," he said finally.

"Is she kind?" I asked.

"Kind enough," he commented in a pouting tone.

"How does she survive in the Quag with so many dangerous creatures?"

"They leave her alone, don't they?"

"Why?"

"They just do," he said with finality.

"And can she help me find Delph?"

He shrugged. "If she can't, no one here can."

"Can you show me the way there?"

"What! In this bloody storm?" he said in a protesting voice.

"I can fly," I added.

His eyes widened. "Fly? What rubbish!"

I strapped Harry Two into the harness.

"I'll show you. Come on. We haven't a sliver to lose."

He rose and followed me to the cave entrance. The rain was still bucketing down and Seamus gazed out ruefully, but I didn't care. I just needed to find Delph. Though it wasn't night, it was dark because of all the black clouds. Clouds. Like the one that had taken Delph.

I said to Seamus, "That flame you conjured, can we use it to see?"

He seemed surprised by my request but nodded, reached in his pocket and pulled out another little blue ball of fire.

"Climb on my shoulders," I said.

He drew back. "I'm too heavy."

I hoisted him up effortlessly.

"Now, when we fly you can hold on to the straps of the harness, okay?"

"Up there is where we're going?" he said fearfully.

I nodded and said, "But don't worry, I've never had a crash that killed me."

I stepped out into the rain, slid my goggles on, kicked off, and we went in search of the one Wug I could not live without.

The Cottage of Astrea Prine

THE STORM HAD grown in intensity. Even with my goggles, I was flying half-blind. Yet Seamus was holding the ball of blue fire out in front of us, and the rain and wind had no effect on it.

"That way," roared Seamus over the fury of the storm that caused me to roll uncontrollably every few slivers. He pointed to his left and I veered that way.

"How much farther?" I yelled. From his earlier words I imagined the cottage to be far closer.

"Well, it's moved, ain't it?" said Seamus.

"That's bloody wonderful!" I shrieked.

"Down there!" he suddenly shouted.

I looked through my fogged and smeared goggles and beheld a sight that even in the Quag seemed extraordinary.

It wasn't a cottage. It was a dome of emerald green. And it didn't seem solid. It was . . . well, it looked to be simply a glow, like a pulse of a huge heart. But it was unmistakable and it shone clear through the utter madness of the stormy darkness.

I shot downward and saw a landing path next to a small stand of ash trees. I swung my legs down and touched feetfirst. I could hear Seamus mutter, "Never again will me feet leave the ground, so help me, hobsey."

I freed Harry Two from the harness as Seamus gingerly climbed down from his perch on my shoulders. We three stood there staring at the green glow. I looked at the hob.

"So how does one get in?"

"Tricky, tricky, dearie, dearie."

I whirled on him. "If you start that load-a tosh with me again, you're going to see a dicky fit, Seamus the hob, that you will never bloody forget!"

His face fell and he said tersely, "All right, all right, don't wad your knickers. Follow me." We strode single file toward the glow. We stopped within a foot of it and even in the dark I could perceive the outline of a structure within.

"The cottage?" I said, glancing down at Seamus.

He nodded and said with a heavy breath, "The cottage."

"What now?" I asked.

I watched as Seamus took a tentative step forward, but then he stopped and turned to look back at me.

"Well?" I said expectantly. "Budge along."

"Give me a mo'," he said. "Why are you in such a bleedin' hurry anyways?"

"Oh, I dunno, maybe because we're standing in the middle of a raging storm IN THE BLOODY QUAG!"

"Okay, okay, I sees your point." He took several deep breaths.

"Oh, for the love of Alvis Alcumus!" I walked straight into the green glow.

"Oi! Wait!" he shouted.

Harry Two instantly followed and we passed clean through. I turned and looked back at Seamus, who was jumping up and down and gesticulating madly. I reached back through the greenish glow, gripped his hand and pulled him through so he stood next to us inside the emerald dome.

I let go of his hand and stared down at him. His eyes were scrunched closed and he was shivering like he'd been pitched into icy water.

"Uh, Seamus?" I began.

He made a frantic motion for me to shush. Then, little by little, he opened his great, bulbous eyes and stared around. When he realized where he was, he exclaimed in a scolding tone, "Now look what you gone and done."

"*You* brought us here."

"But I didn't tell you to just barge right in. Why, when I think what coulda —"

"What exactly was I supposed to do?" I interrupted sharply.

"Why, you barmy git, wait while I got things sorted out, that's bloody what."

"Well, they're sorted out. We're inside. Now, where's the cottage?"

I had been looking around, but the outline of the structure I had seen from outside the green glow was no longer evident from inside it.

He pointed to his left. "Let's try over there."

"Try over there?" I said blankly. "I thought you'd been here before."

"Well, I have. I mean I been to the green glow, o'course."

"Wait, are you telling me you've never been *inside* the green glow?"

"G'on with ya, what cheek. Why, I ask you."

"I *am* asking you. How many times have you been inside the green glow?"

He looked upward and seemed to be counting off something in his head. He held up a solitary finger. "Well, countin' this time, it comes to, um, one."

"One!" I roared.

He leapt back at my shout. "Well, did you give me a chance? No. You just charged on in. Coulda killed us all."

"So when I walked through the green glow, I could have been killed?"

"And on your head it would have been too."

"Oh, bugger off!" I cried out, and went in search of a cottage that may or may not contain a "nice" female who might or might not eat us the sliver she laid eyes on us.

"You're a right shonky git, Seamus," I called back over my shoulder.

"Trog!" he yelled back.

"Pillock," I screamed in return before hurrying along. Then I stopped. I had just realized something. It was not raining in here. I looked up. There was no storm. No wind. I felt like I was walking along a heated path. It made me feel . . . comforted. We kept walking and cleared a knoll. When we raced down its other side, I saw it.

The cottage. It had a thatch roof, mortared stones for walls and an oval solid-wood door with a light shining through the small square opening at the top of it. There was a short, crazy-angled flagstone path that led to the door.

Gathering my courage, I stepped up onto the block of old blackened stone that formed a rough porch and looked cautiously through the window in the door. Then I suddenly leapt back off the stone and stood there shivering. The door had opened, apparently all by itself.

When I thought things could not get stranger, I heard an imperious voice.

"You may enter," it said. I looked around for the source of the voice, but saw nothing. Still, the voice hadn't sounded particularly threatening. I looked behind me once more and there was a goggle-eyed Seamus standing barely ten feet away. The bloke looked ready to vomit. I probably looked the same.

"It said to enter," I told him nervously.

"W-well, then y-you b-best do what it s-says, eh?"

"Are you coming?" I demanded.

He puffed out his chest and said in a strident voice, "I think I'll keep watch out here, dearie, dearie. Don't want nothing sneakin' up on you, does old Seamus." He gave a crisp little salute.

"Prat," I muttered under my breath, and then I let out a long, resigned sigh. Of all the hobs I could run into, I had to run into *this* one.

I stepped forward into the cottage, Harry Two right next to me. As soon as we had done so, the door swung closed and I heard a lock click into place. I grabbed at the door handle and tried to open it. But even though I had Destin around my waist and my strength was greatly enhanced, the door wouldn't budge.

I turned back around. "Hello?" I said, first in a low voice that could barely be heard even by me. Then I said more loudly, "Hello!"

Nothing.

I looked around. The furniture I saw — a table, a chair and a cupboard — was all small and low to the floor, which was wooden and looked about a thousand sessions old. There was a large clock on the wall whose hands never stopped moving. They whirled around and around the face of the clock. I drew closer and saw that the hands were actually two black snakes inexplicably hardened. Then, when I saw that the face of the clock was actually the flattened countenance of a garm, I leapt back and nearly upset the table, on which was a plate, a cup and utensils all made from tin.

Maybe the female here was actually evil. Maybe Seamus had tricked me. I promised myself if I got out of this cottage alive, I would strangle him.

Gathering my nerves, I said sharply, "Oi, is anyone about in this ruddy place?"

I nearly jumped to the ceiling when it, or she — I wasn't exactly sure what — appeared directly in front of me.

Harry Two barked once and then went silent. I grabbed my chest to try and push my heart back into its proper place. "Holy Steeples," I panted, bent over, all my breath suddenly gone. "Where the blazes did you come from?" I wheezed.

She — now I was sure it was a she — looked back at me. She was small, barely taller than Seamus, which put her at right about my belly button. She was young, maybe twenty sessions, and her black hair hung limply around her shoulders. Her face was oval and her nose, eyes and mouth all small and finely drawn. Her expression was one of mild curiosity mixed with indifference, which struck me as quite odd. I mean, how many Wugs did she have turn up in her digs with a canine in tow? She wore an emerald-colored shawl over a long black cloak.

She kept staring at me with that same curious yet ambivalent expression.

"I'm Vega," I said. "This is my canine, Harry Two."

She looked first at me, then at Harry Two, and then her gaze returned to me.

"I am Astrea Prine," she said, in the same voice that had told me to enter.

"Seamus the hob told me about you and your cottage. I need you to help me find my friend, Delph."

"Delph?" she said questioningly.

"His full name is Daniel Delphia but everyone calls him Delph. He's out in this storm. There was this dark cloud and it covered us and he was gone and . . ."

"Why did you venture here?" she said sharply.

"I don't have time to explain. Delph is out in the storm and I'm worried about him. I don't want anything to happen to him."

She suddenly turned and left the room, this time using her feet.

We hurriedly followed her into the next room, which was far larger than the first and, indeed, appeared much bigger than the entire cottage had looked from the outside. In the very center of the room was a round table.

Astrea strode over to it with quick, short steps and then stopped. We followed. On the table were two identically sized pewter cups. And in each cup sprouted an emerald flame.

"What's that for?" I asked curiously.

She pointed to the cup on the left. "The Quag," she said, and then she took from her pocket what looked like sand and threw it on the flames. They instantly shot much higher. Then she tipped the cup over and the flaming liquid spread across the tabletop.

"Look out!" I exclaimed, reaching out to smother the fire with my cloak.

A moment later, it was as though I had run into an invisible wall. I was frozen, my outstretched hands inches from the molten liquid.

"There is no need, Vega," she said, pointing to the tabletop.

The flames had vanished and the water had spread to engulf the tabletop, with the exception of the other cup, which the water did not touch.

"This is a Seer-See," she said. "A prophetical eye."

Confused, I looked down at the tabletop and my breath seized in my lungs.

It was as though a picture, a *moving* picture, had formed on the table. I scanned it frantically for Delph.

"Amarocs," I said sharply. There was a herd of them in full gallop. They jumped and leapt and galloped and swerved around obstacles with a grace I could barely imagine. They would be beautiful to look at if they weren't so murderous.

"Can you see what they're after?" I was terrified that the something was Delph.

She waved her hand once more and the image leapt ahead of the amarocs. It was a herd of deer. But they were all as white as snow. They were fast, but the amarocs seemed to be gaining.

"The amarocs are swifter than the deer," I said worriedly.

She nodded. "But as you can see, 'tis no matter."

I glanced back at the Seer-See and gasped. The deer were no longer there. In their place were little bits of light that flew into the air and then disappeared, leaving the amarocs rushing around in all directions and roaring in fury.

"What happened to the deer?" I said.

"They were not deer."

"Then what were they?"

"Fairies having a bit of fun at the expense of the amarocs. And more's the better, I say. Bloody troglodytes."

"Can you see Delph on this thing?" I said impatiently, my insides frozen with thoughts of what might have happened to him.

She waved her hand over the tabletop once more.

I caught a breath when I saw him, but then let it out slowly and with relief.

Delph was fast asleep in the huge crook of a towering tree whose canopy was so thick that not one drop of rain could penetrate it. I could see that he had used a bit of rope to secure his perch. That way he could not turn in his sleep and tumble down.

"Is he safe?" I asked worriedly.

In answer, she reached in her cloak pocket and drew something out. She lifted up her hand and let the things she'd drawn out fall onto the tabletop. They looked like grains of rice. They hit the water without making a splash. But I could see the ripples caused by the tiny collision of rice and water. These ripples carried over Delph and formed a circle around him. And then they hardened, becoming still and fixed in the water. It was like he was now in a cage.

"He is free from harm now." She turned once more. "Please come with me, Vega Jane."

As I followed her, it occurred to me that I had never told her my last name was Jane.

A Room with a View

ASTREA USED A large iron key shaped like an arrowhead to open a door and led me into a room that was clearly a library, for every inch of wall was taken up by books in large, ornately carved cases that rose all the way to the ceiling a good fifteen feet above us. In the center of the room were lumpy chairs and scuffed tables scattered hither and thither.

As I gazed around, there was a distinct *click*. A section of the bookcases had opened, revealing a patch of darkness beyond. We entered the space, which was completely black until we had moved into it. Then the room was awash in light that cast the objects in the room into exaggerated relief.

There were comfortable-looking overstuffed armchairs and small tables upon which rested contraptions unrecognizable to me. There was a large wooden desk cut from timber so aged that it looked petrified. Behind the desk was a leather chair with a high wooden back with gleaming nailheads visible. On the desk were papers and parchments and scrolls, stacks of books and glass inkwells and a rack of old-fashioned quills that I had once seen my grandfather use to write a letter.

There was a small fireplace surrounded by brick, with a thin copper-edged chimneypiece upon which sat a clock that, thankfully for my nerves, had no serpents on its face. In front of the empty fireplace were two equally decrepit-looking chairs with the stuffing falling out and tiny footstools in front, where one's feet could draw closer to the warmth if there had been a fire burning.

The next instant, Harry Two and I leapt back as the fireplace, which had been empty not only of fire but also of logs, sprang to life and roaring flames leapt forth. The room, chilly when we had entered, quickly became warm and comforting and, despite my excitement, I felt my eyes droop a bit. I suddenly realized that I was beyond exhausted.

My eyes snapped wide open when I glanced at the floor. It was wooden, the boards worn down over the sessions from the tread of innumerable footsteps. But I was not focused on the planks. I was looking at the square of tattered rug upon it.

More to the point, my gaze held on the images on the rug.

"What are those creatures?" I asked breathlessly.

Harry Two went to stand on the rug, and I watched as he reached out a tentative paw and touched one of the figures woven into its surface.

Astrea pointed to the one on the left. "That's a unicorn. Its horn of course can cure all known poisons."

I had no idea what a unicorn even was. "And the other?" I asked, looking at it. Though undoubtedly aged, the colors of the rug's images were extraordinarily bright, more vibrant than anything I'd ever created at Stacks.

"A firebird," she said casually. "So named because of its exceptionally brilliant plumage. The feathers of the actual bird can be used to light the way and also for warmth against the cold."

"Wait a mo', I've seen one," I said. "It chased me into a cave."

"Indeed? 'Tis not usually dangerous."

"Are you sure Delph is safe?" I blurted out.

"He *is* safe. You care much for your friend?"

"I care everything for him."

"It is a dangerous thing to place so much of one's self in another."

I ignored this and, summoning up courage, I said, "How did you know my surname was Jane?"

Instead of answering, she seized my hand with surprising strength and exclaimed, "That mark? How did you come by it?"

I looked down at the inked three hooks, which I had drawn there.

I jerked my hand free from her grip. I had just endured imprisonment from Thorne. I was not going to make the same mistake with her. Until I knew she was a friend, she would be considered a potential enemy.

"It's the same mark as on this ring." I took it from my cloak pocket and showed it to her. "It belonged to my grandfather," I added warily.

"So he had this ring? You're absolutely certain?"

"Yes." I wasn't about to tell her that it could make me invisible.

She studied the ring for a few more moments before pointing at my hand. "That's only ink."

"I know, because I inked it," I replied promptly. "My grandfather had the same mark on the back of his hand, though it wasn't simply inked."

She waved her hand over mine and the mark vanished.

I stared down at my clean skin and then back up at her.

"Do you know what it means?" I asked.

"No."

I knew she was telling an untruth, which made me ever warier of her.

Before I could ask another question, she walked over to a large blank wall and Harry Two and I scurried after her.

She raised her hand and an astonishingly bright light blasted from it and hit the wall a direct blow. I immediately squatted down and shielded my eyes from what I thought would be a terrific blast emanating from the collision of wall and light. But there was no explosion. I opened my eyes and stood.

And gasped.

The entire wall had come to life. If the little table in the other room was impressive in what it had shown me, this spectacle was like a mountain versus a knoll by comparison. Every inch of the great wall, which must have measured fully fifty feet in length, was now ablaze with images, *moving* images.

Astrea turned to me and said simply, "The Quag. In all its glory. And in all its depravity, which runs deeply. Very deeply indeed."

When I had first seen the extent of the Quag from the top of the plateau where Delph, Harry Two and I were chased by the garms and amarocs, I had been gobsmacked by its breadth and dark, sinister beauty. I had thought I was seeing to the very horizon of the Quag, but I apparently had been wrong about that.

As I watched, spellbound, I could see herds of unknown creatures bounding across open plains and up rugged ridges. Flying creatures, some I knew, most of which I didn't, soared across a sky that was as black as a lump of coal. Trees trembled and creatures crept and I could hear sounds, some gentle that tickled my ears, and others fiercely foreboding that gnarled my nerves and chilled my courage. I saw the majestic peak of the Blue Mountain. And there was the dark river that snaked across the face of the Quag to places unknown and probably hostile. With a thrill that reached all the way to my toes, I thought I saw a small boat with something or someone inside it, slowly making its way across the water's wide, blackened width. That image vanished and was replaced with a frek devouring what looked to be a goat. And then a creature stepped from the trees into the clearing and came into full view.

It was tall and powerfully built, and though it stood on two legs like I did, it had fangs and claws and long, straight hair over its body.

I glanced quickly at Astrea. "What is that ghastly thing?"

"'Tis a lycan," she said.

"I don't know what that is."

"Its bite makes you become like . . . *it*."

We watched as the lycan, with a tremendous leap that covered yards of dirt, attacked the frek. There was a furious battle, for they seemed fairly equally matched. Yet finally the lycan won out and its fangs bit deeply into the frek's neck. The latter howled in pain and fury and then, bloody and beaten, it broke free and fled into the trees.

The lycan stood there, dripping blood from wounds inflicted by the frek, and then it reached its clawed hands to the darkened sky and roared in triumph. It was a terrifying spectacle to witness and yet I found I could not look away.

"The frek's bite drives one mad," I said in a hollow tone.

"The lycan is *already* mad, Vega. A frek's bite will not make a spot of difference to its tortured mind."

A long sliver of silence passed. "What is beyond the Quag?" I asked.

"Why did you enter the Quag?" she asked me once again.

"I don't see why that matters," I said stubbornly.

She looked back at me impassively. "The difference between what I think matters and what you think does could likely fill a bookcase."

"Do you know what's beyond the Quag?" I persisted.

I glanced at her in time to see her face seize up like she was in pain. But before I could say anything, she replied, "It is late. And I'm very tired."

"Well, I'm not tired," I said in a strident tone.

"I will show you your digs and then you can stay up or sleep, as you like."

"And I can go where I want? I mean inside the cottage?"

"You can go into any room that will *let* you. Mind you, not all of them will."

I looked at her like she'd gone completely mental. "The *room* mightn't let me?"

"Rooms have opinions," she said. "And feelings too."

"Feelings!" I exclaimed.

"Feelings I said and feelings I meant," she reiterated forcefully, and then turned and strode away.

I hurried after her, wondering what madness awaited me in this place.

A Question of Doors

M Y DIGS TURNED out to be a large oval room with not a stick of furniture in it. I turned to Astrea and said, "It's all right. I have no problem sleeping on the floor."

"Now, why would you do that, I wonder?" she asked.

I gazed around the room to make sure I had not somehow missed a hulking bedstead lurking in a corner. "Well, I'd need a bed to —"

Harry Two and I jumped back to avoid being crushed by a mammoth four-poster that seemed to drop from the ceiling.

"Bloody Hel," I cried out, my chest heaving and my limbs quivering. Harry Two started barking madly until I held up one hand and he instantly quieted.

"One must be careful what one asks for, at least in *my* cottage," said Astrea casually, as she fluffed up the pillows. She turned to me. "Or at least move quickly on one's feet, as you did, my dear," she added benignly.

"B-but where did that bed come from?"

"It comes from wherever such things exist before they're needed. And it saves no end of cleaning time to have the things go away while they're unnecessary."

"So," I said, "you simply ask for something and it appears?"

"I told you, did I not, that rooms have views and opinions? Does it not logically follow that they can hear what you say?"

"Well, a stout wardrobe would not be unwelcome for my things."

I was ready this time. I had already jumped out of the way when an oak wardrobe with two big doors and a drawer underneath landed with a thud against a wall across from the bed. As I stared at it, the doors opened, and inside were nice cubbies and metal hooks for hanging clothes.

Astrea gave me an appraising look. "I see you're getting the gist of things."

"Should I wish for a table and chairs?" I said, ready to jump.

However, they simply appeared in the corner of the room with a lighted candle in the center, burning brightly. I looked at her inquiringly.

"There's no rule that all things *must* drop from the ceiling," she said. "Now, are you hungry? I daresay things can be scrounged up in the kitchen. It does an excellent trifle, in fact, if you fancy such."

I shook my head, though in truth, as usual, I could have used something in my belly. "I'm full up. You can toddle off to bed while I put my few things away."

She looked at me curiously but also intently. A bit too intently, I thought.

"Well . . . if you're . . . sure?" she said in a drawn-out way.

"Quite sure," I replied, perhaps a bit too quickly. "And we'll go for Delph at first light?"

She said, "Yes."

After she left my digs I turned out my tuck. The cavernous wardrobe swallowed my meager possessions with plenty of room left over.

I jumped up on the bed, which I found quite comfy. Harry Two hopped up next to me and I scratched his ears. He rewarded me with a soft whimper of pleasure. I looked at the door, which had closed when Astrea departed. I jumped down, strode over to it and tried to tug it open. It wouldn't budge.

I looked in disbelief at Harry Two.

"She's locked us in. Well, how do you like that?" I was miffed beyond belief.

I stepped away from the door and sized it up. Then I backed up to get a running start. I glanced at Harry Two. "Don't worry, I want out of here and we *will* be in a mo'."

I started to charge forward and then stopped dead.

The door had swung silently open.

I want out of here. That's what I'd said. And the door had just opened.

I cautiously peered around the corner into the darkened corridor. There was no sign of Astrea. I stepped out of the room, Harry Two right with me. I looked down at him. I guess he could tell I was anxious because he gave my hip a nudge with his snout as though to say *Let's budge along, shall we?*

I looked to the right. I had been down that way. Thus, I turned left.

A door stood on the right side of the passage. I tried the handle, but it was locked. I stepped back, drew up my courage and said in the most polite voice I could muster, "Might I come in, please?"

The door swung open, revealing nothing but darkness.

I looked at Harry Two, who stared back up at me. Now *he* looked anxious.

"Okay, right," I said confidently, though I was feeling not a jot of it actually. I stepped through the doorway. Harry Two followed. As soon as we did, the door shut behind us, and the room brightened.

There was only one object in the room. It was an enormous clock that rested on one huge wall. Attached to it underneath were twin chains with large metal balls affixed to them. The chains disappeared through holes cut in the floor. I crept forward and stared at the clockface. It was unlike any I had seen before. Wug timepieces were divided into the different sections of light and night. There were numbers and words on this one. I drew even closer.

"Century," I read off. That word was under each number etched on the clockface at regular intervals. There was only one hand on the clock. It was now pointed at eight centuries. I had no idea what any of this meant. I stared down at the holes in the floor, into which the chains disappeared. I had no idea where they went. Well, I could learn nothing more here, it seemed.

The next door we reached was about ten feet down the hall.

I stepped in front of it and said, "Might we come in, please?"

"GO AWAY!" The scream was nearly ear-shattering.

I jumped back so far I hit the opposite wall and slumped down, dazed.

"Bloody Hel," I muttered.

I staggered up and we hurried along to the next door.

It opened at my request, though I did cover my ears in anticipation of a negative response. We walked inside and I looked around as the room was illuminated by a source of light that remained invisible to me.

There was a small cradle in one corner. I rushed over to it, but it was empty. It was also covered with cobwebs. So was the entire room, which was filled with old, moldy furniture. While I stood there, I was slowly filled with deep despair, as though only sadness reigned in my heart. Then my despair grew fathoms deeper and I felt tears creep to my eyes. I looked down at Harry Two and I could tell he was having similar emotions. He had lain on the floor and covered his snout with his paws.

When I could stand it no more, I rushed from the room, with Harry Two closely following. When the door closed behind us, the awful feelings instantly vanished. I drew a small knife from my cloak pocket and cut a tiny notch in the wood directly above the door handle. I rushed back and marked in the same way the door that had screamed at me. Now I would know which to leave alone.

The next room shouted at me to GO AWAY! I marked it as well.

The door after that didn't budge at first and I thought the room was going to scream at me. But no sound came. Except finally a tiny click as the door swung open.

I crept inside and looked around as the darkness was dispelled by a wash of light, again from an unknown source. On every single wall were hundreds of paintings. I moved forward so I could see them more clearly.

Groups of females had on long gowns with low-cut necklines revealing far more of themselves than I was used to seeing. Their hair was beautifully styled and layered and piled on top of their heads. The males wore dark cloaks with embroidered stitching and what looked to be gold leaf on their shoulders. Some held short sticks of wood and others had swords in holders on gilded belts encircling their waists. One male clutched a long leather lead attached to a canine that looked like a far larger version of Harry Two. The thing looked proud and noble staring off into the distance as it sat obediently beside its master. I looked down at Harry Two and found him staring at his counterpart cast in oils on canvas. He seemed awestruck.

My gaze kept roaming until it finally stopped and held on one female. She was taller than the others, her flaming red hair pooled luxuriously around her broad, muscled shoulders. I instantly recognized her. She was the one I met on my trip through the fiery portals into the past, which I had discovered at Stacks. I gazed back up at the painting. This female had saved my life and given me the Elemental before dying on the battlefield. Curious though I was about her, my gaze again began roaming to the other paintings, which held landscapes of broad, lovely countryside, towns with towering stone buildings and smoothly laid cobblestone streets. Sleps and carriages were pictured on the cobblestones and there was an air of prosperity and, well, peace.

As I moved around the room, though, the air of hope and prosperity faded. The paintings turned far darker and the lovely gowns, piled-up hair and stately carriages on fine cobblestones were no more. Replacing them were scenes of bloody battlefields, smoldering ruins and abject carnage. Along with this change in subjects, the bright colors of the earlier paintings had disappeared into the shadowy and depressing hues of blacks and grays, displaced only by the garish thrust of bloody red, as someone lay dying. Flames leapt from the stone towers, and everyone looked frightened and confused. In one small painting, there was a young female alone on a street, her face uplifted to the dark sky and her mouth open apparently in a scream as tears fell down her dirty cheeks. The sense of loss was awful.

We left this room and reached the next one. The door opened at my asking. Darkness again. I expected the lights to come on, but they didn't. I did hear something. Something breathing.

The breaths were uneven, harsh, and sounded painful. I felt my own chest tighten as I listened to them. I looked wildly around for the source of the noise.

There was a large four-poster bed set in the deepest crevice of the room. As I drew closer, the room lightened a bit, allowing me to see more clearly.

My jaw dropped when I saw him.

He was the oldest male I had ever laid eyes on, even older than ancient Dis Fidus back in Wormwood. He had not a hair on his head. His beard was snow white and curled down his chest and then past it by a good two feet. His eyes were sunken, hollow and brushed liberally with red. His nose was long and horribly misshapen. His cheeks were flat. When he rose up a bit on his pillow, I could see his hands. They were wrinkled claws with large brown spots across them.

He said in a gasping whisper, "Who . . . are . . . you?"

"I'm . . . I'm . . ." I frantically realized I'd forgotten my own name. *Think, think, you git!* "Vega. I'm Vega J-Jane," I said in a rush.

"J-James?" said the creature, now trying to prop himself up higher.

I hurried to aid him. When I gripped his shoulder through the nightshirt, I could feel it was not much more than bone. His breath was foul and his skin was like the chilliest of water. I easily lifted him because he weighed almost nothing. I stepped back. *"Jane,"* I said more loudly. "Vega Jane."

He looked up at me out of those cavernous eye sockets. "How came you to be here?" he said croakily, though he seemed to be breathing a bit easier.

"A hob named Seamus told me of the place. So I came."

"But why?"

"Because I heard that Astrea Prine would help me."

He gave a shuddering breath and said, "Help you with what, my dear?"

I sprang back as a hand passed by me.

Astrea laid her youthful palm on the aged creature's chest and he instantly calmed, his breathing becoming regular. He thanked her with a smile.

Astrea turned to me and said, "I see that you've met my son, Vega."

The Keeper

I STARED FROM ASTREA to — her *son?*

"You mean he's younger than you are?" I exclaimed. "But —"

She cut me off. "Come with me."

"I thought you were tired?" I asked.

She turned back to her son. "There, there, Archie. Try and get some sleep now, luv, okay?"

She kissed him on his withered forehead.

Harry Two and I followed her out and down the passageway. We returned to the place with the old desk and fireplace that one reached through the secret doorway in the library. She sat down behind the desk and motioned for me to sit across from her.

"If Archie is your son, why is he so old and you're so young?"

In answer she pulled out a small glass flask. "Because of this."

"Is it medicine of some sort?"

"It is an elixir so potent that it keeps one young for as long as one takes it. It is devilishly tricky to make. It requires the blood of a garm and the venom of a jabbit, among other special ingredients."

"How do you get blood and venom from those vile creatures?"

"I keep one of each in cages here at my cottage."

I cried out, "A garm and a jabbit in your cottage!"

"If you tried to enter the rooms where they are kept, they would have told you to 'Go away!'"

I shivered after discovering how close I had been to another wretched jabbit.

"Archie is dying because he chose not to take the youth elixir."

"Why?"

"He no longer sees a point to it."

"Then he'll die?" I asked.

"And soon," she said coldly.

Well, I thought, she was rather heartless. "How old are you?"

"Did you find the room with the clock on the wall and the chains going through the floor holes?"

"Yes."

"What did it read?"

"Eight centuries, whatever that is."

"A century is a hundred sessions."

"A hundred sessions! But what is that clock keeping track of?"

"My time here."

My jaw dropped. "You mean you're eight hundred sessions old?" I could barely process what she was saying. It was all unbelievable.

"A bit older actually. I came here when I was already fully grown."

"I also saw a room with many paintings."

"You were no doubt told about the Battle of the Beasts back in Wormwood?"

"All Wugs were told about it. The beasts attacked Wormwood long ago but were beaten back and thereafter remained in the Quag."

She said emphatically, "Well, that was a lie. There was never such a thing."

"But I've seen the paintings at the Council building —"

She shook her head impatiently. "There *was* a war that took place over a great many sessions. However, it was not with the beasts." She paused.

I was now squeezing both my legs so hard they felt quite numb. "Who was it with, then?"

She gazed at me so strangely I felt myself involuntarily shaking.

"It does not matter. Not now."

"It matters to me," I retorted.

"It was a battle between two opposite forces. One won and one lost. That is all I will say on the matter."

"You tell me nothing," I said forcefully.

"I will tell you this, Vega. We created the village of Wormwood. And then we managed the building of the Quag. And the decision was made to wipe away our history and replace it with another. We called ourselves Wugmorts." She paused. "Do you know why we chose that name?"

I shook my head.

"There is a plant that is universally considered bitter. It is called the Mugwort. We altered it slightly to Wugmort. The survivors carried that feeling of guilt, of bitterness, every time they uttered the word."

I sat forward, my mind filling with questions and possible connections. "I met a creature named Eon. Through him I went back in time. Not just my past. But further back. I was on a great battlefield. A female warrior, while she lay dying, gave me something she called the Elemental, that I could touch using the glove she also gave me. She knew my name. She said I had to survive. And she was in one of the paintings back in that room."

Astrea looked gobsmacked by this information. "You . . . you met her? As she lay dying?"

"Yes. Who was she?"

Astrea didn't look nearly so formidable now. Her eyes held a faraway look, and I could see tears clutching at their corners. She said slowly in a trembling voice, "Her name was Alice Adronis, one of our greatest sorceresses and my dearest friend. The Elemental was her creation." She paused and swallowed. Astrea seemed to be trying very hard not to burst into tears. "She could only live as a victor or die as a warrior, could Alice."

"But why would she know my name? Why would she say I had to survive?"

"I have no idea, Vega. I . . . I . . ." She looked away.

"What happened after that?"

Astrea took a moment to compose herself. "As the first century went by, the magical powers with which we were imbued faded drastically. It was at that point that the decision was made to let them die completely."

"How do you let magic die?" I said slowly. I didn't know why, but I felt a great sense of loss at this.

"By not using it. By not believing in it anymore. Belief, having faith in something, is a very powerful thing, Vega. Perhaps the most powerful thing of all. And as the sessions went by and we started dying off, our descendants knew little of what we were. And finally, virtually no Wug in Wormwood knew anything of us a'tall, but accepted as their history the lies that had been created for them."

I took a deep breath, put aside my misery and told Astrea about the Adder Stone and Destin the chain and how I had come by them at Stacks.

She nodded and said, "Stacks was the castle of our leader, Bastion Cadmus."

"You took his castle with you?" I asked, wondering how this was possible. But, I supposed, anything was possible with blokes who could do magic.

"We had to create another place to live. Every bit was precious to us."

"And the Stone? And Destin?"

"Objects possessed by Bastion."

"And the Quag? And what we were told about it? You haven't explained that."

"I have no need to explain it," she said, her tone sharp again.

I bit back my anger and groped around for something else to ask her.

"But why are you here?" I asked.

"I am, quite simply, the Keeper of the Quag."

"So you had your family here with you at the cottage?"

"Yes. My mate, Thomas, and I came to live here with our sons and daughters." She paused and for the first time I could see her features soften, just a tiny bit. "Thomas never did take the elixir. He was the first of us to go. After Archie passes, it will just be me."

"Why do you do it? Stay here?"

Her eyes flashed. "It's my duty, Vega. I gave an oath as Keeper and I mean to keep it."

She rose, came around the desk and stood next to me. I tried to imagine her as more than eight centuries old, older than poor dying Archie, but I couldn't.

"How much did you know about your grandfather?" she asked.

"He was very nice. But stubborn too."

"He is far more than that. He is an Excalibur."

"A what?"

"Those who are born with their magical powers intact and an innate and profound knowledge and understanding of our real history embedded in their minds. They are terribly rare, but he was one of them."

"My grandfather left Wormwood."

"I know he did."

"And you couldn't stop him?"

"Excaliburs do not carry a sign on their foreheads proclaiming them as such. It was only after he left that we truly became aware of what he was and could do."

"So you saw this, what, through your Seer-See?"

"Yes."

I felt my anger rising. "Then I suppose you saw Morrigone blast me with a blue light, and Delph with a red light that turned his mind to mush and left him jargoled for ten long sessions!" My voice and fury rose as I spoke. "You saw all that, did you?"

"I did," she replied calmly, which made me even more furious.

"She argued with my grandfather. She wanted him to stay."

"Doubtless she did. But against a true Excalibur, she was but nothing."

I stood. "And did you see my parents disappear in a ball of flames? Did you see me crying my heart out? Did you see that, Astrea bloody Prine?!"

Her gaze never wavered. "I did, Vega. I did indeed."

"Well, good for you. I hope you enjoyed it, because I sure as Hel didn't!"

I was halfway to the door when she called out.

"Do you know where they went, Vega?"

I slowly turned and looked at her questioningly. "No, I don't."

She scrutinized me closely before saying, "Let's apply a bit of logic, shall we? If they're not in Wormwood and they're not in the Quag?"

"They're beyond the Quag," I said.

"Yes."

"So why can my grandfather leave Wormwood without ever stepping one foot into the Quag like I have to?"

"Leaving Wormwood and bypassing the Quag would have been easy enough for someone like him."

"And my parents? I suppose they made the decision to leave me?"

"No, Virgil summoned them."

"*Summoned* them? Why?"

"Did he never talk to you about it?" she said fiercely. "Tell me the truth!"

"No, never," I said, taken aback by her harsh tone. Was she as nutters as Thorne?

"You do not know of his plans? Tell me if you do. Tell me!"

I took a step back, for her face had twisted into a furious mass. I thought for a moment that she was going to attack me.

"I have never heard from my grandfather since he left," I said calmly. "And he never told me anything about any plans. All he ever told me was . . . that he loved me."

This was a lie of course. My grandfather had actually told me something about Wormwood. He had said that the most bitterly awful place of all is one that Wugmorts don't know is as wrong as wrong can possibly be. I had no idea what he was talking about then. But now I believed that I did.

Her expression became normal once more and she sat behind her desk and steepled her hands in front of her. "I think that is enough for one night. At next light, we will fetch your friend. And then all will be right again."

She smiled at me in a way that made my skin crawl.

I walked slowly back to my room, wondering who I really was and concluding that I was nothing. If Astrea was right, my grandfather had been able to leave Wormwood because he was magical, this Excalibur thing in fact. And he had summoned my parents to join him, which showed that he could bring others to him if he so desired. But he hadn't summoned me. He had left me behind, in Wormwood. He apparently considered me of no importance whatsoever.

So no matter whether I made it through the Quag or died here, I was nothing. Sometimes the truth helps. Sometimes it hurts.

And sometimes it destroys you.

Reunited

DESPITE NOT WANTING to, I slept like a stone. I was finally awoken by something tugging at my sleeve. At first, I didn't focus on what it was. Then, with a start, I bolted straight up. Harry Two let out a yip and leapt off the bed.

I was eye to eye with . . . Seamus. His bulbous eyeballs seemed horrifically huge.

"Bloody Hel! What are you doing here?" I gasped, holding my chest.

"Came to fetch you to eat. Madame Prine asked me to."

I composed myself. "You were taken care of last night?"

"Fed like a king, mead to drink and a soft bed."

"I'll be along. I need to get dressed."

He shuffled off and I slowly pulled on my clothes.

Then it struck me. Vega, you git!

I rushed out of my room with Harry Two at my heels. I found the kitchen by following the smell of food. Seamus and Astrea were already there. He was standing next to a large round, wooden table, while she was standing in front of an enormous and ancient blackened stove where several fat pots sat bubbling and two skillets were sizzling.

"I hope you're hungry," Astrea said to me.

"I am. And I'm sure *Delph* must be famished."

She shot me a glance. "I suppose you would like to break bread together?"

"I would, yes, please. I really, really would."

"Well, then let's be off," she said decisively.

She moved so quickly that Harry Two and I barely had time to react. A cloak appeared out of thin air and settled neatly around her shoulders as she headed down the hall. We hurried after her, with Seamus bringing up the rear.

The front door opened of its own accord and we all passed through it. The green dome remained over the cottage although through it I could see that the sky was now clear and bright. She passed through the emerald wall and we scurried after her.

She took out of her cloak pocket something that looked like a shiny stick and pointed it at the sky. Her lips moved, though I couldn't hear the words coming out of her mouth. A few moments later, soaring across the clear sky was Delph, still asleep and still inside the web that Astrea had configured last night. He settled gently upon the ground in front of us, curled up and snoring. Astrea gave a final wave of the stick, and the web, which I could see as a number of lines of vivid lights, disappeared. As we watched, Delph started to wake up, stretched, yawned, opened his eyes and . . .

"Holy Steeples!" he screamed as he jumped nearly three feet in the air before landing upright, his body contorted into the sophisticated fighting stance I had seen him employ in the Duelum.

"Delph!" I cried out and launched myself at him, squeezing him tightly.

But Delph, while he hugged me back, was still staring warily at Astrea and he was still fairly in his fighting stance despite our hugs.

"It's okay, Delph," I said. "This is Astrea Prine."

Delph was obviously mightily confused by what was happening. Well, I knew what would take his mind off that. I said, "Are you hungry? We're about to take a meal in Astrea's cottage."

As I knew he would, Delph focused very quickly.

"Well, that sounds all right, then, eh?" he said, straightening up and dropping his fighting stance.

I led Delph toward the emerald light, which he drew back from until I walked through it and beckoned him to follow. As we approached the cottage, Astrea gazed up at my tall friend. "So you're Daniel Delphia, are you?"

"I am," he said, shooting me a quizzical look. "Friends call me Delph."

"And you're traveling with this one?" she said, hooking a thumb at me.

"I am," Delph said again.

Astrea turned and headed into the cottage without another word.

When she had gone into the cottage with Seamus, I screamed, once more jumped into Delph's arms and squeezed him so tightly I thought either he might burst or my arms would fall off.

I gushed as I felt tears rise to my eyes, "You're all right, Delph. I . . . I was so scared. That bloody cloud. You just disappeared."

He hugged me back and then slowly set me down on the ground.

"I don't know what happened, Vega, to tell the truth. I was talking to you one sliver and then the next thing I know, I'm in the middle of some trees with no idea how I got there. It was weird-like. What happened to you?"

"After you vanished, I met a hob named Seamus. He took me to Astrea's cottage."

"And how'd I get back here?"

"I'll explain everything, but it's going to take a while. So be patient."

"Well, let me eat first and then I'll be *more* patient."

We held hands all the way to the cottage. Part of me didn't want to ever let go of Delph. I would rather die than lose him again. I had lost my parents and my brother. I could not lose Delph. I just couldn't.

With him I knew I could face anything.

Together.

I led him into the kitchen, where Seamus was already seated in a chair by the stove, on which the pots and skillets were still bubbling and sizzling, respectively.

"So who's the little bloke?" Delph asked as he sat down.

"Seamus, the hob I mentioned."

"Hob?"

"Remember, in Quentin's book. A hob!"

"Oh, right. Helpful blokes."

"Well, actually, he isn't really all *that* helpful," I whispered.

Astrea had swept off her cloak and hung it on a wall peg and now was once more overseeing the stove. She called out, "Vega, please set the table."

This puzzled me for a moment before I figured what I needed to do. "Plates, cups, goblets, forks, knives and napkins. Please," I tacked on at the end.

Delph nearly fell out of his chair when all these things came plummeting from the ceiling to land softly on the table all lined up proper-like.

"What the —" he began.

"And bowls," added Astrea. "And spoons."

The bowls and spoons alighted next to the plates, making Delph jump again.

I put a calming hand on his arm. "Patience, remember?"

I noted that on the floor a pan of water had appeared in front of Harry Two, along with a bowl of food. He looked at me as though waiting for permission to begin. I smiled and nodded at him and he started to gobble and slurp.

"'Tis ready," announced Astrea.

She swept a hand across the pots and skillets and then pointed at the table. What was on the stove was thus transferred to our plates and bowls. We looked down and saw fried eggs and bacon and ham and brown toast and sausages and kippers, and porridge in our bowls as well. Jams, butter and honey pots also appeared in front of us. Our goblets were filled with milk. Our cups nearly brimmed over with hot tea.

I looked at Astrea inquiringly. "Aren't you eating too?"

"I've not much of an appetite. You two eat. We'll talk later."

She walked out of the room. Seamus followed.

As we ate, I told Delph everything that had happened to me. As I did so, his jaw dropped so low it was almost resting in his pile of smoked kippers.

"Are you telling me that all that happened in the course of one bleedin' night?"

I finished a bit of bacon. "Well, that doesn't count the time I was asleep."

"Bloody Hel," he said, cramming two fried eggs and a kipper into his mouth. He drank down his milk, and his features turned somber.

"What is it, Delph? Do you want some more food? I'm sure —"

"It's not that, though I could go for a few more eggs and maybe a half dozen bits of bacon and another kipper or two and I wouldn't turn down a few more fried biscuits and another cuppa tea, I can tell you that."

He again nearly leapt out of his chair when this exact amount of food and drink appeared on his plate and in his cup. When he'd righted himself and begun to eat once more, I said, "So what's on your mind?"

"It's all rubbish, ain't it? All we've known. Bloody lies!"

He was right. They *were* lies. But there was truth out there. And we would find it.

Trapped

AFTER WE FINISHED eating, Astrea led us into the room located off the library. She sat behind her old desk, staring at us and drumming her fingertips on the wood.

"I want to be sure that I understand your true and sincere intent," she said.

Delph and I glanced at each other.

I spoke up. "I thought I made that clear enough. We mean to get through the Quag. The three of us, including Harry Two of course," I added, scratching his ear.

She looked at Delph. "And you?"

"Like Vega Jane said. We want the truth. Done with all the lies, ain't we?"

Astrea nodded and drew out the sticklike thing she had used to bring Delph here. I could now see that it wasn't clear. It was actually made of crystal.

"What is that?" I asked.

"My wand. It is a necessary element to perform magic."

I said slowly, "I did magic sort of back in Wormwood, but I had no wand."

"You mean with the Elemental or the chain," she said.

"No, I made a window that Morrigone destroyed put itself back together."

"Indeed?" said Astrea, looking quite interested by this.

"Why would I be able to do that?" I asked.

"If power runs down the line, it touches all in that line."

"My parents couldn't perform magic," I said emphatically.

"And how do you know they couldn't?" she asked.

"Well, they never did."

"That is not the same thing as being unable to."

"If my parents were powerful, why would they have been in the Care?"

"Maybe the fact that they *were* powerful caused them to end up in the Care."

My brows knitted together as I thought over this strange possibility. "Are you saying their power made them sick?"

"No, I'm saying that their power made them dangerous to others."

As the meaning of her words sunk in, I rose on quivering legs, my face flushed, my chest swelling with fierce emotions. "Are you . . . ?" I faltered. I made another attempt. "Do you mean to say . . . ?" Again, I could not finish. Delph reached over and put a supportive hand on my shoulder.

Astrea said, "That they were cursed to prevent them from escaping Wormwood? Yes, that is exactly what I mean."

My eyes flashed. "*Morrigone!* She's the only one that could have done it."

"I agree," she said so casually that my suspicions soared.

"And you knew about it!" I yelled.

"Of course I knew about it," she replied so calmly that I wanted to hit her. "Our goal was to stop anyone from leaving Wormwood."

"So you had Morrigone curse my parents into . . . into . . . what they became?"

"I saw what she did."

"You could have stopped it, then," I pointed out heatedly.

"But I did not want your parents to use their power to escape."

Now I pounced. It was stupid, but I couldn't help myself. "So then, why are you helping us to escape the Quag?" I demanded.

"Who said that I was?" she replied instantly.

Suddenly, I read all in her look. How I had so misjudged her I didn't know.

Delph gave voice to what I was thinking.

He leapt up, grabbed my arm and yelled, "Run, Vega Jane."

Before I could even rise from my chair, she pointed her wand at Delph and said, "*Elevata.*"

Delph soared up into the air, stopping right before he hit the ceiling. She gave her wand a bit of a wiggle and he spun upside down.

I stood, my eyes wide and my heart racing. "Stop that!" I screamed. "Don't hurt him. I'm the reason we're here. Leave Delph alone. Please!"

Astrea flicked the wand downward, uttered one word, "*Descente,*" and Delph turned right side up and fell heavily into the chair.

Astrea laid her wand upon the desk and stared at both of us expectantly.

"I may not be what I once was, but let me assure you, my powers are still far beyond your comprehension." She paused, and I knew what she said next would have monumental impact on us. I was not mistaken.

She said, "You shall remain here in my custody."

"For how long?" I snapped, though I well knew the answer.

"For the rest of your lives," she said calmly. "It gives me no great pleasure to do this. You are obviously brave, and your motives are genuine and deeply felt, I'm sure."

"But?" I exclaimed.

"But as Keeper of the Quag, I have a job to do, and I mean to do it. Now, you will have the run of the cottage and the land inside the dome."

"And if we try to get past the dome?" Delph asked.

Despite him asking the question, Astrea's gaze held on me. Her eyes seemed to swell to match the size of the room. "Not pleasant," she said. "A'tall."

I really couldn't believe what was happening. We had escaped Thorne and his bloody kingdom only to be imprisoned once more by this cow! And while Thorne was dangerous, he wasn't magical. Astrea, to my mind, was a hundred times more formidable than the git Thorne.

Astrea rose, and without another word, she left the room.

I slumped back in my chair. Delph, however, remained rigid in his.

"She is a sorely tried female," he observed.

"*She's* sorely tried? What about us? We're going to be here until we're bloody well dead."

"Lot of sorrow in her, Vega. Easy to see."

"I think she's evil!"

"She's not like Thorne. He woulda just killed us and put our bones on his wall. Not keep us fed with a roof over our heads."

I supposed Delph was right about this, though our bones would end up here eventually, I thought miserably. "Well, Astrea said we had the run of the cottage and the land inside the dome."

"So what do we do with that?" asked Delph.

"We are not staying here, Delph. Thorne couldn't stop us and neither will Astrea Prine. We are escaping this place."

"Okay, but how do we do that?"

"I say we start with Archie."

Looking Back

DELPH AND HARRY Two followed me down the hall. I opened the door to the room and walked in. We gathered at the side of the bed and looked down.

I said solemnly, "This is Archie Prine, Astrea's son."

Delph gazed at the shrunken man in total bewilderment. While I had explained to Delph about the elixir, it was altogether something else to see it for yourself.

I pulled up a chair and sat down next to the bed.

"Hello, Archie," I said softly, hoping to rouse him gently from his sleep.

He stirred and his eyes slowly opened. He blinked, but though he'd seen me before, no recognition came to his features.

"I'm Vega. And these are my friends, Delph and Harry Two." Archie kept his gaze on me. I bent lower. "We've come to stay with you and Astrea."

"Y-you . . . h-have?" he croaked.

I nodded. "She told me about you. And her. And this place."

"Sh-she . . . did?"

I nodded again. "She said you'd grown tired of taking the elixir."

"S-sacrifice." He shook his head and when he tried to sit up, Delph and I helped him. Now he was looking at us from a far more comfortable position.

I nodded knowingly. "Sacrifice," I said. "And the Battle of the Beasts. And Bastion Cadmus." I was saying these things in the hopes that something would jog Archie's memory.

"Load-a t-tosh," he said. "Beasts? P-piffle."

"That's right. Astrea said so too. She said there was a war, though. She said one side lost and the other won."

Archie gasped and pointed to the bedside table, where sat a cup of water. Delph grabbed the cup and handed it to me. I helped Archie drink from it, wiping away some drops that dribbled into his beard.

He sat back and cleared his throat. "Ma-Mal-Maladons."

"Maladons?" I said, shooting Delph a glance. "So you fought them?"

He nodded and a tear slid down his cheek. "F-fought. And I-lost. W-we . . . lost."

Delph exclaimed, "You mean *your* lot got beaten?"

Archie slowly nodded. "Fled here. H-hiding. M-mice in a h-hole." In a moment of anger, he turned and spat on the floor before resettling against his pillow. "C-cowards."

Delph and I exchanged disturbed glances. I said, "And you knew Bastion Cadmus?"

"Our l-leader. K-killed."

He swallowed funny and then started to cough. I gave him some more water.

"D-dad wanted to keep f-fighting. B-but M-Mum . . ." He shook his head. "B-bloody K-Keeper. What's th-the

159

p-point. Bloody Keeper. S-sacrifice. What's the p-p-point?" He looked up at me with pleading eyes. "E-eh?" he said. "Eh?"

I didn't know how to answer him. He closed his eyes and a moment later we heard his gentle snores.

We rose and quietly left the room.

When we got to my room, Delph, his eyes as big as saucers, said, "Blimey! Bloody Maladons. War and killin'."

"And hiding," I added. "Like mice in a hole."

"What?"

"Don't you get it, Delph? They created Wormwood as a hiding place. Because these Maladon blokes were trying to hunt them down. And they conjured the Quag around it to keep them out."

"And to keep us *in*," Delph added. "Like the Wall round Wormwood."

We looked at each other. I'm sure what I saw in Delph's features mirrored my own — complete and utter despair.

I said, "Astrea wanted to know about Virgil. What he was planning, whether I had talked to him."

"How could you when he's been gone since you were a wee thing?"

"He's a powerful sorcerer. An Excalibur, in fact. Which means he's always known everything, including things Astrea has withheld from us."

"Blimey, I guess that explains a lot. So what do we do?" asked Delph.

"Keep learning things. It's all we can do, for now."

"But if we're never to leave here, what does it matter?"

"The truth always matters, Delph."

THAT NIGHT DURING a sumptuous meal that Delph and I lingered over, I drew up the courage to ask Astrea a question.

"Can you show us Wormwood? In your Seer-See?"

"Why?" she asked suspiciously as she took a sip of her tea.

I glanced at Delph, who immediately attended to his custard. He might've been thinking about Astrea sticking him to the ceiling.

"Well, since we're going to be here forever and everything, it would be nice to see our home." I added quickly, "I don't suppose you'd let us go back there. We'd promise never to enter the Quag again."

I was lying of course. I would never stay in Wormwood, not now.

She set her cup down. "Let you go back to Wormwood? Knowing what you do now? Do I look barmy to you?" She glanced down at her wand, which lay beside her plate. "Although, I could wipe away your minds of course. Then you could return. Would you like me to do that?" She raised her wand.

"Er, no," I said quickly.

"I l-like my m-mind where it is," added Delph.

Well, I thought, she had certainly called my bluff.

"But can we at least see our village?" I pleaded.

She contemplated this for a few moments and then rose.

A sliver later, we were in the room with the two cups on the table. Astrea did what she had done before, only this time with the other cup. I had to hold Delph back when the flaming liquid shot across the table.

"Wormwood," said Astrea simply, with a wave of her hand.

And there it truly was.

The cobblestones, the old buildings. There were Wugs I knew walking along. Hestia Loon, her shopping bag in hand. Herman Helvet at his window. With a rush of excitement, I saw mighty Thansius marching purposefully along.

He passed by another Wug I knew, Julius Domitar, who ran Stacks. He was tottering along seemingly full in his cups. He raised a hand in greeting to Thansius. Then another Wug came into view.

"Me dad," cried out Delph.

Sure enough, there was Duf Delphia making his way on his two timbertoes. A whist pup was striding next to him, tethered to a leather cord that Duf gripped.

I brightened and looked at Delph. "He looks good. Happy."

But my smile faded, for Delph didn't look happy, only homesick. I reached over and took his hand and squeezed it. He looked down at me and attempted a smile, but I knew his heart wasn't in it. It was a lot — to be kept from your family, and didn't I know that.

I glanced back at the tabletop when I heard the clattering sound of hooves on cobbles. The blue carriage! I drew closer, wanting desperately to see who was in it. As I watched, the driver, Thomas Bogle, reined the sleps to a stop.

The carriage door opened and out stepped Morrigone.

"Cor blimey," exclaimed Delph, who was looking over my shoulder. "She don't look like herself, does she?"

Morrigone had always been tall and queenly, perfect in both mind and body. Before our differences had been made clear to me, I had always admired her. I had wanted to emulate her. But this Morrigone was far different.

162

She didn't seem as tall. Her hair, normally bloodred with every strand in harmony with its neighbor, was now disheveled and thinning, the luster gone. Her face looked sessions older, with lines and sags prominent. Her tall, well-shaped body had a sunken appearance — fragile where she had always been robust.

I glanced at Astrea. She had a puzzled look on her face. This was startling to me because it's the first time I had ever glimpsed uncertainty in her features.

"What's wrong with Morrigone?" I asked.

She shook her head slightly. "She . . . she looks a bit tired is all."

I looked back at the image and saw him step out of the carriage.

It was my brother, John. And though Delph and I had not been gone from Wormwood very long, John also looked different.

His step was brisk, his manner authoritative and supremely confident. And, dare I even think it, cruel? But then again, he had been cruel to the Wugs working on the Wall.

I said, "My brother became very different under Morrigone's tutelage."

"Different how?" she asked. But when I looked at her, I could tell she already knew the answer.

"He was sweet and innocent. And then he wasn't," I said bluntly. "What did she do to him?"

She didn't answer right away. "'Tis complicated."

"'Tis my brother," I shot back. "The answer should be simple."

I looked back at John, my thoughts whirling so fast I thought I might simply pass out. Instead, fierce emotions building large in my chest and head, I walked out. Then I started to run. I sprinted through the cottage and out the front door. I sped down the crazy-angled path, across the lawn, and, with Destin around my waist, I took to the air and flew straight at the emerald dome.

I don't remember anything after that.

Words

WHENEVER I'D BEEN knocked out before, Delph was always there.

This time he wasn't.

Instead, Astrea stared down at me.

I blinked and slowly looked around. I was in my room on the bed.

Astrea didn't look unduly worried. "I suppose you had to try it."

I sat up and rubbed my head. "What happened?"

"You hit the dome and the dome did not give. You did."

I said nothing to this, both my pride and a rising anger making me mute.

I wanted to ask her again about John. And Morrigone, why she looked so different. But I had a strong feeling that my questions would go unanswered. Before I could say anything, she broke the silence.

"I understand that you talked to Archie?"

"You said we could go where we wanted," I said testily.

"And what did he tell you?"

Ignoring her query, I said, "I feel sorry for him."

"Why? He's lived a good, long life."

"He's lived a long life. I'm not sure how *good* it's been."

She looked like I'd slapped her, which bolstered my spirits greatly.

"I'm sure I don't know what you mean," she said icily.

"Archie spoke of sacrifice. Whose sacrifice? His? Because he didn't really have a choice, did he? Or his father? You made the decision for all of them. Just like you're doing with *us*."

"You know nothing whatever about it, Vega. You're throwing out words that make absolutely no sense because you are ignorant of the facts."

"Well, they'd make sense to Archie, I'm sure. I mean he's the one who lived all this time and never really lived at all. That's probably why he's so bitter. And who can blame him, really?"

I wanted to make her hurt. I wanted to make her feel . . . something for what she was doing to us. For her taking our lives away too.

"I thought I understood you, Vega. Now I know that I don't a'tall."

"It's quite simple, really. You've taken my life away and I'm not happy about it. I'm sure you'd feel the same."

"For the greater good, it —"

"Please don't try and justify it. And I won't believe you anyway. It's like the lie about the Battle of the Beasts. What did Archie call that? Oh, right, piffle. So that's what your greater good is. Piffle. I'm sure Alice Adronis would have seen it the same way. She died as a warrior. Not as a mouse in a hidey-hole. So that's what you are, Astrea, despite all your grand power. A frightened mouse in a dirty little hole."

I never took my gaze off her as I said all this. And I said

it in the maddeningly calm tone she had employed with me the whole time I'd been here.

"You are a stupid Wug," she snapped.

"Alice didn't think so. She gave *me* the Elemental. She told me that *I* had to survive. If you call me stupid, then you're calling your best friend stupid as well."

Astrea got up and left without speaking another word.

Delph immediately burst into the room with Harry Two in tow.

"You okay?" he said anxiously while Harry Two leapt up onto the bed and licked my hand.

"I'm okay. What actually happened?"

"Found you knocked out on the ground, didn't we?"

"I tried to get through the dome. I knew it was stupid. But I . . . I . . ."

"Just wanted to get out of this place," Delph finished for me.

I sighed and lay back against my pillow.

I gripped Delph's hand. "We will get out of here. We will. I swear it."

He met my eye, but I could tell he didn't completely share my optimism.

"Course we will," he said, tacking a smile on to the end of his words.

I sat up and hugged him and felt his warm breath on my cheek. He hugged me back. It was just us against, well, everything. But for some reason, I felt like we had a chance, a fighting chance. I'd never asked for anything more than that.

I got off the bed and shook the collywobbles from my head.

"You saw what was happening?" I asked.

"What, you mean in Wormwood? Morrigone? John?"

I nodded. "Astrea was shocked by how Morrigone looked. Something is going on. But she doesn't know what. And it's scaring her."

"Well, if it's scaring the likes of her, we ought to be terrified, I reckon."

I could always count on Delph for spot-on observations. But terrified or not, I didn't come into the Quag to finish my life as a prisoner. Every part of my body was burning with one desire.

To be free.

THE NEXT LIGHT, we cornered Seamus outside of the kitchen. The little hob had kept his distance from us ever since Astrea declared us to be no longer free.

"So can you leave if you want, Seamus?" I asked, as Delph and Harry Two hovered in the background.

He looked at me nervously, his huge eyes twitching.

"I don't knowsey what yousies is talki —"

"Seamus!" I said warningly.

Harry Two gave a low, throaty growl that I could tell was making the hob very anxious.

"I can go if I want to," he said warily. "But you can't."

I studied him closely. "Seamus, why do I think that meeting you in the cave was not a coincidence?"

I could tell right away from the look on his face that I was right. He blustered and denied and blustered some more, but I persisted and would not let him leave.

"Well, it might've not been," he finally conceded.

"Because Astrea sent you?"

He looked around cautiously before giving a brief nod of his large head.

"And the flying creature that made me run into the cave?"

"Well, she might have sent that too."

"And the cloud that took Delph away?" I added bitterly. "She conjured that too, didn't she? Didn't she!"

Seamus slowly nodded, though I had never seen him look so frightened.

Delph said, "But why?"

I glanced at him before looking back at Seamus. "Because Astrea saw us in the Seer-See. She was afraid we might make it across the Quag. She manipulated things so Seamus and I would meet. And one thing led to another and then here we are — prisoners forever."

Seamus gave a resigned sigh. "She is very powerful, is Madame Prine."

I leaned in closer to the hob. "Well, you know what?"

"What?" he said, his eyes as huge as supper plates.

I snarled, "I'm powerful too."

LATER, I LED Delph to the library. My thought was that in some of the books, we might find things that would better explain what Archie had already told us. If there was a terrible war between our kind and the Maladons, someone had to have chronicled it somewhere.

I told Delph to start at one end and I would begin at the other. However, it was not to be.

I reached for a book and tugged. It would not come out. I tried with both hands. The same result. I looked over at

Delph, who had one big foot placed against the front of the shelf as he pulled with all his might on one thick volume.

"Blimey!" he finally cried out, sounding winded and letting go of the book.

"It's Astrea's doing," I said, my fury rising. "She doesn't want us finding out anything else from the books. Which of course means that these books *do* explain things."

I gazed longingly at the thick tomes. Just inches from my hand and they were of no use to me. Their pages might as well have been blank.

We went to Archie's room. When I tried to open the door, it screamed at me, "GO AWAY!"

"Holy Steeples," said Delph, who had jumped nearly to the ceiling, though I didn't because I was used to this "greeting," though not at Archie's door.

"Well," I said. "It seems that Astrea is certainly limiting our run of the cottage. Which is actually a good thing."

"Why do you say that?" asked a stunned Delph.

"She's afraid we might find something useful. Which means there's something useful here."

But as much thought as I had given to this, the way we would get out was one I had never even considered.

The Sign

I DIDN'T MEAN TO intrude upon her. But I simply walked in and there was Astrea looking at her Seer-See. In the image was Morrigone, still looking bedraggled. She was waving her hands around as she had done when performing magic. I didn't know what she was doing until Astrea waved her wand over the image and it rippled as though someone had tossed a handful of pebbles in a bucket of water.

Morrigone nodded and lowered her hands.

Now I understood.

They were communicating. And then I knew that Morrigone must have told Astrea all about me and to be on the lookout. That I could do a bit of magic, that I had learned some of the truth about Wormwood and that I had escaped from Morrigone and Wormwood. My anger at Astrea increased a thousandfold. She had led me right into her trap.

The next thing I knew, Astrea had turned and was looking up at me, her wand uncomfortably pointed in my general direction.

"What are you doing here?" she asked sharply.

"You said I could go where I wanted in here," I said innocently. "So did you have a nice little chat with dear Morrigone?" I said acidly.

With a flick of her wand the images were gone and the wood was now simply wood once more.

Astrea and I locked gazes.

"You really should keep your nose out of things that do not concern you," she said in a tone that managed to send chills up my spine.

However, I stiffened my resolve and snapped, "Well, it is my business if the consequences will affect me. And Wormwood. It might not be your home, but it is mine. Did you know that bloody King Thorne intended to invade and destroy Wormwood? Do you even care?"

"I would not have allowed —"

"Bollocks!" I shouted out. "You don't care!"

"I would remind you —"

But I was not to be denied my say. "You may be safe under your emerald dome; not everyone has that opportunity, Mighty Keeper of the Quag."

"You are safe here," she retorted.

"Not by my choosing," I shot back. I had anticipated her response. "And I did not enter the Quag to be safe. Only a fool would do that. And I'm no fool."

The door was thrown open and Delph and Harry Two appeared. Behind them I could see Seamus's huge eyes peering at me.

They came fully into the room and Delph shut the door.

"Everything okay?" he said nervously.

"No, everything is *not* okay," I barked, keeping my eyes on Astrea.

"You're acting very foolishly, Vega," she said darkly.

"Oh, so it's foolish in your eyes to care what happens to others? I suppose you didn't care when Alice Adronis died in battle, then? I did. I cared. I was there. I guess you were already in your hidey-hole here by then, were you?"

"Better to hide than die!" she retorted.

"Better to fight and die than live as a coward!" I screamed in her smug face.

"Fight!" She chortled. "You wouldn't last a sliver."

"I *can* fight!"

"You are nothing! Even your grandfather understood that. It's why he didn't bother with the likes of you. He left you behind. Where you belong!"

I pointed a finger right in her face. "I am more than you will ever be, you insufferable cow!"

Her wand moved so fast I barely followed the motion. She said something I couldn't quite catch and then I was catapulted across the room, slammed against the wall and fell to the floor, bleeding from innumerable slashes and cuts all over my body.

"Vega Jane," screamed Delph as he raced over and knelt next to me. He looked up furiously at Astrea. "What did you do to her? What!"

Harry Two barked and growled and looked like he was about to attack her.

Delph held my head up. "Vega, the Adder Stone, where is it? In your pockets?"

I was in so much pain that I couldn't tell him that the Stone was back in my room. I could see my blood pooling on the floor. I felt sick and light-headed.

Delph screamed at Astrea. "Help her!"

"Madame Prine," said Seamus in a pleading voice.

Through my half-closed eyes I could see the horror-stricken look on Astrea's face. To her credit she seemed unable to comprehend what she had done to me.

"Help her!" yelled Delph. "Please."

But then something happened inside of me that I couldn't fathom. It came from a place apparently so deep inside me that I had never before visited it. I had no idea it was even there. The pain was gone. My head cleared. Everything I had been feeling, all the anger and loathing, seemed as nothing to what was now swelling inside of me. It was as though I was no longer myself. I was someone else.

I easily threw Delph aside, rose on steady legs, waved my arms and screamed, "You will not beat me!"

Waves of light came out of my hands and exploded across the room. Everything seemed to have slowed down such that I could see exactly what was happening although it was occurring at tremendous velocity.

Astrea was lifted off the floor and thrown across the entire width of the room. She crashed into the wall and slid down battered and bruised, her wand falling from her fingers.

The vortex of light waves emanating from my hands engulfed Delph, Harry Two and Seamus. They were blown off their feet, sailed across the room and landed hard against the wall, crumpling to the floor. Every stick of furniture in the room, including the Seer-See, was blasted into smithereens. Wood and glass swirled around the room like confetti.

And then, as quickly as it happened, it was over.

I stood in the middle of the room, my wounds healed, my hands now at my sides. I gazed around at the devastation I had involuntarily wrought.

"Delph, Harry Two!" I screamed.

I was at their side in moments. I gripped Delph's arm and Harry Two's front paw. "Tell me you're okay. Tell me, please. Oh my holy Steeples, what have I done?"

Tears poured down my face until first Delph and then Harry Two stirred.

My canine licked my face, and Delph gripped my arm, his smile crooked, but leaving me vastly relieved. I helped them up.

"Cor blimey!" exclaimed Delph. "Where did THAT come from?"

Tears still sliding down my cheeks, I said, "I don't know. I just don't know, Delph."

I turned to see Astrea still lying on the floor, but conscious. She was staring up at me with emotions so complex flitting across her face I had no way of interpreting them.

She slowly rose, as did Seamus across the room.

Astrea took a few halting steps forward, her gaze never once leaving my face.

I walked over to her so that we stood toe-to-toe.

I was determined to let her speak first.

"How did you do that?" she demanded.

"I *can* fight," I said quietly. "All I need is the chance."

Her face sagged and I saw her eyes blink rapidly. Her free hand went to her trembling mouth. And before I could get out another word, she had rushed from the room. We heard her clattering down the hall.

I raced after her, but she was already out of sight.

She wasn't in her room. She wasn't in any room of the cottage to which I had access.

I finally found her outside. She was over by the dome, sitting on a large rock, her wand held loosely in her hand.

I slowly walked up to her and sat on the ground next to her.

She had heard me approach but didn't look at me.

I said, "I hope I didn't hurt you. I didn't intend to."

"You very clearly did," she replied calmly. "But then I certainly hurt you first."

"It just came upon me," I said slowly. "I still don't understand it."

Our gazes fixed on each other. "Don't you, Vega? Well, I understand it quite clearly."

A few slivers passed before she spoke again.

"I do care, Vega. I care very much. I have spent the last eight hundred sessions of my life caring about others."

"I know," I said quietly.

"Do you know why I'm so small even though I take the elixir?"

I shook my head. "I just assumed that you were always short."

"I was nearly as tall as Alice once."

"What happened?" I said in a perplexed tone.

"Eight centuries of responsibility have literally weighed me down, Vega. And taking the elixir, while it gives one life, robs you of other things, important things."

"Like what?"

"Perhaps compassion. Perhaps understanding of others'

points of view. Perhaps things that I need more than ever right now."

I said nothing because I sensed that she just needed to get this out.

"And I also know that one can reasonably dispute my methods, even my goal, as you did."

"But I did it in the wrong way. I shouldn't have used the words I did."

"You were actually quite eloquent, Vega. Perhaps more than you know. And my words to you were equally harsh."

She gazed up at the sky again.

The next words I said, though, got her full and rapt attention.

"The Maladons?"

She turned to look at me. "Archie told you?"

I nodded.

"Yes, the bloody *Maladons*."

She said the word as though it were the most disgusting one ever conceived.

"They are powerful, I take it."

"Yes, so much so that they destroyed us and everything we believed in. Utterly and completely."

"Maybe not so completely," I replied.

She gazed at me. And I thought I saw just a hint of a smile.

"What can be done?" I asked.

She considered this query for a bit. "You said you want to fight?"

"Yes."

She looked back at the cottage. "What you did in there, Vega?"

"I don't know how I did it."

"Doesn't matter. You did it; that's what counts."

"Well, my grandfather is an Excalibur. And you said that power follows the line."

"It is actually more than that. Much more." She turned on the rock to face me and her tone became quite deliberate. "An Excalibur is born with everything he or she will ever have in the way of power. That made your grandfather very mighty indeed. But there is a greater power even than that."

"What?" I said breathlessly.

"For those who are not so powerful when young but grow into more formidable power as they become older. With such power so deeply rooted in them that they can sometimes perform large feats of magic without a wand. Without actually uttering a spell. You have no idea how remarkable that is. I think that you are one of those. And they are even rarer than the Excaliburs. They are so rare, in fact, that we do not even have a name for them. Perhaps I will commence calling such a phenomenon . . . Vega."

With that, Astrea fell silent and I could think of nothing else to say. I thought we would simply sit together under a beautifully clear sky, apparently contemplating the absolute worst of futures. I was about to be gobsmacked as I never had been in my life.

"If you want to cross the Quag and take up the fight once more, you will need to be trained up," she said. "We will commence at next light."

Before I could say anything, she rose and walked back to the cottage, leaving me sitting there, alone.

The Other Elemental

I COULD NOT SLEEP that night. I tossed and turned and squirmed and dreamed. Finally, in a cold sweat, I rose, dressed and went outside and sat on the stone slab by the door with Harry Two and stared up at the emerald dome and beyond that to the sky over the Quag. This coming light, Astrea said, we would start our training. I had no idea what that would entail and it was a bit unnerving. Well, more than a bit actually.

As I sat with Harry Two, the door opened and there was Delph in his long nightshirt. He didn't look like he had slept either. In his bare feet, he sat down next to me.

"Like old times," he said. "When we were up your tree."

Though that wasn't very far in the past, it seemed so long ago that I could barely remember it.

"Yeah," I said absently, still staring at the dome.

"You said Astrea wants us to go across this place now."

"She wants us to fight."

"These Maladon blokes?"

"Right."

"But we don't know nuthin' 'bout 'em."

"I guess that will be part of the training, Delph."

He looked down, his brow creased with concern and his expression one of frustration. "But I ain't magical, Vega Jane. What you did, blasting everything like that, I can't do that. You know I can't."

I took his hand. "What I know, Daniel Delphia, is that you and I are in this together. We were separated once. And we will never be separated again. I can't do this without you. You know that, don't you? You must."

"That female from the past said it was you what got to survive, right? Well, I 'spect she knew what she was saying. So, if it comes to it, I'll do whatever it takes to make sure you do. And I mean *whatever* it takes!"

I felt swells of cold dread filling me. I looked at Harry Two. He reached out a paw and placed it squarely on my shoulder. The look on his face was somehow perfectly clear to me.

I will die for you too.

That look seized me with terror. I glanced over at Delph and then back at Harry Two. *If they died for me? No, what if they died because of me?*

WE FELL ASLEEP on the stone and were roused only when Astrea appeared at the door and called to us. We put on our clothes, ate our breakfast and assembled in the library.

"What will the training consist of?" I asked.

"Learning magic."

"But that means a wand."

"Indeed it does."

"Where did you get yours?"

"It was given to me by my father."

"Where did he get it?"

"He took a bit of himself and formed my wand by the proper incantation and passed it down to me. It is how such things are done in our world. It gives a connectivity among families that is largely unbreakable. In this way I have the full force and power of all my ancestors."

"He took a bit of *himself*?" I repeated.

"Blimey! What bit would that be?" said Delph, voicing what I was thinking.

Astrea said, "His blood. That is often used. You can see the hardened drops of it embedded in the base here."

She looked at Delph. "Have you ever done anything magical, Delph?"

Delph gaped at her for a long moment. "I'm not magical," he finally said, as though it should have been obvious.

"And you base this conclusion upon what precisely?"

"That I ain't never done ruddy magic, that's what."

"Neither had Vega Jane, until the opportunity presented itself," she retorted.

Delph said, "Well, I've never done magic, though I've been in situations where I wish I could've done. So's that means I'm just a big lug."

"You're *not* a big lug, Delph. I'd be dead back at Thorne's but for you. You think of things I never could. And you're strong and so very brave."

"Shall we commence?" interjected Astrea.

At that moment the door opened and I nearly fell out of my chair.

A young male, not much older than us, stood there. He was dressed oddly in a long nightshirt with his bare calves and feet visible. His face was unlined by care or worry and his dark hair was long and swept helter-skelter over his head. His eyes were so dazzling blue they seemed like ice chips reflected against a cloudless sky.

I saw Delph looking at him, as puzzled as I was.

"Archie!"

I turned to look back at Astrea, who had called out the name. She had risen from her chair and was staring goggle-eyed at the fellow.

Archie? I thought. But Archie was in bed, ancient and dying. Then it hit me.

"You took the youth elixir," I blurted out.

Archie smiled and strode forward. He was far taller than his mother, but not so tall as I was. And of course he was much shorter than Delph.

"Correct, I partook of the elixir of youth," he conceded.

His speech was oddly formal and his tone that of a much older male. Which made sense since a bit ago he had been very ancient indeed.

He stretched like a cat and then shivered. "Feels absolutely splendid. Far better than lying in bed, gasping for air."

"What in the world made you do it?" This query came from Astrea, who was still staring at her son.

In answer, Archie pointed at me. "She was my motivation."

"Me?" I said, bewildered.

He nodded. "Mum sat with me last night. Don't think she expected me to last much longer. And she told me that she was training you to take up the fight once more. I wanted to help you!"

"Thanks, Archie," I said, giving him an appreciative smile. Then I turned to face Astrea. "But we have a problem."

"Such as?"

"I have no wand. Without one I can't do magic."

Archie said, "She clearly has a practical mind, Mum."

It was disconcerting having Archie call her that, when she looked not that much older than he was.

She glanced down at my pocket. "What about the Elemental?"

"What about it?"

"Take it out."

I pulled my glove out and started to put it on.

But she stopped me. "There's no need for that, Vega."

"But Alice Adronis told me —"

"I'm sure she did, but she was also in great distress when you met, and I doubt that she was thinking clearly. So just trust me. For I have given this much thought and believe I am correct. Just take it out with your bare hand."

Yet despite her words, I noted that she was keeping her wand at the ready.

I cautiously slipped my hand into my pocket. My fingers inched closer to where the shrunken Elemental lay. My breathing got heavier and my heart started to beat faster. Alice had worn the glove. She had told me . . .

I felt my fingers an inch from the wood of the Elemental. I looked first at Delph. He was staring dead at my pocket. I glanced at Astrea. She was looking not at the pocket of my cloak but directly at me.

"Believe, Vega," she said quietly.

"Believe in what?" I asked, bewildered.

"In yourself."

I caught my breath, swallowed a huge lump in my throat and decided that taking this slow was only making it worse; it was better to just get it over with. I thrust my hand forward and my fingers closed around the Elemental.

I had closed my eyes at the moment of collision of flesh and wood. Now I opened them because nothing had happened. I drew the stick out and looked at it clutched in my hand. It looked tiny and impotent. I glanced at Astrea.

She was staring at the thing as if it was a frozen serpent.

"What?" I said.

"I haven't seen the Elemental for over eight hundred sessions," she said, her voice both awed and sad. "I saw Alice hurl that at so many of our enemies." She glanced up at me. "Would you, please?"

I instinctively understood her. I willed the Elemental to its full, golden size. I held it up as though I was about to hurl it.

Astrea took a step back, her eyes filling with tears as she stared at the Elemental. Then when she glanced at me, she did a double take.

"What is it?" I said, glancing down at myself.

"Nothing," she whispered. "'Tis nothing. You just reminded me of . . . never mind. You can shrink it now."

I did so and said, "Now what?"

"Tell it to lengthen to nine inches precisely."

I was surprised by this but conjured the thought and watched in satisfaction as the wood grew to what seemed the proper size.

Astrea drew closer and examined my hand in relation to the Elemental. "Good, good. Yes, that will certainly do."

"Do for what?"

She stepped back. "Now *that* will be your wand."

My face screwed up. "My wand? You just said that a wand had to be passed from a family member. And that it had to have something of that person inside it."

"And those conditions have been met here," she replied.

"How?" I exclaimed. "I got this from Alice Adronis on a battlefield hundreds of sessions before I was even born. She . . ."

"She what?" interjected Astrea. "She couldn't be related to you? She couldn't have put something in the Elemental of herself?" She paused. "Wrong on both counts."

"That's impossible!" I shot back.

"Look at it. Look at it *closely.*"

I stared at the Elemental. There was nothing to see. But then, then there was something. I bent my face nearer. It was a dark red line, like a thread weaving through the wood.

Astrea said, "It's a strand of her hair, Vega. Alice's beautiful auburn hair."

I looked up to see her watching me. "It can't be."

"A simple test will suffice." She pointed at the wall of books. "The incantation is '*Rejoinda*, book.' Roll the r and make a slow, deliberate back sweep with your wand toward you. And let your mind focus only on the book. Like this."

She pointed her wand at the first bookcase, uttered the phrase "*Rejoinda*, book" and drew her wand slowly toward herself.

A book shot off the shelf and zoomed right into her hand.

She set it down and turned to me. "Now you do it."

I looked down at the Elemental. "I can't."

"Yes, you can. Place your thumb over the top of the wood and your index finger below. Let about six inches of the wand extend out from your hand. And not too tight a grip. It won't slip."

"Why not?"

"Because it has become a part of you now."

I stared down at the thing, expecting to feel horrified. But I actually felt warm . . . and safe.

I glanced at Delph. He was staring at me. "You *can* do it, Vega Jane. You know you can. You've done things. THINGS! You can bloody well fetch a book."

I turned back to look at Astrea.

"Just believe, Vega. As you did when you plucked the Elemental from your pocket without need of that glove."

Well, she had me there. I *had* done that.

I took a deep breath, readied myself, looking at my hand, the books, the wand. Wand! Maybe I *could* do this.

I focused on one book in particular. I let my mind see only it. I said in a firm voice, "*Rejoinda*, book."

I got the word right, rolling the *r* just as Astrea had, but in my excitement I snapped my hand and, with it, the wand toward me.

The entire bookcase flew from the wall and shot right at us, books cascading from it. I screamed and dove to the floor together with Delph and Archie.

"*Embattlemento*," cried out Astrea.

I looked up in time to see the bookcase halt in midair as though it had hit something solid. Then it shot backward, settling neatly against the wall. All the fallen books picked

186

themselves up and zipped back onto their original places on the shelves.

I slowly rose along with Delph and Archie. I gazed shamefacedly at first the bookcase and then Astrea, and then gazed ruefully down at the Elemental still clutched in my hand.

When I glanced up, Delph was staring at me with such astonishment that it was quite unsettling.

"I guess I'm not very good at magic," I said miserably.

"On the contrary," said Astrea, "you have surpassed my expectations. I believe that you can be a first-rate sorceress."

This made me feel euphoric. And that feeling lasted until what she said next.

Astrea held up five fingers. "These are the numbers of layers to the Quag, Vega. Each layer, or circle, as we refer to them, is a world unto itself, separate from its neighbor. Each holds unique and deadly challenges. Each changes all the time, growing and evolving, feeding off the magic that created and inspired it." She paused and then added, "And please understand one thing quite clearly. Despite your magical prowess, each circle could well be your graveyard."

And with this final chilling pronouncement, she turned and left us.

The Education of Me

THE NEXT LIGHT after we had our meal, Astrea led me, Delph, Harry Two and Archie to a large room, of which the cottage seemed to have an ample number. Along one wall was a huge blackboard like the one we had used at Learning back in Wormwood. Astrea closed the door behind us and then took out her wand and pointed it at the board. In an instant, writing started sprawling across it.

"Your first lessons," announced Astrea.

She gave her wand another flick and a small ball appeared in her hand.

"Now, Vega, remember the incantation from the last light?"

"*Rejoinda*," I said eagerly, desperate to prove myself in her eyes.

She nodded. "I want you to take this ball from me, using that spell." She held up her hand before I could do anything. "But first, we need to go over some basics so that what happened before will not repeat itself." She pointed with her wand to a section of the blackboard. "Read that," she instructed. "Out loud."

I looked at the section and commenced to read.

"*Proper spell work involves performing a number of things at the same time, but always employing the principle of MBS, or Mind, Body and Spirit. That is to say focusing the mind, preparing the body and engaging the spirit so that all three elements come together at the appropriate time. Merely saying the incantation does nothing if these elements are not properly combined.*" I turned to Astrea. "So how do I do that?"

"Keep reading," she replied.

A bit put off, I returned my gaze to the board. "*Combining MBS with the proper incantation and the appropriate wand movement will result in the desired result. Nothing less than that will work.*"

I finished reading and turned back to her. Well, okay, I got *that*.

She held up the ball. "You jerked your hand before. You need to be slow and deliberate in the movement. But far more importantly, you need to employ MBS appropriately for any of this to work properly."

"Which is why I asked you how to do this MBS thing," I said irritably.

"Becoming upset with me will not result in your mastering incanting," she said politely. "So calm yourself, focus your mind on this ball and nothing else. When you have done that, you will next summon your physical side such that all your bodily energy is congregated in your wand hand. Lastly, your spirit should be in complete harmony with your mind and body."

"Bloody Hel," exclaimed Delph. "That's not asking a lot, is it?"

Astrea turned to him. "It *is* asking a lot. But when you're attempting to do something truly extraordinary, isn't it fair to ask a lot in return?"

Delph blanched and looked at his boots. She turned back to me.

I said, "How will I know when I've achieved the proper balance?"

She held up the ball. "When this rests in your hand of course."

I squared my feet and shoulders. I looked at the ball and did my best to push out all other thoughts. I looked at my wand hand, trying to force my physical side to move itself completely there. I had no idea in what part of my body the spirit resided, but in my head I told it to get comfy with my mind and body. I held my wand loosely and then, remembering my mistake from before, I gave it a slow, deliberate back sweep and said, "*Rejoinda*, ball," rolling my *r* perfectly, or at least I thought so.

Absolutely nothing happened. The ball continued to reside firmly in Astrea's hand. I stared openmouthed at her, but she didn't seem surprised at all.

"It was only your first attempt."

"But I did it before," I said in more of a whine than I intended.

Archie said, "Well, actually, you nearly crushed us all with that bookcase, luv. Mum got the book."

I gave him a surly look before saying, "Can I try again?"

Astrea nodded and said, "You will try many times, I daresay."

Thirty-seven attempts later, the little ball flew to me and fit snugly into my quivering hand. I wasn't expecting it because I had pretty much concluded by the eighteenth attempt that I was never going to be a proper sorceress and maybe Delph and I should return to Wormwood and beg for our jobs back.

It didn't sink in that I had succeeded until Delph clapped me on the back so hard I very nearly toppled over.

"You did it, Vega Jane. You did it."

He picked me up off the floor and crushed me in his embrace. When he made no sign of freeing me, Astrea said, "Um, Delph, it would be good if we can move on, which will require you of course TO LET HER GO."

Blushing madly, Delph dropped me on the floor.

Astrea's focused expression had not changed. "Let's do it again, shall we?"

My enthusiasm faded because from her serious look, I understood exactly what she meant. Being able to retrieve a little ball on my thirty-seventh attempt was hardly going to get us through the Quag. But I couldn't help but smile inwardly. I *had* performed wand magic after all. Maybe I *could* be this sorceress thingy!

I pursed my lips, focused my MBS, and said the incantation as I slowly and deliberately moved my wand.

The ball came to me fourteen times in a row. It was only then, when seeing it in the palm of my hand wasn't nearly as exciting as it had been the first few times, that Astrea said, "Let's move on, then." She motioned to Archie. "I'll need your help to demonstrate this one, dear."

Archie nodded and slipped from his cloak pocket a long, thin reedlike piece of what looked to be blackened wood. He saw me eyeing it and said, "My dad gave this to me when I was far younger than you."

"With a bit of him in it?" I said.

Archie nodded. "A tooth. If you look close, you can see just a hint of it near the handle. Family history has my mum knocking my dad's tooth out over a wee argument, and he decided to save the tooth for passing a wand down."

"It wasn't like that, Archie," said Astrea firmly, two splotches of color on her cheeks. "Your father had a toothache and wanted some relief. That is all." Astrea cleared her throat and moved to the center of the room before pointing with her wand once more at the blackboard. "Do you recall the incantation I used when the bookcase came flying?"

Surprisingly, Delph spoke up. "*Embattlemento*," he said quickly before gazing around and looking stunned that the correct answer had come out of his mouth.

"Precisely," said Astrea, eyeing him closely. "It is a defensive blocking spell used to protect oneself from harm. We will demonstrate."

She motioned to Archie. "On the count of three."

"Which curse, Mum?" he asked.

"Oh, whatever you like, Archie, dear. Surprise me."

Blimey! It was like they were discussing what tea they wanted to drink.

They simultaneously raised their wands.

She said, "One, two, three."

Archie said, "*Injurio*," and whipped his wand at her. What looked to be a skylight spear burst from its tip.

At the same instant, Astrea slashed her wand in front of her from right to left and said, "*Embattlemento*."

The blast of light hit an invisible barrier conjured in front of her and ricocheted off, ripping a hole in the ceiling.

Delph, Harry Two and I had dropped flat to the floor. We looked up to see the gaping hole in the wood.

Astrea pointed her wand upward and calmly said, "*Eraisio.*"

The hole vanished.

We rose on trembling legs and stared at the pair.

"I'm not sure I'm ready for that one," I said.

"Which is why we will begin with this." She took the ball from her cloak pocket. "I will throw this at you. You conjure your barrier with the incantation. The sweep of the wand is from left to right, the movement sharp and clean. Make yourself believe that the ball will injure you."

"Okay, but your movement was *right* to *left*," I corrected.

Her eyes twinkled. "I'm glad you were paying attention."

I readied myself while Delph, Harry Two and Archie took collective steps back. Even though it was just a ball, I guess they were recalling the bookcase fiasco.

"On the count of three," said Astrea. "One, two, three."

She heaved the ball right at my head with great force.

I swept the air with my wand and said, "*Embattlemento.*"

The ball bounced off my conjured wall so hard that Astrea had to duck as it hurtled back at her. When she straightened, she looked at me in some amazement.

"That was quite good, Vega. Quite good indeed."

I couldn't hide my smile. But I *could* hide the fact that I had pictured in my mind a jabbit coming at me instead of the ball.

Yet I *had* done it. On my first try. I wanted to scream with joy. Until the next four times, when the ball hit me full in the face. We worked at it for a long while until every third time my conjured wall held.

"That is good enough for now. Let's move on to something a bit more serious." She pointed her wand at a corner of the room, gave it a flick and said, "*Golem Masquerado.*"

There appeared a large male. I was shocked at first, but then I could see that he was made of clay. I had used that material back at Stacks.

"Why do we need that?" I asked.

"I would much prefer you practice on something non-living," said Astrea.

My smile faded as, without warning or preamble, she made a downward slashing motion with her wand and hissed, "*Jagada!*"

The clay male was suddenly covered in cuts. Had it been a real person, he would have been bleeding from innumerable wounds.

I stared from the slashed clay male to Astrea.

This is what she had done to me before. She knew it. And she knew that I knew it.

"Not pleasant," she said grimly.

"You want me to do that?" I asked, my voice tremulous.

"Do you want to do it?" she shot back.

I looked at the clay figure and imagined it to be Delph or Harry Two instead.

I looked back at Astrea. "Not now."

She looked at me for a long moment. "Then let's move outside."

As we trooped down the hall, Archie came up behind me and whispered in my ear. "It's okay, Vega. Most of us couldn't have done that our first time. In fact, some could never achieve it."

194

"Why is that?" I whispered back.

"You have to really want to hurt someone."

"Well, your mum seems to have no problem with it."

"She was in a *war*, Vega. She's killed before. And she's had eight hundred sessions to brood. It gets to you, doesn't it?"

We exited the cottage and passed through the green dome.

Archie stretched his arms and looked to the sky. "Been ages since I've been out of the cottage. Just breathe in that air."

"How long ago did you stop taking the elixir?" I asked.

"The light you showed up on our doorstep."

I was stunned. "You mean you age that quickly?"

"You age pretty much right away when the effects of the potion wear off. It just takes a bit of time before you actually die."

He said this so casually that I could only stare.

"Well, I'm glad you decided not to die."

He smiled. "Me too, Vega. Me too."

Astrea raised her wand, gave it three parallel flicks and said, "*Crystilado magnifica.*"

Three feet away from us appeared an amaroc bounding through the fields, evidently in pursuit of prey. It was so close that I could see the red eyes, huge chest, bared, yellowed fangs and the cold breath bursting from its nostrils.

Delph screamed and jumped back. I yelled and pulled my wand, about to will it to full Elemental status so I could hurl it at the beast.

But Astrea held up her hand. "The amaroc is many miles distant. This spell allows you to see things far away as if they were very close. A useful device in the Quag, don't you think?"

As I stared at the amaroc I said, "Very useful indeed."

She waved her hand once more and the image vanished. She pointed toward where a forest was located.

"Now you try."

I raised my wand, gave it the requisite three flicks and said, *"Crystilado magnifica."*

It was as though we were in the forest. I could see everything. Everything!

As I watched, a deer came soaring into view. I had loved to watch them from atop my tree as they ran through the woods back in Wormwood. I grinned at Delph but faltered when his reciprocal smile turned to a look of horror.

I whipped back around and stared at the deer once more.

From out of nowhere a ghastly, quasi-transparent creature had appeared. With astonishing speed and unerring accuracy, it had plunged right at the beautiful deer, catching it in its ethereal grasp. The deer looked as stunned as I felt. Here it was running blithely along . . .

Then . . . then it was torn to shreds. And the thing consumed it. I tried to turn away, but something grabbed me by the shoulder and held me in place.

I looked around to see Astrea there, holding me, making me watch.

I turned back around. And the most astonishing thing happened. The monster that had killed the poor deer had become . . . the deer, albeit a ghostly, filmy white version of it.

Astrea waved her wand, said, *"Finit,"* and the entire image disappeared. She turned to me and said, "That was a wendigo. A malevolent spirit that can possess whatever it devours. Creatures such as this lie between you and your destination at the end of the Quag."

My voice shaky, I said, "And you helped create all these horrible things."

She looked taken aback by my comment, which, I had to admit, had been somewhat accusatory. "Not all of them, no. But by conjuring what we did, we laid the foundation for these creatures to spawn even greater horrors than the originals. The effects of magic can often be unpredictable, Vega. You must come to understand that."

"And do you think it was all worth it?" I asked in a firmer voice.

"The answer to that is still to be written," she replied just as firmly.

A Sorceress of Sorts

THE TIME RACED by as my education continued. My *true* education.

By saying the phrase *"Pass-pusay"* and tapping my wand against my right leg, I had disappeared from the room we were in and transported myself to the hallway outside. I don't know how I did it or why I had traveled to that particular spot, but Astrea was very encouraged that I had accomplished this on only my fourth attempt. I had even worked out some reverse curses with a degree of success. But I had also very nearly drowned poor Delph by miscasting the confounded spell *Engulfiado*.

I now lay exhausted on my bed. It didn't seem that saying words and waving a little stick around could be tiring, but it actually involved far more than that. This mind, body and spirit requirement was much harder than laboring at Stacks.

Someone knocked on my door and I wearily raised my head. "Yes?"

"It's Delph, Vega Jane. Can I come in?"

"Give me a mo'. I'm not decent." I jumped up, threw on my cloak and then opened the door.

"You look . . . very, um, *decent*," he said shyly.

"Thanks, Delph. But how can you tell? Your eyes are closed."

He opened them just a bit as though to test whether I was truly decent. Then he opened them fully.

"Now, what was it you wanted?"

He took the chair next to my bed while I perched on the corner of the mattress. He was curling and uncurling his large hands, something I knew he did when he was both nervous and upset.

"Just say it, Delph."

He nodded. "The thing is, Vega Jane, the thing is . . ." He stopped, stood and started to pace. Harry Two and I swiveled our heads back and forth as he did so, following his long gait as he crisscrossed the room. He whirled around, looked at me and said, "I . . . can't . . . do . . . this magic. So what bloody good am I to you?"

"What good are you to me? You're joking, right?"

He made a huge muscle with his arm, but it wasn't intended as a show of strength, a fact made clear by his next words. Pointing at it, he said, "This is all I have. I'm strong in Wormwood, pretty much none stronger. But here I'm a bloody weakling, Vega Jane. I can't help you. And if I can't help you, I'll end up hurting you."

He suddenly slumped to the floor and just sat there looking spent.

As though he could sense Delph's pain and anxiety, Harry Two used his snout to lift Delph's hand and perhaps his spirits. As Delph stroked Harry Two, I said, "Okay, Delph, let's say you can't do magic and I can."

"'Cause it's the truth!" he said fiercely.

"But I'm just learning how to do this. You saw that."

"What I saw, Vega Jane, was a sorceress or whatever you want to call yourself, getting better and better. You'll soon have the stroke of this magic stuff."

"And do you really think all you have to offer are muscles?"

He looked surprised by this comment. "Eh? What else, then? All I got."

"So it wasn't you who came up with the strategy for me to win the Duelum?"

"Who cares about the damn Duelum? Ain't you been listening? I *can't* do magic."

I rushed over and seized his shoulder. "Neither one of us came into the Quag thinking we could do magic. But we still came here. And you know why we did."

I grew silent because I wanted to hear him say it. I wanted to know, for certain, that he wanted it as much as I did.

He said, "To find the truth."

I nodded and let go of him. "That's right. Maybe I'll be a good sorceress and maybe I won't. Maybe you'll never be able to do magic, I don't know. I don't know much about anything in this place because it's so *unknowable!* But that won't stop *us* from finding answers, Delph. And if *we* die trying, well, I'd rather that than live a life that's not even my own."

Delph slowly nodded and said, "Okay, Vega Jane. Okay."

"So are we good?" I asked, peering at him closely.

"We're good," he said with a smile.

MORE TIME PASSED and my lessons continued unabated. I muttered so many incantations that it seemed I could recall none. I made intricate moves with my wand. I employed my mind, body and spirit together in ways I couldn't have even fathomed before. And it was all done under the strict tutelage of Astrea Prine. She seemed to enjoy the role of teacher far more than jailer.

I had my share of victories and a nearly equal number of total disasters.

One terrifying moment had come when I directed a curse at the clay male.

"*Jagada*," I called out, whipping my wand at the target, but my enthusiasm had led to a momentum in my arm that badly threw off my aim. My curse hit poor Archie and he started to bleed from gashes all up and down his legs.

I screamed, Harry Two yipped and Delph raced over to him to help.

But Astrea calmly said, "*Eraisio*," and waved her wand at Archie. The slashes immediately healed, though his trousers were still ripped.

I apologized profusely, but Archie took it in stride.

"There's not been any of us that hasn't made mistakes, Vega," he said encouragingly. "And you're doing just fine."

However, I was so shaken that I could do no more that light. Later, I cried myself to sleep, the image of bloody Archie refusing to leave my thoughts.

The next light, I crushed the clay man by invoking the spell *Impacto*. I very warily performed the *Impairio* curse on Archie and struck him blind, but the reverse curse worked just fine too, restoring his sight instantly.

"Mind, body and spirit," Astrea kept stressing to me.

"I'm getting the hang of it," I said confidently.

"The basics at least."

I looked at her, knowing that something else was dwelling on the tip of her tongue. "But?" I said.

"But you've had to do none of this while an opponent is casting spells back at you, trying to hurt or even kill you. That changes everything, Vega."

"But how can I practice that?"

"You will practice that, when you are ready."

"You mean truly fighting?"

"Yes! You will have to do so to get through the Quag."

That night I lingered in front of the fire with Astrea and Harry Two while Delph and Archie went off to bed.

"The first night I was here I saw the room covered in dust and cobwebs. It was set up like a nursery."

She slowly nodded. "It *was* a nursery, Vega. For my children."

"It . . . it must have been difficult for them," I began.

She gave a hollow laugh. "As you so astutely pointed out, I took their lives from them."

I remained silent. I shouldn't have said that to her. I'm sure she had meant the best. But sometimes decisions come at a great cost. For others.

"They never had the chance to meet anyone. Never had the chance to fall in love, marry and have a family. See their children grow up and have their own children." She let out a long breath that I could sense was chock-full of remorse. She glanced at me before looking away. "My youngest, Ariana, was the first to die. She was so full of life when she was a child. Then she grew into a bitter old biddy, and who could blame her? This cottage, her brothers and sisters. And me.

That was all she had. Then one by one, the others went. Tired of not living. A decision I had made for them."

She lapsed into silence, a quiet I was hesitant to break. But the fact was I had another question to ask her, and it would have a great impact on me personally.

"You said you had killed?" I began.

She was staring into the depths of the fire. She looked so young that it was difficult for me to accept that she was over eight centuries old.

"To defend myself. I was quite good at it. As you will have to be."

I drew closer. "When I threw the Elemental at the males attacking me on that battlefield, I didn't know it was going to *kill* them."

"And you wonder if you have it in you to consciously do so?"

"I cried when I hurt poor Archie."

"It is not a natural thing to kill another. At least it is not for us."

"Do you think that's why, well, why they beat you? The Maladons?"

"Do you know how they came by their name? Did Archie tell you that?"

"No."

"In our ancient language it means 'terrible death,' Vega."

"Terrible death. So you named them that? Because of what they did to you?"

She shook her head. "No. They named themselves. To inflict terrible death on others is the highest calling they have."

"That's . . . awful," I said, nearly unable to process how anyone could be that evil.

"The Maladons have always been remarkably good at killing. Although toward the end, many on our side became quite adept at it as well. Alice Adronis killed scores of them and seemed to care not a jot."

"I don't think that's true."

She turned to face me. "And how could you possibly know that?"

"I saw her on that battlefield. She was honorable. Noble. I'm sure the killing *did* bother her. As it would me."

"And your point?" asked Astrea curiously.

"Well, if we didn't care, we would be no better than the Maladons. And then what would be the point of defeating them?"

This comment seemed to surprise her. "You figured that out without any help whatsoever from me."

"I've had to figure out a great many things on my own," I said quite seriously. "But that still doesn't answer the question of whether I can kill if I need to. I don't even know what the spell is to do it. Is there a particular one?"

"*Rigamorte*," she said immediately, her features deadly serious. "It is the most powerful of all curses. While we have other spells that can eventually lead to death, that is the one guaranteed to produce it."

"It even *sounds* hurtful."

"Point your wand at me and say it."

"What?" I exclaimed in astonishment.

"Point your wand at me and say the incantation."

"But I can't do —"

"Now," she screamed, "or I will do it to *you*. Now, Vega!"

Terrified, I raised my wand and cried out, *"Rigamorte!"*

My wand gave what amounted to a little sneeze and that was all.

"I guess I need work," I said lamely. "But you would have blocked it or countered it if —"

"There is no shield. Only inevitable death."

I was horrified. "Then if it had worked?"

"It could not possibly have worked, Vega. You were scared. It was why I screamed at you. One cannot perform the curse while scared. It is not the emotion required."

"What is, then?"

"Something more than loathing. Or even hatred. An emotion so strong that it blocks out every other feeling you have. It must be like molten lava in your blood vessels. You must *want* to kill above all other things. To end the life of another living thing, Vega. Otherwise, you're simply wasting your breath. It is horrible to kill someone. So to take the life of another, you *must* become horrible."

I cleared my throat and said slowly, "I don't know if I could ever feel that way about anyone. I mean there were blokes in Wormwood that I didn't much care for. But I couldn't kill them. I mean I just wouldn't."

"Would you rather it be you dead, or your enemy?" she retorted. "For I can tell you quite plainly that a Maladon confronting you will not hesitate to kill."

I sat back and thought this through. To get through the Quag and do what I needed to do, would I have to become a killer?

It seemed that I would.

A Warning

I ROSE EARLY NEXT light and dressed quickly. I could hear no one stirring yet. Even Harry Two was still asleep at the foot of my bed. I walked down the hall and stopped in front of one of the doors that had refused me entry my first night here. I took out my wand, gave it three parallel flicks and said, *"Crystilado magnifica."*

I jumped back so far that I actually slammed into the opposite wall.

Full in my face, burning a hole in my brain really, was a jabbit curled up in a cage made of brilliant light. The terrible creature was fast asleep, its hundreds of eyes closed. But sleeping or not, I wanted to run away shrieking.

Instead, I tapped my wand against my leg, hissed *"Passpusay"* and thought of my destination. Anywhere but here, actually.

Moments later I was outside the cottage and also free of the green dome.

I looked around at the peace and quiet of an early morning's light. I got a running start and took to the air with Destin firmly around my waist. I kept my gaze swiveling back and forth both above and below, my wand at the ready.

A sudden gust of wind hit me and I went into a dive. I

caught myself in plenty of time, at least a hundred feet up in the air. Righting myself, I looked ahead and paled. The clear sky had turned to a towering darkened mass. Jagged skylight spears were being cast out of the black clouds. Accompanying thunder-thrusts pierced my ears. I had no choice but to flee to the ground.

I landed hard and stumbled a bit before regaining my balance. I looked upward. The sky was once more crystal clear.

What the Hel?

I bent my knees and shot upward. I was immediately engulfed in horrendous wind and torrential rain. I was flipped and shoved all across the sky, the rain hitting me so hard it felt like whacks from a piece of wood. The water blasted in my eyes and down my throat, making me gag.

I shot downward and sprawled on the ground, soaked to the bone.

I rolled over and looked up once more. The sky was all blue again.

I twisted my hair, wringing the water out of it, and did the same with my clothes. When I looked to my right, I was so astonished I touched my arm to make sure I was still where I thought I was. Because it was *me* approaching me! Barely ten feet from me, it stopped and stared. Now, I've had experience with a maniack, a despicable creature-thing that can take the form of someone and then clutch on to you and make you relive your worst fears while it slowly crushes you to death. But I had never been confronted by, well, me.

Of course I knew it wasn't me. It had to be some creature that was intending to do me harm. Well, I was prepared for that. I would just do something to scare it off. I raised my

207

wand, pointed it at the creature, gave my wand a flick, kept my eyes on the thing's right arm and said, *"Injurio."*

The pain was so immediate and so intense that I gasped, bent over and grabbed my right arm. That had really hurt. I must have done the spell wrong.

I pointed my wand at my arm and said, *"Eraisio."* The pain stopped.

I looked at the creature. It had drawn closer. It was my exact double. And now my fear was mounting. Though it had done nothing threatening, every instinct I had was telling me to be very afraid.

Focusing my mind, body and spirit, I pointed my wand at its leg, gave a slashing movement with my wand and said, *"Jagada."*

Four rips in my leg appeared and I howled in agony, dropped to the dirt and clutched my wounded limb. Tears in my eyes at the pain, I looked up to see the creature now standing barely a foot from me.

The thing's mouth opened and I saw inside hideous rows of blackened, sharpened teeth. Then a tongue flicked out and licked my face. But it wasn't a pleasant touch. I could instinctively tell it was *tasting* me. Blind with pain and fury and not wanting to be eaten, I raised my wand, gathered my hatred for the thing, focused my mind, body and spirit and screamed, *"Rig —"*

I never finished because my voice was gone, which meant I couldn't complete the spell. This thing must have done it. And without my voice, how could I stop it from eating me?

The thing opened its mouth wider. All I could see was

this impossibly large black hole big enough to actually swallow me whole.

"Impairio," a voice said.

A blindingly white light hit the thing full in the face. It instantly changed into a blackened husk that was all teeth and gnarled limbs with a single massive eye.

Then the same voice said sharply, *"Rigamorte."*

A coal-black beam shot out and hit the creature directly in the chest. It burst into a huge ball of smoke and then was gone.

I turned to see Astrea standing there, her wand still upraised. She looked down at me, pointed her wand at my leg and said quietly, *"Eraisio."*

My cuts instantly healed. I stood on shaky legs.

She pointed her wand at my face and said, *"Unmutado."*

"What was that thing?" I asked, my voice now returned.

She looked at where the creature had been. The grass underneath was burned.

"A dopplegang. A creature that can become whatever it sees. In this case it became you."

"But when I tried to cast a spell on it, the spell hit me instead."

"That's the primary strength of the dopplegang. Its prey will strike out at the thing, never realizing that it is, in fact, attacking itself. The dopplegang will wait patiently for its prey to kill or incapacitate itself, and then it will eat the unfortunate one."

"So when I tried to use the *Rigamorte* curse?"

"I stopped you. Because you would have killed yourself."

"But how *did* you stop me?"

"*Mutado.* A spell that takes your voice away. I just performed the reverse curse, which is why you can speak once more."

"And you struck the dopplegang blind because if it can't see, it can't become something else? Meaning it reverts back to its true self?"

"And with that defense gone, I was able to kill it." She added sternly, "You're quite fortunate that I found your room empty and came looking for you."

"I was flying around when a storm struck."

"Of course it did."

"Because the Quag doesn't want me to fly over it?"

Her angry look faded. "Excellent, Vega. You are treating the place as a living, breathing, evolving organism, as well you should." She looked at the spot where the dopplegang had been. "You actually learned a valuable lesson this light, Vega. You must be prepared for anything. I can teach you much, but I can't teach you all that you will face in the Quag." She pointed ahead with her wand. "The first of the Five Circles lies just out there. Destin's flying ability will be limited from now on."

"But not impossible?"

"No. But you should use it only in extreme circumstances. And even then the danger you're fleeing may be as nothing to the peril you create by attempting to fly." She looked pointedly at me. "But speaking frankly, please do not think that all three of you will make it through alive. The odds against that are so enormous as to approach the miraculous. And while

I do obviously believe in magic, I do not and never have believed in miracles."

She turned and walked off. But I stood there, as though rooted in the dirt of this awful place. I'm not sure the dopple-gang could have hurt me any more than Astrea just had.

Lessons from Hel

I SAT IN MY seat and stared up at the blackboard. Delph sat to the left of me, while Harry Two was at my feet. He wasn't dozing. My amazing canine was paying attention! Archie sat in the very back. At the head of the room and standing in front of the blackboard was Astrea, clothed in a long cloak.

She tapped her wand at the blackboard, and writing appeared on it. "The Quag, as I told you before, is divided into Five Circles."

Delph had his ink stick poised over his parchment. It appeared to me that he was even more focused on this lesson than I was. And then it struck me why. He couldn't do magic. But he could know the circles as well as anyone. That might prove important later on.

"The First Circle," began Astrea, "is named the Mycanmoor."

I flinched. The Mycanmoor had been mentioned on Quentin's map.

"The Mycanmoor is a maze of startling complexity and populated with creatures that might well prove lethal in any encounter."

"What is the maze made of?" I asked after I wrote all this down.

"It can be many and various. Thick, living hedges and forests of trees. Walls of stone so high you can't see the tops of them. Vines of poisonous plants. Battlements of bones. And these elements can change on a whim."

"Bones?" I interjected. "What of?"

"Bones only have one source," she said. "The dead."

"Yes, but dead what?" I persisted.

"No Wugs, if that's what you mean. Other creatures that were killed in there. The principal threats in the Mycanmoor are the chontoo and the wendigo. Also the manticore is nothing to be trifled with."

"So what's the secret of getting through the mazes?" Delph asked.

In response, Astrea tapped the board and on it appeared a mess of pathways that seemed to have no end. She pointed her wand at it and said, *"Confuso, recuso."* The maze lengthened out and became as straight as a poplar tree.

I turned to her in amazement. "That's it, just the one spell?"

"It's not simple if you don't know what it is. In fact, if you don't, you'll wander the maze forever, for it is what is deemed a perfect maze."

I looked curiously at her. "What does that mean, a perfect maze?"

"One with no detached walls, and no isolation sections, which refer to a passel of passages totally encircled by walls. These are completely unreachable because there is no trail to those sections from any starting spot in the maze. There is exactly one solution to a perfect maze and only one. And there is only one path in the maze from one spot to another spot. Making it utterly perfect, hence the name."

She tapped the board once more. Instantly, another maze appeared there. As I looked at the thing, I could make neither head nor tail of it.

However, as though in a trance, Delph rose and went over to the board. He ran his eye up and down the drawing and then picked up an ink stick that lay on Astrea's desk and started to draw a line. Around and around he went, up and down, side to side, down this path, down another, left here, right there, and the whole time, Delph was staring at the board, his focus complete. Finally, his line of ink ran itself right out of the maze.

He turned to see both Astrea and me watching him in amazement.

"What?" he said, eyeing us warily.

"How did you do that?" Astrea exclaimed.

"Do what?"

"Get out of the maze," I blurted out. "Ruddy brilliant it was, Delph."

He looked at what he had done as though he was seeing it for the first time. "I . . . I just went the way that would get me out of the bloody thing."

Then it occurred to me that Delph had always been like that. He had found the most efficient paths through the forests in Wormwood better than anyone. He had come up with a strategy for me to prevail in the Duelum. He had come up with a diversion so that I could escape from Thorne's room. He had a mind that grew large thoughts from small things.

"Well," said Astrea. "I think that you might do very well in the Mycanmoor even without the spell I just gave Vega."

I was glad she had said that, for I could see Delph's spirits lift immeasurably.

"Now we must move on to the beasts that will confront you in the Mycanmoor. You must be prepared for them." She looked at Delph. "*Both* of you."

She waved her wand. Appearing on the blackboard was something that made me jump up, my wand at the ready, and Harry Two to bark and then attack.

Astrea waved her wand once more and my canine was whisked gently back to where he had been sitting. She looked at me and said, "This is a chontoo."

I was staring at a head without a body attached to it. The face was foul with jagged fangs, flames for hair and eyes that were utterly demonic.

"What does it do?" I asked fearfully. "And where is the rest of it?"

"That is all there is," she replied. "The chontoo was spawned over the centuries by different creatures and species *intermingling*, as we call it here. It is said that the chontoo will wildly attack anything in the hopes of using its prey's body parts to replace the ones it does not have. As this is not possible, it will always fail. But its bloodlust never wavers."

Delph said, "So if it can't use the body, what does it do with it?"

Astrea replied calmly, "It eats it of course."

"O'course," parroted Delph, his face growing a bit pale.

"The chontoo can fly, as you might note, since it has no legs with which to walk. It can appear in quite a rush and can do so silently. One must be prepared."

"And what do we do when it does appear?" I asked.

"You must stop it, Vega," she said emphatically.

"You mean kill it?"

"This particular incantation is effective." She lifted her wand and then snapped it downward like it was a whip, right at the image of the chontoo. She cried out, *"Enamelis fixidus."* A purple light shot out of the wand and collided with the image of the chontoo.

The creature had been baring its fangs. Now its jaws clamped together and its mouth no longer opened.

"What exactly did the spell do?" I asked.

"Cemented its jaws together. And if it can't eat, it will die."

I swallowed nervously and looked down. I knew Astrea was staring at me, but I wasn't prepared to meet her eye. Not yet.

She waved her wand and the chontoo disappeared and another creature took its place on the board. Astrea said, "The manticore."

I was looking at a thing with the head of a lion, the tail of a serpent and what looked to be a goat in between. The jumble of animals was positively terrifying.

"It is swift of foot, with immense strength, and its flaming breath is unquenchable," she said.

I glanced at Delph, who was staring at the manticore like it had somehow possessed his soul.

"And how does one defeat it?" I asked.

"Any number of spells I taught you will do nicely. But it's tricky because a manticore can read minds. So it knows what you are about to do and will take appropriate evasive action."

"Well," said Delph. "That's a bit of a problem."

"So how do we beat the manticore?" I asked again.

"There are two of you, so Delph will have to distract it. Let it read *his* mind, Vega, while you perform the appropriate spell to rid yourselves of the thing."

I looked at Delph once more. I thought he would be shaking his head and looking mortified. But he was nodding and said, "Now, that's a right good plan."

"It's a right *bad* plan if the manticore ends up killing you before I can take care of it," I said forcefully. "It's dangerous, Delph."

He looked at me like I was a nutter. "Dangerous! We've nearly died, what, six times already since we've been here? Dangerous? Har!"

Something nudged my hand. I looked down to see Harry Two pushing it with his snout. I thought he just wanted to be petted, but there was a look in my canine's eyes that spoke something else.

It was as though he was saying, *There are* three *of us, Vega, not just two.*

"Moving on," said Astrea. She waved her wand again and the manticore vanished and was replaced with an even more odious creature, which I had already seen once before.

I thought Astrea shivered just a bit too as she said, "The wendigo."

Having already seen this spectral creature devour a deer from the safety of Astrea's Seer-See, I knew that it ate flesh.

Astrea said, "This creature doesn't simply kill. It can possess you by eating your mind."

"It eats your mind?" said Delph, looking horrified.

She said, "You saw what it did to that unfortunate deer."

I nodded, my mind holding the image of a wendigo running away in *my* body.

Astrea said, "Now, it's crafty. You must always be on the lookout for the warning signs that a wendigo is nearby."

I poised my ink stick over my parchment, ready to write down these warning signs. When she said nothing, I looked up. "What are they?" I asked. "These signs?"

"A vague feeling of terror," she said.

"Well, now, that's right helpful," scoffed Delph. "I mean I doubt we'd be feeling that way otherwise, eh?"

She continued, "And a sense that the facts stored in your head are drifting away and being replaced with strange, often horrible memories that are *not* your own."

"How can it do that?" I asked.

"You are being imprinted with the residual memories of the prey that the wendigo has killed in the past and which linger in its own mind."

It all sounded horrible enough. "Then what do we do?" I asked.

"There is one and only one incantation that will defeat the wendigo." She held her wand in front of her and then made a slashing motion that resembled the letter X. She said in a very firm, very clear voice, "*Omniall.*"

"What does that do?" I asked.

"It removes the mind utterly and irreversibly."

"It removes the mind? Then what happens to the wendigo?" I asked.

"It dies of course. That is just how it must be here."

And I supposed she was exactly right.

For the Ages

W E SAT BEFORE the blackboard for long periods of time. I also practiced my spells and incantations, and performed reverse curses when Astrea tried to attack me. I could tell that she always held back some. But as the time passed, I could also discern that she didn't have to hold back quite as much. What I had found, to my pleasant surprise, was that in combat I had certain instincts that served me well. I could adapt after sizing up my opponent's strengths and weaknesses. I was quick on my feet, both literally and in my mind. I had done the same thing in the Duelum back in Wormwood on my way to becoming champion.

She also made me work through mazes she conjured inside the cottage. I had great difficulty in doing so, and often resorted to the *Confuso, recuso* spell. But Delph was never at a loss and was able to get us out of every single maze that Astrea created. Yet I wasn't overly worried. So long as I had the spell, no maze could defeat us.

Over tea in the library, Archie told us that he had once thought of venturing across the Quag.

"Why?" mumbled Delph, his mouth full of biscuit.

"Well, mate," began Archie, "when you've lived in the same cottage with the same person for hundreds of sessions, it gets to you. You want to try something different, don't you? A breath of fresh air."

"I'm not sure I'd call the Quag a breath of fresh air," I said.

"Well, anyway, it didn't happen."

"Why not?" I asked.

"My mum found out about my plan and put a stop to it."

"How? You can do magic too," said Delph.

Archie's expression became forlorn. "Yes, but I'm not as good as she is. She'd win every duel, hands down."

"But she wants to help us get across the Quag," I noted.

"Bloody ironic, ask me," said Archie.

AFTER OUR LESSONS were finished each light, Delph worked on maps tracing routes and learning everything he possibly could to help us. And I practiced my spells and incantations over and over. At night, Delph and I would study, talking back and forth as we sat in the book-laden library. My notebook was full with what Astrea had taught us, and the margins were heavily cluttered with additional thoughts. I'm sure that Delph's looked the same. Most nights we fell asleep in our chairs, our parchment upon our chests, and Harry Two snoring on the floor next to us.

We were told that the Second Circle was known as the Withering Heath. It was not any sort of heath with which I was familiar. Instead, it was a vast forest with trees so densely set side by side that Astrea said it was sometimes difficult to breathe. This circle had such creatures as the deadly and quite mad lycans, which I had glimpsed through the Seer-See, and the hyperbores, which were blue and could fly, and might be an ally or an enemy. Astrea also impressed upon us that the Second Circle was full of depression and that if we allowed it, that feeling would come to dominate.

The Third Circle was the Erida Wilderness, which was actually the opposite of what I thought a wilderness should be. Astrea had said, "It's a vast flat expanse that stretches seemingly forever. And jabbits and cucos inhabit the Third Circle."

I well knew what jabbits were. But I had never heard of cucos.

"They will provide light in the gloom, when you might very well need it," she said. "And, as I previously mentioned, there is the unicorn, whose horn will defeat all poisons."

Delph and I had looked at each other. I said, "How do you get the horn?"

"There are two ways. One, you simply kill the unicorn and take it."

I didn't much like that way. "And the other?"

"You convince the beast to freely give it."

"How?"

"That, you will have to figure out for yourself when the time is right."

"But how do we figure it out?" I asked.

She had given me a disdainful look. "Not everything can be learned safely in a classroom, Vega. Education is not so neat and tidy." She lifted her hand and pointed to the wall. "Out there is where you will learn your most valuable lessons. If you survive them, that is." She paused and said, "There is another creature which dwells there, called Eris. He has one duty in life, to cause trouble and strife. He will do you mischief if you let him."

"How do we defeat him?" Delph asked.

"You must learn to trust your instincts. That is the only way."

I had looked at my ink stick as though hoping it would write down a far better answer of its own accord, but it didn't. Lately, lessons were not going as well as they might. I was looking for precise answers and she was giving us "instincts."

The Fourth Circle, we learned, was dominated by the Obolus River. I had sat up straight when she mentioned this. I remembered seeing the long, squiggly waterway and what looked to be a small boat upon it.

"Rubez is the boat's pilot. He will carry you across the river, for a price."

"What is the price?" I asked.

"The pilot is the one who sets it. You will have to ask him."

"And what exactly is Rubez? A male?"

"Not exactly," she answered. And I thought she might have shivered. "The river holds perils of which I am not familiar, but they are perils nonetheless."

"How do we avoid them?" I asked.

"Stay *out* of the water" was her ready reply.

NEXT LIGHT, WE walked into the classroom to find Archie there but not Astrea.

"Where is she?" I asked, setting my bound parchment on my desk.

Archie said, "She'll be along. Just finishing up some things for this lesson, I reckon."

"The Fifth Circle," said Delph. "That's what we have left. The last one."

The door to the room opened and Astrea stepped through. At first I couldn't think what was wrong. But then it struck me. She looked older. Her dark hair had some white in it around the roots. Her face was a little heavier, a bit saggy.

"Are you all right?" I asked.

She nodded curtly before striding up to the blackboard.

She took out her wand and tapped it against the board as Delph and I quickly took our seats. Harry Two also sat up and came to attention.

"The Fifth Circle," she said in a weak voice.

I waited for her to conjure something on the board, but instead, Astrea sat down at her desk and clasped her hands in front of her. She said, "It is called the Blue Range. My term for it anyway. It is mountainous. It has deeply carved valleys." She stopped speaking and her gaze took on a glassy expression, as though she were looking so far into the distance that her eyes had failed her.

"Astrea?" I prompted.

With a jolt she came back to us. She coughed and then stared directly at me. "The Blue Range is the last obstacle before the end." Again, she stopped.

I said in an encouraging manner, "And it's mountainous with deeply carved valleys? And . . . ? What else?"

She shook her head slightly as though attempting to dislodge a very disturbing memory. "That is all I can tell you. I do not know what dwells there."

"But you said that you created the Quag?"

"I created *parts* of it. The Blue Range was not one of those parts."

"Well, who created it, then?"

"A fellow named Jasper. His full name was Jasper Jane."

My head snapped up so fast it hurt my neck. "Jasper JANE?"

She nodded slowly. "Your ancestor many times removed. He crafted the Blue Range. He was an immensely talented sorcerer with a flair for the dark sphere."

"The dark sphere?" I said, slightly repulsed by saying the words.

"It is what we call that haven of our magical minds that holds sinister thoughts and impulses. Our kind has them. But we can control them, whereas they predominate with the Maladons. Jasper was a curious hybrid of our two races."

"You think he might have been evil?" I said, horrified by the thought.

She shook her head emphatically. "Oh, no, he fought valiantly on our side, and his knowledge of dark sorcery made him a particularly efficient combatant. He created the last and, I would have to say, most difficult circle."

"And he never told you anything that was in it?" I asked in a breathless tone.

She brooded over this, then said, "He told me one thing, right before he died."

"What?" I said, in a near gasp.

"He told me it was meant to be the land of the lost souls. And that was all he would say on the subject. A curious male. He was a loner; he kept himself to himself."

"What does that mean?" I asked, thinking that I was a loner too, really. But I couldn't be part evil, could I?

"I suppose it means that once you enter it, you will be lost there for all time. And when your physical body perishes and falls to dust, your imprisonment will not be over. It will really just be commencing for your soul, Vega, for your soul can live forever."

I felt crushed by this. "Does that mean that all of this is for naught?"

I looked over my shoulder at Archie. He sat with his gaze downcast. I looked back at Astrea and got quite a shock. She seemed to have aged a hundred sessions. The youth elixir! She had stopped taking it!

"I wish I could help you more," she said. "But it is what it is."

Then she rose on unsteady legs and left us.

When the door closed, I glanced back at Archie. "Why is she doing this?"

He shrugged and said unhelpfully, "She doesn't really confide in me, Vega. She thinks I'm too *young* to understand." He gave a rueful laugh and then fell silent.

I looked at Delph. "She's stopped taking the elixir. She's going to die soon."

He took this in and said, "We can't let her do that, Vega Jane."

I stood. "We won't, Delph. Come on."

Betrayal

WE FOLLOWED ASTREA'S slow treads down the hall and watched her open the door and go inside. A few moments later, I was knocking on that same door.

"Please go away," she said from inside the room.

"We'd like to talk to you," I answered.

"I have talked enough. Please go away."

"We'll stay here for as long as it takes."

The door slowly swung open.

I had never been in Astrea's room. As I glanced around, I was struck at how barren and empty it looked. I had expected a haven of comfort and clutter.

Astrea was in the bed with the covers pulled up high to her rapidly softening chin.

I sat in the rickety chair next to the bed while Delph stood next to me. She didn't look at us. She simply stared at the ceiling.

"Well? What is it?" she said.

The ancientness of her voice was painful. As powerful as the elixir was, its effects wore off rapidly.

I glanced down at her. "We need you."

"I have instructed you as best I can. Now it is up to you."

"But we're not ready." I glanced at Delph. He shook his head in agreement.

She glanced at me. It wasn't a harsh look. She let out a long breath. "Do you know why we build walls? Either real ones or ones simply in our minds?"

I mulled this over. "To keep folks in or out," I said at last.

"We build walls because we are afraid. We do not like change. We do not like it when others who do not look or think like us come along and try and change things. Thus we run from it. Or, even worse, attack it."

I thought back to my time in Wormwood. I had seen that very thing.

"It was awful, really, what we did to all of you," she said, tears welling up in her eyes.

"You . . . you took away our . . . history," I mumbled.

She lifted herself up on the pillows. "We took away your *identities*. It was as bad, actually, as anything the Maladons could have done to you. I see that now."

"They would have killed all of you."

"We also took your lives, and then *merely* required that you keep on living."

"But you're letting me cross the Quag. You're giving me a chance to make things right."

She lifted a hand and touched my cheek. "I did that for one reason only, Vega." She drew in a long, painful breath. "Because You Will Not Be Beaten."

Her hand fell away.

Tears filled my eyes. "But we still need you, Astrea. *I* need you."

She closed her eyes and shook her head. "The youth

elixir has been exhausted. Archie took the last of it. And I was so busy teaching you that I waited too long to get more. I am not up to dealing with the needed ingredients."

I saw that befuddled expression on her features once more. She gripped her head. "It's not . . . pleasant," she said. "Aging this quickly."

"If you tell me how to get the ingredients, I will make the elixir."

Her face took on the expression of awful sadness. She looked over my shoulder. I turned to see who was there. It was Archie. He stood there seemingly frozen.

When I turned back around, her eyes were closed and she was apparently asleep. But from under her eyelids I saw a tear emerge and trickle down her now heavily wrinkled cheek. I gently shook her by the shoulder, but she didn't wake. I shook her harder. I gripped her face and spoke very close to her ear, trying to rouse her. But it didn't work.

I raced over to Archie. "Can you make the elixir?"

"No. She never taught me. And truth is, I'm a complete muddle with potions."

I ran out into the hall with Delph hard on my heels. But I had no idea where I was going. I just wanted to be doing . . . something. Delph hooked me by the arm. "Wait, Vega Jane," he said. "What are the ingredients?"

I hesitated and then decided it would be best just to tell him.

"Two important ones are the venom from a jabbit and the blood of a garm. But we don't have to hunt them. They're in two rooms of the cottage."

A long sliver of silence passed until it was ended by Delph's shouting, "There's a bloody jabbit AND a garm in here somewhere?"

"I know which rooms," I added in what I hoped was a calm, helpful tone.

This only made him look as if he would be sick to his stomach. "You . . . you KNOW!"

"I can get the blood and venom. You need to search through Astrea's desk to find the rest of what we'll need and how to make it."

I took out my wand and ran down the hall. A few moments later, I was in the kitchen. I sorted through the cupboard until I found a small metal bowl and a glass bottle. I pocketed them, turned and ran back out.

Down the hall I stopped at the door with the little mark on it. The jabbit, I knew, was behind this portal, trapped in his cage of light.

I raised my wand, made the three parallel strokes with it and said, "*Crystilado magnifica.*"

Instantly, the image of the jabbit appeared directly in front of me. I knew it was coming, but it still took all of my willpower not to scream.

Okay, I thought. The thing is in there. *But wait, how was I going to get in the door? It would shout "GO AWAY!"*

Then I forced myself to calm down. Astrea had taught me that one. I tapped the door's lock with my wand and said, "*Ingressio.*"

The door immediately swung inward.

I stepped forward into the room, my wand at the ready.

The jabbit was across the space, curled up, its multiple heads lowered, all the awful eyes closed. It was asleep. All around it I could see the lights of its cage swirling. The jabbit was a truly enormous serpent, thick as a tree trunk, with two hundred and fifty venomous heads running the length of its body. It was the most fiercesome beast in all of Wormwood. And yet there were even more terrifying ones out there in the Quag.

I had a plan. I didn't know if it would work, but I was going to try. I raised my wand, pointing it at the body of the giant serpent.

I flicked my wand and said, *"Paralycto."*

The spell I cast hit the wall of light and rebounded. I ducked just in time and it flew over me and hit the opposite wall with a crash.

When I rose, I knew that my spell could not get past the lighted cage. This was a problem. When I heard multiple hisses, I knew I had another problem.

I turned to look. The jabbit was awake now and five hundred eyes were upon me, each of them filled with malice. I swallowed, and it seemed most of my courage drained with it. Now I would have to undo the cage, *then* cast the spell. But that would free the jabbit, at least momentarily. And I knew better than most how quickly they struck. However, unless I did this, Astrea was going to die.

I decided to act fast because the longer I waited, the more time the jabbit had to fully awaken. As I looked at the serpent, something remarkable happened. I grew calm. I don't know why, but I felt a confidence I had no reason to have. I pointed my wand at the bars of light and, focusing my MBS, said, *"Eraisio."*

The light bars instantly vanished.

I could tell the serpent was not yet fully aware that it was free.

Seizing this opportunity, I pointed my wand once more and said, *"Paralycto."*

It was truly remarkable to see such a gigantic creature become instantly frozen. It had reared up right before the spell struck, but now its hundreds of eyes were glazed over and its fangs were conveniently bared.

Still, I walked toward it with great caution, hoping with each step that my spell would hold. I pulled the metal bowl from my cloak pocket and drew close to the nearest set of fangs.

I held the bowl under one of the open mouths, pointed my wand at the fangs and prepared to cast a spell that Astrea had taught me for drawing liquid from various objects like stones and trees, since we would need a source of water.

"Springato erupticus."

A yellowish liquid poured from the fangs and collected in the bowl. It was amazing how much venom could come out of a single pair of fangs.

Once the bowl was fairly full, I pointed my wand at the fangs and muttered the reverse spell to stop the flow of venom.

I stepped back against the far wall, set the bowl down and prepared myself.

Two spells back-to-back.

MBS, MBS. Focus, Vega, focus.

I whipped my wand down the length of the serpent and said, *"Unparalycto."*

The jabbit immediately came back to life. It fixed its gazes on me. I could see exactly what it was planning to do.

"Incarcerata."

The jabbit struck at that instant. And slammed right into the white light bars that had reemerged around it. They held fast and the creature retreated into vast, windy coils, its fury evident in its hideous eyes and the angry twitches of its tree-trunk body.

I smiled. And then turned to pick up the bowl. I never got there.

The jabbit struck with the bloodcurdling shriek that I had always been told was the last thing you would ever hear.

"Pass-pusay," I screamed, slapping my wand against my leg.

I was instantly on the other side of the room and the jabbit had slammed into the wall with its two hundred and fifty heads. The roof of the cottage shook with the impact, and a long crack appeared along the wall.

How the Hel had it escaped my cage of lights?

It turned and with a massive whip of its tail, it was charging straight at me. My thoughts turned back for an instant to Stacks, where a pair of jabbits had been hunting me down. I had escaped behind a little wooden door with a screaming Wug for a knob. There was no such escape now. No door, no screaming Wug.

The jabbit struck again.

"Embattlemento."

The serpent hit the conjured wall with such force that the entire room shook. I fell back, but I quickly regrouped as the jabbit rebounded off my spell and was flung backward against the far wall of the room.

It was slow to shake off the impact.

I could hardly believe my eyes. I had *hurt* a jabbit.

Before it could attack once more, I shouted, "*Incarcerata.*"

The white bands shot from my wand and encircled the creature.

I prayed that it would hold this time. I stepped carefully around the jabbit as its five hundred eyes followed my every move. I slowly bent down, keeping my gaze on the thing, and picked up the bowl of venom.

Then I was out the door in a flash and closed and secured it behind me with a locking spell. Breathless, I hurried down the hall, where I nearly collided with Delph coming the other way. He was carrying an old journal.

"Found it," he said. "The instructions for the elixir."

"Brilliant!" I held up the bowl. "And I got the venom."

"Bloody Hel," he gushed, taking the bowl gingerly.

"And now for the garm." I rushed down the hall to the other door that had told me, "GO AWAY!"

I cried out, "*Crystilado magnifica.*"

I blinked. "*Crystilado magnifica,*" I said again.

The room was empty. There was no garm in a white-light cage.

I heard the growl behind me. I didn't even have time to turn.

I screamed. The garm roared.

I saw a flash of something and I was knocked heels over arse.

As I slid along the floor, I looked behind me.

The garm was on its hind legs, just about to expel a chest of flames that would burn me to cinder.

And there was Harry Two. He must have knocked me down.

He leapt directly at the beast and then the impossible happened. My canine clamped his strong jaws around the garm's snout, forcing it shut. The garm screamed in fury, though the sound came out muffled because it could not open its mouth.

It flung itself around, slamming Harry Two into the wall. But still Harry Two hung on, even with his legs dangling uselessly and blood pouring from the side of his head. The garm reached up with its forelegs to rip Harry Two to pieces.

I had another vision. Of my first canine, Harry. He had also saved me from a garm and sacrificed his life in doing so. I had no intention of letting that happen again.

There was a powerful feeling surging through every bit of me. It wasn't hatred. Or loathing. It was far more than that. I don't believe there is even a word to adequately encompass it. I said it before I even realized saying it. It came out of my mouth with such force that it seemed the words alone could do what I wanted done.

I pointed my wand directly at the garm's chest.

"Rigamorte!"

The black light hit the garm with such power that the many-tonned beast was lifted right off its clawed feet. Harry Two let go in midair and fell away from the hideous thing as the garm was flung along the hall, hit the wall and slumped down with an enormous, cottage-rattling thud. It was quite dead as it rolled over, its tongue hanging out, its bloody chest still. I sprinted down the hall and knelt next to Harry Two, who lay sprawled on the floor, his damaged legs useless, his head bleeding badly.

I pulled the Adder Stone from my pocket and waved it over my precious canine. A second later he was licking my face, healed and his legs functioning. I hugged him so tightly I could feel his heart pounding against mine.

"I love you, Harry Two. I love you so much. Thank you for saving me."

I looked over at the garm. Its blood, which perpetually ran down its chest, would make my task easy. I plucked the glass bottle from my pocket and froze.

Archie stood there, his wand pointed at my chest.

Now I knew what had happened with the jabbit and the garm, though I could barely believe it.

His eyes turned to slits. He started to say, *"Riga —"*

But a huge fist came down on the top of his head and Archie fell to the floor, unconscious, his wand falling from his hand.

Behind him stood Delph.

He looked at me and flexed his muscle. "Sometimes you don't need magic, Vega Jane. Har!"

Adieu

D ELPH!" I GASPED.

He bent down and pocketed Archie's wand, which had rolled across the floor.

"Bloke can't do much without that," he said.

"He was going to kill me," I said.

"I reckon he was." He looked at the dead garm. "Your doing, I 'spect."

"I used the *Rigamorte* curse, the same one Archie was going to use on me."

I stared down at the unconscious Archie and shook my head in disbelief.

As he started to stir, I pulled my wand, aimed it at him and said, *"Ensnario."*

Thick ropes appeared out of the air and wrapped themselves around Archie.

When he came fully around and realized what had happened, he looked up at me and unleashed a torrent of foul language.

"Mutado," I snapped, and my spell hit him full in the mouth, silencing him. Then I picked up my flask, while Delph easily lifted Archie off the floor and slung him over

his shoulder. "We best get on with the potion making," he said. "But we need something called Breath of a Dominici."

"Breath of a Dominici? What's a Dominici and how do we get its breath?"

"Haven't the foggiest," said Delph as we walked down the hall together with Harry Two at our heels. Archie had struggled at first but now just lay slumped over Delph's massive shoulder.

When we reached the kitchen, Delph set Archie on the floor. Harry Two sat next to him, guarding the bloke.

Delph took me over to a table where he had lined up a row of bottles and other objects. There was a piece of parchment tacked to the wall. I set the flask of garm blood down next to the bowl of jabbit venom.

"It's all here," said Delph. "'Cept the breath thing." He tapped the parchment. "Took this outta that journal. Tells you how to make it. Steps you got to do. Figgered you'd be good at that, like at Stacks. I heated up some water, 'cause we'll need to mix some of it hot."

I looked over the parchment. "Okay, the Breath of a Dominici goes in last. Why don't I start putting it all together and you can try and figure out this breath thing?"

Delph set off while I turned to making the elixir of youth. I took my time because I was afraid of making a mistake. There was a lot of heating up of ingredients at just the right temperature and then letting them cool down for exact times. I had brought in an old timekeeper from Astrea's desk and used it as my timer.

The mixing and grinding and cutting and stirring were

exhausting. When I poured in the jabbit venom, a huge ball of smoke shot up from the pot I was using to hold the potion. Luckily, I got out of the way in time. When the smoke hit the ceiling, a hole opened up there, which I quickly repaired with my wand.

Now the mixture had to stew for a bit. Then I would add the blood of the garm, a handful of something called tendrils of tawny, which looked like frozen worms, and a small jar of liquid labeled PETRIROOT PUSCLES.

I would rather die than drink this mess. Eternal youth couldn't be worth it.

Twenty slivers after that would come the Breath of a Dominici. If Delph managed to find it somehow.

I turned and looked at Archie, who was staring across the room at me.

I pulled up a chair and sat across from him.

"If I let you speak, will you promise not to scream foul things at me?" He looked surly but slowly nodded. I did the reverse spell but kept my wand ready.

"I know you set the jabbit and garm on me. And then you were going to kill me. Why?"

"Isn't it obvious?"

"Not to me, it's not."

"Well, then you're clearly not very bright. You'll probably perish in the First Circle."

"Maybe I will. But at least I'm going to try."

"Exactly," he roared. "For eight hundred bloody sessions, my dear mum has been saying that no one can cross this place. No one! We sacrificed our lives for that. When I learned what you were going to do and that the old bat was going to help you do it, I thought she must be mad. I took the elixir and then threw the rest away."

"But why couldn't she make more?" I asked.

"Because I cast a befuddlement hex on her."

"So you *wanted* her to die."

He screamed, "I wanted to make sure that you did not cross the Quag!" He grew silent and drew several deep breaths. "And over eight hundred sessions is long enough to live, don't you think?" he added quietly.

A minute later, Delph came charging in with Seamus in his wake.

"Do you have it? The Breath of a Dominici?"

"I don't but Seamus here does."

I looked at the hob. "Seamus? How can you have it?"

"Ms. Prine sent me out for it, before she became, well, old." He reached in his pocket and pulled out a long-stemmed flower that had a bloodred bloom as large as my fist.

"That's it? A flower?"

He wrinkled his nose at my abrupt comment. "Well, it might be just a flower, but the only place it grows is in a nest of vipers that don't much like to part with it."

"So how did you manage it, then?" I asked.

"The vipers don't much like fire either, do they?" His face crinkled into a smile. "So's a little blue ball of it just happened to fall into their midsts and then it just happened to become a *big* blue ball of flames that they wanted no part of."

"Brilliant, Seamus, absolutely brilliant. Well done."

Looking happy with my praise, he handed over the flower. I put my nose close to it, took a whiff and nearly gagged. It smelled like slep dung.

"Holy Steeples," I said, rubbing my nose.

"Aye, you don't want to stick your nose in that thing," Delph said. "Seamus says it reeks."

"Thanks, Delph," I replied crossly. "Next time, why don't you tell me something like that *before* I do it?"

I cut up the flower petals according to the parchment, waited five slivers and then threw it into the steaming pot. The resulting smell was beyond horrid.

"Bloody Hel," exclaimed Delph, lifting his shirt to cover his face. Seamus had run from the room. Harry Two put his paws over his snout. But I had to stir the thing in precise motions, so I stood there, two fingers pinching my nose, my eyes running with the stink of it. A few slivers later, it was done. I poured a flask of it, corked it and then we bolted down the hall and into Astrea's room. She was so small and frail-looking now that I feared she was already dead.

"Astrea, I've got it, the youth elixir."

She made no response.

We tiptoed over to the bed and looked down at her. She had faded incredibly fast. Her hair was stark white, her skin translucent and covered with large spots, and her features elongated and craggy.

"How do we do this?" I asked Delph.

"When I was little and me dad wanted to get some medicine in me, he just opened my mouth, pinched me nose and poured it in."

And that's what we ended up doing. I got the contents of the flask down Astrea's throat, and then stepped back. At first, there was nothing and my spirits plummeted to my boots. Then she gave an almighty gag, sat straight up in the bed, and her eyes opened. And, as though the sessions were being peeled away like the skin of an onion, all the elements of old age gave way. Her hair darkened, her skin grew firm, the features shortened and tightened, the body filled out. It was like I was watching her entire life in reverse.

Finally, she sat there looking as she had before.

She drew a long breath. "Thank you," she said. And in her voice I could tell that she knew exactly what had happened.

"Where is my son?" she asked wearily.

"We have him tied up. He used a befuddlement hex on you. And he tried to kill me."

She nodded slowly and rose from her bed. "It's entirely my fault," she said. "How did you manage the potion?"

"Seamus got the Breath of a Dominici. The rest of the ingredients were here."

"But surely the garm and jabbit?" she began.

Delph answered. "Vega Jane got those all right. They were no match for her, even when Archie let them loose on her."

"Archie let them loose?" she exclaimed. But then her expression calmed. "Of course. He would have been jealous. And confused. And angry."

I said, "I had to kill the garm. It was going to kill Harry Two. So I killed it. And I had no problem doing so," I added firmly.

Astrea looked at me pointedly. "I see, Vega. I see."

And I could tell that she really *did* see.

She patted my arm. "In bad times, wisdom is so often born, Vega. Now I need to go and see Archie."

THE DOOR OPENED a bit later and Astrea appeared. When I saw an unbound Archie behind her, I leapt off the bed and pulled my wand.

"There is no need, Vega," she said, her voice strong and firm.

I looked at Archie. His features were docile, ambivalent even.

"What happened to him?" I asked.

She drew close to me. "The *Subservio* spell. He is quite harmless now. But I did speak with him before I did the incantation. I tried to make him see my side of things. But I'm not sure we're there yet."

"About the Fifth Circle," I began. "Since Archie placed a befuddlement hex on you, you didn't tell us all you knew of it."

"Oh, but I did tell you everything I know of it. Not even my Seer-See will allow me to glimpse the Fifth Circle."

"Blimey," muttered Delph.

"Now it is time for you to be on your way," she said.

"On our way . . . where?" I asked warily.

"To cross the Five Circles of course," she said.

"What, now? Right now?" exclaimed Delph.

"But you need to know that escaping from here will come with a price."

I shook my head. "A price?"

"To put it simply, escaping the Quag means imprison-ment forever."

I shot Delph a glance just at the same moment he looked at me.

I turned back to Astrea in time to see her wave her wand.

"Good luck," she said.

I felt my eyes roll back in my head.

And then everything went black.

A Surprise

W OTCHA, VEGA JANE?"

I opened my eyes and glanced up. Delph was looking straight down at me.

"You okay, Vega Jane?" he said anxiously.

I automatically nodded, though I didn't know if I was actually okay or not. I sat up slowly, trying to gather my wits. Harry Two put out a paw and gently touched my arm as if to make sure I really was all right.

I looked around. "Where are we?"

"Dunno for sure, but I figure right close to the Mycanmoor."

"How can you tell?" I asked.

"Over there," he said, pointing to the right.

I squinted and in the darkness I could make out a high wall.

"The maze," I said, glancing at him.

"What I figger. Yeah."

My temper flared. "Why would she do this, Delph? Just send us here with no warning a'tall?"

"Dunno, Vega Jane. Suppose she had her reasons."

Cataclysmic thoughts suddenly hit me. Our things? My wand! The Adder Stone. Destin. I looked wildly around and let out a breath of relief when I saw our tucks sitting side by side. I opened them and saw neat bundles of food and jugs of water. I looked down. The leather harness was strapped to my torso. On my thumb was my grandfather's ring. I lifted my cloak. Destin was around my waist. I felt in the cloak pocket and my hand closed around first the Stone and then my wand. I took out the latter and gripped it loosely. I could feel it instantly become a part of me. I had done it so many times now that it felt natural and right.

"Do you think we have to be in the maze for the counter-spell to work?" I asked.

Why hadn't I thought to ask Astrea that? There were suddenly hundreds of queries to which I was sure I needed answers to survive.

"Might help to find the entrance before we do," Delph replied.

We shouldered our tucks and started forward.

I pointed my wand up ahead and said, "*Illumina.*"

A bead of light shot out of my wand and hurtled toward the dark shapes that we took to be the wall of the maze, where it lit up everything in front of us.

An instant later, Delph and I could hear hooves smacking the ground and wings flapping and sharp cries of unknown creatures. I held my wand at the ready, unsure if I was about to encounter an army of hideous beasts. I hadn't practiced such an eventuality with Astrea, and I doubted my ability to fight off a mass attack.

Thankfully, the sounds and chatter died down and were replaced by quiet.

I looked over at Delph. "Actually, I think I liked the noise better," he said.

I agreed with him. It might have been only the weaker creatures that had fled the light. The ones that could kill us might be just ahead, waiting.

We moved forward, my gaze darting in all directions. I took a mental tally of my emotions for the signs of the wendigo — vague terror coupled with something else's memories. But my thoughts, terrifying though they were, all seemed to be my own.

"Vega Jane, how about you use your wand to see what's up ahead, eh?"

"Good idea." I pointed my wand, made the proper motion and said, "*Crystilado magnifica*."

Now directly in front of us was an enormous wall. A battlement, Astrea had called it. And it was made entirely of bones. It made the wall back at Thorne's look puny by comparison. "I think we found the maze."

"And there's the entrance, I reckon," he said, pointing to a dark, oval shape.

We marched on, drawing closer and closer to this image.

Before we got to the wall, we encountered a large wrought-iron gate that suddenly appeared in front of us. Written out in scroll were the words *Wolvercote Cemetery*.

"She didn't mention a cemetery, did she?" I said. He shook his head.

Delph peered through the gate. "It's a graveyard in there all right," he exclaimed. He pushed on the gate, but it would not open.

I tapped the lock with my wand and said, "*Ingressio*."

The huge gate swung back.

We passed through with Harry Two bringing up the rear.

We came to the first row of graves.

"Look at the names on them, Delph," I said as I eyed them. *Mullins, Dinkins. And* KRONE?

Jurik Krone's ancestors were buried here? They let *anyone* in here, didn't they?

Delph said, "Look, there's a Picus and a Mulroney. And . . . and . . ."

His voice trailed off and I could see why.

The name on the lichen-stained gravestone was Barnabas Delphia.

He read the epitaph out loud. *"Barnabas Delphia, loving father and devoted husband to Lecretia."*

"Did you ever hear of them from your father?" I asked.

Delph shook his head. "Never. Not once. I can't hardly believe I'm seeing it."

I left Delph standing there and moved down the row of graves. When I saw the name on the simple gravestone, I caught a breath and moved closer.

ALICE ADRONIS, WARRIOR TO THE LAST BREATH

I looked down at the sunken mound of dirt and then back at the leaning gravestone. I held my wand up high and gazed at it. Alice had given me the Elemental on a great battlefield far, far in the past. She had done so with her dying breath, telling me that I had to survive.

I suddenly jerked because the wand had started to move in my hand. As I watched, shocked, it bent forward so that its point was directed at Alice's grave.

I didn't understand for a moment, but then I did.

The thing was *bowing* to her, its former mistress.

I felt the tears cluster in my eyes. But I also, for the first time, felt a powerful connection between Alice and myself. Astrea had said that Alice and I could be related, and that was why the Elemental worked as a wand for me. As I looked down at that sunken mound of dirt, it occurred to me that I had a great deal to live up to. Alice had evidently thought that I needed to survive for an important reason. I hoped I was up to the challenge that the Quag was certainly going to present.

The grave I saw next was that of my ancestor Jasper Jane, the creator of the Fifth Circle. His gravestone simply held his name with no accompanying description. A sorcerer steeped in dark magic, Astrea had said. I shivered when I thought about what he might have put in the final circle.

The next two graves also captured my attention.

Bastion Cadmus. His epitaph read THE ONE WHO LEADS US. The other gravestone read THE STRENGTH OF LOVE, THE FALLACY OF YOUTH. I could make neither head nor tail of that. The name on the gravestone was Uma Cadmus. I didn't know if it was Bastion's mate or perhaps his daughter.

"Vega Jane!"

I turned and saw Delph farther down another row of graves. He was frantically motioning for me to come. Harry Two and I raced over to where he stood.

"Lookit that, Vega Jane," he said.

He was pointing at a number of graves.

I read down the list of names. I exclaimed, "They're all Prines. This is Astrea's family."

"Too right. So if she knew about this place, why didn't she tell us, eh?"

"So what else hasn't she told us?" I asked. My belly felt like it was full of ice.

I was going to say something else, but I never got the chance.

Something had reached up through the ground, grabbed my ankles and pulled me downward, through the dirt and below to where the dead lay.

Orco

J UST AS I had in falling into Thorne's labyrinth, I endured the sensation of plummeting a long way. However, this time I remembered I had on Destin and thus was able to lessen the impact when I hit bottom.

I was up in an instant, my wand at the ready in the pitch-darkness.

"*Illumina*," I cried out.

The place was instantly lit and I saw Delph and Harry Two slowly getting to their feet.

"Are you okay, Delph?"

He brushed off his clothes and nodded, though his face was ashen. I looked down at Harry Two. His hackles were up and his fangs were bared. I looked wildly around, certain that my canine had sensed danger coming.

We were in a low, darkened tunnel with stone walls that were awash with age and slime. I looked in one direction and saw a blank wall. At the other end of the tunnel was an opening. I looked at Delph to find him staring at the same spot.

I glanced up expecting to see dirt above us, but there was only stone.

"What grabbed us?" I said breathlessly. I looked down at

my ankles. "That's blood on my trousers," I exclaimed. "But it's not mine."

"Same with me," said Delph, indicating his legs.

I looked at Harry Two and saw red streaks on his forelegs.

I once more gazed at the stone ceiling. "The graves are up there," I said.

"What's below a grave?" asked Delph, miserably. "Nothin' good, I wager."

"If something yanked us down here, it must still be around."

"And the only way out looks to be through there." He pointed ahead.

I squared my shoulders and tried to make myself feel confident and brave though I felt neither. I held my wand in front of me and marched toward the opening with Delph and Harry Two alongside me. We reached it and, deciding that waiting would just make it harder, I walked right through it.

At first, there was nothing. Then there *was* something.

Set into the walls were little beads of light that blinked on and off. For a moment, I thought they were pieces of glass or metal. But when I wandered closer to the wall, I leapt back in horror.

They were eyes. Blinking eyes!

I looked over at Delph. He was obviously stunned as well.

As I looked again, I could tell there weren't just eyes on the wall. There were mouths. They were opening and closing along with the eyes, but no words were coming out. It was as if they were silently screaming.

I turned and ran.

Right into him.

He was a little taller than I was and so lean that he looked like bone with a bit of skin lying over it. Yet he was as hard as a tree, and I toppled over from the collision. My wand fell to the rock floor.

He was dressed in a long coat of black, trousers and a slimy shirt. His face was as pale as goat's milk. His beard was blacker than his coat and lay tightly to his face where his cheekbones protruded like hard nuts. A strip of black fuzz arched over his mouth, which was set in a grim line. He also had on black boots up to the knees.

I looked madly around for Delph and Harry Two. To my horror, they both were pinned flat against the wall. Delph's mouth was open, but no words were coming out. I scrambled to my feet and started to run toward them.

"No," the creature said in a raspy voice.

It was like my feet were sunk into the rock.

I looked back at him over my shoulder. In his hand was a wooden cudgel intricately carved with evil-looking figures I did not recognize. He smacked one end of the cudgel on the rock floor, and my feet were released.

I turned to face him.

He leisurely circled, looking me over.

His nose was unlike any nose I had ever seen. It had three openings instead of the usual two. And it had two humps in the bone as though it had been broken more than once. And it was so long it very nearly overtook the mouth on the way to the chin, which was as sharply angled as a cutting knife. And the eyes above the elongated nose were solid black. Not just the little orbs in the middle. Where I had white, his entire eye was black.

I glanced down at the hand curled around the cudgel. It wasn't really a hand. It was a claw, nails longer than my fingers. And they were covered in blood. That answered the question of where the blood on our clothes had come from. This bloke had pulled us down here.

He pointed one claw at me. Destin seized up around me, lifting me off the ground, and I hung there in midair. My spine was nearly cracking as I was forced backward, my head growing perilously close to my heels.

He croaked, "The chain of Destin 'tis indeed."

And then he stamped the floor with his cudgel once more and I fell hard to the rock. I lay there breathless. I glanced over at Delph. His mouth was still open, but his eyes were looking not at me but at a spot on the floor. I looked there.

You idiot. Your wand!

I snagged it, pointed it directly at the creature and cried out, *"Impacto!"*

He instantly swept his cudgel across the air and my spell hit an invisible barrier. The collision caused dust and rock to fall from the ceiling of the tunnel.

Although he'd blocked my incantation, the creature was now regarding me in a new light, it seemed to me.

"You are a sorceress," he hissed.

I rose to my feet. "I know I am. What the Hel are you?"

He said nothing, but continued to watch me.

"Release my friends. Now!" I raised my wand threateningly.

254

"I will see you again, *certe*," he said.

"What does that mean, *certe*?" I asked.

In answer he pointed to the walls where the eyes blinked and the mouths opened. He opened his own mouth in a gruesome smile and I saw his teeth. They were black like his eyes. He hissed, "All come to me in the end. *Certe*."

He stamped the cudgel against the rock floor a third time, and I braced myself for another attack. But he simply pointed again to the wall where the eyes and mouths were. And now I could hear them! They seemed to be pleading with me to save them. Their cries rose and rose until I had to put my hands over my ears.

He shouted out some word I had never heard and there was instant silence.

When he turned back to me, he opened his mouth wide and out came his tongue. Only it was not really a tongue, not like mine, in any case. It was long and black and had three arrow points at the end of it.

"I am Orco," he said. "These are my offspring. And I will see you again, the timing of which remains with you, for now. But not always so. Something will intervene." He smiled maliciously. "It always does."

With his free hand he reached inside his coal-black coat and pulled out an enormous timekeeper on a rusted chain. He held it up so I could see. Across the glass of the timekeeper, faces were swirling like shooting stars traversing the heavens. They came and went with astonishing speed, too fast to count, almost too fast to see at all.

Orco intoned, "Life. And then death. *Certe*."

Everything went black again. I felt propelled upward. At last, I hit something hard and lay still. When I opened my eyes, there was Harry Two.

I sat up and hugged him. Then I slowly rose and staggered over to where Delph lay on top of the grave of his ancestor Barnabas Delphia.

"Delph! Delph!"

I gripped his shoulder and pulled him up. He came around and looked at me.

"D-did . . . did that just really h-happen?" he asked in a disbelieving voice.

I nodded, my breaths coming in bunches.

"It . . . it was horrible, Vega Jane. Them faces. Pleading-like."

"They were dead, Delph," I said quietly.

"But what did that thing want with us?"

"Astrea said that escape from this place means imprisonment forever. I wonder if she meant down there, on that wall?"

"So we'll end up there? No matter what we do?"

I couldn't believe that Astrea would have trained me up just so I would end up stuck on a wall by that evil creature.

I straightened and looked out ahead of us. "The First Circle," I said.

It was our only chance.

The First Circle

I T DID NOT take us long to reach it.

The battlement of bones, I instantly termed it, harkening back to the description Astrea had used.

It was so tall that I could not honestly see to the top of the walls. It just appeared out of the gloom like a malignant giant blocking our path. Every last inch of it was built from bones of all sorts, taken from things once living.

"I think . . . I think some of 'em are like us, Vega Jane. The bones, I mean."

I nodded but said nothing. It was too horrible to even think about.

Delph saw it before I did. I don't know if I expected some grand entrance, but the doorway was barely bigger than the one I had at my old home in Wormwood. It was battered planks with blackened hinges and a rusted, twisted iron handle for a latch.

We approached it stealthily because that just seemed the natural thing to do here. When we reached it, we stopped and looked at each other.

Delph reached out and opened the latch.

The door swung inward, revealing, if it was possible, even greater darkness within. Taking the same tack I had underneath the graves, I stepped quickly through. Delph and Harry Two immediately followed. As soon as we were inside, the door slammed shut. And I doubted that any spell I cast would reopen it. From this point we could only go forward, not back.

We were inside the First Circle. We were inside the perfect maze.

I looked ahead of us and suddenly the place was awash in light. The walls in here were exactly like the ones out there: bones. From every nook and cranny, skulls with empty eye sockets stared back at us.

The corridor turned sharply to the right about ten feet down. We walked ahead a bit, turned that way and were immediately confronted by eight different passages bleeding off the one we were on.

I held up my wand and was about to say the *Confuso, recuso* spell to straighten out the maze.

I never got the chance.

The battlement of bones changed suddenly. The skulls became long vines that shot out and ensnared me, ripping my wand from my hand. I tried to call out, but a vine wrapped around my mouth. I looked over in terror to see Delph being lifted into the air like a small child, the vines pinning his arms and legs together.

Then I saw something flash past me.

It was Harry Two! My canine was dodging and leaping over the vines that clutched at him. When a vine grabbed his hind leg, he turned and bit it in half with one chomp of his strong jaws and razor-sharp teeth. Try as they might, the vines could not capture my canine. I wondered for a moment where he was going, until I saw him returning with the thing clamped between his teeth.

My wand!

He raced toward me and leapt between two vines, which shot out to intercept him.

My hands were bound by vines, but my fingers were still free. Harry Two reached my outstretched right hand and my fingers closed around my wand.

But my mouth was still covered by a vine and another had encircled my neck and was squeezing the life literally out of me. My mind felt dark and dizzy as my chest started to heave with the effort of staying inflated.

I could not cast a spell without saying it. I didn't know what to do. I closed my eyes and felt the wand begin to slip between my fingers.

I opened my eyes when I heard him.

Delph was looking up at me even as a large vine encircled his body and started to tighten.

"Your wand," he cried out. "The Elemental!"

The Elemental.

I willed the Elemental to full size and though my arm was still bound tightly so I could not throw it hard, it didn't matter. I had known for some time that I controlled the Elemental with my mind, not the strength of my arm.

Do it, save us.

The Elemental blasted off from my hand and hurtled down the passage. As it did so, the power of its mighty wake tore apart the vines holding us, throwing huge chunks of them against other vines, which in turn were smashed by the weight of these projectiles.

Freed from the grip of the ravaged vines, Delph and I plummeted toward the ground. I was ready, though, because I doubted we would get a second chance. The Elemental had turned and was racing back to me, and I caught it before I hit the ground. I willed it to its normal size, made a slashing motion with my wand at the towers of vines and shouted, "*Withero.*"

The vines instantly turned brown, shrank and collapsed.

But I wasn't done yet.

"*Confuso, recuso.*"

The maze straightened out.

"Run, Delph. Come on, Harry Two."

We rushed past the dead vines because I had no idea if new ones would take their place. We ran and ran until, although we were not out of the maze, we had to stop, bend over and suck in long breaths to replenish our lungs. When I looked up, I was glad we had stopped. But that was the only thing I was glad about.

The manticore was barely twenty feet from us, barring our way.

The conjured image back at Astrea's did not do the creature justice.

It was twice as tall as Delph and three times as broad. It must have weighed a ton. Its lion's head had a full mane of tawny fur; its serpent's tail swished across the ground. The goat's body in the middle did not seem substantial enough to merge these two fierce creatures.

Mesmerized by all this, I never saw it coming.

"Look out, Vega Jane!"

Something hit me and knocked me down.

The blast of flames passed over us an instant later.

I had forgotten that the bloody beast could do that.

I looked over to see that it was Delph who had pushed me down. And saved my life.

I sat up, pointed my wand at it and prepared to send it to Hel.

Only it wasn't there.

Blast, that's right. It can read minds.

Harry Two barked. I whirled.

The manticore was behind us, barely five feet away.

It roared and flames shot at us, but I had acted at the same moment, not giving the thing time to read my mind, which was racing like a runaway horse.

"Embattlemento."

The ball of flames hit my shield spell, ricocheted off and hit the wall of the maze.

A skull hit me in the head and I realized that the bones had come back. Other bones toppled down around us.

I raised my wand and pointed upward. *"Embattlemento."*

The skulls hit the shield and bounced off.

But I had taken my eyes off the manticore. Where was it?

There it was, to my left, closer to Delph.

I raised my wand to blast it, but then it was gone again. The bloody thing could move faster than my eye could follow.

It reappeared on my right.

"Hey," shouted Delph. He was waving his arms at the manticore. He picked up a skull and hurled it at the beast. It shot out a lungful of flames and the skull disintegrated.

"Impacto!" I screamed, my wand pointed straight at the manticore.

The thing was blasted off the ground, soared backward and slammed into the wall of bones behind it. It slid down the wall and lay still. And dead.

"You did it, Vega Jane," gasped Delph. He was kneeling on the ground, holding his arm.

The walls on either side of us shook and then started to tumble down.

"Harry Two," I screamed and struck the harness. He leapt and I attached him to it. I grabbed Delph and took to the air. We soared along, dodging and spinning past bones, skulls and other debris. Chunks and pieces still hit us, but I kept my gaze resolutely on the end of the maze.

And then a tower of bones collapsed in front of us and the small square of black that I knew represented the end of the maze disappeared.

I pointed my wand and shouted, *"Engulfiado."*

The bones were blasted out of the way by a tidal wave of water and we soared through. I landed too fast and we all sprawled on the ground. I unhooked Harry Two from his harness and stood.

"Delph, you okay?" I said urgently.

When he didn't answer, I looked at him. "Delph?"

He turned his face to mine. It was a sheet of pain.

"Delph, what is it?"

I ran to him, then stopped dead when he held up his arm.

"G-guess it got m-me."

The manticore *had* gotten him. His left arm was burned nearly black, the skin was bubbled and cracked.

I immediately pulled the Adder Stone from my pocket, waved it over his arm and thought good thoughts.

"Thanks, Vega Jane," he said. "Pain's all gone." He stretched his limb.

Well, the pain might have been gone, but the arm was still blackened. The skin was still popped and cracked like meat kept too long over the flames. When Delph followed my gaze and saw the state of his arm, his face turned pale.

"Delph," I said. "I'm sorry. I guess the Stone can't fully . . ." I could not finish.

"'Tis okay, Vega Jane," he said softly. "No more pain. That's what's important, eh. Like you done for me dad. Even if it don't look . . . if it don't look so good no more."

I felt tears creep to my eyes, but his look told me they were unwarranted.

He gripped my arm. "We're alive, Vega Jane. We're ALIVE."

He opened his tuck and slipped on another shirt.

I looked around as the walls of trees sprouted on either side of us, soaring up so high they seemed to touch the sky. In a few moments, we were totally engulfed in another maze.

"Oh no!" I said, my spirits plummeting. I drew my wand and prepared to say the spell that would straighten the maze, when I started to feel funny. No, *funny* was the wrong word. I was feeling *terrified*. But what was making me terrified were things that I knew had not happened to me. I was a beast and then something was tearing me apart. I was a bird and I was being devoured. I was transformed into a hideous lycan and then I was disemboweled.

With a rush, my mind cleared.

A wendigo!

I looked behind us and there it was, soaring straight at us.

I grabbed Delph's hand at the same time he scooped up Harry Two.

"Go, Vega Jane. Go!"

We shot upward until we had nearly cleared the maze's treetops. Then I pointed us forward. I looked back. The wendigo was right behind us. The skylight spear and the resulting thunder-thrust hit so close to us that it nearly knocked us out of the sky. And I knew why.

I was flying over the Quag. The storms had arisen to stop me, as Astrea had said they would.

"Delph!" I screamed. "I can't fly up here. The storms will stop me. We'll have to go back into the maze."

Delph had been gazing down from his high perch. "Before you drop, light up the maze down there," he called over the punishing noise of the storm.

I had been glancing behind us to see the wendigo gaining, but I did what Delph asked.

"*Illumina.*"

The maze was suddenly brilliantly lighted. I saw Delph run his gaze over all of it. Another skylight spear hit a tree directly behind us. The force of the collision sent shock waves out that tumbled us across the air.

I lost my grip on Delph's hand, and he and Harry Two fell away from me.

At the same instant, my mind was filled once more with the terror of another. When I glanced back, the wendigo was within twenty feet of me. The storm seemed to have no impact on the ghastly thing.

I forced my mind to clear and shot downward into the darkness, scanning everywhere for the falling pair.

"Illumina!"

I saw them and blasted toward them, the crown of my head pointed nearly straight to the ground. I had never gone this fast before and still it didn't seem it would be fast enough. I was convinced we were all going to die and the bloody wendigo would feast on us.

I put on a burst of speed at this thought, reached out my hand and snagged Delph by the back of his shirt. Harry Two was still in his arms. I started to head back up, but Delph cried out, "Keep in the maze, Vega Jane. Keep in the maze."

I looked at him and then back at the wendigo, which was still right on our tail.

I could feel my mind seizing up with terror, none of it mine, but that didn't make it any less horrible. I must have slowed down because I heard Harry Two let out an enormous growl that made every hair on my neck stick straight up.

"No!" I screamed, as Harry Two leapt from Delph's arms and directly at the wendigo, which was so close now that I could see its ghoulish, transparent shape nearly next to me.

I snagged Harry Two with my hand and redoubled my speed, leaving the wendigo behind, at least for now. When I looked down at Harry Two, I gasped. Part of his left ear was missing. While Delph held on to my leg, I put my canine in his harness, snatched the Adder Stone from my pocket and waved it over the spot where Harry Two's ear had been. The stone could not regrow parts of the body, but it ceased the bleeding. And my canine seemed all right otherwise.

"Left, left!" screamed Delph.

I hung a left so sharp that our boots smacked against the trees.

"Right, then another right," directed Delph.

I did as he said. I marveled that he had apparently memorized the maze from looking at it for only a few moments.

He kept barking out directions and I followed them. But the wendigo was still behind us and I intended to do something about that right now.

"Hang on, Delph," I said, lifting up his hand until he was able to clutch part of the harness that was keeping Harry Two affixed to my chest.

I pointed my wand behind me and cried out, *"Embattlemento."*

Then I went into a dive. The wendigo managed to avoid the spell shield by veering to the left, but it had allowed me separation. I flipped over so that I was flying on my back, made the mark of the *X* in the air with my wand and shouted, *"Omniall."*

The light hit the wendigo directly on its transparent chest and then it literally went berserk. It immediately spun out of control and slammed into a wall of the maze. I watched it plummet and crash into another section of the wall. It kept doing this over and over, its mind and thus sense of direction gone, until it fell to the ground in a crumpled heap, dead.

I turned back around and soared off.

Twenty slivers later, following Delph's directions, we shot free of the maze and into the open air. I quickly landed and detached Harry Two from his harness. I immediately hugged my canine and gingerly touched the spot where part of his left ear had once been. It pained me as much as Delph's arm.

But when I looked over at Delph, he was grinning broadly. And when I focused on Harry Two's features, I could see the mirth in his mismatched eyes.

"We did it, Vega Jane," exulted Delph. "We made it through the First Circle."

Suddenly, my wand was snatched from me.

"But it'll be the last thing you do," said a deep voice. "Or me name's not Lackland Cyphers."

Captaining the Furinas

THE LARGE BLOKE who had taken my wand was holding an old rusted but still deadly sword. His companion, a female, held a crossbow loaded with an arrow pointed at us.

Lackland Cyphers had a short black beard and long hair the same color, but his eyes were a bewitching shade of green. He was dressed in old clothes and a pair of dirty, calf-high boots. His features were handsome, but also haggard. He looked to be about twenty sessions old.

The female was around Delph's age. Like me, she was tall and thin, with wiry forearms revealed because her shirtsleeves were short and ragged. Her face was lovely but dirty. She had on muddy canvas trousers and lumpy, torn boots that were near the end of their useful life. Her hair was the color of corn and wildly pitched in the swirling wind. She held her wooden crossbow with a practiced hand.

"Who are you?" I asked, eyeing my wand in Lackland's hand.

"Now, I should be asking *you* that," he blustered.

"I'm Vega Jane. This is Delph and my canine, Harry Two."

Lackland nodded in turn at the other two and then looked back at me.

"Now tell me who you are," I said.

"I told you me name, Lackland Cyphers." He pointed to the female and said, "And this is me fellow Furina, Petra Sonnet."

Delph said, "What's a Furina?"

"I just told you," said Lackland sharply. "*Us*. Where do you come from? Another part of this place, no doubt? Eh?"

"You mean the Quag?" I said, mostly to get his reaction to the term.

"Where else?" He held up my wand. "What is this thing?"

"What does it look like? It's a stick."

"Liar!" snarled Petra.

I glanced at her curiously. She seemed awfully sure of herself. But maybe she was always so disagreeable.

Lackland barked, "And does this *stick* allow you to fly, then? Eh? Because we saw you up there."

"No, it doesn't."

"What, then?"

"I just *can*. Can't you?"

Petra said, "Lack, we shouldn't be out in the open this long. Let's just take what we can and get on."

"Did you see the wendigo?" I asked.

Both of them stiffened. Lackland said, "A bloody wendigo?"

"It was after us. We had to kill it."

"You . . . you killed a wendigo?" said Petra. Her hands trembled.

"It was either kill it or let it kill us," I said. I looked around. "This is the Withering Heath, the Second Circle."

"Heaths and circles? Gibberish," said Lackland.

"Maybe to you, but not to us," barked Delph.

"Where are you headed, then?" he asked.

"Out of here," Delph said back.

Lackland looked at him cross-eyed. "Er you daft? There's no such thing."

"There is such a thing and we intend to find it," I chimed in.

When I glanced at Delph, he was staring fixedly at the pretty Petra.

I felt my face instantly flush.

Petra looked at our tucks on the ground. "What do you have in there? Food?" She took a step toward them.

In a flash, Harry Two leapt in front of our tucks and started growling, his long fangs bared.

"Call that thing off," ordered Lackland.

"Why, so you can nick our stuff?" I shot back.

"We're Furinas; that's what we do, steal," said Lackland.

"Why?" Delph asked.

Lackland looked him up and down. "Why do we steal? Well, it's a bit of a bloody nightmare surviving round here, mate, in case you hadn't noticed."

"How did you get here?" I asked.

"Born to it," said Petra.

"Don't tell 'em nothin'," snapped Lackland.

"Why? Are you ashamed or something, Lack?" she retorted.

Before Lackland could reply, Delph said in a calm voice, "We were born in Wormwood, which is surrounded by this place. It's a little village. Very poor. I worked at the Mill lifting stuff. Vega Jane worked at Stacks making things."

Petra scoffed, "Poor, eh? You look fed and cleaned proper to me." She wasn't looking at Delph when she said this. She was gazing directly at me!

I stared right back and said icily, "That's because we spent time with Astrea Prine at her cottage back there." I added in a more neutral tone, "Do you know her?"

They both shook their heads, and I believed them.

"Are there others like you?" Delph asked.

Lackland's gaze fell, but Petra said sternly, "Used to be. We're all that's left."

I said, "But you're not that old. Where are your parents?"

"Dead," barked Lackland. "Dead and gone."

"It was beasts," said Petra. "A while back. We lived in a village too, a proper one, not that far from here. Furinas have lived here for, well, forever, I guess. Used to be a lot more of us. A lot more. But over time, the beasts round here just . . . just . . ."

"I'm sorry, Petra," said Delph earnestly. This drew a surprised glance from Petra. I think she might have even blushed! For some reason, my hand curled to a fist.

Petra continued. "The last time they attacked us, they killed everyone. Except us. We've been on our own since then."

"Petra," snapped Lackland. "What did I say about telling her stuff?"

"She's not a beast, Lack! Does she look like a lycan to you? Use your eyes. They're like us." She gave me a withering look. "Well, in looks maybe. Can't speak to how tough she is."

I felt my face burn before glancing away. I looked in the near distance and saw confronting us a vast forest of dense, towering trees. The Withering Heath, as Astrea had called it. A place full of depression. We had barely survived the First Circle and Delph and Harry Two had been injured. We needed a place to rest and feel safe for a while, if there was such a place to be had in here.

"We need to find shelter," I said, turning back to them.

"You're not giving orders," said Lackland. "And who says we want you coming with us anyway? I say we take what you got in them bags and then *you* can be on *your* way. How's that for a plan, eh?"

Right at that moment, the ground shook under our feet.

"Bloody Hel!" cried out Petra and Delph together.

We could see the thick trees shake. And then the trees on the fringe burst apart. And there it stood.

I whirled around and looked at Lackland. "You have colossals here?"

His face was pale, but I saw determination in his green eyes.

"We got lots of things here. But they're slow, so's we can get away from 'em. We just have —"

"A colossal?" exclaimed Delph. I'd forgotten he had never seen one.

I had confronted one of these giants on the battlefield in the past. It had almost crushed me then. I hoped never to face another. But this colossal was only about half the size of the ones I had seen before, about thirty feet tall and broad as a cottage. Which, to my mind, was plenty huge enough!

"Lack!" screamed Petra. "Behind us."

We all turned to see another colossal within twenty yards

of us. How a creature that enormous was able to get that close without us knowing was unthinkable.

"Give me my wand!" I screamed.

"What?" said Lackland, clearly stunned by the second colossal.

"The *stick*. Give it to me."

"Why, what can you do with —"

"Oh, for the love of Steeples." I snatched my wand from his hand, turned to Delph and said, "Get them out of here." I pointed to my right. "Toward the tree line."

Delph grabbed our tucks and shoved them at Lackland. "Take these and get to the tree line," he shouted. He snatched the crossbow and satchel of arrows from Petra before she could stop him.

"What the Hel are you doing?" she screamed.

"Delph," I cried out.

"I'm not leaving you, Vega Jane," he said in a voice that brooked no opposition.

"But," spluttered Lackland, before Delph grabbed him by the collar and nearly threw him in the direction I'd indicated. "You heard her, now go!" Petra gazed stubbornly at Delph. "Please," he added. "Please go."

She paled and her stubborn expression vanished. I saw her put a hand on Delph's shoulder. "Good luck," she said. Then she ran after Lackland.

My teeth gnashing at what she had done, I had almost forgotten we were facing two colossals. I heard a bark and looked down. Harry Two was right next to me. I knew my canine would stay and fight with me. And die most likely.

I looked ahead and behind me. The colossals had not been waiting while we dithered. They had been moving, and despite what Lackland had said, they moved pretty fast simply because their legs were so long.

Delph called out, "Vega Jane, you take to the air. I'll stay on the ground with Harry Two."

"What are you going to do?" I asked breathlessly.

He held up the crossbow. "Like Thorne. Another distraction."

I kicked off and soared into the air. I looked down and saw that Lackland and Petra had reached the tree line about a hundred yards distant. They were now crouched there watching me flying through the air with the greatest of unease because I had not one but two colossals to face. My mind went back to the great battlefield where I had seen these horrors crush large men and steeds in their hands. But I had also seen colossals defeated. All it took was strength, skill and, I imagined, a good dose of luck.

I flew as high as I could, well above the tallest trees because I knew what would happen when I did.

The mighty storm blew in because I had taken to the air. Skylight spears hit and thunder-thrusts deafened me. And then the rain started. All of this was good because the colossals were high up in the air too. And the rain and storm was blinding them, I was sure, as it was me. But not for long. My goggles were in my tuck, but I didn't need them.

I held my wand in front of my face and said, "*Pristino.*"

Instantly my field of vision cleared.

I looked down. The colossals were within ten feet of each other, looking all around for their prey.

Then one of them cried out in pain.

Delph had just shot it in the leg with an arrow.

The next instant, Harry Two was dancing around the legs of both colossals. The second colossal saw him and started to spin around, trying to catch my far more nimble canine, and bumping into the other colossal as he did so.

My plan came together in a moment. I pointed my head and shoulders downward and raced toward the ground. Then I leveled out, swooped to my left, turned and zipped forward. Lined up directly in my sights was the back of one of the colossals.

Well, here goes, Vega.

Ten feet from the two giants, I pointed my wand, made a whipping motion and exclaimed, *"Impacto!"*

A light shot out from the tip of my wand and hit the first colossal directly in the back. He grunted from the punishing blow and fell forward. And, just as I hoped, he smacked right into the second colossal, knocking the thing off its feet. When both of them hit the ground, it was as if the heavens had opened, releasing a thunder-thrust.

When I looked down, I saw the colossal on top slowly rise. Underneath him the other colossal was lying quite dead, crushed by the sheer weight of his companion.

And then something hit me a glancing blow in the shoulder, nearly knocking me out of the air. I felt sickened when I saw what the object was.

It was the head of the dead colossal, which his brethren had ripped off his body and flung at me. Covered in the thing's blood, I soared upward as the remaining colossal reached a great hand up and tried to snatch me out of the air.

I felt a bit of my cloak being tugged, and then a piece of it was ripped off.

The colossal howled again. Delph had managed to shoot the thing in the eye. Quite a feat, considering how tall the creature was. His hand over his bloody face, he started to chase after Delph and Harry Two, who were sprinting for their lives.

The colossal reached down to a belt around its waist and pulled out the largest ax I had ever seen.

It threw the ax and the vicious weapon whirled at Delph with blinding speed. It was stunning to see something that large move that fast. Mesmerized for a moment, I regained my senses, pointed my wand and shouted, "*Embattlemento.*"

The ax struck my shield spell and there was a mighty explosion. The shield held and the shattered ax fell to the ground in pieces.

The colossal seemed stunned by this development and I aimed to take advantage of his momentary confusion.

"*Jagada!*" I cried out, and made the proper motion with my wand.

The light hit the enormous creature and small wounds sprouted over his gigantic chest. But it seemed only to irritate rather than incapacitate him. I looked down at my wand. What spell would work against this thing? One spell had knocked it down. The other spell had cut it. But neither had stopped it. I didn't want to try the *Rigamorte* spell. If it didn't work, I knew I couldn't beat the thing.

"Look out, Vega Jane," Delph cried out.

I glanced at him and then looked at the colossal. He had picked up a boulder like it was a pebble and hurled it directly at me. I was so surprised by this that I barely ducked in time. As it was, I could feel my hair being whipped back by the wake of the projectile.

Then he picked up a handful of large rocks and chucked them at me.

I had to dodge, dive and cast spells in order to survive this attack. My *Impacto* spell exploded a hurled stone that was so close to me that a part of it broke off and hit me in the thigh, cutting it deeply.

With my wound and being exhausted from dodging death, I knew I had to finish this as fast as possible. While the colossal looked around for something else to throw at me, I glanced at a towering tree about thirty feet away. Gauging all necessary details in my head, I pointed my wand at the base of the tree and screamed over the storm, *"Withero!"*

A light from my wand hit the tree right where it met the ground and the base and roots weakened and then crumpled under the weight. It teetered for a few moments and then fell forward, all hundred-odd feet of it. I flew far away from its reach. By the time the colossal realized what was happening, it was too late.

The massive trunk hit him directly on the head with such force that it drove him ten feet into the ground before the enormous tree collapsed on top of him.

It was such a bloody awful sight that I could only look for a second to make sure the thing was dead before I flew toward Delph and Harry Two and landed.

I took the Adder Stone out, waved it over my bloody thigh and thought good thoughts. I could feel the wound healing up, and the pain vanished.

"Are you okay, Delph?" I asked.

"Yeah, right nice flying." He grinned.

"Nice shooting." I patted Harry Two. "Good job, Harry Two."

As we hurried toward Lackland and Petra, I tried to use my cloak to wipe the blood and gore off my face and shoulders where the slain colossal's head had splattered me.

Then I stopped dead.

Lackland was on his knees and was, well, *bowing* to me.

He gazed up at me with a look of awe. He said breathlessly, "Will you take us with you, Vega Jane? Please?"

Petra wasn't bowing. She looked disgusted by this show of adoration.

When Delph handed back her bow and quiver, she gave him a radiant smile, rubbed his arm and said, "That was amazing, Delph. Truly." She slowly let her hand drop and then looked back at me with a defiant expression.

I took a deep breath and then let it go.

I think I would have taken ten more colossals over her.

A Pact

WE FOLLOWED THEM back to their camp, which was about a mile away. We had to wend our way through a forest that became so dense that we could barely squeeze between the trees. At least, I thought, there was no way a colossal could attack us in here. They were simply too big!

Unlike the woods around Wormwood, these trees were not all tall and straight. Many of them were twisted and warped and shrouded in dreary colors. There was not a bright green leaf to be seen on any of them. And their bark reeked of smells that were not fresh or sweet. Indeed, I could detect only fear and death in the air somehow. Every sound made could be predators coming. Every step we took might be our last. The end of our lives seemed to lurk beyond every shadow of every grotesque tree. Every branch seemed to bend toward us, wanting to strike.

I would have liked to close my eyes or look away, but I knew I couldn't. I had to remain vigilant. As I looked at my companions, I could see they were doing the exact same thing. Petra and Lackland looked especially subdued and nervous. Well, I would be too if my entire village had been wiped out.

Their camp was nothing much. There was a strip of tattered oilcloth stretched over some low tree branches, and beds made largely from leaves inside a little wooden lean-to. It made Loons back in Wormwood seem positively luxurious.

Their food and other important possessions Petra had pointed out were kept in a burlap bag tied to a tree branch. I doubted they were safe up there, but then again, where was safe in this place?

We sat around a small fire that Lackland built and warmed our bones from the chilly air. When I saw how little they had, I opened my tuck and shared some of our food and water. After we had been fed so well at Astrea's, it pained me to see how they gobbled the few morsels I offered. Not that long ago, I knew I would have done the very same thing.

Lackland finished the pieces of bread and hard cheese I had given him and drew closer. "Blimey, how did you do all that . . . stuff back there?"

I took my wand out of my pocket. "Sorcery. Magic. I was taught it."

I glanced over at Petra. From the corner of my eyes, I had seen her flinch when I drew out my wand. Now she was staring at it, her eyes widened, I think, in fear.

"Don't worry, I won't use it on you, Petra," I said disarmingly. I tacked a smile on to this to show I was joking. Mostly.

I had imagined she would look frightened, but she didn't. She just stared back at me for a sliver with contempt.

I could feel my temper starting to get the best of me.

Perhaps sensing this on my features, Delph said quickly, "But Vega Jane was magical to begin with. It's not like you can just wave a stick around and fight huge blokes like them back there."

"Are you magical, Delph?" asked Petra, taking a moment to smooth out her hair and rub a spot of dirt off her arm. She touched his shoulder with her hand and let it stay there for a wee bit too long, at least in my mind. I felt my hand curl to a fist. It was a struggle not to take a swing at her.

"Not a drop of magic in me," said Delph with a crooked grin. "I'm just big."

"And smart," I added quickly, because I saw that Petra was about to say something simpering to him, I was sure. "It was Delph that got us out of the maze. He remembered it all when the wendigo was chasing us. And he was the one who distracted the colossals so I could finish them off."

Petra looked at Delph with admiration. "That's right bonny of you, Delph. Big, and smart too. And not half-bad-lookin' neither." She again touched him on the arm. When she noted the blackened skin near his wrist, she exclaimed, "What happened to you?"

He shrugged and said, "Manticore got me. Vega Jane got ridda the pain, but me arm's a bit the worse for it."

"You beat a manticore too?" Petra said, her look full of awe.

Lackland let out a loud burp and said, "Well, all's we got is a sword and a bow. Right easier to beat beasts with that stick thing."

I was staring at Delph, who was blushing as Petra rubbed his arm. I quickly rose and threw another stick on the fire. When I sat back down, I somehow ended up between Delph and Petra. She had to quickly move her hand out of the way.

281

"So who do you nick stuff from?" I asked. "Blokes like you?"

"Like we said, ain't no blokes like us left," replied Lackland. "Leastways not that I know of."

"So who, then? Not the beasts in here surely?"

"No, not the beasts."

"Well, if it's not blokes or beasts, what's left?" asked Delph.

"Hyperbores mostly," said Petra, with another glance at my wand. I finally put it away. "I guess one could call them beasts, but they're closer to us than the other ruddy things in here."

I nodded thoughtfully. *Hyperbores*. Astrea had told us about them. Blue-skinned and they could fly. And that they could be an enemy or an ally.

"What are they like?" I asked. "Do they try and attack you when you nick from them?"

"No," said Petra. "I think they let us steal from them because they know we have nothing."

Lackland scowled at her. "As if anything in this place would 'let' someone steal from 'em. We stole it fair and square."

I didn't think anyone could *steal* something "fair and square." But I didn't say this.

"Well, we've never been caught or hurt doing it," pointed out Petra.

"'Cause we're good, ain't we?" said Lackland with a satisfied look.

"Where do the hyperbores live?" I asked.

"Oh, they have nests here and there," said Lackland.

"Nests?" Delph exclaimed. "What, like birds?"

"Yep, way up in the trees. Pretty big nests too. Lots of 'em live together. Safer that way, I 'spect."

I said, "How do you nick from them, then, if they're way up there?"

"Petra can climb something fierce," said Lackland proudly. "And she drops the things toward the ground, where I catch 'em."

"What sorts of things?"

"Vegetables, meats, spare cloth we make into proper trousers and shirts. And water. They keep it in jugs made from tree bark. Catching them can be a bit difficult. Broke my nose and two fingers so far."

"Not a bad price to pay to keep from starving," pointed out Petra.

Lackland turned to me. "You can get us out of here, you said?"

"I didn't say that," I shot back. "I said Delph, Harry Two and me are getting out of here."

"But what's beyond here?" asked Lackland.

"I don't know," I said truthfully.

"Then why do you want to go there?" Petra said.

"'Cause it's no doubt better than this place," replied Lackland, the scowl returning to his features. "I mean, what place could be worse than here, eh?"

I said under my breath, "Well, we'll find out." In a louder voice I said, "What do you know of where you came from? We're called Wugs, or Wugmorts. You look just like us. I wonder if you could have been from Wormwood too at some point."

Delph looked at me questioningly. I shrugged. I had just thought of this. I didn't see how Wugs from Wormwood could have ended up this far in the Quag and started another settlement of sorts. But I didn't know it wasn't possible either.

Lackland looked unsure. "I mean we're just here. Always just been here. Always been Furinas. Least it's all we've known."

Petra added spitefully, "Never enough to eat. And always something ready to kill you!"

Lackland agreed. "Aye, me dad told me all the remaining Furinas finally banded together for safety. Our last settlement was over to the west. About five miles from here. There were only about twenty-odd of us left, when the bloody beasts came that night." He looked down and threw a twig on the fire. "Blasted things."

"And your parents never told you anything about where you came from?" I asked.

"Well, there's the parchment, o'course," said Lackland.

I said quickly, "What parchment?"

Petra said sternly, "Now who's telling stuff?!"

Lackland said, "Eh, you're the one said they looked like us. And they saved our skins. So show 'em the parchment. It's in the bag hanging on that there tree," he added, pointing.

"I know where it is, Lack!" Petra rose and scampered up the tree with impressive nimbleness. I snatched a glance at Delph and saw him watching her with similar admiration. And maybe a wee bit more than that. I felt a scowl creep to my mouth. At that instant, Delph glanced over at me, saw my expression and dropped his gaze to the dirt.

Petra brought the bag back down and carried it over to us. She sat cross-legged next to Delph — of course — and opened it. She drew out a bunch of withered pages of bound parchment and passed them across to me.

I looked through them. The writing was beautiful, but the language was not something I had ever seen.

"What does it say?" I asked.

Both Lackland and Petra shook their heads. "We've never known," she said. "Nor did our parents."

"So why carry it around?" asked Delph.

Grinning sheepishly, Lackland said, "When you ain't got much, hard to part with anything." He paused, then added, looking at me, "Now, we know things that can help you. And we'll pull our weight. Tough as anything we both are. You won't regret this, never one bit." He looked pleadingly at me.

Delph glanced at me. I nodded. He turned back to Lackland and Petra and said, "'Tis done, then." He held out his hand and we shook all around.

I said, "You have to understand that it will be dangerous."

"Well," said Lackland. "What a change that'll be, eh?"

We all laughed.

And it felt good.

Until I realized that we might well never laugh again.

Positive Parchment

IT WAS NIGHT. I had taken the first watch. My wand beside me, I kept my gaze going back and forth. As the time passed I saw someone stir. Delph rose from his bed of leaves and strode over to me, carrying a loaded crossbow that was Petra's weapon of choice but which Delph had used to devastating effect against the colossals. I passed Destin over to him and watched as he slung the chain around his waist. I also handed him the Adder Stone. I would always hold on to my wand of course.

"Nothin'?" Delph asked as he took up the vigil.

I shook my head.

He plopped himself down and said, "Get some sleep, Vega Jane."

"Who's taking the third watch?"

"Petra. She and me worked it out."

"I'm sure you did." My harsh tone surprised me and it seemed to startle Delph.

"You okay?" he said.

I didn't look at him. "I'm fine, Delph."

"No, I think there's more to it," he insisted. I scowled at him until he said, "Sit, Vega Jane, and talk to me."

I plunked down next to him. "Okay. Petra and you seem to have become good friends really, really fast."

"I feel sorry for her and Lack. They've had it rough. Lost everything."

"Yes, but she keeps . . . well, rubbing your arm and looking at you." I knew this sounded positively stupid, but they were the only words I could think of.

To his credit, Delph didn't laugh or make me feel like I was being silly.

"I saw you staring at me when I was looking at her once," said Delph. "But there was a point to it, see."

"What point?"

"It was when Lack asked where we were headed."

I looked at him curiously. "Right. And you said we were heading out of here, meaning the Quag. And he called you daft."

"Right. But see, I looked at Petra when he was saying that, and she didn't look like she thought it was daft, gettin' outta here, I mean."

"What did she look like?"

"Like she wanted to leave this place."

I snorted. "Well, who wouldn't?"

"No, 'twas more'n that. It was like she knew it was *possible*. It was like she knew there was another place to go to, see?"

This struck me like a hard slap. "You could read all that in her face?"

"It was pretty obvious, Vega Jane. I may not talk much, but I don't miss much neither."

His words embarrassed me. It seemed I often took Delph

for granted when I should consider myself the luckiest Wug there was, to have him with me.

"Then it seems there's more to Petra than we thought," I commented.

"But I still feel sorry for her," he said.

I sighed. Males. They couldn't see everything, could they?

"Thanks, Delph. I'm glad we had this talk."

"Right you are."

I strode over to the others and lay down on my cot of leaves, my tuck as my pillow. Harry Two was next to me. I closed my eyes. However, I quickly found that I could not fall asleep.

How could Petra know there was a place to go to?

I opened my eyes, reached in my cloak pocket and pulled out the wrinkled parchment pages. I pointed my wand and muttered, "*Illumina.*" But mere light was not going to make the strange inkings understandable. In frustration I smacked the parchment with my wand and said, "Make sense."

Next moment, I almost dropped the thing. The words on the first page started swirling around and around, like water going down a drain. But the words didn't disappear. And yet they didn't re-form into words that I could understand either. Instead, they came together and out of their midst a face materialized on the parchment. It was the aged, wrinkled, heavily bearded countenance of a male I had never seen before. He seemed to look directly at me.

"Who holds the parchment?" he asked.

Well, blimey, I thought. With my voice quavering, I said, "I do."

"Your name?"

"Vega Jane."

He seemed to consider my response for a few moments. I took the opportunity to glance around. Lackland and Petra continued sleeping. Delph was far away, sitting on the rock, his back to me. Harry Two panted quietly next to me, staring at the face.

"I do not know you," said the male.

"Well, I don't know you either."

"How came you to have the parchment?"

"Lackland Cyphers and Petra Sonnet. They're Furinas. They had it. Or you, rather."

He nodded, but said nothing.

"The parchment was all gibberish before. They could never read it."

"Then you must possess a wand."

"I do."

"A sorceress, or a witch if you prefer. From where do you come?"

"Wormwood. But I was trained up as a sorceress after I left there."

"For what purpose would you be trained up?"

This bloke was too nosy. "Why so many questions, eh?"

"I have been part of parchment for a very long time with no one with whom to converse. You would be inquisitive too in this position."

That seemed reasonable enough. "Well, who are you? And how came you to be in the parchment in the first place?"

"You would not know me, as I do not know you."

"Perhaps I know some of your descendants if you are so very old."

"I meant I am not a real, living thing."

My eyes widened. "Then what are you?"

"I am a remnant."

"A *remnant*? What is that?"

"A collection of memories from an assortment of folks. A record, if you will, of their remembrances."

"So you have recorded in you the information from the Furinas?"

"Not them, no. I do not know how these Furinas came to possess me."

"Who else, then?"

"I go far back. To the ones who created this place."

I took a deep breath. This bloke *could* be of help. In a lot of ways.

"Okay. But why gibberish on parchment?"

"That was for protection, in case the parchment fell into the wrong hands."

"I see. Smart, considering the Maladons can do magic too."

Now the bloke settled his gaze on me and I knew he could see me as well as I could see him. "And how do you know about *them*?"

I said, "Astrea Prine. Do you know Astrea?"

"I can know no one. I am a remnant. But I have heard the name. She is a powerful sorceress. The Keeper of the Quag in fact."

I looked around again, but Lackland and Petra still slept and Delph still kept watch. I glanced down at Harry Two and found his gaze remained directly on the image.

"You say you cannot speak unless someone has a wand. But what if the wand holder was a Maladon?"

"I can tell."

"How?"

"For me, the wand of a Maladon produces only darkness. Yours was, by comparison, a bright, shining light."

"We're traveling across the Quag. Can you help us do so?"

He shook his head. "It is impossible."

I said defiantly, "We reached Astrea's cottage. We cleared the perfect maze back in the First Circle and defeated both a manticore and a wendigo in the process. And now we're in the Second Circle, where I have killed two colossals."

This seemed to give him pause. "Impressive," he said at last.

"So can you help me?"

"I'm not sure how."

"You said you have remembrances from those who created the Quag."

"'Tis true."

"The Second Circle," I said. "It's full of beasts that want to do us in. But are there creatures that can aid us?"

He said immediately, "Hyperbores live here. You'll want to befriend them."

"How?"

"Hyperbores will respond to the same things that make friends everywhere. Respect and kindness. Now, I am tired. I haven't spoken this much in, well, never."

"But I can call you back, right?"

"If you desire. Just tap your wand as you did before."

"And you have no name?"

"You may call me Silenus, Vega."

And before I could utter a response, he was gone and the gibberish had returned to the paper. I got up and raced over to Delph and told him everything that had just happened.

His jaw dropped farther and farther as I recounted the story.

"Silenus, a bloody remnant?" he said when I had finished.

"Yes. So what do you think?"

"I think we need to find these hyperbores." He glanced at where Petra and Lackland lay sleeping. "And maybe they can help us, eh? They know about hyperbores. They nick from 'em."

Despite the truth of his words, my spirits sank a bit for an obvious reason.

Bloody Petra.

Hyperbores

I AWOKE TO A sight that made me close my eyes and groan.

Delph had his shirt off and Petra was rubbing his blackened arm with some stuff she had mixed in a small pail and was applying with a wet cloth. They were chatting amiably and she laughed at something he said.

I glanced over at Lackland to find his gaze fixed on the pair. He looked like I imagined I did. I didn't know if he had any particular feelings for Petra, but they had been together for a while. Or maybe he was only having a difficult time adjusting to our presence.

I scrambled to my feet and walked over to them.

"Delph, aren't you cold without your shirt?"

I expected him to look embarrassed and quickly don his clothes. But he didn't. He looked up at me and said, "Pet's been cleaning up me arm. Whatever that stuff is, it feels right good, Vega."

I felt myself do a double take. Never in all his life had Delph called me simply Vega. It was always Vega Jane. But not this light.

And there was something else. "Pet?" I said.

She gave me a look that had a coy smile tacked on to it. It was all I could do not to pull my wand and turn her into a, well, I don't know what, but it would be pretty disgusting.

"That's what my friends call me," she said. "Petra is a bit formal." She looked around. "And I don't think formal is what we are. Not me and Delph here." She looked at her pail. "I could use some more water. Would you like to fetch some, *Vega Jane?*"

Okay, two could play this game.

I told Petra to hold her pail next to a nearby tree. I pointed my wand at a spot above the pail and said, "*Springato erupticus.*"

Water flowed into the bucket.

"That's amazing," said Petra.

I gave my wand a bit more of a flick and my mind, body, spirit a bit more of a kick and the water came out like a gusher, blasting her so hard she was knocked off her feet and doused.

"Whoops," I said. "I'm so sorry."

But she was laughing. "'Tis fine, Vega. Haven't had a proper bath in forever."

Despite how I loathed her, I had to laugh. It sounded like something I would say myself.

I glanced at Delph before telling her, "You need to take us to the hyperbores."

This statement caused Lackland to join the discussion. "The hyperbores? Why?"

"We'll need their help to make it through the Second Circle."

"But how can they help us?" Petra asked.

"I won't know until we meet with them. You said they live in nests?"

"Aye, way up in the trees," said Lackland.

I said, "And *I* can fly. Now let's get on with it, shall we?"

WE MADE OUR way through the denseness of the trees. Petra gripped her crossbow. Lackland was armed with his rough-hewn sword. Delph wielded an ax that Petra had provided him. And I had my wand.

Lackland held up a hand and we all stopped.

We drew together in a little cluster behind some bent trees. In a whisper Lackland said, "The nest is up that way about fifty yards. And they're up there."

"How can you be sure?" I hissed back.

In answer he cupped his hand behind his ear. "Have a listen."

I cupped my ear too and strained to hear. What reached me was a low buzzing sound. I looked at Lackland. He nodded and attempted a smile, which faded quickly. "How they talk," he said. "Like bees."

I gripped his arm. "How do they defend themselves?"

Petra said in a low voice, "Amarocs were after some of them collecting water down by a stream. Came on 'em fast, no time to fly away. Me and Lack were watching from a stand of trees a little ways away. The amarocs were just about to reach their prey, when out of nowhere came a dozen fully grown hyperbores. They were on the bloody amarocs before they knew what hit 'em."

"What did they do to them?" I asked.

Petra said, "They beat them all to death with their wings and then ripped them apart with their claws. Then they carried the carcasses to their nests."

"Why?" I asked.

"To eat them," she said simply.

"They . . . they eat meat?" I asked breathlessly. Petra nodded. "But they've never attacked you?"

Lackland said, "Well, we were never stupid enough to try and attack *them*."

"But you take things from them," I pointed out.

Petra said quietly, "But just odds and bits. Nothing they would truly miss. And like I said before, I think they feel sorry for us."

"Do you think they know what the beasts did to your families?" I asked.

Lackland shrugged, but Petra nodded. "I think you've hit the nail on the head, Vega. I think they do know."

This positive comment from her surprised me. But when I looked at her, she had already turned away. I would much rather have simply loathed her. If she was going to turn out to be all complex, that was going to make me even more ruddy upset!

Delph looked at Petra. "Do you think the hyperbores care about you and Lackland?"

"Why does that matter?" Lackland asked as I glanced at Delph in surprise.

"'Tis important. Do you?"

She said slowly, "Once when I was up there, one of them came back to the nest. I had just gotten hold of some provisions when it flew in. It was male and he was very large. He could have wrung my neck easily enough if he wanted."

"Pet, you never told me that," Lackland said sharply.

"The thing is, he just looked at me. It seemed that there was sadness in his eyes. He saw the things I'd nicked and then reached down and handed me a few more odds and ends." She gazed earnestly at Delph. "So, yes, I'd say they *do* care."

Delph turned to me. "Then we might have a chance."

I nodded and said, "Okay, but we need a plan."

"Oh, a plan, eh?" said Lackland sarcastically, eyeing me severely. "You just thinking-a that now? What a leader you turned out to be, you useless twit!"

I bit my lip and with it my tongue. I was so hotheaded sometimes and Delph was calm. If I was going to be their leader, I wanted to be more like —

WHAM!

Delph had slammed Lackland against a tree. He put his face to within an inch of Lackland's and snarled, "Was it my imagination or did you not beg Vega Jane to 'lead' you out of this here place? And just so you know, she's 'led' me and Harry Two all the way through to this very spot. And case you forgot, Vega Jane saved your arse from those colossals. So if you ever talk that way to her again, I will rip your bloody head off."

I stood there and stared at Delph, my heart fluttering weirdly, and my mind all jargoled.

Delph let Lackland drop to the dirt, but he quickly scrambled up, looking both angry and embarrassed. He scooped up his sword where he had dropped it, and for a moment, I thought he might be contemplating something very stupid. I stepped forward and said, "If you're not with me and Delph, then just say so and we can go our separate ways. No hard feelings."

I glanced at Petra to let her know she was definitely included in this ultimatum as well. She took a step closer to Delph as her answer.

Figured.

I turned back to Lackland. "And you?"

Rage and calm seemed to compete across his features. Finally, the latter won out. He lowered his weapon. "So what's the plan?"

Delph answered, "To begin with, Pet has to climb a tree." He looked at me. "And you, Vega Jane, have to fly."

TWENTY SLIVERS AFTER Delph explained his plan, Petra had climbed sixty feet up the massive tree where the hyperbores had one of their nests. Then she stopped and looked down at me. I looked up at her. We waited for a count of five. I could see in her eyes a wariness that I would have felt too if I was in her position.

She screamed. Another forty feet above her I saw three blue feathery heads poke out from the branches.

I gave Petra the signal. She drew a quick breath, closed her eyes and let herself fall. I pushed off the ground and shot upward.

Up above, I could see two hyperbores fling themselves from their perch and soar downward. Their wings were surprisingly compact and did not spread very wide from their lean, muscled blue torsos.

They were fast.

But I had the advantage that Petra was falling *toward* me.

I saw Petra open her eyes. She looked dead at me as she plummeted.

I saw fear in her eyes, which was to be expected when one was falling a long way to, potentially, one's death. But was she afraid for another reason? Namely, that I was going to let her die? And what was I feeling? Well, I wasn't feeling so much as I was *seeing* her and Delph together. I held on this image for a moment too long.

"Vega!"

I had let her pass right by me. I turned in midair and shot downward. The image of her and Delph had been replaced by one of her lying crumpled and dead on the ground, due entirely to me. I was not about to let that happen.

I passed her, swooped back underneath and caught her smoothly in my arms.

I looked at her and she looked back at me. Fear receded and gratitude returned to her features.

For my part, I felt incredible guilt.

"I'm . . . I'm sorry about that, Petra."

She studied my features, and in her look I thought I could see that she knew exactly what had happened. "'Tis okay, Vega. I might have done the same if I'd been you." Was it my imagination or did I see something in her eyes that told me she would not have chased after and caught me?

As I carried her in my arms to the ground, the pair of hyperbores caught up to us and landed. I put Petra down and looked at them.

They were both males. Their skin was the blue of water when the sunlight hits it just so. Their heads were lightly feathered. Their wings, when not in use, retracted nimbly behind their shoulders. They wore tight leggings and no shirts. Their torsos were heavily muscled.

One of them looked at me. "You can fly? How?" he asked. I was both stunned and immeasurably relieved that he could speak Wugish.

I pointed to my chain. "This is how. My name is Vega Jane. This is Petra Sonnet." I pointed over at Delph, Lackland and Harry Two as they emerged from the trees, and introduced them too.

"I am Troy. This is Ishmael," said the larger of the two.

Troy looked at Petra. "Were you coming for food?"

She nodded. "And then I fell."

Troy looked at me. "And you saved her."

"She's my friend," I answered. "Friends have to help each other, especially here."

Troy said, "You speak wisely for someone so young."

Ishmael said, "We have not seen you before. From where do you come?"

"A village. Wormwood."

Troy said, "We do not know this place."

"Most don't. We left Wormwood and entered the Quag."

"Why?" asked Ishmael.

"In order to travel through it." I paused. "And beyond it."

"Beyond it," repeated Troy. "And what do you think lies beyond it?"

"I want to find out. Can you help me do that?"

The hyperbores exchanged a glance. Then Troy pointed up. "Come with us."

Without another word, they spread their wings, kicked off and soared straight upward.

I looked at Delph, my heart hammering in my chest. I had no idea if the hyperbores were going to eat me or not. "If

I'm not back in sixty slivers, just head on without me. I'll find you."

"If you're not back in sixty slivers, I'll find *you*," he said.

I pushed off with my legs and rose quickly to join the two hyperbores aloft. A sliver later we alighted on the edge of the largest nest I had ever seen. It was not made of bits and pieces of twigs as normal bird's nests were. It was made of logs chinked with hardened clay and packed leaves. I looked around and saw dozens of small encampments where groups of hyperbores, young, old and in between, were working, playing, talking. They all stopped what they were doing and stared at me.

Troy pointed to the far end of the nest, where I could see a large canvas tent had been erected.

"You will talk to Micha. He is the chieftain of our race."

When we reached the tent, Troy called out, "Micha, we have one who seeks your counsel."

"Enter," said a powerful voice.

Troy pulled back the tent flap and motioned me in.

"Aren't you coming?" I said.

Troy shook his head. "Micha will see you alone."

The tent flap dropped, and I turned to find myself in a surprisingly large space. There was a sleeping mat on the floor. In one corner was a big wooden table with chairs around it. A huge tree trunk rose up in the middle of the space, and thick ropes tied to it supported the tent. Perched on a thick branch sticking out from the tree trunk was Micha. His feathery head was as white as his skin was blue. He peered imperiously down at me.

He said, "Your name?"

"Vega Jane," I said, as firmly as I could.

With a leap and a short flap of his wings Micha descended smoothly to the floor and stood erect. His torso was still powerfully developed, but the muscles, I could tell, had passed their prime. Still, he was an imposing figure.

He motioned for me to sit at the table. I did and he joined me. He passed me a bowl of fruit and then poured out water into wooden cups. I contrasted this with King Thorne, who had servants do all this for him, and my impression of Micha became instantly more positive.

I bit into an apple and drank some of the water.

"What counsel do you seek?" prompted Micha.

"Passage through the Second Circle."

Micha became instantly rigid and there was a guarded look in his features.

"You speak of circles?"

"Because Astrea Prine taught me of them. I want to pass through them so that I can leave this place."

"Indeed?" He picked up an orange from the bowl and used his claws to tear it open before putting a chunk of it, skin and all, into his mouth. He chewed slowly.

"So Madame Prine wishes this?"

I pulled out my wand. "Yes. So you know her?"

Micha held his gaze on my wand. "Of course. She is the Keeper of the Quag."

"We will accept all the risk. We only . . . we only seek to be better informed."

"It is always a good thing, to be better informed." He paused, seeming to choose his words carefully. "There are many challenges in this place."

"Which is why I'm here." I held up my wand. "Astrea has trained me up, yet I would never turn down either helpful information or any element or other tool that might prove advantageous to us."

He considered my words carefully. "One hears of things that reside in the Quag. And I do not mean simply beasts."

"What sorts of things?"

"Things hidden here and there that might prove useful to one such as you."

This piqued my curiosity. Astrea had never mentioned anything like that. Perhaps this was why Silenus had directed me here. "Do you know of any specific things like that?"

He nodded slowly. "There is a magical element known as the Finn."

"What does it do?"

"It can do a great many things. Useful things," he added.

"Did Astrea create it?"

"No. Not all things in here were created by those who made the Quag."

My spirits plummeted. "Are you saying that a Maladon created the Finn?"

"So you know of Maladons, do you?"

"As, obviously, do you."

Micha said, "It could be that the Maladons created the Finn. I am not sure about that. But I am sure that it is heavily guarded."

"By what?"

"A coven of alectos. Creatures with vile serpents for hair, and blood dripping from their eyes. They have the power to drive one to kill themselves through the hypnotic sway of the serpents upon their heads."

Oh my holy Steeples. "Where is this coven?"

"Two miles from here in a cave upon a knoll. I will take you, if you so desire." He eyed me curiously, obviously awaiting my answer.

I was feeling confused and terrified that there were Maladons in the Quag. This made me suspicious. Of everyone. Voicing this thought, I said, "Why are you helping us, Micha?" I demanded. "You don't know me."

"But I do know Madame Prine. And I admire courage, particularly in one so young. To be frank, I doubt you will survive. But I admire your courage nonetheless."

Why did that not make me feel any better?

The Mighty Finn

I COULD NOT USE Destin without another storm commencing, so Micha was carrying me. Other hyperbores, including Troy and Ishmael, had ahold of all the others. When I looked over at Lackland and saw his panicked expression, I had to smile. Petra, on the other hand, seemed perfectly comfortable.

We started to descend and when I looked down, I saw why.

There was the knoll. From here I could not see the entrance to the cave, but that was probably because it was also growing dark even though it wasn't night yet. The bloody Quag! We landed gently and Micha set me down.

The others landed next to us. When we were all gathered around, Micha warned, "Remember never to look the snakes in the eyes. That way you will not be fooled into killing yourself." He put a hand on my shoulder. "Good luck."

"Thank you," I said.

He unfolded his wings, and the hyperbores soared upward.

"Okay," I said, and turned to the others. "I'll go into the cave while you stay out here and keep watch. If I get into any trouble —"

"Are you mental?" interrupted Delph. "I didn't let you have a go at the colossals on your own. Do you really think I'm gonna let you go in there alone to face these alecto things by yourself?"

"There's four of us," added Lackland forcefully. "Better we all fight."

Harry Two immediately let out a bark.

Lackland looked down at him and said with an amused expression, "All right, five, then."

"I've got a wand," I pointed out.

"And I've got me sword," countered Lackland.

"And me my crossbow," added Petra.

Delph hefted the ax and said, "And in a dark cave, you need someone good with directions and that's me."

I started to protest, but looking at their faces, I knew it would do no good. I would have to knock them all unconscious to keep them out of the blasted cave. And then another emotion hit me: gratitude. They were willing to risk their lives to help me do this. I should appreciate that, and I bloody well did.

"Okay, but when we run into these alectos, don't forget what Micha said." We headed to the cave.

"*Illumina.*" The inside of the cave instantly became lighted and I went first, looking in all directions for evil creatures with vipers for hair and blood for eyes.

"Stay close," I said over my shoulder. "And stay ready."

"What does this Finn thing look like?" Delph whispered. Still, it sounded like he had shouted as his words echoed through the confined space.

"I don't know. Micha didn't say. But I assume it will be pretty obvious what these alectos are guarding when we get —"

I couldn't finish because we were tumbling downward; the once level floor had now become sharply angled. I hit something hard and stopped. Then the others crashed into me. We lay there for a few moments in a mass of arms, legs and torsos.

And then we heard it. I leapt up, my wand in hand.

The others scrambled to recover their weapons.

"*Illumina,*" I said again. When I saw what was there, my lungs seized.

A dozen figures surrounded us. They were all clad in black rags. But I didn't really focus on that because of the swaying serpents astride their heads. And, as Micha had said, the creatures' eyes were dripping blood.

Over their shoulders in a small niche in the rock wall, illuminated by a light source not readily apparent, was a tiny wooden peg with a loop of twine wound around it. The twine was knotted in places.

Was that the Finn? I wondered. The thing we had risked our lives coming down here for? A peg and string! *For the love of Steeples. Had Micha deliberately led us on a fool's errand to our doom?*

"Vega Jane!" cried out Delph.

I came around in time to see an alecto launch at me. At the very last moment, I remembered Micha's words of caution.

Don't look at the serpents. Look at the alecto's eyes.

"*Impacto!*" I cried, making the motion with my wand.

The alecto that had nearly reached me was thrown backward against the wall, where it slumped to the ground, its serpents dangling limply.

I turned in time to see Delph swing his ax and behead another alecto that had attacked him.

Petra fired an arrow into the chest of another. It fell dead at her feet.

Lackland swung his sword with surprising skill, taking out two more alectos with deft thrusts into their torsos.

"Delph, no!"

It was Petra screaming.

I whipped around, even though I had two alectos bearing down on me, to find Delph — his eyes full on the swaying serpents perched on another alecto's head — raise his ax with the clear intent of plunging it against himself.

"Lassado!" I exclaimed. A rope shot from the end of my wand, spun around the ax handle, and I gave a tremendous pull. I ripped the ax from Delph's hand and guided it smack against the neck of the alecto that had duped him.

The head of serpents fell neatly to the ground.

Then I felt the impact with my shoulder, turned and saw the serpent prepare for another strike against me.

An arrow hit the alecto square in the face and dropped it dead.

I flashed Petra a grateful look and then checked where the serpent had bitten into me. It had struck the leather harness, but fortunately its fangs had not penetrated my skin.

I spun around and leapt over three alectos who were at that moment charging me. As I somersaulted over them, I aimed my wand at their backs and said three times, *"Severus."*

Their torsos separated from their legs and they all fell dead.

I looked around for something else to attack but found that the others had finished off the remaining alectos.

I ran to the niche and cautiously looked at the Finn. It glowed brightly under the light. Delph joined me and said, "You figger that's it?"

"Has to be."

I reached up and gripped the thing, half expecting something bad to happen to me. But nothing did.

I grinned at Delph. "We did it."

"Vega!" screamed Petra.

I turned around. A section of wall had opened up. And charging through it were at least a hundred alectos.

Delph yelled, "We're goners!"

I gaped. I had no idea what to do. I looked at the Finn. My hand was trembling so badly that I nearly dropped it.

Petra raced over and snatched the Finn from me. She undid one of the knots.

The next moment, I was hit by a force of wind so powerful that it lifted me off my feet and knocked the senses clean out of me. I closed my eyes and saw nothing but a swirl of darkness.

I thought I must be dead. Because this must be what death looks like.

Nothing.

Enemies beside Me

VEGA JANE? VEGA Jane?"

I heard my name and slowly opened my eyes.

I had expected to see the darkness of the cave or the black of death, but I saw neither. Instead I saw light.

I looked up at Delph, who hovered over me with such a look of fear that my heart went out to him. I gripped his hand.

"I'm okay, Delph."

I sat up and looked around.

Petra was tending to Lackland, who had a gash on his head.

Then I saw with a rush of fear that Harry Two was covered in blood.

"Harry Two!" I cried out and tried to jump up.

"'Tis okay, Vega Jane," said Delph, pushing me back down.

"It's *not* okay. He's covered in blood."

"Used the Stone on him. He's fine. His chest got caught on some rock when we got blown from that place. But he's all healed up." He looked over at Petra and Lackland. "Tried to use the Stone on him, but Pet wouldn't let me. Don't trust it, I guess."

I rose gingerly. "How did we get out of that place?"

In answer, Delph held up the Finn and handed it to me. I could see that the twine was once more tightly looped around the peg, but the first knot was still undone.

"I 'spect it has something to do with this."

I looked down at the Finn and thought back. "The wind that blew us out of there and saved our lives. It came from this?" Then I remembered something else. I stared over at Petra.

"You undid the knot and that caused the wind. How did you know to do that?"

She looked at each of us nervously. "I don't know. I was just fumbling with it. To make it do something. I was just lucky."

I glanced at Delph. He was nodding. "Right glad you did, or else we'd be dead."

Lackland too was nodding and grinning. "Pet keeps her head when things get rough, I know that."

But I wasn't smiling. I didn't believe her. Even if Delph and Lackland hadn't seen it, I had. Petra wasn't "fumbling" with the Finn. She knew exactly what she was doing. But how? I was still staring at her when she glanced at me. She could easily read the suspicion in my eyes. And I didn't care if she did. Because I *was* suspicious.

"Yeah . . . lucky," I said slowly, before putting the Finn away in my cloak pocket.

Delph said, "But how will a big wind help us get through the Second Circle?"

"No idea," I said quite truthfully. I looked at Petra. "Any thoughts on that, *Pet?*"

"No," she said, staring right back at me.

"Close enough call," said Lackland, rubbing at his injury while Petra was trying to swipe his hand away.

I took the Stone from Delph, rose, walked over to them, waved the Stone over the injury, thought good thoughts and the wound vanished.

"Bloody Hel," exclaimed Petra as Lackland ran astonished fingers over the now repaired skin.

He looked at the Stone and said, "What is that thing?"

"In this place, it's our best friend."

I put the Stone away and said, "We need to push on before it gets much darker. Then we can camp for the night and get an early start."

Lackland eyed the dense trees that lay ahead. "What do you think is in there?"

"Ruddy things that can kill us," said Delph. "That's what."

We grabbed our tucks and trudged on. I would have liked to fly, but while the hyperbores apparently could do so with no storms to trouble them, I knew what would happen if we took to the air.

We wended our way through the trees and forest paths so dark that I was compelled again and again to illuminate our way with my wand. Finally, when our legs could carry us no farther, we settled in for the night in a tiny clearing.

Petra and Delph gathered some wood, which I then lit with my wand. Lackland used an iron skillet he had brought to cook up some of our provisions.

I filled the goblets that Astrea had given us and then poured some water into a bowl for Harry Two.

We had escaped death from the alectos by such a slim margin, yet I was also heartened because we had all fought well together. But then a depression set in and all I could see were dismal outcomes, all of us lying dead while a herd of ugly creatures hovered over us, eagerly awaiting the coming feast. And what if these awful beasts ever invaded Wormwood? My brother and every other Wug would die. I shivered at the thought and tried my best to think of other things.

Later, after everyone had settled down — Delph had drawn the first watch — I slipped over to Lackland and sat cross-legged next to him where he lay on a bed of leaves.

"You fought well," I said.

"But that wand-a yours. 'Tis quite a weapon, it is."

"Have you ever been this far before?"

He shook his head. "Never needed to, never wanted to, till you lot came along." He grinned, though the look died on his lips as he gazed over at the fading fire. "Scary thing to leave what you know." He glanced at me. "But look at me telling you that. You left everything behind to come to this place."

"To come *through* this place," I amended.

"Aye," he agreed.

We both grew silent, listening to the soft pops and crackles of the dying fire.

"Do you think we'll really make it?" asked Lackland in a resigned tone. And it was then I fully realized that he was not that much older than I was.

I shrugged. "I don't know, Lack."

He nodded and idly rubbed at his beard. "What do you think is beyond here?"

"I just hope whatever it is, it's better than this place."

He chuckled. "Well, it would have to be, wouldn't it?"

I wasn't nearly as sure as he was about that.

I bid him good night and went over to sit next to Petra.

She gazed up at me from her bed of leaves. I wanted to broach the subject of the Finn again, but she probably sensed what I was going to do and was quicker.

"You say there are three more circles after this one?" she asked.

"Yes."

She let out a breath and looked toward where we had come.

"Having second thoughts?" I said.

"It was only a matter of time before me and Lack were killed back there. So if we die here, what does it matter?" She paused and said, "So are you and Delph . . . just friends?"

Were Delph and I more than friends? In some ways we were like brother and sister. In other ways? Well, we had kissed.

"What does it matter to you?"

"I like him."

"I like him too."

"So I guess that answers my question," she said, eyeing me steadily.

I rose and looked down at her. "I guess it does." I felt cold chills in my belly.

To ward them off, I took the Finn out. "I never would have thought to undo the knots, and yet I'm a trained sorceress."

I let that statement hang there like a storm cloud between us.

"Well, maybe you need to be trained up better."

314

I almost smiled at her sarcastic remark. Almost. Because again Petra's words reminded me of something *I* would have said.

I left her and lay back on my bed of leaves with my tuck under my head. I didn't drift off to sleep. My mind wouldn't allow it. I plucked the parchment from my pocket, made sure no one was watching and then tapped it with my wand.

An instant later the image of Silenus faced me once more.

I said quietly, "We befriended the hyperbores and managed to get the Finn from the alectos."

He looked at me with raised eyebrows and an expression of surprise.

"The Finn. Did you indeed?"

"We know if you undo one of the knots, it makes a big wind. What else does the Finn do?"

"It will defend you against the greatest threat you will face in the Second Circle."

Okay, I thought, *that was a little vague.*

"Do you have it with you?" he asked.

I pulled it out and held it up for him to see.

"Very good," said Silenus. "Now, there are three knots."

I looked at the twine. "I know. Undoing one knot created a mighty wind."

"The Finn is a particular magical element with a specific power. As you discovered, undoing one of the knots creates a powerful wind. Undoing the second knot produces gale force winds."

Well, I thought, *if it were much stronger than the first wind, that was something indeed.*

"And the third knot?" I asked.

"A wind of unimaginable strength, equal to many times that of the most powerful storm you have ever encountered."

I looked down at the peg and twine. *Blimey.* All that from something so small and simple? And if undoing the first knot had been what had blown us out of the cave, I couldn't imagine ever undoing the third one.

"So it will save us from the gravest danger here. What might that be?"

"Alas, you ask something to which I do not know the specific answer. But I do know that the Finn will be very helpful to you."

I looked over at Lackland and Petra.

"Where do they come from?" I asked. "The Furinas we came upon in here?"

Silenus took some time considering my question.

"When Wormwood was created, so was the Quag, surrounding it certainly and completely, making escape impossible."

"*Nearly* impossible," I corrected. "But go on."

"There was a transition from the great battlefields to the village of Wormwood whilst the surrounding territory representing the Quag was being conjured. One could not have expected a totally seamless migration."

"Meaning what, exactly?" I said.

"Some were trapped in here and never made it to Wormwood."

"Trapped in here?"

"Yes. And no doubt some were killed. But some survived. And they bore descendants. And some of those survived and some didn't. So really the very fittest, or perhaps the luckiest, are still with us."

I was horrified. "How could they be left behind?"

"It was a time of great chaos and confusion, Vega Jane."

I decided to ask him something that had been bothering me. "Could there be descendants of Maladons in here?" The image of Petra held steady in my mind.

"I cannot say for certain. If there are, they may not even know it."

"Tosh! How could they not know it?"

"Well, you didn't know you were a sorceress, did you?"

Okay, he had me there.

I slowly put the parchment away in my cloak, rolled over and stared at Petra. I could tell she wasn't asleep. She was staring upward, apparently lost in thought.

I lay back and closed my eyes. But I knew I could not sleep. I understood quite clearly that there were creatures in here that would kill me simply because they were wild beasts.

But if Petra was a Maladon? What if she was leading us into some sort of trap?

It seemed my most dangerous enemy could be right here beside me.

An Unexpected Visitor

W E WALKED ALONG meandering forest paths for three full lights and nights without encountering a single threat. This should have made me feel better. But it didn't. In fact, I was feeling more and more depressed because I was certain that around the next bend, we would be attacked by something we could not defeat.

Each time we stopped to eat, to rest or for water, I could tell the others were thinking the very same thing. After nearly dying at the hands of the dreadful alectos, it was no surprise that we were all on edge.

Another two lights and nights passed and we saw not a single living creature, either friend or foe. I would have taken a right good fight over the sea of endless trees, placing one foot in front of the other and feeling my spirits continue to ebb away. The forest here was so dense that all we saw were twisted trunks and tangles of branches and dark leaves with not one bird on them. They wedged in on us the farther along we went, to where I had to use the *Illumina* spell as soon as we set off. There was something very disconcerting about being in darkness all the time. And combined with how tense we were already, the effect was one of suffocating melancholy.

It got to the point where we dragged ourselves up at first light, ate a bit of food, packed up and set off without a word to one another. As we trudged along, glances were sullen and the few remarks were short and abrasive. Our body language was that of defeat.

Lackland almost never talked; he just glared at everyone.

Petra didn't glare, but I could tell she was not happy.

Even Delph was not himself. He once snapped at Harry Two just because my canine accidentally bumped into him and caused him to spill a bit of water. Only my canine seemed to be able to rise to the occasion. He trotted along, his smile wide but his senses, I knew, on high alert. He was the only thing during that time that could lift my spirits. But still, it wasn't enough.

We had stopped for our night meal and were clustered around the campfire, when Lackland finally erupted. "This is bloody stupid, this is," he snapped.

"What is?" I demanded hotly.

"We have no idea where the Hel we're going. We could be going in circles, for all you know. Or can you tell one ruddy tree from another?"

"Well, I don't see you jumping up to lead us," snapped Delph.

Petra barked, "He's just saying what we're all thinking." She pointed a finger at me and added, "Do you know where we're going? Really?"

I eyed her and when I did, I felt a degree of malice rise to my chest that almost made my skin burn. I stood and held out my wand. "This makes me the leader," I said. "If you want to strike out on your own, then go ahead. You'll last a sliver, if that."

Lackland jumped up. "We can't do that. You took us from what we knew."

Now Delph leapt up and together we faced off against Lackland and Petra.

Delph shouted, "You begged to come with us."

"'Cause I thought you knew what you were doing," roared Lackland.

He held up his sword.

Delph hefted his ax.

Petra pointed her crossbow.

I raised my wand. But then something popped up in my head. Something that Astrea had said, that I had not really focused on. But now I did. Because now I understood what she meant.

The Second Circle is full of depression, and if we allow it, those feelings will come to dominate.

I looked at Delph. "It's the depression of the Second Circle that Astrea told us about. It's in the air. It's everywhere. It's driving us mad!"

Delph half lowered his ax. "Blimey."

At that moment, his senses evidently stricken clean from him, Lackland suddenly shouted, "Pet, shoot the canine. I'll take care-a them two."

I raised my wand and shouted, *"Embattlemento."*

His sword and her arrow hit my shield spell with such force that the reverse concussive blow knocked Lackland and Petra off their feet.

I next said, *"Ensnario."*

Thin ropes of light shot out of my wand, enveloping them both, and with a cast like that of a fishing pole, I flicked my wand to snatch them up and deposit them by the clump of trees. I cried out, *"Impacto."* One end of the rope drove itself deeply into the ground.

"Vega Jane," shouted Delph. "If it's in the air, you can use the —"

"I know, Delph, I know what I have to do." I grabbed his arm. "Hold on to me. Come, Harry Two!" I patted my harness.

My canine jumped up and I buckled him in. I pointed my wand at the ground and said, *"Ensnario."*

Thick roots emerged from the ground and wrapped themselves around our legs.

I pulled the Finn from my pocket and looked at Delph. "Silenus said this would be far worse than what we experienced in that cave."

Delph swallowed a lump in his throat and then put one huge hand on me and one on Harry Two.

"Ready?" I said.

He nodded. "Ready."

I said a silent prayer and untied the second knot.

It was akin to a mighty, raging river that had been turned into air. Pretty much every tree in the forest was pushed nearly sideways by the force. I had to close my eyes and then cover my mouth and nose because the wind was so strong I could barely breathe.

I had never felt such force as this. Even with the bindings around our legs, I felt myself lifting off the dirt. My fingers were being pulled off my wand. And if I lost that in this gale, we were done for. In unleashing the second knot of the Finn had I ruined any chance we might have to survive? Delph screamed as he started to lose his grip on me and Harry Two. My canine was being pulled away from me. I could hear my magical snares tearing one by one.

I glanced over at Petra and Lackland. They were completely off the ground with only one magical tether holding them from oblivion, for anything that was swept loose in this maelstrom would be smashed against the trees.

I had just killed us all.

I watched as the last strand of magical rope broke. I couldn't say another spell because the force of the wind prevented me from even moving my mouth. We were done for. The three of us shot up into the air. I looked to my left and saw Petra and Lackland propelled upward like they'd been shot from a morta.

And then the wind stopped, and we plummeted back down, landing hard on the dirt, but otherwise alive.

I cautiously rose and peered around. Petra and Lackland were slowly rising. Some trees had been uprooted and lay toppled in the dirt. Others were still bent over, perhaps permanently so. Most, though, had returned to their original positions, which was a testament to their strength.

I touched my head and, despite my aches and pains from the long fall to the dirt, I broke into a smile. The terrible depression that had engulfed me was gone. It was like a —

"Like a refreshing wind drove it all away?"

I spun around to see who had spoken.

It was Seamus. He was perched on a fallen tree. He was no longer dressed shabbily. He wore black trousers, a white shirt, a vest laced with golden threads, shiny shoes and a well-brushed top hat.

"Who the Hel is that?" Lackland and Petra exclaimed together.

"Seamus the hob," Delph answered. "We know the bloke."

The truth struck me. I said, "Astrea's been following us in the Seer-See, hasn't she?"

"Well, of course she has," said Seamus, as though that was the most obvious fact ever uttered. He hopped off the fallen tree and walked toward us.

"You made good use of the Finn." Seamus scratched Harry Two behind the ears. "Canines are immune to the depression, you know."

"Astrea sent you here?"

"Yes, but not to interfere. If you perished, I was instructed to give you proper burials in the Wolvercote Cemetery."

"Well, that was ruddy nice of her," I said sarcastically. I drew a deep breath. "How is Archie?"

"He no longer remembers anything about you."

I looked at him curiously, taking in the new clothes. "You seem different."

His eyes twinkled. "Hobs are actually quite a formal lot. But we are also quite good at playing other roles when circumstances require it." He bent over and added in a croaky voice, "Seamus is a good hob he is, dearie, dearie." This made me smile in spite of myself.

"Does this mean we're at the end of the Second Circle?" asked Delph anxiously.

"I think you can presume that, yes," said Seamus, eyeing Lackland curiously. "The Third Circle commences just beyond that rise in the dirt." He added in an admonitory tone, "But the Third Circle, as you well know, has its own unique challenges." He smoothed down his clothes and tipped his top hat. "And now it is time for me to depart. I doubt you will see me again. I wish you luck."

"Wait, I have more questions," I began.

But right before our eyes, Seamus vanished.

A Second Sorceress

WE PICKED UP our tucks, and with our spirits greatly improved, we made good pace. We soon cleared the trees at the spot Seamus had indicated.

Then we all stopped. We had to, just to take it all in.

"Blimey," exclaimed Lackland.

Blimey indeed, I thought.

If we were tired of trees, we had come to the right place, because there wasn't a single one ahead of us. It was as flat and open as any piece of land I had ever seen in my life. In the distance was a huge block of what looked to be granite, miles wide and a mile high. But except for that, the land just stretched on past the horizon, flat.

And bright.

The forest had let in no light.

This place seemed incapable of leaving any out.

It had been cool though foreboding among the trees.

Here it was hot and glaring, the air seemingly seared with the heat from above. We had been used to the darkness for so long that all of us put a hand to our eyes to shield them from the harsh light.

I looked at the others. "I guess we best get a move on."

I went first, with Harry Two at my side, Lackland and Petra following and Delph bringing up the rear. We had gone barely a mile when I took off my cloak and then my overshirt. The others did the same as the heat continued to build. Then I rolled up my trouser legs. My boots felt like blazing rocks around my feet.

On we trudged, mile after mile, as it became hotter and hotter. We stopped for water, but as soon as we finished our fill and started to walk again, we sweated it away. Harry Two was panting so hard I thought he might pass out.

Delph came up next to me after we had trudged what I calculated to be twenty miles. In a low voice he said, "Do you see that rocky outcrop over there?"

I nodded.

"Well, it's as far away as when we started walking, Vega Jane."

I stared at the thing and realized that he was exactly right.

I looked up to the sky and got another shock.

Though we had been walking for a long time and the light should have been well turning to night, the sun was in the same position it had been when we first stepped into the Third Circle.

"Delph, the sun."

He nodded. "I know."

I thought back to what Astrea had told us about this place.

A vast, flat expanse that stretches seemingly forever.

Forever. I shuddered. Maybe her meaning had been quite literal. And what did that bode for us?

After more trekking, we stopped and set up camp. If anything, it was even hotter. I looked up at the sun and then down at our little campsite.

I raised my wand directly over the camp and said, *"Embattlemento."*

The large shield spell rose from my wand and hovered in the air over where we would be sleeping. It suddenly grew darker under the shield, and the air became much cooler.

"Thank you!" exclaimed Lackland as he rubbed the sweat off his face and let the cool air wash over him. Then he collapsed onto his back and just lay there.

Later, we made our meal, and sat around cross-legged on the ground. What worried me the most of course was what Delph had already observed: We weren't getting anywhere. If Lackland and Petra hadn't realized this yet, they soon would.

Delph took the first watch while the three of us slept. Well, Lackland and Petra slept. I tried for a long time but then gave it up as a bad job. I took out the parchment and summoned Silenus. We looked at each other over the span of several inches.

"You live," he said in mild surprise.

"I live," I said. "Barely. We're now in the Third Circle."

He nodded benignly. "I am glad."

I cocked my head. "Why? You're a remnant. I wouldn't think a remnant would have emotions."

"Well, very clearly, you do not know everything," he said in an even tone.

I refocused on the matter at hand. "Do you mind if I show you to a friend of mine?"

"Is he a good friend?"

"He's my best friend."

Silenus nodded and I carried the parchment over to where Delph was keeping watch, sat down next to him and introduced him to Silenus. It took Delph a bit of time to get comfortable with seeing the face on the parchment, but he finally settled down after a few "Cor Blimeys!"

I said, "We have a problem, Silenus."

"Just the one? I'm positively astonished."

"We walked for most of the light, but the sun remains overhead bright and hot. I used a shield spell to give us some relief from it."

"Very smart of you, Vega Jane."

Delph added, "The thing is, we walked all that way and didn't go anywhere. It's like we're not even moving."

Silenus nodded. "I can see that that would be a problem."

"You can say that again," interjected Delph.

I said, "Astrea told me that the Quag moves. I mean, it really doesn't. It's just a hallucination spell." I suddenly blurted out, "*Transdesa hypnotica.*"

"Pardon?" said Silenus.

"It's the incantation that makes the Quag appear to be moving. But it's really not. It's all in our heads. Astrea told me about it." In a rush of panic I realized something else. She had never told me how to counter it. How could she have forgotten to do that? How could I have forgotten to ask her?

Then something else occurred to me. I looked wildly around.

I couldn't see the mountains in the distance. Nor the ridges, nor anything else that Delph and I had seen before.

I looked back at Silenus.

"Bit of a pickle, eh?" he noted imperturbably.

"Yeah, a bit," I mumbled, my spirits falling out through the bottoms of my boots. I stared down at my wand. "But I've got a wand."

"Quite so. Then you know the reverse incantation?" asked Silenus.

"No, I bloody well don't," I admitted miserably.

"Are you sure?"

"Yes, Astrea never said."

Delph spoke up. "But, Vega Jane, Astrea never told you how to summon this bloke Silenus. And remember when you knocked us all silly back at her cottage? You done that all on your own, eh?"

Silenus smiled at Delph. "Your 'best friend' is quite perceptive."

"That's right. I . . . I just said, 'Make sense.' And you showed up."

"Magic and spells conjured are borne *of necessity*," explained Silenus.

I shot him a glance. "What, you mean I can come up with the spells that I need to get through this place? Not just the ones Astrea taught me?"

"Of course. That is part of being magical, after all."

And with those parting words, he disappeared.

Delph said encouragingly, "You'll figure it out, Vega Jane."

"No, I think *we'll* figure it out, Delph." I smiled.

He held my gaze. "So you told the bloke I was your best friend?"

"You are my best friend, Delph."

He gave me the biggest smile in return. I started feeling very warm. He touched my arm and leaned toward me. I closed my eyes and —

The growls reached our ears. We leapt up and looked around. Yet all I could see was vast open expanse.

"Use your wand," urged Delph.

"*Crystilado magnifica*," I cried out.

Now revealed as though they were dead in front of me were four beasts moving with alarming speed and heading our way.

Delph screamed, "Get up. Lycans. Wake up!"

I glanced behind me. Lackland and Petra had already grabbed their weapons.

I withdrew the *Embattlemento* shield from overhead so we could see better, and the sun burned down brightly once more and the temperature soared.

I was about to incant my magnification spell again, but then I gasped because the lycans had risen out of the dirt right at my feet. Before I could strike with my wand, an arrow hit one of the creatures in the chest. It screamed in fury, and recoiled as blood flew everywhere. Then it toppled over and died.

There were three more to deal with, however.

"*Jagada*," I cried out, pointing my wand at the second lycan.

Huge gashes sprouted all over its body. It thrashed about in great pain before it collapsed. I was knocked back by its flailing, and landed in the dirt so hard that all the breath was forced from me.

I scrambled up in time to see Delph use his great ax to cut the creature in two. Then he fell back as the third lycan attacked. I pointed my wand and yelled, *"Rigamorte."* But the lycan abruptly turned and my spell missed.

The next moment I was hurtling backward as the fourth lycan crashed into me. I came within an inch of being bitten by the thing. My wand fell from my hand and our combined struggles kicked it away.

Without Destin and my wand, I would be no match for a lycan. But I was not going down without a fight. I rolled away and jumped to my feet. He leapt at me, but I managed to dodge out of the way. I pulled my cloak off, rolled it up between my hands and held it out in front of me. With a snarl, the thing attacked again. I dodged it again, jumped on its back and wrapped the cloak around its throat.

Before I could start to squeeze, its claws grabbed my hair, yanked and threw me off. I landed on my bum five feet away. When I looked up, the lycan was leaping right at me, its fangs poised for the kill.

"Rigamorte!"

The black light hit the creature square in the back. It froze for a moment in midair and then plunged, landing full on me. I managed to push it off and scrambled away from the dead thing.

Then I looked over and saw a very pale Petra clutching my wand. *She* had cast the spell. And it had *worked*.

She looked at me with terrified eyes, even as Delph and Lackland stared at her too, obviously having witnessed her slaying of the lycan with the wand.

The next moment, she dropped my wand and clutched at her hand, tears streaming down her face.

I rushed over to her and picked up my wand.

Delph and Lackland had also hurried over. Lackland said in amazement, "You . . . you can do that . . . stuff what Vega can do."

"Sorcery," added Delph breathlessly.

She was still clutching at her hand and she was still crying. I looked down at her hand. "Petra, let me see."

She shook her head and kept her hand covered.

"Let her see, Petra," said Delph. "Vega can sort you out with the Stone."

I had already pulled it from my pocket. But I had to pry her fingers open. I shivered and my stomach lurched when I saw it. Her hand was blackened as if it had been forced into a fire. It looked painful and stiff indeed. I stared at it and then at Petra. There was both pain and confusion in her features.

I waved the Adder Stone over the wound and thought good thoughts. Nothing happened. Surprised by this, I held my wand over her hand and tried several different spells to heal the wound. Not a single one worked.

She jerked her hand free and snapped, "Just leave it."

As she walked away clutching her injured hand, I looked at my wand. Why had it burned her? Because the wand didn't belong to her? I already suspected her of being a Maladon. She had cast the death spell. She had known how to use the Finn, a magical element created by dark sorcerors.

I glanced up to see Delph watching me curiously. I wanted to tell him what I was thinking, but Lackland was standing right there.

"Thank the Steeples for Petra being a sorceress," I said with a forced smile that I'm sure Delph saw right through.

"Aye," said Lackland, who appeared still to be dazed by the whole thing. "I'll just nip over and see how she's doing." He headed to where Petra sat slumped over.

I so wanted to tell Delph that Petra was our enemy. Then maybe the admiring look in his eyes whenever he glanced her way would be gone for good. But there was just one problem with all I was thinking.

Petra had used the wand to save *my* life.

"What is going on with Petra, Vega Jane?" asked Delph.

"I don't know, Delph," I answered. And I really, really didn't.

One Good Deed

I CAST THE SHIELD spell over us as we walked along the next light. It kept the sun and heat off us, but that was not our major problem. The granite outcrop was still as far away as ever. And when Lackland finally walked up to me, I knew what he was going to say.

"Vega, we don't appear to be moving a jot all this time."

"I know, Lackland."

He scowled. "And do you have a plan to take care-a this wee problem?"

I looked up into his bearded face. Then I glanced behind us to see Petra and Delph walking together. They were talking in low voices. I turned back to Lackland. "I'm working on it."

He looked at me skeptically. "Oh, well, there's a relief."

"Do *you* have any ideas?" I countered.

He held up his sword. "You want something run through with this, I'm your bloke. This wand and words stuff, that falls to you."

I glanced back again. "And to Petra, apparently."

His features clouded. "Never knew that about her."

"Are you sure? There were never any signs?"

"Well, what sorta signs would there be?"

"Did she ever do something inexplicable?"

He shook his head. "Not that I can remember. But then again, till our village was attacked we didn't spend all that much time together. I mean, we're not family or anything. Just Furinas."

"Who was left of your family?"

His gaze became downcast. "Me mum and me sister. Me dad and older brother were killed a long time ago."

"How?"

"Colossal. There . . . there was nothing I could do. Bloody lycans killed the rest of the Furinas. 'Cept for Pet and me. When I saw them things charging us, all I wanted to do was slaughter 'em all!" he added fiercely. He paused and looked once more at Petra. "Pet and me been together a while now. Like having me sister back, I guess. Nobody wants to be alone. Not in here."

"No, they don't," I said, thinking of Delph and Harry Two.

We had been walking as we talked. When I looked ahead, I stopped dead. Lackland bumped into me.

"Look!"

He stared ahead of us and I felt him stiffen.

"What the devil is that?" he asked.

Delph and Petra had joined us by then. Delph said, "It's a unicorn."

It was indeed a unicorn. Brilliantly white with a mane of gold, shiny black eyes and a regal horn the color of silver. It was large and muscular, with a huge chest. And it was standing right in our path. It looked so noble, almost like a polished statue but with a pulsing heart. And it was also really the first beast we'd encountered in here that wasn't trying to *murder* us.

"Harry Two!" exclaimed Delph.

My canine had ventured forward and was within a couple yards of the unicorn. The creature snorted and drew back a bit. Harry Two stopped and then wagged his tail and smiled. The unicorn then stepped forward a few paces. Harry Two closed the gap and the pair faced each other across the span of a foot.

The unicorn tossed its mane, and Harry Two barked, but I knew it to be a friendly greeting. My canine then walked forward and rubbed his muzzle against the right foreleg of the unicorn. The latter lowered its head and grazed Harry Two's ear with its soft golden mane.

Harry Two looked back at us and yipped, as if to say, *Budge along.*

I crept forward, then glanced back at the others, who hadn't moved.

"Too many of us might scare it," Delph explained lamely.

I looked back at the unicorn and kept walking forward, though ready at an instant to retreat if it showed any fear or anxiety. I put out my hand and let it sniff. Then I stroked its mane and it rubbed up against my shoulder. I looked closely at the silver horn. What had Astrea said? *The horn of the unicorn can defeat all poisons.* That would come in handy, I reckoned.

But then I recalled how one got the horn of a unicorn.

Talk it out of the horn.

Or kill it.

There was no way I would ever harm this creature. It was so beautiful and gentle and . . . It nudged my hand with its snout, lifting my fingers from its mane to its head, just as Harry Two so often did. My heart melted even more. I very gently touched the horn. Though it looked solid, it was so soft against my fingers.

Then I noted that it wasn't putting its full weight on its front foreleg. I knelt down for a closer look.

"Something has injured it," I said. I stroked the leg gently, careful to not touch the gash there. I reached in my pocket and pulled out the Adder Stone and waved it over the wound and thought especially good thoughts. The wound completely healed. I rose and stroked the unicorn's mane.

"Good as new," I said to it.

I found the unicorn gazing at me, its black eyes darker than the deepest cave. Set against the brilliance of the white coat, the effect was remarkable.

"You're beautiful," I said in a low, awed voice. "Absolutely beautiful."

I gently rubbed its horn one more time and then withdrew my hand. My fingers were tingling. I looked down at them. They were the cleanest they'd ever been. Not a speck of dirt could I find on them. I looked at the unicorn's coat, horrified that I had transferred my dirt to its immaculate hide.

But there wasn't a bit of it there.

I once more found the unicorn gazing at me. It opened its snout and if a creature such as this could smile, it just had. As I watched, it turned and trotted off. The farther away it got, the faster it moved, until it was just a blur. Then it was gone.

I turned back to the others and rubbed my fingers where I had touched the horn. Something appeared in my pocket. At first, I was terrified, for I feared dark sorcery.

I pointed my wand and said, a bit lamely, "*Rejoinda*, uh, bloody thing in my pocket."

When it soared out and landed in my hand, we all gathered around in wonder. I caught a breath.

It was the unicorn's horn.

But hadn't the creature had the horn when it disappeared? I . . . I couldn't be sure.

"How did that get there?" I said.

Delph looked at me and smiled. "You took care-a its leg. Showed it kindness. Dad would be proud-a you for that. Nursing beasts like that."

I grinned and rubbed the horn. I knew it must be very hard, but it felt so very soft. I put it away in my pocket and glanced down at my fingers. They still tingled and it seemed that this sensation was spreading over me.

I looked toward the granite outcrop that was as far away as ever and an idea suddenly popped into my mind, and I wondered why it hadn't before.

I raised my wand and said, "*Confuso, recuso.*"

A shimmering wave seemed to pass in front of us. When it was done, we were within barely a mile of the granite outcrop.

I heard Lackland exclaim, "Bloody Hel."

Astrea *had* taught me the counterspell after all, only I didn't know that. But clearly, what was a hallucination but a confusion of the mind?

We marched on, energized by our sudden remarkable progress, and reached the wide rocky outcrop in short order. It was cooler in the shade cast by the granite and we decided to take a rest. As the others made camp and readied food and water, I used Destin to quickly zip up to the top of the big rock and land before a storm knocked me silly.

I looked behind me. The sun was shining, the heat intense. In front of me was the gloomiest gloom. No sun, no light, just clouds, soupy fog and chilly air.

The Quag was certainly living up to its reputation. It was the most insanely frustrating place I could ever have imagined. I hoped soon to have it at the back of me.

I jumped and landed on the dirt below and rejoined the others.

"What did you see?" asked Delph eagerly.

"It looks like it will be cooler than here," I remarked.

We ate our meal in silence and then Lackland asked if we should push on.

I decided not to. It would be silly to waste time going around the outcrop when, using Destin, we could just go over it. But I wanted to do a little scouting first, and I didn't want to do it alone. I set Delph to take the first watch with Harry Two and then I beckoned Petra over.

"I'm going to fly over the rock and go ahead a bit into the next part of the Third Circle," I said. "Would you like to come with me?"

While I had given few direct orders to any of them, Petra seemed to understand that declining to come was not an option. I harnessed her up and then kicked off. I had never flown with her before, but she took to the journey with ease.

When we arrived up top and I released her from the harness, she said, "Why don't you just fly over this place? That way you can avoid all the dangers below."

"If I take to the air with the intent of flying over, then a huge storm blows up. But a hop here and there seems to be acceptable."

"You sound as if this place is a living thing."

"Oh, it is very much a living thing." Astrea had taught me that, and I had certainly seen evidence of it firsthand.

We stepped to the other edge of the outcrop and she peered ahead.

"It's so different from back there," she said.

I glanced down at her blackened hand. "Does it still hurt?"

"No, not really." She hastily pulled her sleeve lower to cover it.

"It's okay, Petra. We're all carrying scars from this place. And we'll probably have more before all is said and done."

"I guess you're right," she said softly, but she kept her hand covered.

"Can you tell me about your family?"

She glanced sharply at me. "My family? Why?"

I kept my voice calm. "Because they may have known some things. Things that could help us get through here."

She was shaking her head. "They knew nothing, Vega."

Put off by her answer, I said testily, "They clearly knew something if they survived all this time in here. As we've both seen, it's not that easy." I paused for a moment and then added, "And they didn't have magic, did they? Not like *us*."

She gave a long, penetrating look. "If you're asking me how I did what I did with your wand, I can't tell you because I don't know."

"Yet you grabbed it and said the incantation."

"I heard you say it before, when the lycans attacked," she said quickly. Too quickly, I thought.

"It's the killing spell. The only one that does it outright."

She gave me a condescending look. "Well, lucky for you, then. Otherwise, you'd be dead."

I ignored this. "And even though you said it was just luck, you clearly knew how to use the Finn."

She rubbed at her burned hand. "It was just luck," she insisted.

"So, your family?" I persisted. I'm sure my look told her I was not going to yield on this.

She let out a quick breath and scowled. "All right, damn it. I had an uncle. My father's brother. He was a bit odd. Kept himself to himself, but he took a liking to me. We used to take walks together. And we would talk."

"About what?"

"He said, well, he said that we didn't belong here. That he thought there'd been a mistake."

"A mistake? How so?"

"I don't know. But he seemed angry about it. He said that we should be living somewhere else."

I thought back to Delph's remark about Petra seeming to understand that there was another place outside the Quag. And this also might be what Silenus had alluded to — that some Maladons had been trapped in here.

"Maybe your uncle thought you belonged in my village."

"Maybe," she said doubtfully. "But the thing is . . ."

She looked away, unable to meet my eyes.

"Petra, please just tell me."

"Will you promise not to tell the others? Not even Lack knows."

"I promise."

She eyed me severely, as though measuring the sincerity of my words.

She pointed at my wand. "My uncle had one of those."

"A wand! Your uncle?"

"I didn't know back then that that's what it was," she cried out. "I swear I didn't."

"But how do you know *now* that it was a wand?"

"Because of what he did with it."

"What did he do with it?"

"He could move about. Go from one spot to another."

"*Pass-pusay*," I said.

"Yes, I remember him saying those words."

"What else?"

"He could make a fire with it. We would cook what we killed over it."

I gripped her arm. "How could your uncle do things like that and no one other than you knew? Why didn't Lack know, your father, your mother?"

"Because he never showed them the wand. He never did anything with it around them. Only with me."

"And why was that?"

She peered up at me. "Because . . . Because . . ."

"Because he knew *you* could do it too?"

She nodded jerkily and her lips quivered.

"How?"

"He let me use it once to bring down some eggs from a nest for my meal."

"So he told you a spell to use?"

"He told me the words."

"Where did he get the wand?"

342

"I don't know."

"What if I were to tell you that he could only have come by it from a family member who gave it to him with a piece of themselves embedded in it?"

She looked utterly astonished by this.

I went on. "So that means someone in his family, meaning *your* family, passed him that wand. What happened to it?"

"I don't know. When the lycans came, we were sleeping. We had someone on watch, but they must've fallen asleep too. My uncle was killed. I don't know what happened to his wand."

I looked at her again, watching every move of her body, every twitch of a facial muscle. I knew something for a fact. I knew that she was lying. Petra had her uncle's wand somewhere. Knowing what she could do with it, she never would have left it behind, lycan attack or not.

"Do you want to go down there?" she asked quickly, looking over the edge of the granite. She obviously did not want to continue this discussion. And I decided not to push it. I had certainly learned a great deal.

I nodded. "You can stay up here if you want."

She shook her head. "No, I don't want you to go down there alone."

"You're sure?" I said. I wished I could trust her. But the fact was, other than Delph and of course Harry Two, I could trust no one.

"Yes."

So I harnessed her up and we leapt together.

Eris

IF ANYTHING, THE gloom intensified on the ground when we landed. I had to light my wand and it still provided only the barest illumination. I didn't like this. An army of jabbits could be sneaking up on us right now and we'd never know it until we felt their fangs against our flesh. I grabbed Petra and pushed her to the ground as something flew over us so close that I felt the wake from whatever it was lift strands of my hair.

"Keep quiet and stay down," I whispered to her.

I carefully lifted my head and looked around, listening intently for anything that might tell me what was out there. The next thing I heard was totally unexpected.

Laughter.

And then a voice from out of the gloom.

"Does my heart good to see the likes of them wallowing in the dirt, right where they belong no less."

I settled on my haunches, my wand ready as I looked around. That was a male's voice. There was someone in here with us who was not a beast. For one wild, panicked moment, I thought Thorne had escaped Luc and the other ekos and caught up to us somehow. But it wasn't his voice.

"Who are you?" I called out.

"Trouble and strife which cuts like a knife. One who enters my ground will be hunted right down." Laughter followed this silly song, along with a whooshing sound like the thing was whizzing overhead.

Trouble and strife, I thought. Okay, Astrea had told me about this bloke.

"Are you Eris?"

The whooshing sound stopped.

"How come you to know my name?" the voice snarled.

I thought I might give him a bit of his own medicine.

I sang, *"I always know the name of one I've come to tame."*

Silence.

O-kay. Maybe I had gone a bit too far.

A figure started to solidify in front of me. He was like a fat baby, only with whiskers, dressed in a gray cloak with his bare feet protruding from it.

"Tame Eris?" he said, a low, malicious undertone to his words now.

I held up my wand. "Astrea Prine sends her best."

His beady eyes on my wand and with sudden understanding in his features, he said, *"Well, good luck on finding your way in the gloom. And that wand of yours will lead to your doom."*

Okay, I could figure this out, I was sure. Astrea had told me much about this bloke and the Third Circle. This place was filled with darkness, though luckily not accompanying depression as with the Second Circle. But there was something that could cut right through that darkness. What was it again? Ah, yes!

I said, *"Rejoinda, cucos,"* and moved my wand back toward me, as though I were pulling something in slowly and steadily.

A moment passed and then an inkling of light came out of the gloom. Then the light grew bigger, brighter and bolder. When a sliver had passed, the light had cut right through the dark.

"Blast!" screamed Eris.

The light was now like the sun coming up and burning off the moist air. The gloom was lifting everywhere. In another few moments, we were surrounded by cucos, small birdlike creatures that fluttered around, their wings glowing with light. They were brilliantly colored, as though they had small bits of rainbows embedded in them. I held out a finger and one of them perched on it. I felt my spirits rise along with the light.

Petra held out her arm and a half dozen cucos alighted there. She smiled as the illumination swept over her. "I don't think I've ever felt this good."

I had to smile, for I felt the exact same way. It was as though the full power and goodness of the sun had come to defeat the darkness.

Holding up a cucos, I looked at Eris. *"Trouble and strife will not trouble my life."* I couldn't help but grin as Eris waved a fat fist at me and then vanished.

We went back and collected the others. I ferried them up to the top of the outcrop and then down the other side. When they saw the clouds of cucos, both Lackland and Delph became giddy little males, running after the small bursts of light and letting the creatures collect on their shoulders and even their heads.

Delph said, "Never thought I'd have any fun in this place."

With the cucos providing light, we made good progress and then stopped to make camp. As we sat around, eating our meal, I more fully recounted for the others what had happened with Eris. Petra enthusiastically joined in and gave me so many compliments that it got to be quite embarrassing.

Delph and Lackland laughed heartily when I mimed Eris's angry exit.

Then I heard them coming.

I screamed, "Jabbits!"

The ground was actually shaking; the hisses pierced our ears. And then there were the shrieks, which could rob anyone of the last vestiges of both sanity and courage.

"What the Hel is a jabbit?" yelled Lackland. He drew his sword and stood his ground. I couldn't say I liked the bloke all that much, but I would never question his courage.

Petra grabbed her crossbow and Delph his ax. Harry Two, as usual, was by my side. The ground was shaking so badly now that I figured there were a hundred or so of the things charging us. I squinted ahead, and though the land was flat and open, I could see nothing.

I called out, "*Crystilado magnifica.*"

I really wished I hadn't.

On the positive side, it wasn't a hundred jabbits. It was only one.

On the negative side, this particular jabbit was larger than a colossal.

The jabbit had reared up right in front of us. A hundred feet high it was, with so many serpent heads along its vast trunk that it would have been impossible to count, certainly in the time we had left to live. It was like a venomous tree with a thousand deadly branches, all of which could move with terrifying speed.

I glanced at Lackland and saw that all the color had drained from his face. He raised his sword, but I could tell by his expression that he knew it was like waving a flower in front of an army of alectos.

I saw the ax whiz past me and strike the jabbit. I looked at Delph. He had heaved the thing with all his strength. It had barely cut the serpent's thick trunk.

Then, it struck.

"*Embattlemento!*" I cried out.

The jabbit had lunged at Delph, who had fallen backward. The serpent crashed into my spell shield, but it was so huge that it pushed the shield back and into Lackland, who was nearest to it. There was an almighty explosion and Lackland lay senseless on the ground. The jabbit reared up, saw me and struck again.

"*Pass-pusay*," I said, tapping my wand against my leg.

The creature slammed into the spot where I had just been, burrowing a hole five feet deep.

Petra came running up and fired an arrow into one of the serpent's eyes. The only problem was, it had hundreds of others.

Harry Two sank his teeth into the tail of the monster. Luckily, Delph was up again and raced forward and pulled my canine away before one of the heads struck out to bite Harry Two. Its slashing tail hit Delph hard and he went flying through the air with Harry Two gripped in his arms. They both landed with a thud a good hundred feet away.

I pointed my wand. "*Impacto!*"

The jabbit was so large that my spell did nothing but crush two of the heads on its lower trunk. When it came out of the hole and turned to me, I could tell that its fury held no boundaries. It struck. But I was gone again. It slammed into the ground once more. It rose again, only a bit dazed this time.

This strategy recalled to me what I had done against my opponents in the Duelum back in Wormwood. I would use the creature's fury and strength against it.

Three more times it struck, and each time, I was gone a moment before impact. The thing rose up the last time, swaying and woozy. We faced off. Hundreds of eyes looked at me. I stared back at it, suddenly not nearly as afraid as I had been. I might just win this fight.

Then the wretched beast did something that totally surprised me.

It went after Lackland, now just struggling to his feet.

"No!" I cried out.

Lackland screamed and threw his sword at the thing, but it merely bounced off.

I called out, "*Rejoinda*, Lackland."

Lackland flew toward me just as the jabbit attacked.

Lackland shouted as he sailed right into me, or he would have if I hadn't ducked. I stood straight again and decided that enough was enough. I marshaled every ounce of mind, body and spirit that I could, pointed my wand and said quite firmly, "*Rigamorte*."

The black light hit the enormous serpent smack in the chest as it turned to face me. For a long moment, it just swayed there, back and forth like the pendulum in a case clock. For one terrifying moment, I thought that my killing spell had not worked. And if this most powerful incantation had failed, then I knew I could not defeat the thing.

The next moment, I shouted out, *"Pass-pusay,"* and tapped my leg with my wand once more.

The spot where I had just been standing was crushed by the falling dead jabbit. The force with which it hit the ground knocked me off my feet and my wand sailed away.

I rolled over and found myself next to Lackland.

"Sorry, I had to do that," I said as I sat up.

That's when I noticed that his eyes were closed and his breathing was shallow. And one side of his face was red and swollen. And then I saw the gash in his skin, where a drop of yellow liquid sat next to it.

The jabbit's venom. When Lackland had flown past the thing. It must have . . . bitten him.

I squatted down next to him. "Lackland? Lack, can you hear me?"

I touched his hand. It was growing cold.

I was in a daze; this couldn't be. Then my senses cleared. The Adder Stone! I reached in my pocket for it. There was nothing there. Delph! I had given it to him.

"Delph!" I screamed. I looked over and saw a dazed Delph stagger up, but then he fell over again. "Delph, I need the Stone. Now!" I said, *"Rejoinda,* Stone," but then I realized I didn't have my wand.

I saw Delph push himself to his feet and put his hands in his pockets. Then he dropped to his knees and started to paw through the ground with his hands. He had evidently lost the Stone.

Petra raced over and knelt next to me. She gripped Lackland's hand. "Lack? Lack, hang on. Hang on!" She looked at me and said frantically, "Can't you help him?"

I didn't understand. The bite of a jabbit instantly killed. But then I looked at his wound. It was not two bite marks representing twin fangs. It was a slash. He must have hurtled by the serpent, and one of the vile thing's fangs must have scratched Lackland's face somehow. As I watched horrified, the yellow liquid riding on his face was absorbed into his skin.

"NO!" I screamed, but I was too late.

Lackland started writhing and convulsing. And then, even more terrifying, he grew still, his breathing slowed, dangerously so. His eyelids started to flutter.

"Lack!" cried out Petra. "No!"

Fighting back tears, I looked wildly around for something, anything, to save him. Only I had nothing. Nothing. Where was my wand? The Stone? The fingers of my right hand started tingling. As if by its own volition, my hand reached into my cloak pocket.

I pulled it out.

The silver horn of the unicorn.

Without thinking, I pressed it against Lackland's wounded face.

The solid horn liquefied and was absorbed, like the venom, right into Lackland's skin. Then, with a gasp and shudder, he sat straight up so fast, our heads nearly collided. I jumped back. He looked at me; his eyes seemed to wobble in their sockets.

He said woozily, "What happened, Vega? Did we kill the thing, eh?"

Petra screamed and hugged him so hard, he fell back over.

I could think of nothing else but to throw myself on top and hug both of them.

When we all sat up, I saw that Lackland's face was still scarred and swollen. Delph came racing over with Harry Two.

"Found it," he said, holding up the Stone. He handed it to me along with my wand that he had obviously also found. I waved the Stone over Lackland's face. While the skin healed some, it was still bad-looking.

I used my wand on him and the healing spell improved his face even more, though it was still scarred some.

I said, "Don't worry, Lackland, we'll get you back to your handsome self."

He laughed. "Badge of honor, way I see it. Besides, a male can be *too* pretty, eh, Pet?"

She smiled and held up her damaged hand. "How about a female, Lack? Eh?"

"Go on with you, but it's right better than being dead, I can tell you that."

"Har," said Delph as a finishing point. We all grinned.

I stood. "I think the Fourth Circle beckons," I said, full of confidence now.

I should not have sounded so gleeful.

The Fourth Circle was where I was going to die.

Rubez

THE LAND IN the Fourth Circle was curious — flat in spots, rising in others. We could make out crags of rocks and spiny ridges leading into the sky. Overhead were no stars, no Noc. I led us by the light of my wand.

We walked as far as we could and then made camp near a stand of tall willow trees. I was on the lookout for the slender thread of the Obolus River, which I knew ran through here, but I never caught sight of it.

We ate and Lackland offered to take the first watch.

Petra and Delph quickly fell asleep but, as usual, I found I could not, at least not right away.

I reached in my tuck and pulled out the map of the Quag that Quentin Herms had left me at my tree back in Wormwood and that I had reproduced on parchment.

There were some points about it that were right, spot-on actually. But many more were absolutely wrong. I thought back to the sequence of events that had led up to this map being in my possession. I had been in my tree when I heard the baying of the attack canines. I had seen Quentin going into the Quag. I had then gone to work at Stacks only to find a message from Quentin telling me to go to my tree that night. There I found that an extra board had been nailed into the trunk, behind which I had found the map.

I sat up. But the extra board had not been on my tree when I saw Quentin fleeing into the Quag. So he had to have come back out of the Quag and nailed the board there sometime later, but before I returned to it that night.

Then I wondered something that I never had before. Why had the Council been hunting Quentin down? Something must have triggered it. We had been told later that Quentin had broken laws but we were never told which laws. And Morrigone and Thansius had never really spoken about the matter to me.

I reached in my pocket and pulled out my grandfather's ring. It had been found in Quentin's cottage, so presumably my grandfather had given it to him. But why had he not given it to my father, his only *son*?

What quality did Quentin possess that would have made my grandfather give *him* the ring instead? Was he simply a messenger, getting to me things that I would need? Was he doing my grandfather's bidding somehow? If so, why?

I pulled out the parchment, tapped it with my wand and said, "Silenus?"

His image appeared instantly on the paper.

"Where are you now?" he asked somberly.

"The Fourth Circle."

"The Obolus River."

I nodded. "And Rubez the pilot. What can you tell me about him?"

"Nothing, I'm afraid."

"Astrea said that he will demand payment to take us across the river, but she didn't say what it would be."

"I have of course never taken the journey, and have no scraps of knowledge from anyone who has."

"Wonderful," I muttered. "Does the river take us to the Fifth and last Circle?"

He shook his head again. "Alas, 'tis shrouded in mystery."

"But there *is* a river, so I would imagine that there might be some water dwellers in it."

"I would not be surprised if there were."

"Hence the boat with Rubez to safely cross it," I noted.

"I would imagine that safe passage across the Obolus would involve more than simply coin for a seat."

"What, then?" I asked.

"It may very well cost more than you are willing to give, Vega. And then it will be up to you to decide. Such is the way of this place. It often demands more than one is either willing or able to give."

And with that ominous comment Silenus was gone.

I slowly put the pages away in my cloak. What would I be unwilling to give up in order to cross the Obolus?

Petra had the last watch. I waited a few slivers after she left to take up her post, and, making sure that Delph and Lackland were asleep, I drew closer to Petra's tuck. I knew what I was doing was in many ways wrong. But it was also what I needed to do right now.

I pointed my wand at it and muttered, "*Crystilado magnifica*."

All the contents of her tuck were immediately magnified in front of me. I saw what I thought I would. My next incantation was spoken just as softly.

"*Rejoinda*, wand."

The wand flew from the tuck and right into my hand. When it smacked against my skin, I realized — too late — that it might burn me. But it didn't. Perhaps it would do so only if I tried to cast a spell with it.

"*Illumina*."

With my own wand lighting Petra's, I looked at it closely. It was made of wood far darker than mine. Technically, her uncle had not given this to Petra. Perhaps he would have, but he'd been killed before he could. She had simply taken it. But someone had given it to him. His father perhaps? I found what I was looking for on the base of the wand.

It was a part of a fingernail. I could make it out clearly against the wood.

Feeling a little guilty, I pocketed the wand, went back over to my bed and lay down. If Petra was my enemy, even though she had saved my life, I did not want her to possess a wand, a wand that could kill both me and Delph. But still, I did not feel good about it. There seemed to be no easy decisions in this place.

I closed my eyes and fell asleep, unsure if what I had just done was right or not.

PETRA ROUSED US when it was time to get up. This was a bit difficult to calculate since the sun didn't rise here. I watched her closely as she gathered her tuck, but she never looked inside it. Thus, she was unaware her wand was gone.

When she did become aware, I knew she would immediately suspect me. How could she not? I was the only one who knew about her magical past with her uncle. But she had not told me that she had the wand. Thus, I doubted she would confront me about it, at least not in front of Delph and Lackland. I could tell she did not want them to know her secret. It was a foul tactic I was playing on her, but right now I could not afford any more surprises.

For three more lights and nights we rambled over the darkened landscape. One time we saw an inficio flying overhead and had to take cover in a cave. Another time, it was a pack of freks doing battle with a herd of creatures for which I had no name. The freks eventually won and lingered over the corpses constituting their spoils of victory. As they ate, we ran for it and were soon safely away.

On the fourth night that I stood my watch on the edge of our campsite, I raised my wand and muttered, *"Crystilado magnifica."* I had done this before with little result. This night was to be different.

Yet I never could have imagined that I would be seeing something like this.

It wasn't some creature way out *there.*

It was Delph and Petra. For some reason my spell was showing me what was behind me rather than in front.

They were very close to each other and were talking in low voices, so I could not hear. Over the last two lights and nights, I had seen them lingering together, whether it was when we were walking or sitting around our meager fire. They tended to sleep near each other as well.

But this vision?

I whirled around and quickly made my way back nearer the dying fire.

I stopped and looked.

Delph was waving the Adder Stone over Petra's damaged hand. I knew he was thinking wonderful thoughts. And then she smiled and touched his cheek.

I turned away and walked back to my original spot, my head lowered, my eyes on my dirty boots. Delph was my best friend. Friends did not act like that with anyone else. It wasn't . . . it wasn't . . .

It wasn't what, Vega?

It wasn't what you wanted to have happen?

Well, it's not your life. It's Delph's. If he likes Petra better than you, so be it.

The next moment, I froze when I heard it.

The sound of lapping water.

I ran to tell the others.

We hurried along, following the sound of water until we reached a clearing, and there it was.

The Obolus River. It was long and snakelike, twisting and turning until it was out of sight at both ends. And it was wider than I would have thought. It was actually impossible to see to the other side. But I just knew on the other side was the Fifth, and last, Circle. The only thing between the last circle and us was this body of water.

"Look there," hissed Lackland, pointing to one side.

To our left was an old wooden pier, listing back and forth on what I supposed were partially rotted support timbers sunken in the water.

The wooden sign hung on a leaning post swung slowly in the breeze. Though we were some yards from it, the words were clear enough, even in the dark. In fact, the words seemed to glow red.

"*Blackroot Pier,*" I read.

"Vega Jane," said Delph in a tone I had never heard him use before.

"What?" I whispered back.

But I needn't have asked. I could see what had prompted his words.

The small, black vessel had rounded the bend and was drawing closer to the pier. At the back of it, holding a long steering oar, was a dark-shrouded figure. The boat glided over the water as if it was riding on the air just above the surface of the Obolus.

The shrouded figure expertly guided the craft to a gentle stop at the warped boards of the pier.

There was a lantern attached to a bent rod affixed to the boat's gunwale. It gave off enough of a glow for us to see the face of the gent piloting when he lowered his hood.

We all took a step back when we saw him. It appeared to me that Rubez was a skeleton, only someone had forgotten to tell him he was no longer alive. Everything about him was bony, hollow and dead.

Yet his eyes glowed fiercely in the lantern light. The glow seemed to be the same as the fiery red of the letters on the sign. He opened his mouth and spoke at the same time that one long, bony hand reached out and beckoned to us.

"Draw close, those who wish to cross the Obolus," he

said in a voice that sounded like the low throaty rumble of an attack canine. "And Rubez will oblige."

We drew close, stepping up onto the fragile pier, which lurched sideways under our collective weight. I thought we were all going to go tumbling into the water, but the thing righted itself and we stood level a couple of feet from Rubez.

I started to step on the boat, when Rubez barred my way with his oar. It was dripping wet and slimy.

"Oi," I called out as I jumped back. "You said to draw close and you'd oblige."

"Rubez is needing his due," he croaked.

I stared at him. "What sort of *due*?"

In answer, he looked at the planks of the small boat and then over at us.

"Got room for four and no more."

I looked at the others and then turned back to him. "But we've got five."

"Four and no more," he repeated.

I pulled my wand. "And I said we've got *five*. Now, I know you want some sort of payment. And I'll be glad to give it. But we're *all* crossing this river."

He smiled at me and his teeth were bloodred. And I noticed for the first time that his arm, exposed a bit as he wielded the oar, was covered in dark scales, like a fish. He raised his oar and then pointed it over my head.

The next moment, Delph screamed. I turned. He was on his knees, holding his head, his face contorted in agony. I grabbed him but he threw me off, fell onto his belly and started convulsing.

"Delph! Delph!"

Petra and Lackland tried to help, but they were thrown backward by some unseen force.

I pointed my wand at Delph to try to incant something that would make whatever was hurting him go away. But it was as if something was gripping my wand and pulling it away. I whirled around to stare at Rubez. He just stood there, his oar still held high, and I knew it was the source of Delph's agony.

"Stop it!" I screamed. "Stop it, please."

Rubez slowly lowered his oar, and Delph instantly ceased convulsing. He lay there panting.

I knelt next to him and gripped his hand. "Delph?"

"O . . . okay, Vega Jane," he mumbled. "Pain's gone. O-kay."

I turned back to Rubez venomously. "Why the Hel did you do that?"

"Four in me boat, no more."

I looked over his vessel. "Okay, then we can make two trips. Three and two. That meets your bloody rule!"

His smile vanished and he held up a solitary finger. "One trip, not two."

I stood, faced him and squared my shoulders. "So what is your due, then, eh?" I truly didn't understand what the bloke wanted.

He glanced down at the dark waters and then back up at me.

"One of you must swim for it if you want to get to the other side. That's me due. If you don't want to swim for it, you can stay here, the lot of you. And you won't be alive in a few slivers." He looked over my shoulder as he said this. "They're coming."

"Who's coming?" I asked sharply.

He lowered his gaze to me and his eyes were like fists of fiery blood. "Death," he hissed. And that sound filled me with a dread that not even the shriek of a jabbit could inspire.

I looked down at the gently lapping waters and then across toward the river's other side, which I still couldn't see from here.

I turned back to Rubez. "Is there truly no other way?"

"Only one."

"What?" I said eagerly.

"I can turn five into four. Then the remainders can ride in me boat!" he ended savagely and raised his oar threateningly. "Which one, eh? EH!"

I held up my hands and cried out, "No. I'll swim for it."

Delph rose on shaky legs. "Vega Jane, you're not that good of a swimmer."

Harry Two danced around my feet and moved his forelegs as if to show how powerful a swimmer he was.

"No," I said. "I'll go."

"No," snapped Delph. "You can't always be the one to go it alone."

Lackland said, "How 'bout the canine, eh?"

"Shut up, Lackland," I barked.

Delph pulled me aside and whispered, "Let's have a go at him and take his blasted boat."

"You saw what he just did to you. And his oar apparently is more than a match for my wand."

Delph said in a normal voice, "Then how do we choose, eh?"

Petra said, "I vote for Lack to go in."

Lackland swore under his breath. "Why me?"

"Well, we need Vega's wand to get through, don't we?"

"That's bloody ruthless of you," snapped Lackland. "What about Delph? Or are you too wonky over the bloke?"

Delph and Petra both looked like they had been walloped by a colossal.

Before Petra could answer, Delph said, "I'll go. I'm a strong swimmer." He added in an embarrassed tone, "And like Petra said, we need Vega's wand to go on."

"No, Delph," snapped Petra. "You're not going in there. Bloody Hel, I'll go."

Lackland interjected, "Look, why not the ruddy canine, eh? Will somebody tell me that? It's a bloody beast."

Delph shoved him. "Harry Two is worth five-a you."

"Enough," I shouted. "I'm going in."

"But we need you to —" began Petra.

I pointed my wand at them.

"No, Vega Jane," screamed Delph. He knew what I was about to do.

Harry Two barked and lunged at me, his mismatched eyes wide with distress.

I said, "*Subservio.*"

Instantly, their eyes became unfocused and they stood rigidly before me. I pointed my wand at the vessel and they all climbed in, Harry Two included.

I drew a deep breath as I looked at them one by one, my gaze holding finally on Delph. Would the last impression I have of him be one of stark betrayal? And there sat Harry Two, frozen, but inside I knew he could see what I had done. I felt deep shame all around. But I had no time to dwell upon it.

I turned back to Rubez, who was waiting expectantly.

"Anything you can tell me before I dive in?" I asked coolly.

He appraised me for a few long moments. Then he glanced overboard. "What's down there needs sorting out, don't it? Whether you're the one to do it?" He shrugged. "Only you can answer that." He gave me a wicked grin, which made my blood boil. I told myself that I would survive this if only so I could face this bloke again and turn him to dust!

Rubez used his oar to push off from the pier. I watched them drift away. It had occurred to me that this might be the last time I would see Delph or Harry Two. I should have felt teary. I should have felt *something*. And truth be known, I did. A terrible, terrible emptiness. As though all I had or had ever felt was gone.

Then they disappeared in the mist that had sprung up over the water. All I could hear was the splash of the oar against the water's surface as Rubez carried all of my companions away.

The *Subservio* spell would only continue to work while I was in relatively close proximity to them. But by the time the effects wore off, it would be too late to stop me.

I held up a solitary hand and said, "Good-bye."

Then I stepped to the edge of the pier and looked down at the Obolus River. Delph was right. I was not a very experienced swimmer. There simply wasn't that much water in Wormwood. I had no idea what awaited me in the foul depths, but standing here thinking about it was not doing me any good.

So, gripping my wand, I took a deep breath and dove in.

Death Becomes Her

I DIDN'T KNOW WHAT to expect when I hit the water. Well, I supposed I thought it would be cold and miserable, but it really wasn't. In fact, it felt warm and comforting.

When I broke the surface of the water that changed.

I took a breath. At least I tried to. But when the air hit my lungs, I thought my brain would explode. I gasped and writhed and when I was about to lose consciousness, I did the only thing I could think to do. I dove under the water.

After nearly suffocating above water, my mouth was still open when I went under. The liquid poured into my lungs and I knew then that I would die when my lungs filled like buckets.

But I didn't die. The pain in my head went away and I gulped breath after breath and as the water poured through my lungs, I felt strangely replenished. I lit my wand and looked around. The water was so murky that even with the illumination, I could see only a few feet in every direction. I swam on, gliding smoothly through the water. I wanted to make sure that I was heading in the right direction, so I broke the surface again and stared ahead. But it was so dark and the pain in my head became so fierce that I had to dive back under again.

A cold chill invaded my insides, even as my outside felt warm and comforted.

If I can't breathe out of the water, how will I escape this place? Was this the due that Rubez demanded? The sacrifice that most would be unwilling to make?

Me imprisoned in the Obolus forever?

I pushed these troubling thoughts away and swam on, hoping I was traveling in the right direction.

Rubez had said that things in here needed sorting out. I had no idea what he meant by that. I assumed that there were vile creatures lurking in the water that would do their best to kill me. If so, I was as prepared as I could be.

I held out my wand and said, "*Crystilado magnifica.*"

What I had expected were water demons whose ferocity and lethality would match those that walked the land. That, I could understand. That, I could fight, and perhaps win. But that wasn't what I saw.

"Nooo," I moaned. I stopped swimming and started to sink to the bottom of the foul river.

The great battlefield on which I had been given the Elemental by Alice Adronis and then nearly killed lay before me. Only, this time I was part of the great battle. I was astride a muscled steed. I was outfitted in chain mail. I carried a great spear in one hand as I flew through the sky. Just as Alice had done.

I had seen this same image before in a dream, thus I knew what was about to come. The blow hit my image full in the chest and I tumbled off my steed. I fell, and as my image fell, it happened.

The image and myself became one. And we were both

falling so fast and so far that my breath was torn from me. I looked down at my chest and there was the wound, deep and bloody. And the pain pierced me so badly that I cried out and my mouth instantly filled, not with water but with blood. My blood. And then I felt no more.

And that scared me more than anything else had.

For there is only one reason a wounded person feels no pain.

This was no dream. This was no image.

This was my death.

Me, Vega Jane.

I was no more.

I hit the bottom of what I supposed was the Obolus River and then a remarkable thing happened.

I kept falling. It was as though the riverbed there had opened, the dirt moving aside, allowing my plummet to continue to a place that was somehow even deeper.

My eyes had been closed all this time because my courage had reached its limits. But now I had to open them. I heard the heavy staff strike the stone floor. I looked up at the tall, lean, near-cadaverous figure.

It was Orco. With his great, long nose, which had three openings. His totally black eyes looked me up and down. His awful mouth opened, revealing both his black teeth and the long tongue with the trio of arrow ends. He hissed and struck the stone again with his cudgel.

This caused me to spring bolt upright and stand before him. I looked down at myself. My clothes were as dry as if I had never stepped foot in the water.

I looked to my right and there it was.

The wall of the dead. The mouths were open, the eyes the same. No sounds came from the mouths, but in the pleading eyes I *heard* more misery than I could possibly bear.

I looked back at Orco. He was smiling in triumph. And I knew why.

I looked down at my chest and saw the gaping hole there, my stilled heart right underneath. I put out my hand toward it but then drew back. I could not bring myself to touch my own mortal wound.

I looked up at Orco.

"*Certe,*" he hissed, a triumphant look on his features.

Was I really dead? But how could I be? I had never really been on that battlefield. So how could I have been mortally wounded?

"I am not dead," I said firmly.

In response he pointed with his clawed fingers to my chest. "*Certe.*"

I shook my head stubbornly. "I am *not* dead."

He pointed to the wall and raised his cudgel. I felt my feet leave the stone floor. I was hurtled across the space and slammed into the wall. I could now hear the words spewing from the poor souls imprisoned there.

The next thing that happened to me was the most dreadful of all.

I was sinking into the wall. It felt like I was being dissolved from the inside out. I could feel myself . . . vanishing, parts of my being disappearing from me. As I looked wildly around, I somehow knew that once my mouth and eyes were the only things left visible of my being that I would be lost, trapped here forever.

My thoughts turned fleetingly to Delph and Harry Two. And even to Petra and Lackland.

And then as I sank farther into the stone a voice came into my ear.

It was not from the death wall.

It was a voice from inside my head.

Vega, death is only fear. Without fear, there is no death. Without death, there are no bars. Without bars, there is only freedom.

A voice speaking in my head at this moment should have driven me completely mad. But it didn't. For some inexplicable reason, it gave me pause. Then it gave me calm. And then it gave me something much, much stronger. Perhaps the strongest thing of all.

It gave me hope.

I looked at my hand, which was still visible. And in it was clutched my wand.

And I recalled that in our first meeting Orco had feared my wand.

Which of course meant that he feared me.

Vega Jane.

I was a sorceress. I had a wand. I had a need. Thus, as Silenus had informed me, I could come up with a spell to fill that need. The exact words weren't important. It was the mind, body, spirit all coming together as one, just as Astrea had said. Just as I had done spontaneously back at her cottage, without even a wand to aid me.

My entire being concentrated on only one thing. I made a slashing motion with my wand and screamed out with all the breath I had left.

"I am not dead!"

There was an enormous crack, like a thunder-thrust, and the wall broke right down the middle, freeing me.

I stepped clear of the rubble, my wand held high.

For the first time in the presence of Orco, I felt no fear. The bars of my prison were truly broken. But in him I saw, with satisfaction, uncertainty in those cold black eyes.

He and I squared off on the stone, circling each other. When he raised his cudgel, I raised my wand, bracing to throw off his attack. He lowered his cudgel, but I kept my wand pointed right at him. He glanced down at my chest. I did the same.

I gaped. The hole in my chest was gone.

I looked up to see that cruel face staring at me.

I could not help myself.

"*Certe,*" I hissed.

And then I was hurtling upward, through stone and dirt and into the crush of water. Up, up, up I went until I thought the pressure I was feeling all around would smash me flat. The next instant, I sputtered and spit and thought I was going to drown. And then I realized something.

I was breathing air once more, not water.

I looked across the surface of the river in all directions. It looked the same to me, which meant I did not know which way to go. I was flopping around in the water, suddenly exhausted from my struggle down below. I went under the water once but managed to push myself back to the surface. Then I went under again. And I didn't know if I could find the strength to keep fighting.

Something grabbed me and I kicked and thrashed to free myself. I tried to point my wand, but my arms were pinned to my sides. I broke the surface of the water, and stopped struggling.

"Delph!"

He was facing me, holding me up in his strong arms.

"What are you doing here?" I asked.

"Are you mental? What the bloody Hel d'you think? I'm savin' you."

He turned on his back, held me under my arms and kicked off.

"Do you know which way to go?" I asked, immensely relieved by his presence.

"We lit a fire on the shore as a landmark. Heading right for it."

"I'm sorry I had to cast a spell over you," I said.

"Figured that's what you done when I came outta it."

"Have you been searching for me long?"

"Long enough."

At last my feet bumped against something and I realized we were in the shallows. Delph helped me to stand.

I looked back in time to see Rubez and his blackened vessel drift past us.

I locked gazes with the creature. After staring down Orco, I knew this bloke could hold no horrors for me. I pointed behind me at the Obolus.

"Oi, Rubez, I think I've got it all sorted out. Thanks."

His face was a mask of loathing. And I didn't care a jot.

We continued on until our feet hit level ground.

Then something leapt on me.

It was Harry Two. He licked my face and pushed his snout against my cheek.

Delph picked me up in his crushing embrace.

"You made it," he said quietly, his breath touching my cheek. His sense of relief was palpable.

"I made it," I said weakly. "Where are the others?"

"Over by the fire."

As we started to walk toward the firelight, he said. "Was it bad swimming across?"

I looked up at his wide, happy face.

"Not that bad, Delph. Not that bad a'tall."

The Lost Souls

WE WERE IN the Fifth Circle now, the last. And it was not lost upon me that this would be our greatest and, hopefully, final challenge.

Petra had offered to take the first watch. Lackland and Delph were asleep. I lay on my lumpy bed with Harry Two beside me.

I had not told the others what happened to me back in the Obolus River. What would have been the point? And besides, what could I say?

Right, so anyway I died from a bloody wound to my chest, but I'm back from the dead now and everything's just smashing. Would you like to see the spot of my mortal wound? It was quite something!

I groaned and put a hand over my face. Then I lowered my other hand to my chest. I had been terrified to do this before, but now I had to. I reached under my clothes until I could feel my skin. I knew exactly where the wound had been. I was scared that I would feel remnants of the awful spot, but my skin was as smooth there as it had always been.

I withdrew my hand. But still, I felt unclean somehow, changed forever. And — the hardest part of all — I felt immeasurably different from my companions.

Delph and I had faced so much in here, together. But we had not experienced this together. Only I had. And I thanked the holy Steeples for that.

I pulled the parchment from my cloak and summoned Silenus. He appeared a moment later.

"We made it across the Obolus and into the Fifth Circle," I mumbled.

"And Rubez's payment?" he asked.

I took a sliver to describe in detail what had happened to me.

"I died, Silenus. I was becoming part of that wall."

"But you fought back and gained your freedom. That is a significant accomplishment, Vega. Never forget that."

"Astrea said she knew little of the Fifth Circle except that my ancestor, Jasper Jane, created it. Apparently, he was keen on dark sorcery. Anyway, she mentioned that it might be the circle of lost souls."

Silenus stared worriedly at me. "Lost souls are a tricky business, Vega. Very tricky."

"How can a soul be lost? Despite what Astrea said I thought if a body died, so did its soul."

"Oh, no. The soul is far more resilient than the body, which is actually quite fragile. The soul can live without the body. And, truth be known, the body can live without the soul, but I would never want to encounter a soulless body. I doubt the meeting would be pleasant. However, a bodyless soul can be quite nice and accommodating. In some ways, in fact, that might be an apt description of me."

"Well, that's not so bad," I said.

"But do not, for one moment, believe that all souls disenfranchised from their bodies are like that, for they are not."

"How do you mean, exactly?"

"An evil soul remains evil, regardless of whether it is wrapped in a foul body or not. Losing the physical does not change the soul. In some ways, it makes it even more evil. Thus it is a good idea to keep a healthy skepticism of all souls, Vega, until you can be sure on what side of the ledger they fall."

"And how does one tell that?" I asked, wide-eyed.

"Well, a good indicator is whether they try and kill you or not."

I had a sudden idea and took out Petra's wand.

"You said you could tell if this is a Maladon's wand?"

"Tap it against the parchment," said Silenus.

I drew a long breath and did as he asked.

Silenus instantly vanished from the page.

I tapped my own wand against the parchment and he reappeared. We stared at each other.

"A Maladon's?" I said.

"Without doubt."

I said good-bye to Silenus and put the parchment away, my thoughts now filled with dread.

I walked over to Delph when it was my turn to take watch.

"Delph, we need to talk."

"'Bout what, Vega Jane?"

"Petra."

He suddenly looked sheepish. "We're just friends. I told you I felt sorry for her."

"I don't care if you like her, Delph. She's pretty and tough, high-spirited and, well, sort of amazing."

"You mean she's like you?" he interjected.

I was about to say something else but had frozen at his words. "Wh-what?" I stammered.

"She's like you. You're all those things. And *more*, Vega Jane. But you're not alike in other ways."

I felt myself turn red and I couldn't look at him.

"What do you mean?"

"You're always helping folks. Back in Wormwood, the way you visited your mum and dad and took care-a your brother. And you were the only friend I had while others made fun-a me. And back at the Obolus with that bloody Rubez, Petra was just fine with Lackland having to swim for it, because she knew she needed you to make it through the Quag. You never woulda done that."

We looked at each other for a long moment. And then we both reached out at the same time and gripped the other's hand. I wanted to do more than that. I wanted to kiss him, but he said, "You wanted to tell me something about Petra?"

I looked at him and then slowly let go of his hand. "It'll keep. Get some sleep," I added.

After he left I sat there thinking.

Petra could be as disconnected from her history as I had been from mine. But, to borrow Silenus's phrase, on what side of the ledger would she eventually fall?

I knew at some point I would have to answer that question. I only hoped it didn't cost me my life.

Vanished

THE SUN ROSE, much to my relief. As soon as we cleared about a half mile of forest, we saw it.

The mountain that Delph and I had seen on our very first night in the Quag — which seemed a century ago now — rose above us, far closer than it ever had been before. The land at the foot of the mountain rose swiftly, forming spiny ridges. These ridges, like the backs of serpents, with deep valleys in between, grew steeper and steeper until they ran smack into the face of the mountain.

I eyed Delph. "Seems like we go over the mountain."

He nodded, his gaze taking in all points. While the mountain still looked blue and stripped of foliage, from our vantage point, we could see the ridges leading up to it were lushly encased in green. However, there was nothing beautiful about this place. After all we had been through, I saw only the stark possibility of death.

We reached the spiny ridge in the middle and started to head up. The going was rough. The trees and other foliage were densely packed and the incline swiftly became steep. The footing was not so good either, and we each took tumbles several times. But we kept going.

Lackland had to use his sword, and Delph his ax, to cut a way through. I finally ended up using my wand to blast a path. Then we arrived at the end and looked down into a broad, flat valley nearly a mile across. I glanced to my right and left. The path had just ended in a sheer rock cliff! There was no way to keep going up.

Delph stood next to me and peered into the valley. He said, "Guess we go down, eh?"

"I can use Destin to take you down one by one," I said. "You first?" I asked Lackland. I knew he was not so keen on flying and would want to get it over with.

He sheathed his sword and tightened the grip on his tuck. "Right," he said, his face already turning gray and his brow sweaty.

I had him hold on to the leather straps on my back. I counted to three and then we leapt. Well, I leapt and dragged a squirmy, heavy Lackland along with me. I had to dodge past tree canopies, but we landed safely and Lackland gratefully placed his feet back on solid ground.

I flew back up for Petra and then Delph.

Harry Two was the last to come down with me. When we alighted, I unhooked him from his harness and looked around.

There was no one there.

"Delph?"

Harry Two yipped and started sniffing around.

"Petra? Lackland? If this is some sort of jolly on your part . . ." But I knew it wasn't. They would never do something like that. Harry Two and I raced here and there, exploring behind trees and dense foliage, but there was not one sign of them.

My belly burned with anxiety. Then I had a sudden thought. I raised my wand and said, *"Rejoinda,* Delph." I prepared to duck when his large body came flying at me, but it didn't. Everything around us remained still and quiet.

I attempted the same spell with Lackland and Petra. Nothing.

"Crystilado magnifica."

All that got me was a close-up of trees with not one living thing in or around them. I looked down at Harry Two, cold dread invading every part of my body. We were alone. I had no idea what to do. I had never felt so frantic. I rushed around screaming their names. I was a mad female, all reason struck clean from me.

Then another thought filled me with fresh panic.

This was the place of lost souls. Silenus had said that the physical could be separated from the soul, though an evil person's soul would remain evil, whether it had a body attached to it or not. Had they been taken and their souls removed? If so, where were their bodies?

Stop it, Vega.

I was acting as if it was certain they were dead. I couldn't think that way. I had to find them. And I would.

"Come on, Harry Two," I screamed.

He jumped into his harness and I sprang into the air. We soared along and I did long banking movements to the right and left as I kept my gaze below, looking for any sign of my companions. I saw nothing and my spirits plummeted and my nerves once more threatened to run away with me. The longer they were gone, the more it seemed they would be gone forever. I could barely breathe. I was so scared, I couldn't even cry. It was like I had been struck by the same spell I had used to freeze the jabbit back at Astrea's.

As I looked up, I saw it materializing. At first I thought it was another storm blowing up because I had been flying for so long. Only it wasn't a storm. I would have preferred a storm, actually.

The sky was suddenly blackened with flying things. As one drew close to me, I could see that it looked like an inficio, only far smaller, about the size of Harry Two. But there must have been thousands of them. And they were all bearing down on us with clawed wings and screeching cries.

I went into a dive. I could feel my canine's rigid body against my chest. I could sense the things right behind me. I even felt the tugs on my cloak as one grabbed it with its claws. I sped up and disappeared through a canopy of leaves. I was praying the creatures would not follow us down here.

My prayers were not answered.

I zoomed along the ground with the swarms closing in.

I pointed my wand behind me and cried out, *"Engulfiado."*

A surge of water shot out and as I looked back, I saw it slam into the wall of creatures, knocking many of them down and scattering the rest.

But I knew they would regroup and be after us again.

Up ahead I saw it. I had no other choice.

I pointed my wand at the huge double doors of the massive stone building that had just appeared in my line of vision.

"Ingressio."

The doors sprang open. I looked back. The swirl of foul

creatures was feet from us. I could see their razor-sharp claws and beaks and the murderous looks in their eyes.

Harry Two and I zipped through the doors. Pointing my wand behind me again, I cried out, "*Securius.*"

The doors slammed shut and bolted.

A split second later, I could hear hundreds of thuds against the thickened doors as the clawed creatures slammed into the wood. But, thankfully, the doors held.

I landed and let Harry Two out of his harness. My chest heaving, I watched the doors just as I had back at Stacks in Wormwood when the pair of jabbits was after me. That door had not opened. It didn't look like these would either.

But those foul things out there, had they attacked Delph and the others? Had they carried them away somewhere to . . . to . . . I couldn't think it. I felt the tears now rush to my eyes. It felt like my heart had been ripped clean from me.

I managed to regain a bit of calm and looked around. The place reminded me of Stacks with its high ceilings, stone stairs, white marble balustrades and arched columns leading into other rooms. I started up the stairs to see what was on the second level, when I heard it.

"May I help you?"

Halfway up the stairs, I whirled around, trying to locate the source of the words. My gaze had passed over a corner on the first floor. But then I came back to it as the, well, whatever it was, moved out into the open where I could see it clearly.

The figure was really just an outline. The light coming in through the high windows shone right through it, as with the wendigo.

"May I help you?" the figure said again.

I slowly walked back down the stairs and stopped as the thing glided over to me. Yes, it was gliding, not walking.

When it drew close enough, I could see that it was the image of a tall male bent with age. He had on boots and a long robe open in the front. With a thrill I saw the image of the three hooks imprinted across the breastplate he wore.

"I'm looking for my friends," I said quickly. "There were three of them. They just vanished. I'm very worried. Please, can you help me?"

"Three friends vanished?" he said. "Dear me, that is not good. I am sorry."

He looked me up and down and then gazed for a moment at Harry Two.

"I haven't seen a canine in ages," he said. He reached down to pet Harry Two, but his hand passed right through my canine. I saw Harry Two shiver slightly.

"Blast," said the male. "I forgot about that. Oh, well."

"Who are you?" I asked. I also wanted to ask *what* was he.

"My name is or was Jasper Jane."

I nearly fell over. And I would have but I was apparently frozen to the spot.

"Well, I'm Vega *Jane*," I managed to say.

He looked at me curiously. "We share a surname. Do I know you?"

"I doubt it." I paused and then continued. "I saw your grave," I said slowly. "At the Wolvercote Cemetery."

"My body *is* buried at Wolvercote. But my soul is not. My soul is right here in front of you. 'Tis all I have left."

My eyes widened. "How do you separate your soul from your body?"

"There are two ways of doing so. For me, I did so because my body was dying but I did not want to fully perish. Thus, using magic I removed my soul before my physical self breathed its last."

"You said there was another way?"

"Yes. But I do not wish to describe it. It is too horrible."

He suddenly saw the ring on my finger. "Where did you get that?" he exclaimed.

"It belonged to my grandfather. What does it mean?" I asked. "The mark?"

"It is our Trinity. Our mantra: Peace. Hope. Freedom. Precisely in that order."

"Look, I need to find my friends. Every sliver that passes —" I gulped.

"I'm not sure I can help you, not sure at all. You see, it's really not my place to help those trying to pass through here."

"I know that! But Astrea changed her mind. She trained me up to escape here. To take up the fight once more against the Maladons."

This all came out in a torrent. He looked stricken.

"Astrea? I . . . Helped you to leave here? Fight again? I can scarcely believe it."

In my mind I searched for something that would make him see that he had to help me. I held up my wand. "And this was given to me by another ancestor, Alice Adronis. She told me I had to survive. To fight. You have to see the truth, Jasper, don't you?"

Jasper was now staring at me, openmouthed. His hand ran up and down the symbol of the three hooks on his breastplate. "See what?" he said breathlessly.

"Eight centuries is bloody long enough to hide. And the Maladons will find us. They will. If they're truly as evil as everyone says, they will never stop looking. Well, I would rather come out of hiding and take the fight to them!"

He looked down at my wand. "Alice . . . Alice gave you that?"

"It was her Elemental. And now it's my wand. It has a strand of her hair embedded in it."

"Alice was the most courageous of us all." He slumped to the floor and sat there cross-legged. "This is quite astonishing," he said. "Quite. We had our plan, you see. And . . ."

"And you carried it out very well. But it's over now. It's over!"

"How came you here, to my castle?" he said sharply.

"I was chased by flocks of very lethal flying creatures."

"Oh, yes, the dreads," he said absently.

"The what?"

"The dreads. My creation. If they followed you here, they'll be waiting just outside. If you attempt to leave, they will cut you and your canine to pieces. They never give up once they have prey at hand. Dreadful things, hence the name."

My patience was exhausted. "Fine. If you won't help me, I'll find my friends by myself." I turned and started to walk off.

"But the dreads!"

I turned and shouted, "I don't care. I can fly, so I have a chance. And they're my friends. I will die for them. And if you won't help me, then go to bloody Hel!"

As soon as I finished speaking, he vanished.

Good riddance.

We rushed from the room and reentered the main hall. I stared at the double doors where the dreads, according to Jasper, still lurked. So I knew this was probably the end.

I knelt down and hugged Harry Two, pushing my face into his fur, breathing in his scent. "I love you, Harry Two. Thank you so much for all you've done for me." He licked my face, and in those wonderful mismatched eyes, I could see that my canine was more than ready to stand by my side, and die with me.

I rose, my wand clutched in my hand. But before I could mouth my incantation, the huge front doors burst open. I was sure the opening would be filled with dreads coming to tear us to pieces. But there was nothing there.

I ducked when something flew past me.

It was Jasper. On a flying steed. It was as transparent as he.

He looked back and motioned for me to join him.

I hooked Harry Two into the harness, leapt into the air and followed Jasper out.

Catching up to him, we flew side by side over the darkened landscapes below. "Where are we going?" I asked.

"To find your friends."

"Does this mean you're going to help me?"

"Obviously." He glanced at me in concern. "You're clearly magical, but you're not, well, *slow*, are you?"

"Do you really think I could have gotten this far if I was 'slow'?"

"No, I suppose not."

I looked around. "If I fly too long, a storm will come out to stop me."

"Not so long as you're with me."

"You can do that?"

"This is the Fifth Circle. I created it. So I can do almost anything. *Almost.*"

We soared for a long time. Below us the night turned to light and then back to night and then back to light even though I knew that could not be possible. It was all so surreal that after a while I just accepted it and it no longer bothered me.

"There," said Jasper, and he started to rapidly descend.

I followed him downward and we touched the ground about a sliver later.

"Take out your wand, Vega."

I immediately did so. Jasper Jane had not struck me as someone easily cowed. But he looked nervous now. Yet, I thought with some measure of pride — we were family after all — that he also looked quite determined.

"Where are we going?" I asked.

"There," he said, pointing ahead.

I could just make it out amid a sea of trees.

It looked like Steeples back in Wormwood, only it was made of the blackest wood I had ever seen. It of course had a steeple and long glass windows. But on the glass were pictures of the most horrible creatures I hoped never to see. And whereas my Steeples had a cross on top, this one had something else. It grew more distinct as we neared the structure. I recoiled in horror when I saw that it was a body split in half.

"What is . . . this place?" I said.

"This is the Temple of the Soul Takers. Their leader is the high priest Bezil," said Jasper. "A truly evil creature."

"But hold on, you created all of this! Which means you created *him*."

"My job was to prevent escape from here and also entry into here," said Jasper. "I could not do so without conjuring dark forces powerful enough to achieve both goals. Once created, these species evolved. They have had eight centuries to turn even more diabolical. They forcibly split the souls from the bodies of those unfortunate enough to cross their path, devouring the latter to nourish themselves and then turning the souls loose to wander aimlessly. That is the *second* way to sever your soul from your body."

"How did you think of such a thing?"

He looked at me. "I based it on the Maladons."

The horror of this left me speechless.

He said, "Your friends are assuredly in there. If you wish to leave them to their fate, let me know now and we can turn back." As he finished speaking, he watched me so closely it reminded me of the way Astrea would look at me. There was a definite air of appraisal in his features.

"I already told you. I am not leaving my friends."

"Capital," said Jasper.

"But how do we defeat these blokes?"

"I can do nothing to them," he said.

"What? Then why did you come?"

"To show you the way. It will be up to you to defeat them."

My spirits sank. "Can you at least give me advice on how to do so?"

"You need to trust your instincts, Vega. And your heart. That did not serve our lot particularly well against the Maladons, but that is not to say we should not trust our heart.

After all, it is the one thing we have that the Maladons do not. Good luck."

"Wait, I have one more question."

He looked at me expectantly.

"Why did you change your mind?"

"If I trusted one 'soul' in my life, it was Alice Adronis. If she wanted you to survive to take up the fight once more, then I will not stand in your way."

And with a slight pop, Jasper Jane was gone.

A Trusting Heart

I STARED UP AT the wooden building whose timbers were so black that they looked to have been charred in some great fire. I glanced at Harry Two. My canine was not smiling, nor was his tail between his legs. He just looked serious. And ready. This gave me a bit of desperately needed confidence.

We approached the enormous pair of doors leading into the place. My wand held tightly in my hand, my gaze darting to and fro, we stopped in front of the doors. I pointed my wand and said, *"Ingressio."*

The doors swung silently open. Though this was what I had intended, it did not make me feel any better that this temple of evil was opening so readily. I pointed my wand again and said, *"Crystilado magnifica."*

For the first time ever, nothing happened. No engorged images appeared in front of me. We stepped cautiously through the opening, and the doors slammed shut behind us. Expecting it as I was, this did not startle me. I had other things to bring me terror. Starting with the interior of the place.

Every single inch of the walls and glass was covered with acts of depravity and slaughter and mayhem. It was like a maniack's mind had been opened up and splattered, like blood, over the walls and windows.

As at Steeples, there were rough-hewn pews lining the floor. But unlike the simple beauty of the Steeples seats, these were carved with images of misery and torture and death. Creatures up and down the wood were depicted killing other creatures and then devouring them. Worst of all were the countenances of the victims, their faces frozen forever in silent horror. As I looked at them, they seemed to move right in front of my eyes, as though the army of foul things and their pitiful prey had suddenly sprung to life.

I could sense this was meant to terrify me. And I *was* terrified.

But that was not the same as being unready to fight.

"*Embattlemento*," I cried out, pointing my wand to the right, where a winged creature with rows of clawed appendages shot at me. It slammed into my shield spell and fell to the floor in a crumpled and — gratefully — dead heap, its neck snapped from the sudden collision.

I looked down at Harry Two, who was gnashing his teeth and growling. An instant later my canine had leapt ahead of me and attacked a figure draped all in black from head to foot, which had appeared directly in front of us.

"No, Harry Two," I screamed out.

But Harry Two had caught the thing right at the neck and his fangs bit down hard. The figure fell to the floor, a pool of green blood draining out of its neck.

I patted Harry Two, who had immediately returned to my side, as we stepped over the thing. Curious, I knelt down and lifted the hood. I wished I hadn't.

The face I was looking at appeared to have been lifted directly from the flames. The skin was burned and popped and cracked. It looked far worse than Delph's damaged arm. And the bulbous eyes, an awful mix of yellow and red, stared back at me malevolently, even in death.

I shuddered, dropped the hood, rose and hurried on.

Up ahead was a monstrously large statue carved from solid rock. I thought this might be Bezil. His cloak was black, his skin was burned, his head was shaved and his eyes were full of malice. He held something in his hands. As I drew closer I could see it was a dead child.

I passed cautiously by the statue, part of me sure that it would suddenly come to life and attack me, but it didn't. Farther on was a pair of huge doors carved with the same malignant images that I had seen on the pews.

I drew a breath, pointed my wand and said, *"Ingressio."* I knew that just beyond this portal, there would be those who would try and part me from my soul.

I knew it would be bad. Only I didn't know how bad.

The doors swung inward and we drew forward. I had achieved good results from not second-guessing myself and stepping boldly into a situation. Unpredictability can be a good thing when dealing with heinous, evil incarnates, I'd found.

So I stepped boldly into the room.

And screamed.

Delph, Petra and Lackland were immersed in three separate pools. The water was not clear, however, but foul, dark and bubbly, and there seemed to be things floating in their depths. Only my friends' heads were visible and their eyes were closed. And while I stood there, they were turning more and more transparent. At the edge of each of the pools were robed and hooded figures who stirred the waters with long, slender silver rods. Yet as I drew closer I could see that the rods were actually clear and that the silver color was coming from the waters, like ink being swept up into an ink stick.

Their souls were being taken! This was the other way of stealing souls that Jasper had told me about.

My screams had alerted the robed figures. They all turned, dropped their hoods and revealed their hideously scarred and charred faces. As I turned to the right I saw another pool that was empty. I ventured that was meant to be mine.

Before I could move, a half dozen of them flew at me, leaping through the air with a speed and agility that was dazzling. Harry Two, though, was not nearly as slow as I was. He met one of them head-on and I saw his lethal jaws clamp around the fiend's neck, and it went limp as my canine bit down. I raised my wand but was knocked backward by two of the Soul Takers smashing into me. Their clawed hands were immediately at my throat, ripping and cutting into me.

"*Impacto!*"

They blasted off me, flew across the room and careened into two of their fiendish brethren who were charging at me. They all fell into the pool containing Lackland.

Four more were at my side in a thrice. Harry Two launched at another and toppled him, tearing at the creature's throat.

"*Jagada,*" I cried out, spinning around, and two of them immediately collapsed with cuts all over their bodies.

I didn't wait for the fourth to launch itself at me. Pointing my wand at it, I simply said, *"Rigamorte."*

He fell dead at my feet.

I pointed my wand at Delph and said, *"Rejoinda,* Delph."

He flew from the waters and soared across the room, crashing into two other Soul Takers who had rushed into the room, knocking them out.

I grabbed at his arm. "Delph, Delph, wake up. Wake up, please!"

I heard Harry Two whine and I whipped around and shouted, *"Engulfiado."*

The powerful torrent of water hit a pair of Soul Takers — who were dragging Harry Two across the room — with such force that it smashed them into the stone and killed them.

"Delph, please. *Rejoinda,* Petra."

Petra soared out of the waters as another pair of fiends attacked me with the long rods they had been using in the pools. One of the rods collided with my face and I felt blood spurt from my nose and cheek. *"Embattlemento."*

The rods shattered against the shield and suddenly Delph and Petra awoke.

"What the —" began Delph.

Petra slowly rose, gazing around, taking it all in, and then looked at me. Lackland was sinking deeper into the depths of his pool. The Soul Taker there had not left to attack me. He was still swirling the rod in the water. Lackland was nearly out of sight. His soul nearly separated.

From another doorway a dozen Soul Takers emerged, all armed with weapons, and charged us.

I looked at Petra. Our gazes locked for an instant, but in that short time, much was communicated. Her look was pleading. She knew I had taken her wand. She *knew*. Part of me didn't want to, but the other part of me realized it was the only way. I fished in my pocket, found her wand, pulled it free and tossed it to her. She gripped it and turned to face the regiment of demons coming at us. I did likewise, raising my wand and shouting, "*Impacto*."

A moment later, Petra screamed the same incantation.

The combined spells produced a force of unparalleled power.

The Soul Takers were not merely blown off their feet.

They were disintegrated.

I turned to look at Petra and smiled. She returned it weakly.

Then she was hurled off her feet and back into her pool, where she immediately was pulled under.

Next I was being thrown through the air and landed in the fourth pool. And under I went as well. I opened my eyes and though the water was dark and foul, I found I could see clearly enough. That was not a good thing.

I knew who was facing me.

Bezil. The bloke from the statue. His cloak was bloodred and there was a heavy chain around his neck with a metal disc at the end of it. The symbol engraved on the disc was that of the body torn in half that was on top of his bloody temple. Now I knew it represented the separation of the soul from the body.

He held a knife in each hand, his expression murderous. I had lost my wand and was looking desperately in the water for it. Suddenly, a hand shot down into the pool, grabbed Bezil by the chain and wrenched him completely out of the water.

I found my wand and used Destin to soar upward and back into the room, coughing and sputtering as I flew.

It was quite a sight to behold.

Delph was slamming his fist into the side of Bezil's head. But Bezil was far more powerful than he looked. He lashed out at Delph and knocked him heels over arse.

I aimed my wand at Bezil but never got the spell off. Two Soul Takers attacked me. As I fought them, I tried to keep Delph and Bezil in sight. They were having a titanic struggle, tossing each other across the room, raining blow after blow on the other.

As I fought off my remaining Soul Taker, Delph ripped one of Bezil's knives free and slashed him with it. The demon sprang back as green blood surged from the wound. Delph did not wait a moment before pressing his attack. He was on Bezil like a garm on prey. Two enormous punches to the head, which I seemed to feel from across the room, and the bloke's eyes closed and his head went limp. Delph picked him up and tossed him back into the pool of water, where he quickly sank.

"Yes, Delph!" I screamed in joy.

He looked at me, battered but grinning as I finished off the last Soul Taker.

Petra had gotten Lackland out of the pool and also smashed the rod that had been used to suck out his soul. Though he was staggering around and gagging, he looked otherwise unharmed.

We've won, I thought. Until I saw Delph.

"Uh, Vega Jane?" said Delph.

I looked at where he was staring.

Bezil had soared free of the pool. He was standing near a foul image on the stone wall. He raised his hands and spoke a stream of words. A moment later, the wall opened and out marched a hundred Soul Takers, with swords, lances, axes and knives, and bloodlust in their eyes.

There was no way we could beat them all, even with two wands.

"Harry Two," I cried out, and patted my chest.

My canine leapt into his harness and I secured him. "Take my hand, Delph. Lackland, take Delph's hand. Petra, Lackland's."

We were all linked together now, with Petra and me at the ends of the chain, our wand hands free. We would need them.

With bloodcurdling screams, Bezil and the Soul Takers attacked.

I pointed my wand at one of the pair of gigantic stone columns that supported the ceiling. Out of the corner of my eye, I saw Petra point hers at the other.

"*Severus.*"

"*Severus,*" repeated Petra.

Enormous cracks ripped through the columns. They started to shake. And then they began to topple. We were already in the air by then. I turned and, like leaves strung out on a vine, we soared for the doorway while the temple began to fall around us. We barely cleared the doorway as the room's ceiling fell in, crushing Bezil and his followers beneath the rubble of their foul temple. How fitting!

But I was terrified that the rest of the temple was going to cave in on us, permanently entombing us here too. We shot through the front doors as they toppled inward. Free of the crumbling temple, we soared up, up until I could maintain flight no longer. Then we fell fast and at a steep angle, slamming into the ground and tumbling painfully across a long swath of dirt until we came to rest in a heap.

As I looked up, I saw the entire temple crash inward on itself. Dust rose into the air and then it was quiet.

I looked over at Delph, who was struggling to his feet. He looked down at me.

"I thought we were goners," he said.

"We almost were," I said back.

I let Harry Two out of his harness and helped Petra to her feet while Delph pulled up Lackland. I glanced at the wand Petra still clutched in her hand.

"I'm sorry I took it from you," I said so only she could hear.

She looked down at it. "I can understand why you did."

"I couldn't have done that alone in there," I said. "I hope you know that."

"Pet!" exclaimed Lackland. "Where in blazes did you get that thing?"

Petra looked at her wand, obviously unsure how to answer.

"I had a spare," I said, drawing an incredulous look from Delph.

"Oh," said Lackland. "Well, thank all that's bleeding wonderful for *spares*, eh?"

I was startled to find that we were at the foot of the Blue

Mountain. Once we cleared it, I reckoned the end of the Quag would be right on the other side.

"How did you find us?" asked Delph.

"I had help. From a friend."

Lackland said, "Well, should we be on our way?"

I glanced up sharply at the mountain. What was left up there to try and stop us? I looked down at my wand. It seemed so tiny and insignificant, yet it had served me well all through the circles. I could only hope that it had enough magic left.

The Last

W E COVERED FIVE miles. All nearly vertical, until we were so weary we could no longer lift our arms and legs. We made camp on a small plateau that allowed a view across the Quag. Or it should have.

I turned to see where we had come from. I had never really looked behind me while here. I had always been concerned about what was ahead of us.

But nothing was back there except darkness, even though it was still light. It was like staring into the heavens on a starless night. There was just nothing. I shivered involuntarily.

I looked over at Delph, who was helping Petra make the meal. They were both scarred from their time here, Delph with his arm and Petra, her hand. No doubt their minds were scarred too, as was mine. I observed with a pang of jealousy that they worked well together, seeming to read the other's mind.

We ate our meal and drank our water. None of us spoke. It was as though the battle with the Soul Takers had robbed us of something important and we were all trying to figure out what.

Lackland carelessly rubbed his injured face. Delph rolled up his sleeve to examine his burned arm. But when I looked over at Petra, she was simply looking at her wand as though she had never seen it before. I knew how she felt. The weight of a wand in one's hand carried with it expectations and a certain responsibility equal perhaps to the tonnage of the mountain we were on.

Petra took the first watch, and Delph and Lackland lay down on their beds. I followed Petra to the perimeter where she would take up her post.

I glanced at her wand and decided to come to the point. I was, above all, a practical Wug. "How many spells do you know?" I asked bluntly.

She seemed taken aback by this but I plunged on. We didn't have time for niceties. "The *Rigamorte* spell is not something you do your first time," I said. "And the other spells you used, though I said the incantation first, your wand movements were spot-on. So how many spells do you know? It's important."

It was like I was trying to determine how many morta rounds we collectively had left to fire at our enemies. I was under no delusion that the Fifth Circle was finished with us. I had relied on Petra's magical ability to escape the Soul Takers. I knew I would need it and her again.

She said sharply, "What does it matter? I couldn't save my family from the lycans, could I?"

I pointed at the bit of fingernail housed in the bottom of her wand. "That was part of your uncle, wasn't it? It's not his wand. He made this wand and gave it to you, didn't he? It's *your* wand." She had used my wand to kill, but it had damaged her. She wielded her own wand with ease and skill, which told me plainly she had used it before.

She looked down at the wand and gripped it more tightly. "So what if he did?"

"So how many spells?"

"A few. A few more than the ones we already used. He wanted to teach me more, but the night the lycans came, we were off getting water. A garm attacked us. And killed him." She looked at me fiercely. "And I killed it. That was the first time I used the death spell. My uncle told me I had to feel —"

"Something more than hatred or loathing? And you had to feel it with every bit of your mind, body and spirit?"

She nodded dumbly.

I thought it interesting that we both had lost loved ones to a garm, she her uncle and me my first canine. And that we had both used our first death spell on a garm.

She looked at my wand. "You can do loads more than I can."

"Well, I was properly trained up," I said, watching her closely.

"Can you properly train me?" she said eagerly.

I had been expecting this request, but I still wasn't sure how to answer it.

I looked over at a distant spot. "Point your wand that way. The incantation is one you've heard me use before. *Crystilado magnifica*." I showed her the proper wand motion.

She readied her wand.

"Focus your mind, body and spirit," I said. "And let that combined energy flow through your wand." Blimey! All of a sudden, I felt like Astrea Prine!

Petra did as I instructed but failed the first three times. She did not grow frustrated, however, as I had when attempting this. She asked more questions and I gave more answers and on her sixth try, the landscape that was miles from us was now mere inches from our faces.

She looked over at me and beamed in triumph. I returned the smile, though not quite as enthusiastically. Then we both gazed at what we would be facing the next light.

"Is that smoke curling up?" she said.

I squinted to see better, though I shouldn't have had to. The image *was* right in front of me. Still, there was something distorted in the picture that made it difficult to clearly make out the details. Perhaps Petra had not performed the spell exactly right.

"It looks to be." I pointed to a spot. "And that might be a little shack where the smoke is coming from."

"So someone lives there?" she said, sounding puzzled and anxious.

I could well understand that, for who would want to live in the Fifth Circle? "I guess we'll find out soon enough." I had an idea and said, "Maybe we can avoid climbing this mountain. Maybe we can fly to the top."

"I thought you said that wasn't possible."

"It might be now."

"How do you figure that?"

"As someone once told me, in here anything is possible."

As I turned to leave her, I stopped. "Petra. Did your uncle ever mention the term Maladon to you?"

I wanted to see her first and true expression.

"No," she said. "What does it mean?"

"It's not important."

THE NEXT LIGHT, we packed our tucks and I buckled Harry Two into his harness. I wasn't going to ferry the others one by one. Not after what had happened last time. For all I knew, others like the Soul Takers were lurking around. We were going to stay together. Die together or survive together. Not alone. Never again.

We held hands in a line like last time and then I kicked off and we soared clumsily into the air. Petra was bringing up the rear with her wand held ready in her free hand.

We soared along and I have to admit that the view from up here was spectacular. Closer up the mountain was even more bluish than it seemed from far away. Parts of it were covered in foliage but other sections were bare rock where for some reason apparently no plants would grow.

So far, no dark clouds formed and the air was nicely calm. I looked down below and spotted once more the curl of smoke that Petra and I had seen using the magnification incantation. From up here, I could make out more details. The shack we had also seen previously was small and made entirely of blue stone. I bent my head forward and we flew lower. Now I could see a patch of blue dirt through the trees. And then I spotted him.

He was a small male slowly trudging across the dirt toward the cottage, carrying a stack of wood nearly as large as he was. This was presumably fuel for the fire that was the source of the smoke. He was dressed in old rugged trousers, a checkered shirt and — I could make it out as I dipped us lower — a red cap whose peaked top bent over a bit.

I didn't fancy an encounter with another creature in the Fifth Circle. I thought we could simply fly to the top of the mountain instead.

As soon as I finished this thought, the storm was upon us so fast I barely had time to draw another breath. Petra screamed and Lackland bellowed as skylight spears shot sideways, so close to us that I thought they must, at the very least, impale us. Thunder-thrusts hit with such force that they knocked us across the sky. I could feel my grip loosening on Delph's hand. Then another scream jarred me back.

I looked down to see Petra tumbling downward.

Lackland stared up at me, shock on his features. "She . . . she just slipped."

It had been him screaming, not her.

"Hold on," I yelled.

I went into a dive that put so much torque on my shoulder with Delph hanging on to me that I thought my limb would part ways with my body.

I saw that I would not reach her in time, but then I didn't have to. I pointed my wand and said, "*Lassado*."

The thin light exploded from my wand tip, encircled Petra's waist, and I whipped it upward. She soared toward us.

"Lackland, grab her foot."

He did so and held on.

"I don't think she's conscious," he cried out. "Her eyes are closed."

"Is she breathing?" I shouted. My first thought was that she had indeed been hit by a skylight spear.

"I . . . don't know. I think so."

I aimed my head downward as the storm raged around us. We slammed into the ground far harder than I had intended, but I was up in an instant and knelt next to Petra. She was on her back, her eyes were closed and her features were screwed up in pain.

"Petra? Petra!"

I slapped her face with my hand.

Her eyes popped open and she looked wildly around. "What! Where? You?"

"Are you hurt?"

I looked her over and saw no obvious injuries. My gaze went back to hers as Delph and Lackland peered over my shoulder, their faces anxious.

I said, "You nearly died. We just caught you in time."

She slowly rose and touched her head. "I . . . I guess I blacked out. The last thing I remember was . . ."

"Hullo?"

We all whipped around and stared at the thing that had spoken.

It was the little male with the red peaked cap. We had landed near his shack. As I looked around, I could see it and the curl of smoke barely twenty yards away.

"Who are you?" I asked. He looked at me with soft brown eyes and a very friendly countenance, which immediately put me on my guard. Friendly did not really exist here. I well knew that. Cunning and murderous, yes, but not friendly.

"I am called Asurter of Muspell," he said, his voice high and squeaky.

"Muspell?" I said. "Is that what this place is called?"

"It is what I call it," said Asurter, who came barely up to my waist. Indeed he was as small as Eon back in Wormwood, though his skin was quite red.

"What are you doing here?" asked Delph.

"I cut wood and I keep my fire hot."

I looked over at the shack.

"It's warm," I said. "Do you really need a fire?"

"I always require a fire," replied Asurter. "Do you need food or watering?"

We looked at one another. I wanted to push on but, though the storm had cleared as soon as we touched ground, I knew we would have to labor up the mountain on foot now.

I said, "That would be very nice, thank you."

As Asurter turned his back, I gave the others a sign to be on their guard. The bloke might be okay, and then again, he might not.

We walked past a truly enormous stack of firewood all neatly cut and cubbied. Asurter gathered up a staggering amount of wood in his arms and led us into the shack. It had looked humble and small on the outside. And it looked the same on the inside. The walls were simply the back sides of the stones that formed the house's outside. The floor was dirt, the furnishings limited to one chair and one table. Dominating the space was a stone fireplace that took up one entire wall from the floor to the peak of the ceiling. As soon as we got inside it was so intensely hot that I started to sweat and I had to shield my eyes from the harsh glare of the flames.

I looked at the others and saw they were having the same reaction. When I took a step toward the flames, I had to immediately draw back because of the heat. Yet Asurter walked right up to the opening of the fireplace and put the stack of wood on it. The flames instantly shot to a full ten feet in height and seemed to threaten to escape the bounds of the fireplace.

Blimey, I thought, *no wonder his skin is so red if he gets that close to the flames.*

He turned back to us and said, "Food and water?"

He pointed to the table and we saw that food had indeed appeared there. And water. Only the food was charred black. And when I went to pick up a goblet of water, I dropped it because the metal was burning to the touch and the water was boiling.

Asurter seemed not to notice this. He went back outside and returned with another load of wood. He threw it on and the flames leapt ever higher.

I looked at the others and saw their concern building. Delph pointed a finger at the door.

"Well, thanks, Asurter, we'll just be going now," I said.

He turned to look at me. "Going? Going where?"

Before I could stop him, Lackland said, "Up the mountain and out of this place, that's where."

I froze because I could sense something building. Just like I had with Ladon-Tosh in the Duelum back in Wormwood. A sensation of energy, of power amassing, only at a rate a thousandfold greater.

"Run!" I screamed as I hurtled for the door.

Asurter was no longer small. In fact, he was growing so fast that he burst through the roof of the shack. And he looked nothing like he had before. He was gigantic, with long hair and a beard that reached to his waist. And if Asurter had been red, this thing was aflame. Truly aflame, his beard was on fire against his chest, his hair likewise.

We dashed outside. As we looked back, Asurter had grown to a height of a hundred feet. And what he did next made my lungs seize up. He reached down to the ground and gripped something metallic that appeared to have been driven into the dirt.

As he pulled it free, we all saw that it was a sword set afire that was fully half as long as Asurter was tall. When he turned to look at us, it was terrible to behold. His face was simply a mass of flames. And when his mouth opened, the scream coming from it could have melted iron.

Fortunately, I had recovered my senses and cried out, "*Embattlemento.*"

The flames met the spell head-on and thankfully the spell held, though the magical shield was white hot and I felt the heat emanating from it though I was twenty feet away.

My victory was short-lived.

Asurter turned, raised his sword and smote the ground behind him a terrific blow. Fire hit the ground and then flames towered a hundred feet in the air. And, as we watched horrified, the line of fire raced right up the face of the mountain, setting afire everything in its path, moving faster and faster as it went, so that it traveled from where we were all the way to the top of the Blue Mountain with such velocity it made my head spin and vanished the breath from my lungs.

And then it happened.

The top of the Blue Mountain blew off with a force so powerful I had never witnessed anything close to it before. Though we were many miles from it, the force knocked us all forty feet into the air, and we rolled and tumbled across ground that was now heaving and pitching like a boat on a storm-tossed sea.

When we finally came to a stop and managed to look up,

the entire mountain was on fire and a wall of flaming mass was roaring down the long slope right at us. It was a thousand feet tall and miles across. It was unstoppable. It was coming right for us.

The Fifth Circle had just won.

The Four Remaining

R UN, VEGA JANE!" screamed Delph.

I could sense him beside me, tugging on my arm. But I didn't look at him. I could hear over the roar of the mountain of fire heading our way that Lackland was fleeing down the side of the mountain, screaming for us to run as he went.

From the corner of my eye, I could see Petra on her knees, her head bowed, awaiting the end. At my feet was Harry Two. He was doing the same thing I was doing — staring at fiery death coming our way.

I looked at my wand and knew, despite its considerable power, that it would not be nearly enough. The flame from Asurter's mouth had nearly buckled my shield spell. What was coming now was a million times more powerful. My *Engulfiado* spell would simply turn to mist in the face of it.

I had Destin around my waist, but I could not fly us high enough to escape the flames. And as I continued to watch, the most amazing thing happened to me.

My panic ceased and a peaceful calm took over. I don't know if it was simply resignation that my life would be ending momentarily. Or something else entirely.

As Delph kept trying to pull me away, my feet seemed to become even more deeply rooted to this spot.

This was my last stand. I would die here. Or I would survive here. It would be one or the other. This I clearly understood.

I put my hand in my cloak pocket and withdrew the Finn. I don't know what made me think of it, for many thoughts were flashing through my mind at that point.

I had retied the knots on the Finn. I looked down at it, unsure what would happen once I did what I planned to do.

I undid the first knot on the Finn.

The wall of flames hit Asurter's shack and it evaporated into steam.

I undid the second knot on the Finn.

The wall hit Asurter and all one hundred feet of the bloke disappeared into nothing.

Now nothing stood between us and cremation.

"VEGA!" Delph screamed.

But I was not listening. I was watching our death coming at us with unfathomable speed and ferocity.

I undid the third and final knot of the Finn. It was the only one that had not been untied before. And when my fingers let go of the freed string, I wasn't sure what was worse: the flames . . .

Or what I had just unleashed.

I was catapulted straight into the sky with such force that I could feel my lungs collapse, my brain spin and my clothes nearly rip from my body. The Finn had been wrenched from my grasp. The wind that was propelling me also shot outward like a titanic wave, and it hit the mighty wall of flames with a cataclysmic blow that I thought nothing could survive. Had I still been ground bound, I was sure I would have disintegrated from the effects of this collision beyond all collisions. It swept over the spot where I had been with such power that I had to close my eyes. I was afraid that my mind could not contain what I was seeing, that it would simply burst if I didn't stop looking.

But finally, I had to open my eyes. I looked down and froze. It wasn't just that trees were bent over. It wasn't that rock was smashed flat. It wasn't that the fire had been quashed.

Truly, all of those things happened.

But something else happened too.

The entire Blue Mountain was gone. It was laid flat as the palm of my hand. There was nothing left. And not only were the flames extinguished, but there was not even a wisp of smoke left. The air was as clear as I had ever seen it.

And I had a bird's-eye view of this, because I was nearly a mile high. It had nothing to do with Destin because all the others were up there with me. Delph, Lackland, Petra and Harry Two. We were all suspended in the sky as though ropes from above had glided down and encircled us. Next to us our tucks floated in the air.

Everything in the path of the Finn's third knot of power was gone. As far as the eye could see ahead, there was nothing. It was like someone had rolled up the Fifth Circle and taken it away.

And then, as quickly as the mighty wind had come, it left us.

And we started to fall as though the ropes from above had been severed.

I confess to having been in a trance as I watched everything below us vanquished. But now, as we plummeted to our deaths, the trance ended.

I flipped over in the air, shot to my left, grabbed Harry Two and buckled him in. The others were below me, falling fast. I pointed my head down and shot toward Delph, who was nearest. I pointed my wand and cried out, "*Lassado.*"

I roped him in and, without missing a beat, zoomed toward Petra and did the same with her. Now only Lackland was left to save. I turned in midair and accelerated toward him.

As I drew nearer, I saw it from the corner of my eye.

A bolt of fire. How could that be? I turned.

Asurter had risen from the flattened earth. How he could have survived the wall of fire and the third knot of the Finn was inexplicable to me. Yet he had suffered, for though he was still a giant, he was no longer aflame. He was but a charred ruin.

But he had some fire left in him and had just hurled it directly at us. I screamed out, "*Embattlemento.*"

The bolt of fire hit my shield and exploded. Then I pointed my wand at Asurter and said, "*Impacto.*"

Asurter was blasted into a thousand fragments and was no more.

It was then that I heard the scream and turned back.

In time to see a flailing Lackland strike the ground with an almighty thud.

And then he lay still.

I pointed myself straight down and raced to the dirt, hitting so hard that we all tumbled down. I ran with Harry Two still buckled to my chest and reached Lackland before the others had regained their footing.

I knelt down next to him. His body looked crushed, but he was still alive.

He looked up at me and a strange smile played over his lips.

"We done good, eh?" he managed to mumble.

My hands fished through my pockets for the Adder Stone.

"Just hang on, Lack."

"Done good, eh," he said again, more weakly.

"Just hang on."

"Done good," he whispered.

I found the Stone and held it over him. "It'll be okay."

"Done . . . eh?" He closed his eyes.

I wished good thoughts, the best I ever had. I waved the Stone over and over his broken body. I kept doing it even as Delph and Petra ran up and knelt down next to us.

"Lack!" said a stunned Petra.

"It'll be okay," I snapped. "I've got the Stone."

Delph looked down at Lackland and then gripped my shoulder. "Vega Jane."

"It'll be okay," I said, tears starting to fall down my face.

"Vega Jane," he said softly.

"It'll . . . it'll . . . the Stone."

Good thoughts, Vega. Lack, you'll be okay. Almost there.

I didn't see Petra reach down and use her hand to close Lackland's eyes.

I didn't see Delph take the Stone from my hand.

I didn't see Harry Two lie down next to Lackland and nudge his hand with his snout. I didn't see any of this because I had closed my eyes. I had closed my eyes because I knew if I kept them open a second longer, I would never move from this spot ever again. That I would just die right here.

Right next to Lackland. Who *had* just died.

The Stone could not bring back the dead. I knew that. I had always known that.

I felt Delph gently help me to my feet and turn me away from the body.

"We'll take care-a it, Vega Jane. It'll be okay."

I went and sat on the ground, my back to them, as they dug the hole and laid Lackland Cyphers into it. Harry Two sat next to me. His snout nudged my hand, but for the first time ever, I did not pet him when he did so.

The sacrifice that everyone had warned me about had just come in the form of a mortal blow to one of us. Death was all around here. But we had always managed to just skirt it. I had known the odds of all of us getting through the Quag were abysmally small. Astrea had told me that. But she needn't have.

I had not known Lackland long. But I had known him long enough.

And his loss ate at me in the way that such a loss always does. In a way that such a loss always should.

When the last bit of dirt had covered his remains, Delph and Petra rejoined me. "'Tis done," said Delph quietly. "'Tis done."

I opened my eyes at last and looked up at him. Tears stained his face. I looked at Petra and saw the same there.

I looked back at the mound of dirt. I rose and walked over to it and looked down. I pointed my wand, and a chunk of charred wood flew forward and planted itself at the head of the mound. Using my wand as an ink stick, I wrote the words on the wood.

Here lies Lackland Cyphers, a good friend to the end.

Then I placed a shield spell over the mound to keep his final resting place safe.

I turned and looked ahead. With a mountain no longer in the way, our path was quite straightforward now. Though nothing was quite as straightforward as it appeared, was it? Certainly not in this place.

I grabbed my tuck from where it had fallen to the ground, and hoisted it.

I passed by Delph, Petra and Harry Two.

I was changed now. I was different. I could feel it in every crevice of my being. I had been the leader. Yet a reluctant, hesitant, unsure one. Then I had grown more confident, piling victory on top of victory. Thorne and the circles. Now something else had happened. Something catastrophic.

One of the ones I had led, who had trusted me to get him through this safely, now lay dead. Yes, I was changed, completely. And forever.

With my wand in hand, I led the way once more.

To the end.

To the bloody, bloody end.

Taking Flight

I SENSED THAT I could now take to the air if I wanted to without the threat of a storm rising to stop me. But even with that, I decided that we would walk through the last bit of the Quag. For some reason, it just seemed like the right thing to do.

So on we marched.

Delph and Petra had not attempted to talk to me after burying Lackland. I appreciated this, because had I been faster, there would be five of us nearing the end of this journey, not four. It was my fault and mine alone that he was dead. Just like Duf Delphia's legs. I had failed.

I glanced down at my hand when it started to burn.

I stood there paralyzed when I saw it.

On the back of my right hand something was materializing.

My hand started to shake so badly that I dropped my wand. I had to hold my burning hand with the other one. Then the pain shot straight up my arm and I dropped to the ground, screaming. I rolled and thrashed. When I felt something grab me, I kicked and punched to make it let go.

I opened my eyes and saw that Delph and Petra had taken hold of me, trying to calm me, trying to see what was wrong.

And then, just like that, the pain was gone. My hand and arm felt normal.

Delph cried out, "Bloody Hel, Vega Jane, what is it? What's wrong?"

I slowly sat up and looked down at my hand where a moment before it had felt like a garm had bitten down on it.

"Holy Steeples," cried out Delph when he saw it.

"What is that thing?" exclaimed Petra.

On the back of my hand were the three hooks. The symbol of Peace. Hope. Freedom.

It was on my grandfather's hand. Now it was on mine.

And this was not ink that could be easily erased. I knew it was burned into me, probably from the inside out. I knew somehow that I would have this mark until my life was over.

I rose on shaky legs and retrieved my wand where it had fallen.

"It's just a mark," I said calmly, though I felt anything but.

"But, Vega Jane —" began Delph.

"I'm fine!" I barked, and then said in a normal tone, "I'm fine. Did you expect that I would escape this place without some sort of scar? Both of you have yours. And Harry Two." I tried to say this in a joking way, but I knew my tone rang hollow. This was not a normal scar or wound. This was something more. Far more.

I felt like I had just been branded. And I'd had no say in the matter at all. I hated this place. I truly hated every square inch of it.

"Let's get on," I said. "Let's just finish this."

419

FOR THREE LIGHTS we walked across a vast plain. It was inconceivable to me that a majestic mountain had rested here for over eight centuries until it was toppled by a peg of unknotted rope, leaving only flatness in its wake.

On the fourth light, I slowed when I saw it just up ahead.

A shimmering glare, as though light was being reflected off something.

As we drew closer, our pace slowed even more. After all we had endured, I did not want to rush headlong into something that would leave us paces short of our goal.

"What do you reckon that is?" asked Delph, at last breaking the silence that hung over us like a funeral pall.

I gazed at the shimmer but could not answer him. As darkness started to fall, the shimmer did not diminish. The light hitting it thus was not coming from the sky.

As we grew closer the answer struck me.

The light was coming from *the other side*.

Which meant, I realized with a thrill, that we had, at last, reached the end of the Quag.

I glanced at Petra and then looked at her wand. She nodded and gripped it tightly.

"Loosely," I murmured. "'Tis a part of you now, Petra."

I saw her fingers loosen around the wand's base.

She stole a glance at me and in that look I realized she had something on her mind. I moved over to her and looked at her expectantly.

"What is it?" I asked.

"Lack," she said.

"It was my fault," I said. "I'm the leader."

"No," she snapped. "It was *my* fault."

"What!"

"You were saving us from that flame bloke. I had my wand. I could have saved him." She looked at her boots. "But I didn't. I froze. I bloody well froze. And now he's dead. Because of me."

She sat down on the ground and started to sob. Delph looked over at us anxiously, but I waved him off. I sat next to Petra, trying to think of something, anything, to make her feel better.

"Do you know why I came into this place?" I said at last.

Her weeping slowed and she said hesitantly, "To escape, get out."

"No. I just wanted to know the truth. Where I lived, there was no truth. I wanted to find it in here."

She looked up at me. "Why is the truth so important?"

"It's the most important thing of all, Petra. Without it, we don't matter. Nothing matters."

I stood and held out my hand for her to take. "You saved my life back there. You saved all of our lives back there. That's the truth. And now all we can do is keep going. That's all. Lackland would certainly have wanted that. I think you know that."

She slowly reached out, took my hand and stood.

We walked on, cautiously, every nerve and sense alert.

Then we saw that the shimmer had turned into something more substantive.

It was a wall. A bloody wall. Like back in Wormwood. Only this one was mostly transparent. But I knew it was also far more impenetrable than mere wood and straps.

What had Astrea told me? I strained my mind to think back to her words as she lay dying in her bed.

We build walls because we are afraid. We do not like change. We do not like it when others who do not look or think like us come along and try and change things. Thus we run from it. Or, even worse, attack it.

With those words in mind, I took a step back. This wall had been built to do two things: keep *us* in and *them* out. It was a stake driven right between two races that had fought a war. One was in hiding. One was on the hunt.

I had a sudden thought.

Was my grandfather out there? My parents? How would I find them? How would we help do what needed to be done?

I sat on my haunches and looked down at my wand.

I had exhibited resources and a pluck in the Quag that had often astonished me. In the midst of the violence of things trying to kill me, I had risen to the challenge and, with the help of my friends, survived, defeating foes that in truth should have vanquished us with little trouble.

Yet I also knew that I had never faced off with a fully trained Maladon who had grown up in the world of sorcery. And despite what Astrea had said about me having exceptional power, the truth was that I was young and inexperienced. And that could prove to be fatal at some point.

Delph squatted on one side of me, and Petra on the other. They both looked at me questioningly.

"What now, Vega Jane?" said Delph.

I pointed my wand at the shimmer and invoked the magnification spell. However, the spell failed me as it had at the Soul Takers' temple. All we saw was exactly what we could see with our eyes. The shimmer, which reflected back our images and present surroundings, like a vast looking glass.

I pointed my wand at the shimmer and tried various spells. Petra joined me in the hope that our combined wands could accomplish what a single one could not.

Nothing happened other than the spells hit the wall and then simply vanished. For one intensely uncomfortable moment, I imagined that we'd come all this way, fought this hard, lost one of our members, only to be forever forestalled by this last obstacle. If sorcery could not overcome it, if the limited spells that I knew could not touch it, then what the Hel had this journey been for?

In my agitation, I kicked off and shot straight up higher, higher, as high as I had ever flown. And then I pointed my head forward and put on a burst of speed. I was repelled so fast when I hit the wall that I was tossed heels over elbows backward a good two hundred feet before regaining my equilibrium. I hovered there in the air. And then I looked down to see the others staring up at me.

"Stand back," I called down to them.

I looked down at my wand, willed it to its full-size Elemental status, and hurled it at the wall. It glanced off, did a slow arc and flew back into my hand.

The Elemental looked undamaged.

But so did the wall.

I had never known the Elemental to fail me. Yet it just had.

I had no spells left to conjure. I had no weapons left to try against it. I had nothing left to throw at the bloody thing.

I slowly headed back to the ground and simply stood there staring up at the wall, wondering what to do. How could I beat it? I had been faced with many such obstacles. I had overcome them all. Until now.

I looked over at Delph and Petra. "Any ideas?" I said, readily conceding by my words that I was completely out of them. They shook their heads.

I wished Lackland were here to give me Hel for not knowing what to do. I needed to hear his taunts. And while Alice Adronis thought I would be the one to lead them in a renewed fight against the Maladons, I wouldn't have followed myself to the High Street back in Wormwood.

I had never felt such depression in all my life. I could barely breathe. I could barely think. And what I did think was all as wrong as wrong could possibly be, to use my grandfather's words. When I looked over at Delph, I could tell he knew exactly what I was thinking. But right now, he could not help me, no matter how much he wanted to.

Yet with all I was feeling, I had to smile when Harry Two licked my hand. I petted him. He licked some more. And then gripped my ring with his teeth. Then he sat back on his haunches and barked once.

"Quiet down, Harry Two," said Delph.

But I put up my hand.

"Wait, Delph. He's trying to tell me something."

I looked at the ring and then I stared up at the wall.

My grandfather had left the ring behind and it had eventually found its way to me. Jasper had said that the hooks represented our mantra, everything we stood for. That was a powerful symbol, perhaps more powerful than I knew.

This ring could make me invisible. But could it do something else too?

I took a few hesitant steps forward and then kept going until I was right up against the wall. I reached out with my hand and first placed the mark on my skin against the wall.

I held my breath. Nothing happened.

I looked back to see Petra and Delph staring at me like I was nutters.

Then I turned back around and placed the *ring* against the wall.

I started to hold my breath. But never got the chance.

The wall instantly moved under my hand. It started to shimmer and wobble and pulse as if it had been turned into a liquid.

And then a slice in the skin of the thing opened up. I put my hands on either side of this opening and pushed. It opened farther like I was parting a pair of curtains. I thrust myself through the opening and plunged onto the other side.

A few moments later, Delph, Petra and Harry Two pushed through and joined me.

As we looked back, the opening closed up.

"Blimey," whispered Delph.

I knelt down and hugged my canine, rubbing my face into his wonderfully soft fur. In the only ear he had left, I whispered, "You're brilliant, Harry Two, absolutely brilliant."

We all took a good long look around. Staring back at us was dark, blank countryside that looked like the landscape I had often seen in Wormwood. It didn't seem frightening or inherently dangerous, as had every bit of the Quag. But I knew that it probably held perils that would dwarf those we had already faced. The absolute enormity of the moment seized me.

"We did it," I said in a hushed tone. I looked at Delph and Petra. "We made it. We're free from the Quag." Part of me could scarcely believe I was saying these words.

In their faces I saw relief, happiness, but also uncertainty and fear. And I'm sure they saw all of those elements in my features as well.

Instinctively, we all three drew together and embraced, our bodies shaking with the pure emotion of having finally achieved the one thing that had dominated our thoughts and our lives, and which had cost us a precious life. Harry Two sidled up next to me and rubbed his body against my leg. I dropped one hand down and stroked his head.

When we pulled apart, we continued to look at one another.

"We *are* free of the Quag," said Delph. "Thanks to you, Vega Jane."

"No, Delph, thanks to all of us," I said, my gaze on him, and then I looked at Petra. "And to Lackland," I said.

"And to Lack," she agreed, giving me the tiniest of smiles.

"Sort of looks like . . . like Wormwood a bit," observed Delph. "Not the village proper but the land round it."

"It does, but don't think it will be like Wormwood," I replied.

"What now?" whispered Delph.

I pointed my wand toward some faraway lights and said, "*Crystilado magnifica.*"

Instantly in front of us was what looked to be a village whose inhabitants were probably fast asleep in their beds at this time of night. Some of the buildings looked like ones I was familiar with back in Wormwood. Others not so much. The streets were cobbled in places but not in others. A clock chimed. A feline screeched. I could hear rumbling noises, but could not see their source.

But despite the sleepy and seemingly peaceful surroundings, I could sense something not nearly as innocent in the air.

Remember, Vega, the most bitterly awful place of all . . .

"Vega!" hissed Petra.

But I had already heard it.

Something was coming.

Someone was coming.

I patted my harness, and Harry Two instantly leapt there and I buckled him in. With my wand I pointed first at Delph, then Petra, and said softly, *"Lassado."*

Cords of light snaked around their waists while remaining connected to my wand. The sounds grew closer and Delph whispered frantically, "Whatever you're going to do, you better do it now, Vega Jane." He grabbed our tucks and stood ready.

I took my grandfather's ring and spun it around so that the three hooks were facing inward. What I had hoped would happen did happen. Because we were connected by my spell, the power of the ring had spread through the magical tether.

We were now *all* invisible.

With Petra and Delph on either side of me, I kicked off and we lifted into the air right as footfalls sounded nearby and we heard the voice. It was low and menacing.

"Around here, I could swear. It was around here. This place has always been . . . funny. You know it has."

"But how could it be?" said the other voice, which was even lower and even more menacing. "It's not possible. I'm telling you it's not possible. Not after all this time, eh?"

Well, blokes, it *was* possible. In fact, it was the truth.

We had escaped the Quag. And we were here. Wherever here was.

We soared upward and set out toward the distant lights. And, in doing so, took another step forward to all that lay ahead.

Like Jasper Jane had said: Peace. Hope. Freedom. In precisely that order. Although, ironically, I knew we would have to achieve the last in order to fully enjoy the first two. It would require a fight. It always did.

And after surviving the Quag, I was damn well ready to provide one.

Our cause.

Our time.

Our destiny.

Precisely in that order.

A Wugmort's Guide to Wormwood and Beyond

adar \ə-'där\
A beast of Wormwood often used as a messenger and trained to perform tasks by air. Although they appear clumsy on the ground, adars are creatures of grace and beauty in the sky, owing greatly to their magnificent height and wingspan. Most remarkably, adars can understand Wugmorts and can even be taught to speak.

alecto \ə-'lek-tō\
A lethal creature in the Quag characterized by serpents for hair and blood-dripping eyes. The hypnotizing sway of the serpents atop the alecto's head can drive its prey to commit suicide.

amaroc \a-mə-räk\
A fierce and terrifying beast of the Quag, known to possess the ability to kill in many ways. Amarocs have upper fangs as long as a Wug arm and are rumored to shoot poison from their eyes. When captured, their hides are used in the production of clothing and boots in Wormwood.

attercop \a-dər-käp\
A type of venomous spider indigenous to the Quag.

Breath of a Dominici \breTH əv ə dä-mən-'ē-chē\
A long-stemmed flower with a fist-size bloodred bloom that gives off the odor of slep dung. The Breath of a Dominici grows only in viper nests.

Care, the \\'ker\\
A place where Wugs who are unwell and for whom the Mendens at hospital can do no more are sent to live.

chontoo \\'chən-too\\
A flying beast in the Quag comprised only of a head, the chontoo is said to wildly attack its prey in the hopes of using its body parts to replace the ones the chontoo does not have. Spawned over the centuries by the intermingling of different species, the chontoo is characterized by a foul face with demonic eyes and jagged fangs, and flames for hair. The chontoo is primarily found in the Mycanmoor.

colossal \\kə-'lä-səl\\
An ancient race of formidable warriors, of an origin largely unknown to the average Wugmort. The average colossal stands about sixty-five feet tall and weighs nearly seven thousand pounds.

Council \\'kaun-səl\\
The governing body of Wormwood. Council passes laws, regulations and edicts that all Wugmorts must obey.

creta \\'krē-də\\
An exceptionally large creature used in Wormwood to pull the plow of Tillers and transport sacks of flour at the Mill. The creta weighs well over one thousand pounds and is characterized by horns that cross over its face and hooves the size of plates.

cucos \\'koo-kōs\\
Small birdlike creatures that inhabit the Third Circle of the Quag. Brilliantly colored as if small bits of the rainbow are embedded in their feathers, the cucos are best known for glowing wings that can illuminate their surroundings.

Dactyl \\'dak-til\\
A Stacks worker whose job entails shaping metal with hammer and tongs.

dopplegang \\'dä-pəl-gaNG\\
A dangerous creature in the Quag, marked by hideous rows of blackened, sharp teeth, that morphs into whatever it sees. The power of the dopplegang lies in its ability to trick its unsuspecting victim into injuring or even killing itself, since striking the beast in its altered form is tantamount to striking oneself.

dread \\'dred\\
A black flying creature in the Fifth Circle created by Jasper Jane. About the size of a canine, dreads are characterized by their screeching cries and clawed wings that they use to cut their prey to pieces.

Duelum \\'dool-əm\\
A twice-a-session competition occurring outside of Wormwood proper that pits strong males between the ages of fifteen and twenty-four in matches against one another. Viewed by many Wugs as a rite of passage, Duelums can often be brutal.

ekos \\'ē-kōs\\
A small creature in the Quag exceptional for the mats of grass that grow on its arms, neck and face, and sprout from its head. The ekos have small, wrinkled faces and bulging red eyes.

Event \\i-'vent\\
A mysterious occurrence in Wormwood that has no witnesses. Wugmorts presumed to suffer from an Event disappear entirely, body and clothing, from the village.

Excalibur \ek-'skal-ə-bər\
A rare type of sorcerer born with extraordinary magical powers already intact and a profound knowledge of Wug history embedded in his or her mind. It may take years for an Excalibur to become aware of his or her innate abilities.

Finisher \'fi-nish-ər\
A worker tasked with "finishing" all objects created at Stacks. Finishers must show creative ability at Learning, as the requirements for the job range from painting to kiln-firing items intended for the wealthiest Wugs of Wormwood.

Finn, the \'fin\
A magical element consisting of twine knotted in three places and looped around a tiny wooden peg. The untying of one knot brings a force of wind powerful enough to lift objects off the ground. Untying the second knot produces gale force winds, and undoing the third brings a wind of unimaginable strength with the ability to level everything in its path.

firebird \'fi-yuhr-burd\
A huge flying creature in the Quag known for its colorful plumage and sharp beak and claws. It's said that the firebird's feathers are so brilliant they can be used to provide light and warmth. A firebird can be a harbinger of tragedy.

frek \'frek\
A huge, fierce beast of the Quag characterized by an extensive snout and fangs inches longer than a Wug finger. The bite of a frek has been known to drive its victims mad.

Furina \fuhr-'ē-nə\
A Wug-like race indigenous to the Quag, made nearly extinct because of continuous attacks from beasts. The Furinas are descendants of a

group of Wugs and Maladons who became trapped in the Quag while migrating from the great battlefields to the village of Wormwood.

garm \gärm\
A large beast of the Quag, thirteen feet in length and nearly one thousand pounds in weight. The garm is a hideous creature, its chest permanently bloodied, its smell odious and its belly full of fire that can cremate its victim from several feet away. Wormwood lore maintains that the garm hunts the souls of the dead or guards the gates of Hel.

gnome \nōm\
A creature of the Quag known for long, sharp claws that allow it to mine through hard rock. The gnomes are characterized by deathly pale and prunish faces and yellowish-black teeth.

grubb \grəb\
A peaceful creature that lives primarily in tunnels beneath the Quag and can eat through rock faster than most any other species. Twice the size of a creta, the grubb is known for its strong, expandable hide; long slithery tongue; enormous jagged teeth; soft, slippery body; and eye color that differentiates males (blue) from females (yellow).

High Street, the \hī ′strēt\
A cobblestone street in Wormwood proper lined with shops that sell things Wugmorts need, such as foodstuffs, clothing and healing herbs.

hob \häb\
A creature in the Quag about half the height of an average Wug, characterized by its thick frame, small but powerful jaw, stout nose, long peaked ears, spindly fingers and large hairy feet. Hobs are typically amicable creatures that speak Wugish and make themselves of assistance in exchange for small gifts.

hyperbore \\ˈhī-pər-bȯr\\

A blue-skinned flying beast indigenous to the Quag characterized by a lean, muscled torso and lightly feathered head. More closely related to Wugs than any other creature, the hyperbore may serve as an ally or enemy and responds favorably to respect and kindness. Hyperbores set on their prey quickly, beating them to death with their compact wings and ripping them apart with their claws. The hyperbores live in nests high in trees.

inficio \\in-ˈfēs-ē-ō\\

A large fiendish beast indigenous to the Quag that can expel poisonous smoke potent enough to kill any creature that breathes it. The inficio has two massive legs with clawed feet; a long, scaly torso with powerful webbed wings; a serpentlike neck and a small head with venomous eyes and razor-sharp fangs.

jabbit \\ˈja-bit\\

A massive serpent with over two hundred and fifty heads growing out of the full length of its body. Although jabbits rarely leave the Quag, little can halt their attack once they are on the blood scent. Jabbits can easily overtake Wugs and have fangs in each head full of enough poison to drop a creta.

Learning \\ˈlər-ning\\

The institution youngs attend until the age of twelve sessions. It is at Learning that youngs gain skills necessary for work in Wormwood.

light \\ˈlīt\\

The time of sunlight between one night and the next.

Loons, the \\ˈloons\\

A boardinghouse on the High Street.

lycan \\lī-kin\\
A beast of the Quag covered in long, straight hair, whose bite turns its victims into its own kind. The tall, powerfully built lycan walks on two legs and wields its sharp fangs and claws to attack its prey.

Maladon \\mal-ə-dän\\
From the Wugish word for "terrible death," an ancient race whose highest calling is to inflict terrible death on others. A sessions-long war between the Maladons and Wugmorts forced the Wugs to found the village of Wormwood, around which they conjured the Quag for protection.

maniack \\mā-nē-ak\\
An evil spirit that can attach to a body and mind, driving a Wug irreversibly mad with every fear he or she has ever had.

manticore \\man-tə-kór\\
A swift, treacherous beast indigenous to the Quag with the head of a lion, the tail of a serpent and the body of a goat. Over twice the height of an average Wug and three times the width, the manticore's most formidable features are its abilities to read minds and breathe fire.

Mill, the \\mil\\
A place of work in Wormwood where flour and other grains are refined.

morta \\mȯr-tə\\
A long- or short-barreled metal projectile weapon.

Noc \\näk\\
The large, round, milky-white object in the heavens that shines at night.

Outlier \aut-lī-ər\
A threatening two-legged creature that lives in the Quag and can pass as a Wugmort. Outliers are believed to be able to control the minds of Wugs and make them do their bidding.

Quag, the \kwäg\
A forest that encircles Wormwood and is home to all manner of fierce creatures and Outliers. It is widely believed among Wugmorts that nothing exists beyond the Quag.

remnant \rem-nənt\
A collection of memories from an assortment of Wugs; an embodied record of their remembrances.

Seer-See \sē-ir 'sē\
A prophetical instrument used by sorcerers to view other places. The Seer-See consists of sand thrown into a pewter cup of flaming liquid, the contents of which are then poured onto a table to display a moving picture of a distant location.

session \se-shən\
A unit of time equal to three hundred and sixty-five lights.

slep \slep\
A magnificent Wormwood creature characterized by its noble head, long tail, six legs and beautiful coat. It is said that sleps were once able to fly, and that the slight indentations noticeable on their withers now mark the spot from which their wings grew.

sliver \sli-vər\
A small unit or brief period of time.

Stacks \staks\
A large brick building in Wormwood where items for trade and consumption are produced.

Steeples \stē-pəls\
A place the majority of Wugmorts go every seventh light to listen to a sermonizer.

unicorn \yoo-nə-kȯrn\
A noble and gentle beast characterized by a brilliantly white coat and mane of gold, with shiny black eyes and a regal horn the color of silver. The soft horn of the unicorn is known to defeat all poisons, but can only be obtained by convincing the unicorn to surrender it freely or by killing the beast outright.

Valhall \val-hal\
The prison of Wormwood, set in public in the center of the village.

wendigo \wen-də-gō\
A malevolent spirit that can possess whatever it devours. This ghastly, quasi-transparent creature lives throughout the Quag but is predominant in the Mycanmoor. Signs that a wendigo is nearby are a vague feeling of terror and a sense that the facts stored in your head are being replaced by residual memories of the prey the wendigo has devoured.

whist \wist\
A large, domesticated hound of Wormwood known for its impressive speed.

Wugmort (*Wug* for short) \wəg-mort\ (\wəg\)
A citizen of Wormwood.

Bring the fight

THE
WIDTH
OF THE
WORLD

Read ahead for an exciting sneak
peek of Vega Jane book three!

THE WIDTH OF THE WORLD

Sneak Peek

We landed, invisible, on the cobbles, and were nearly killed.

Petra Sonnet cried out, Delph Delphia grunted in surprise, my canine, Harry Two, yipped, and I, Vega Jane, jerked back on the magical tether holding us all together, as the deafening contraption charging down on us flashed past.

It was boxy and made of metal and wood with windowed doors on either side. It also had four what looked to be wagon wheels, only there were no sleps pulling it.

The infernal thing was moving of its own accord! It was puffing and wheezing, with what sounded like metal clanking on metal. Bright lights like powerful candles housed in lanterns were perched on the front of the thing, providing illumination. The front piece was shiny metal with ridges. Etched on it was a name: RILEY.

Riley? Was that the bloke who owned it? Or maybe the bloke who built it? We'd had a wagonmaker back in Wormwood named O'Dougall who put his name on the side of each one.

In a few moments the Riley, swaying from side to side and with a belch of smoke coming out its hindquarters, turned the corner and vanished from our view.

A pale Delph looked at me. "What the ruddy Hel was that?"

I shook my head because I had no idea what the ruddy Hel it was. Rattled, I scratched Harry Two's remaining ear.

We all had scars from our journey across the Quag.

Delph's arm had been burned and blackened.

Harry Two had lost an ear.

Petra had injured her hand.

And I had the mark of the three hooks upon the back of my hand. It had been burned into it by some unknown means.

I drew a breath and once more was about to return us to visibility by spinning my ring around when a pair of males appeared.

We froze, each holding our breath, lest they hear even that slight sound.

"You sure it was from here?" the taller of them asked the other male. He nodded.

My mind was whirling. These were the blokes we had seen earlier, after escaping the Quag. How could they have followed us?

I glanced at Delph and Petra. They looked as terrified as I felt.

I pointed to the right and we shuffled off around the corner.

We set our tucks down and I breathlessly whispered, "They followed us. How?"

Petra shook her head. But Delph said, "You reckon they can detect magic? Because you done that to get us here." He pointed to the magical tethers that kept us all invisible.

I looked down at my wand like it had just bitten me. *Could that be true?*

Delph said, "Look." He was pointing to the right. Down the cobbles at the very end of the street was a tall building made of stone and brick and timbers. I stared up at the highest point of the edifice.

"Steeples," I said in wonder.

"It's got a bell too," said Delph. "Me dad said Steeples had a bell once, before it broke."

"Steeples?" said Petra, looking confused.

"The place back in Wormwood where Wugmorts would go to listen to Ezekiel the Sermonizer deliver his very long soliloquies," I explained. "Telling us to be good while scaring us half to death with tales of how badly our lives would turn out regardless of what we did."

But Delph had a point. At night Steeples had always been empty. I wagered this building might be the same.

We shouldered our tucks and crept along the cobbles until we came to the double wooden doors that constituted the entrance to the place.

There was a sign next to it.

"*Saint Necro's*," I read. I glanced at Delph. "What do you reckon that means?"

"Dunno, do I?" he replied. "Never heard-a no Saint Necro. Alls I know is Steeples."

I tried the doors but they were locked. I pointed my wand at the heavy wrought-iron lock and was about to whisper *"Ingressio"* when Delph grabbed my arm.

"Magic," he said warningly.

I nodded and slowly lowered my wand.

Delph tried to open the door, but it was clearly bolted shut.

Then Petra noticed a window on the side. "It's not locked."

Delph boosted her up first and she slid through. I followed. Delph lifted Harry Two through the opening and into my arms, and then he brought up the rear.

We looked around at a vast chamber that was far larger than Steeples, though it was configured quite similarly, with brightly colored windows, rows of seats and a raised area up front where sermons were no doubt given. I wondered whether the sermonizer who spoke here was as depressing as Ezekiel. Petra said in a hushed tone, "Where do we go now?"

I pointed to a set of stone stairs that led upward. "Let's see what's up that way."

"Why not down?" said Petra, pointing to another set of stairs that apparently led to a lower floor of this saint's place.

"No," I said. "Up is better."

She gave me a skeptical look, but I didn't wait for her approval of my plans. They expected me to lead; well, that's what I was going to do! I bustled over to the stairs with Harry Two gliding along next to me. Delph and Petra hurried after us.

That's when we heard the footsteps at the entry.

We ducked down between two sets of pews as I heard someone say, "*Ingressio.*"

The doors flew open.

We heard footsteps approach. I lifted my head a bit so I could see over the backs of the pews. It was the same two cloaked figures.

But this was impossible. I hadn't used magic before they got here. How could they be —

I looked down at the mark on my hand and gaped. Was it that?

As the footsteps drew closer, I heard one of the males say, "Are you sure?"

I peered over the edge again in time to see the other bloke hold up his wand. "See for yourself," he said.

The wand was glowing.

The other man nodded. "Right."

He crept along until he got to where we were hidden.

"There!" he snapped. He pointed his wand and said, *"Infernus!"*

"Embattlemento!" I instantly cried out.

His blast of fire ricocheted off my shield spell, and he had to duck to avoid being incinerated.

The other bloke rushed forward, casting spell after spell our way, each more powerful than the last.

Petra cast a shield spell as well, and his magic rebounded off it and smashed into the pews, destroying them.

Spells were now being cast so fast I could barely follow them. The inside of the building was being pummeled.

Glass shattered. Wooden pews disintegrated, and a small statue of a female exploded when hit by a glancing blow from a rebounding spell. I had never been in such a battle as this one. The sheer ferocity and speed nearly paralyzed me. And though we were still invisible, we were in terrible danger of being killed simply by being in this confined space.

I was hurling spells so fast I could barely remember thinking of the incantation before sending it off. When I glanced at Petra, I saw both terror and fury in her eyes. Somehow, this filled me with resolve.

I slid on my belly, squeezed under a pew, came up behind the bloke and said, *"Impacto."* He was blasted off his feet and flung against a wall.

But the bloke rebounded off it, turned and fired multiple spells in my general direction. I ducked, then threw myself over a pew. I turned in time to see Delph get slammed against another pew by the force of one of the spells.

I heard someone cry out and looked to see Petra fly over another pew and crash into the floor.

I whirled around on the same bloke and fired every spell I could think of. The problem was he was deflecting them left and right. My arm was growing weary, and Petra had not recovered enough to help me. When a spell hit so close to my head that it made me wonky, I ducked under a pew for a moment to catch my breath and clear my senses.

When I looked back up I almost cheered as I saw Delph slam into the male, lift him up, turn him upside down and pile drive him into the floor. I had seen Delph use that same move in the Duelum back in Wormwood. The bloke went limp.

The next instant a light shot right past my face, hit the wall behind me and knocked a hole in it. The concussive force of the spell knocked me heels over arse and broke the magical tether keeping the others invisible.

"Got you!" roared the other bloke who had shot at me as he pointed his wand right at Delph's exposed chest.

Before I could regain my feet and aim my wand, a voice called out, "*Subservio.*"

Petra's spell hit the bloke square on, and he instantly went rigid and his wand hand dropped. He then simply stood there looking blankly ahead.

We rose on shaky legs and approached him.

"Thanks, Pet, you saved me," said Delph weakly.

"Yes, you did, Petra," I said. "That was quick thinking."

She let out a long breath. "I'm . . . I'm just glad it worked. I couldn't let him hurt you, Delph."

They locked gazes for a moment, and I felt my face begin to burn. I was glad that she had saved Delph, but did she have to give him that look? And did he have to give it right back?

"Look at this, Vega Jane."

While I had been thinking all this, Delph had gone over to check on the other fellow. Petra and I rushed over with Harry Two next to us.

Delph pointed at the wand still held in the bloke's hand.

I stared down at it, stunned.

Etched on his brightly glowing wand was the mark of the three hooks! The same mark that had been burned onto my hand. The mark on the wand was pulsing as though alive.

Delph said, "That's how they managed it. Your mark, it must give off a signal."

I nodded, for he was assuredly right about that. But then what was I to do? I couldn't very well cut off my hand.

"Vega Jane, your glove!" said Delph.

"My what?" I said distractedly.

"Your glove. It has powerful magic. See if it can block the signal."

I plunged my hand into my cloak pocket and pulled out the glove Alice Adronis had given me in order to handle the Elemental, which was now also my wand. I had once thought I needed the glove to hold the Elemental, but Astrea Prine back in the Quag had shown me that this was not the case.

I hastily pulled on the glove, covering the mark. I hoped whatever magic the glove had was enough.

I looked at the fellow's wand and breathed a sigh of relief. The mark of the three hooks was gone from it, and the wand was no longer glowing.

"That was brilliant!" said Petra to Delph.

She gave him a hug and a peck on the cheek. I saw him smile. Yet when he glanced at me and saw my expression was one of granite, he coughed, turned red and said, "'Twas nothing really."

"It was actually very smart of you, Delph." I turned to Petra. "But if we give out hugs and kisses every time someone does something smart, I reckon we might not have slivers for anything else."

Petra gave me a haughty look and rubbed Delph's arm.

Gritting my teeth, I turned, pointed my wand at the unconscious bloke, performed the *Subservio* spell and removed any memory he might have had of this. I did the same with his mate. Next, Petra and I repaired the damage to the building.

Finally, I turned the ring back around, attached the magical tethers, and we became invisible once more. It was only then that I released the blokes who had attacked us from the spell.

They both looked around.

One said, "What the blazes are we doing here?"

His mate looked down at his wand. "I don't know. Was it something to do with my wand?"

The other fellow shook his head. "Last thing

I remember I was in me bed. And that's where I'm going back to," he added angrily.

He turned and left. His mate gave the place one more searching look and joined him, shutting the doors behind him.

I let out a long breath. "Now let's go find a place to hide."

Acknowledgments

A novel does not come into being solely by the hand (and imagination) of the novelist. *The Keeper*, and before it *The Finisher*, are no exceptions to this rule. Many talented folks were involved in making the Vega Jane journey available to a global audience. And here is where I have the welcome pleasure of thanking them.

To Rachel Griffiths, David Levithan, Kelly Ashton, Julie Amitie, Charisse Meloto, Dick Robinson, Ellie Berger, Lori Benton, Dave Ascher, Lauren Festa, Emily Morrow, Elizabeth Parisi, Rachael Hicks, Emily Cullings, Sue Flynn, Nikki Mutch and the whole sales team at Scholastic for believing that a thriller writer could move to another genre and tell a good story.

To Venetia Gosling, Kat McKenna, Catherine Alport, Sarah Clarke, Rachel Vale, Alyx Price, Tracey Ridgewell, Helen Bray, Trisha Jackson, Jeremy Trevathan, Katie James, Lee Dibble, Sarah McLean, Charlotte Williams, Stacey Hamilton, Geoff Duffield, Leanne Williams, Stuart Dwyer, Anna Bond, Jonathan Atkins, Sara Lloyd and Natasha Harding at Pan Macmillan for following me with unbridled enthusiasm wherever I go in my literary pursuits.

To Steven Maat and the entire Bruna team for being with me step-by-step as we released a brand-new character on an unsuspecting world.

To Aaron Priest for listening to my cryptic mumbles at a London book party about this "book" I was writing and for calling me on Sunday after he read it, as opposed to Monday!

To Arleen Priest, Lucy Childs Baker, Lisa Erbach Vance, Frances Jalet-Miller, John Richmond and Melissa Edwards for being so wildly enthusiastic about this series.

To Mark and Nicole James for all you did for me. Here's to attending the premiere together one day!

To Caspian Dennis and Sandy Violette for crowing to the heavens about the book on the other side of the pond.

To all my other publishers who took a chance on this and trusted me to get it right.

To Hannah Minghella, Lauren Abrahams, Matt Tolmach and Kate Checchi at Sony/Columbia Pictures who have shown so much enthusiasm in building a movie franchise around Vega Jane and her world.

To Emma Frost for sitting in a restaurant in New York with me for several hours in preparation of your crafting a terrific script.

To all the libraries where I discovered books that introduced me to the world of fantasy, and to all the librarians who guided a little boy in finding ever-new stories and original voices on the shelves.

To all my friends and family, who have supported me over thirty novels.

To Kristen and Natasha for performing your own magic in keeping Columbus Rose and me running smoothly.

And last, but clearly not least, to Spencer and Collin, who, though you're now adults, help me always to retain the childlike wonder in life that allows me to do what I love.

DAVID BALDACCI is a global #1 bestselling author. His books are published in over 45 languages and in more than 80 countries; over 110 million copies are in print. His works have been adapted for both feature film and television. He is also the co-founder, along with his wife, of the Wish You Well Foundation®, which supports literacy efforts across America. David and his family live in Virginia.